EAT
POST
LIKE

EAT
POST
LIKE

A Novel

Emily Arden Wells

AVON

An Imprint of HarperCollinsPublishers

EAT POST LIKE. Copyright © 2025 by Assemble Media. All rights reserved. Printed in the United States of America. No part of this book may be used or reproduced in any manner whatsoever without written permission except in the case of brief quotations embodied in critical articles and reviews. For information, address HarperCollins Publishers, 195 Broadway, New York, NY 10007.

HarperCollins books may be purchased for educational, business, or sales promotional use. For information, please email the Special Markets Department at SPsales@harpercollins.com.

Avon, Avon & logo, and Avon Books & logo are registered trademarks of HarperCollins Publishers in the United States of America and other countries.

FIRST EDITION

Interior text design by Diahann Sturge-Campbell

Part opener illustrations provided by the author

Library of Congress Cataloging-in-Publication Data has been applied for.

ISBN: 978-0-06-330743-8

25 26 27 28 29 LBC 5 4 3 2 1

For my mother, Bonnie

EAT
POST
LIKE

New York

1

Cassie stepped out of the car and looked up into a magnificent archway flanked by sets of Corinthian columns—here was Capitale, one of New York City's famous historic buildings turned event hotspot, located off the Bowery. The façade was bathed in red and purple lights for tonight's event, with a luxurious red carpet rolled out to the sidewalk. James, Cassie's boyfriend, looked like a movie star in a tux. He had a tall, lean build, and the black suit accentuated his broad shoulders and his trim waist, bound by a black cummerbund. Cassie's heart fluttered, excited to be at such a glamorous New York party. She looked up at him nervously, meeting his large, green eyes, shining with excitement. She held his gaze for an extra moment, appreciating how his eyes changed from green to amber in the center, and his striking black hair, which was slicked back, shiny with pomade. He picked up her hand and kissed the back of it, putting Cassie at ease before they stepped onto the red carpet and toward the illuminated entrance.

"You look absolutely gorgeous," he said, kissing her again, but this time deep in the nook of her neck, sending tingles up Cassie's spine.

"Thank you," she replied. "You clean up well, yourself." She had never seen James in formal attire, and he looked incredibly handsome. He had shaved right before the event, making his skin seem to glow, his chiseled jawline even more prominent. "I can't believe this place," Cassie said. "You're sure we're supposed to be here tonight?" She slipped her hand through the crook of his elbow and placed her other hand on top of his bicep, which felt especially firm after his morning workout.

"Of course," he said excitedly. "This is the ceremony for the Viand Awards, where they announce the best restaurants in the world. All the leading chefs will be here too. It's one of the biggest nights in food—think of it as the Oscars for restaurants. I'm confident we're in the right place."

"Wow. How did we make the guest list?" It was entirely possible that James had already explained all of this to her, but she had a bad habit of scanning emails when they were talking, half listening.

"Friend of a friend," said James, before leading her inside.

Cassie looked around, surveying the party. The building was filled with gastronomic delights and well-heeled chefs in sparkly gowns and tuxedos, the sound of their glasses clinking punctuating the hum of conversation. In one corner of the room was a massive block of ice with fish frozen inside, topped with different kinds of seaweed and large tins of fresh caviar. In the other was a tower of champagne coupes glittering under the party's spotlights. Across the room, she saw a mountain of stacked Parmesan cheese wheels, in front of which chefs were preparing freshly made pasta. Next to them, a truffle purveyor surrounded by a crowd of people was holding out fresh truffles for chefs to smell, before shaving the delicacy onto small plates of risotto.

Someone handed Cassie and James thinly sliced pieces of prosciutto, cut off a whole leg poised on a cherry red flywheel slicer. She held the piece of meat up to the light—it was cut so thin that it was pellucid and almost crystalline, the color deep and rich from the curing process. She gently placed the bite on her tongue, letting the fat and salt melt for a moment before she started chewing. She felt her knees buckle. "That is so delicious," she said, unable to find the words to describe why.

On another side of the room, a sushi chef presented a gigantic whole tuna and began to carve the fish in front of a growing crowd of onlookers. Fellow chefs applauded the fishmonger's skill before being offered tastes of the freshly sliced tuna, served on the chef's Yanagiba Sakimaru knife.

"I'm just so glad I could get the night off," said Cassie. She had also been excited to get dressed up, and she loved how James looked in a tuxedo. "I'm on call, but I can't see how the deal could close on a Friday night."

He handed her a flute of champagne. "Me too." He wrapped his arm around the small of her back, walking his fingertips up and down her bare spine.

Cassie shivered once—and then again—before James whispered into her ear, *"I love this dress on you."*

"I found it in a thrift store! Forty bucks!" Cassie always took pride in her great thrift-store finds. The value made her love those things even more.

"I was there, remember? I told you to buy it. It fits you perfectly."

Cassie had a notoriously bad memory. It was easy to blame her spaciness on late nights at the office and the stress of her job, even if she knew those were excuses. She knew that she was a frustrating partner, but somehow James was unwaveringly sweet to her, and in this moment, she was grateful for it. She smiled and leaned in to kiss him.

CASSIE AND JAMES walked around the room, working their way from one dish to the next. Sea bass with a miso glaze, bites of Japanese Wagyu beef on skewers cooked in sesame oil and soy, and shrimp with snap pea coconut curry served over black rice. Cassie was surprised by how many people James seemed to know; he was constantly shaking hands and talking about his old job at the *New York Times*. He was an accountant now but a self-proclaimed foodie with a passion for New York's restaurant scene. It was not lost on her that they always ate incredibly well, even if the intricacies of cuisine were over her head most of the time.

"Oh! Kumamotos! These are divine," he told her as they passed by a gigantic bed of ice covered in oysters on a half shell, lemon slices, and strands of green popweed, freshly harvested from the ocean. He handed her a tiny oyster that was slightly bigger than a quarter, its shell almost as deep as it was wide. She topped it with a pink mignonette and a squeeze of lemon before clinking his shell with hers and sluicing the briny delight into her mouth.

"It tastes like the ocean," said Cassie. "I don't think I've *ever* had an oyster that good. I truly didn't know oysters had such—"

"Range?" James interjected excitedly. "That's because I usually order oysters from above the Mason-Dixon line. I like them salty. Did you know that oysters are one of the most nutritionally rich foods on the planet?"

She picked up his hand and gave it a squeeze. "I never fail to be surprised by how much you know about food. Aren't you supposed to be a numbers guy?"

"One can't live on numbers alone," he said.

"Ain't that the truth."

"I'm not as diligent as you. I need more than my job to keep me satiated."

"I know, I know," Cassie said, rolling her eyes. "I do work too much. It's going to put me in an early grave."

"You said it, I didn't."

"I would also like to remind you that every tax season you work one-hundred-hour weeks too."

"Yeah, but that's twice a year. Look, we've been through this. I only say it because I care. There's more to life than a promotion."

"What would I even do with all that spare time?" she asked genuinely, remembering the strange, vacant moments in between finals at school and her next internship when she'd felt like she was floating aimlessly through life.

"There's so much we could do. Walk across Manhattan, stopping in at any restaurant that piques our interest," James said, sweeping one arm around the small of her back and pulling her close, bringing her ear to his mouth. "A glass of rosé here, a pickle plate there."

She kissed him on the lips, still salty from the oyster brine. "You—forever the foodie."

"What can I say? It's my element," he said with a shrug, and released her, now distracted by the party. "Gah, these oysters are just so—gorgeous."

James snapped a photo of the oyster spread from above, capturing the abundance of the display. He took photos of each of the name cards. "So I can remember what is what," he explained to her with a wink. But he didn't stop there. He took a video scanning over the top of the oysters, then panning around the party.

Cassie rolled her eyes. "What are you going to do with that video? It's just taking up memory on your phone."

"I like to have memories of things. You know what they say—a video lasts forever."

He then turned the camera on her, scanning up and down flirtatiously.

"Stop!" she said, laughing and pushing the phone down. "Let's enjoy the party. It's so nice to have a *civilized* night out," Cassie teased, and she took his phone out of his hand, dropping it into his jacket pocket. As she pulled her hand away, James grabbed it and kissed its back, then her cheek, then her lips. The kiss became passionate, and for a moment she forgot about the party swirling around them.

"Thank you for coming with me tonight," said James, pausing and looking her directly in the eye. "I'm having such a nice time."

"Me too," said Cassie, but she knew what he was really saying. He wanted her around more. She had a habit of running away—a habit of avoiding intimacy.

Then her purse buzzed.

> Cassie, we're going to need you to come in. The Regalius deal is on.

Cassie sighed. Without fail, she got called into the office when she was having fun and had just started to forget about the day-to-day drama of work.

"I'm really sorry, James, but I have to go into the office. Sounds like the Regalius merger is happening, so I'll be glued to my desk all weekend doing due diligence."

James looked down, disappointed. "Really? Tonight? I had really hoped you'd be here with me. Everything is just so . . . ." His eyes, full of disappointment, scanned the party.

Her phone started to ring—it was her boss. James knew she

had to make herself available for a big deal. It was an essential part of her job.

"I know, I know," he said, looking down at the ground, defeated. "You want to make partner in the next five years."

She smiled at him and put her hand on his cheek. "I love you. Thank you for supporting me."

He kissed her and gave her a friendly tap on the butt.

"Go get 'em, tiger," he said with a wink. "Let me know if you want me to bring anything to you at the office."

She kissed him goodbye and walked out of the party. Looking back over her shoulder, she felt a pang deep in her chest. She wished she could stay at the party with him. She swallowed her disappointment, then ran down the red carpeted stairs and got into a taxi waiting outside. Time was of the essence.

"Midtown, Forty-Eighth and Park."

2

A free weekend was sacred to Cassie, and it felt like she only had one a month. She forced herself to unplug as much as possible and avoid social media—and sometimes her friends—just to give herself the headspace to regroup. She worked for Stevens & Sweeney, a law firm that specialized in mergers and acquisitions, and she was constantly on call. It was relentless. Days sometimes started at seven o'clock and didn't wrap up until three the next morning.

Her mother had been the head of a major New York law firm that represented the big art museums—MoMA, the Met, and the Frick—and some of the big names in the art world. Like any little girl, Cassie had looked up to her mother and wanted to make her proud. She was seven when her mother got terminal cancer, and Cassie felt like she only knew her through reputation. In those early years, her mother had exposed her to the institutions she worked for and some of the now-famous artists, as well as the nonprofits that supported artists. She'd admired how passionate her mother had been about her career—not only the written word of the law, but the *people* she represented. Cassie hoped that one day she would feel as passionate about her clients as her mother had, and that one day she too would be able to choose her clients and have the freedom to do pro bono work for foundations she admired. Until that day, she had resigned herself to the grind.

But this weekend, she was free.

Cassie weaved her way through the dense Saturday crowd until she was at the door of the Strand, a multilevel bookstore in New York City that was both an institution and an oasis from the bustling city outside. She took a deep breath, savoring the familiar musty smell and the absence of noise, now that she was insulated by stacks of books. There was something viscerally comforting about the store, the hush of the storekeepers, the regulars tucked into their favorite reading chairs, and the smell of freshly printed ink.

After wandering through the towering aisles, Cassie found herself in the photography section. She used to love perusing the photography books. Ansel Adams, Robert Mapplethorpe, Irving Penn—she loved black-and-white photography. But lately, those books just made her feel guilty. Guilty for not picking up her camera. Guilty for abandoning one of her true loves.

When Cassie first moved to New York, she was entranced by the city and enjoyed losing herself in the crowd. She loved exploring new neighborhoods and snapping photos, taking in the beauty of a singular magnolia tree in the springtime, feeling the air dance across her skin. In college, Cassie took a black-and-white photography class and shot film with her father's vintage Leica. She loved the weight of the camera, heavy around her neck and cool in her hands, and the meditative practice of framing an image, focusing, re-framing, focusing, re-framing, and then *click*. New York was picturesque to begin with, but she thought that it looked even better in black and white, from the grit of the subway to the grandeur of the buildings off Central Park. Even more exciting than shooting was when a roll of film came back from the lab. There were never thirty-six flawless images, but instead maybe one or two that stood out and a few that were beautiful for their flaws—light leaks, grainy images, or a motion blur when her shutter speed wasn't set correctly. She loved them nonetheless, how they captured something intangible, a singular moment. It was as though one photograph could bring her back to a specific moment, like a time capsule.

These days, her camera sat on her bookshelf along with her favorite novels, collecting dust. She was past the point of being infatuated with New York, instead immersed in routine.

Cassie meandered over to the travel section, as she usually did, losing herself in glossy books about exotic places. She loved looking at the photos in the guidebooks that captured the essence of a place—the art, the architecture, the food, and the beautiful landscapes.

One of her favorites was a little white travel book about Florence, Italy. She slid the book off the shelf and sat down on the floor in the stacks to flip through its familiar pages. She looked at photos of picturesque vineyards, bowls of handmade pasta, white marble sculptures of contorted bodies, and paintings that she remembered from the art history seminar she'd taken in undergrad. Maybe she was ready to go on vacation with James. Maybe to Italy?

Cassie and James had been dating for almost two years, a tipping point for most relationships. It was when most couples started to talk about marriage, but the thought of a wedding made Cassie anxious. She knew deep down that James wanted to get married, and truth be told, he was perfect on paper; he had a great job, and he was consistent, loving, and doting. He was sure to be an ideal husband and a great father.

From the outside, they had a very normal relationship—a flawless pair. An accountant and a lawyer, destined for a stable life with consistent paychecks, a house in Connecticut, and a few kids. But that vision of the future didn't feel like *her*.

Still, something kept her coming back. Each month would turn into another, time slipping by as it does. They would go out to eat once a week and would frequent a handful of restaurants—their "locals." She liked the fact that he was so responsible—he had put himself through college, read the *Wall Street Journal* every morning, and was one of the most disciplined humans she had ever met. He'd bought his apartment years ago with a family inheritance and was diligent about investing and saving.

Although James had never formally asked Cassie to move in with him, she felt like he wanted it more than anything. A year ago, he'd given Cassie a dresser, which was mostly empty except for the top drawer, which held her toothbrush, a few nightgowns, underwear, one change of clothes for work and another for the gym. It had taken her a few months to bring items over to his apartment, but she eventually figured she might as well, since she was spending two to three nights a week there.

Just like Cassie, James worked a lot, and part of his job was to take clients out for dinner. He would call her after, incessantly talking about how delicious the meal was and how much she would love it. Inevitably, Cassie would be at her desk, stabbing at a Sweetgreen salad, which was better than something from the bodega but by no means on par with the gorgeous meals he recounted in great detail.

Occasionally, James traveled for work, stints where he was gone for two or three days, and he would come back with a small trinket for Cassie. He was very sweet like that.

Cassie audibly sighed, closing the Florence guidebook with its photos of the iconic sculpture of David, the Uffizi Palace, and Aperol spritzes, put it back on the shelf, and left the store.

CASSIE DESCENDED INTO the subway, feeling the rush of air coming from the express train whizzing by, excited to get home to her retreat high above the city streets.

Climbing the stairs to her sixth-floor walk-up, she found herself daydreaming again about traveling to Italy with James—where they would go, what monuments they would visit, all the romance of a European getaway. It would be just like *Roman Holiday*, she thought. Vespas, two-hour lunches followed by gelato, and leisurely tours of museums and picturesque fountains. She'd admired Audrey Hepburn, with her classic beauty and timeless style. Cassie could almost see in her the kind of woman she might be someday—one day, when she would have the time and resources to travel and not work so much. But that wasn't her life yet.

Cassie walked through the door, set down her keys on the side table, dropped her bag on the sofa, and dug out her phone. She knew that she was infamously bad at checking her phone on weekends when she wasn't on call. It was a strange form of protest, and she knew it infuriated James, but it was her way of making her time *hers* and no one else's.

JAMES: Hello, beautiful, are we still on for dinner?

CASSIE: Hi! Yes, home now and about to jump in the shower. What time do you want to meet and where?

JAMES: The usual. 6 p.m.

She looked at the mirror and felt the self-loathing creep in; she never felt feminine or beautiful enough, and at a young age she'd realized that clothes could be like armor, providing a newfound sense of security and confidence. Cassie put on her favorite outfit—a black-and-white polka-dotted dress that reminded her of her mother. Mom would have liked it; it was timeless and made Cassie feel strong every time she wore it.

Her mom died before Cassie reached the age when a girl really needs a mother—someone to teach her the simple things about being a woman. While her friends spent their weekends brunching and getting their nails done at the salon with their mothers, then going shopping for beautiful handbags, Cassie spent her time at the gym, which was both therapeutic and an escape from reality.

Cassie checked her phone as she gathered her keys and wallet into her purse.

JAMES: I'm at the bar.

Shit. She was late.

3

Cassie walked into Olivia's Osteria and scanned the crowd. James was perched at the end of the bar. He was always easy to spot. He was tall at six three and looked like he should be famous. He was the kind of handsome that people took comfort in: it was as though they were naturally attracted to him, but he looked common enough not to be too memorable. People felt like they had met him before, or that he looked like someone they knew—he had one of those faces. James wore the same thing every day—navy blue jacket, navy trousers, white shirt. One less thing to think about, he would say. He waved to Cassie and went back to reading on his phone, taking in a few last moments as she made her way across the restaurant.

Olivia's was a charming neighborhood spot run by a husband-and-wife team, situated on a corner in the West Village. It was famously busy every night of the week, but they consistently had good luck getting a table, even on a Saturday night.

"Hi, I'm sorry I'm so late," Cassie said while pulling out a barstool.

He was used to it, and he tolerated it because he loved her. "It's fine," said James. "We're already on the list, and they have a new spring menu. Ramps are coming into season."

"Delicious," Cassie said. Cassie had no idea what ramps were or why people were so obsessed with them. She covertly typed *ramps?* into her phone under the bar, making sure James didn't see.

Olivia, the restaurant's namesake, came over to them, welcoming Cassie with an air kiss on her left cheek. "Wonderful to see you, Cassie! How are you? We haven't seen you in a while." Olivia was always so kind and warm to Cassie.

"Yeah, I've been busy at work. The Regalius account has been kicking my ass and I've been working late," Cassie explained.

"She works so hard, it's unbelievable," said James. "There are some weeks when I barely see her." His tone was inscrutable.

Was he upset? Of course he was upset. Cassie felt her face get hot.

"Work hard, play hard," said Olivia, trying to ease the tension. "Well, your table is ready. Grab your wineglasses and I'll transfer your tab."

Cassie and James got up from their barstools and made their way through the crowd. Cassie overheard the hostess tell a few guests that the wait was running about two hours. What timing, she thought. James had only been there for about thirty minutes.

Like clockwork, a charcuterie plate landed on their table just moments after they sat down. "From the kitchen," said Olivia.

"We come here too much," said Cassie, "especially since they feel obligated to send us freebies."

"Maybe," said James, "but I think they just like us."

"How are they profitable if they give things away? And Olivia is so nice. I worry we're taking advantage."

"There is nothing a restaurant wants more than regulars—not to mention, regulars they actually like," he said before picking up his fork and stabbing at the thin slices of meat, popping three into his mouth at once.

The platter was a gauntlet of temptation. It had everything

he loved: salty, cured meats, soft cheeses, hard cheeses, and a stinky blue cheese with a distinctive "funk," served with a bowl filled with a rainbow of pickled veggies and a little dish of quince jam. Cassie bit into a pickled carrot, crunchy, sweet, and briny. She looked up and saw James looking down at his phone. It was the one thing about him that she really hated—so often when there was a quiet moment when she finally felt herself begin to relax, he drifted off onto his phone. And then it triggered that uneasiness, a doubt, a need to run.

"Honey, we talked about this."

James quickly turned off his phone. "Sorry," he said, looking up at her and smiling. "I was just checking the score of the game."

"So. There's something I want to talk to you about. I . . . I was thinking, maybe this summer, that we could travel to Italy," Cassie said while looking into her glass of wine, avoiding eye contact. She spun the stem slowly between her thumb and middle finger, feeling the glass against her skin, watching the light from the table's candle catch in the liquid. It would be the first time they traveled together—a big step for any relationship. Cassie recalled some of the pages from the guidebook, talking quickly. "We could visit the Uffizi in Florence or the Colosseum in Rome, rent Vespas, and eat gelato. It would be so romantic."

James didn't say anything. He looked into his lap, and the blue light of his phone illuminated his face from below. Just as quickly, it switched off. He looked up at her, paused, and said, "Would you even be able to take time off? It seems that every time we try to do something special, you're called into work."

Cassie said nothing, surprised. He was usually not so confrontational when he was frustrated.

"Are you . . . *annoyed*?" she asked. Now *she* was annoyed.

"No, I'm not annoyed. It's just the truth. You work a lot, and your job is your priority."

He had a point, and his honesty dug into her chest like a dagger.

"Every time we try to plan a trip, you get called back in, and we end up canceling, or I go by myself. Remember when we were supposed to go to Tulum, and your boss called—"

"Yes," Cassie interrupted. "I know."

"You could set better boundaries, you know." James took a sip of his wine and looked across the room.

"That's easy for you to say," she snapped back, out of habit.

"You don't have to defend yourself, Cassie. I understand the situation."

But did he understand? Cassie got quiet again and looked past his shoulder at a young couple seated at the bar, sitting facing each other, their legs affectionately intertwined. She felt herself longing for those early days, when everything was simpler—they had just met, and their attraction was electric. When they first started dating, she felt like they were truly in sync—their minds, their bodies, and the path toward their future. Recently, they had become so relaxed around each other. The relationship was more about the comfort of companionship than the passion they once had. She missed the old them.

"Cass," said James, and he reached out and held her hand tenderly.

Cassie could feel tears start to form in the corners of her eyes. Her throat felt dry. She might cry right here at the table. She knew all the sacrifices for her career would be worth it—but *when*? These days it felt like all she did was work, with no reward. She took a sharp breath. "I'll be right back."

She hurried off to the bathroom, trying to catch her tears before they caused her mascara to run. Once inside, she planted her hands on the sink and looked at herself in the mirror. What was she doing? James was a great guy, and she was going to fuck it all up if she wasn't careful. He was supportive of her, her career, and her dreams. Why couldn't she simply *let him in*? And now—now that she was trying to move things forward, *he* was resisting.

Once Cassie had gathered herself, she made her way to the bathroom door. She took a deep breath, opened it, and returned to the cacophony of the restaurant. She looked across the dining room and saw James patiently waiting for her, unfazed. He was a rock—reliable in all the ways that she wasn't. In a flash, she was overwhelmed with feelings of gratitude, desire, and love for him. But instead of rushing back to the table, she tucked herself against a wall and took a moment to study him from afar. Even when he was relaxed, he had a way of carrying himself that exuded confidence, but in a uniquely quiet and humble way. Part of his beauty was that his body was harmoniously proportioned—as though he were a Roman sculpture come to life—fit, trim, and chiseled, thanks to the fact that he was on his road bike three to four times a week doing laps around Central Park. He sat back in his chair, one arm dangling behind, and his other held his phone as he casually scrolled with his thumb. His face caught the blueish white light of his phone, making him glow against the dim yellow lights of the surrounding restaurant.

Cassie came back to the table to find James still looking down at his phone, scrolling quickly. She stood behind him and leaned over to whisper something into his ear. Cassie's hair fell forward and softly grazed his shoulder, creating a veil of secrecy. She slowly licked his ear, starting at his lobe, until she reached the top of his ear, and then blew, sending tingles of excitement up her spine. The phone went black, and he looked up at her.

"Oh yeah?" he asked with a hungry look in his eyes.

"Let's get out of here," said Cassie, nodding toward the door.

"But the food just got here," said James, gesturing for her to sit down.

"I've lost my appetite," said Cassie, while playing with the top button of her dress. "Let's get it to go."

"You're right," he said, gesturing in their server's direction. "You're always right."

Cassie sat down, taking pleasure in James's newfound urgency to leave the restaurant. While they waited for Olivia to bring the bill, Cassie looked around the restaurant. She realized how this little neighborhood restaurant was so important to all these people; it was the stage upon which they lived out their lives. Where they broke bread, made friends, fell in love, and celebrated life. It was beautiful.

"Another emergency at work?" asked Olivia, as she brought the check and boxes for their food.

"Yes, I just got the call," Cassie lied. Once Olivia left the table, she winked at James, who had just signed the tab.

He grabbed her hand and pulled her through the restaurant, past the crowd of people at the door and outside into the crisp air. They turned the corner and headed toward a main avenue where they would be able to catch a cab. But once they passed the glass windows of the restaurant and were in the shadows, James dropped the bag of food and picked her up, bracing her against a brick wall, meeting her mouth with his. She wrapped her legs around his waist, returning the kiss, deep and wet. He put her down and pressed his body against hers.

"Simmer down," she said, and kissed the tip of his nose. "I can't wait to get you home."

"So, you're feeling better?" he asked.

"You make me better."

THE NEXT MORNING, Cassie woke up late, but James didn't seem to mind. He was busy in the kitchen making coffee and frying eggs for breakfast. He was a man of habit, who liked to stick to his routine, no matter the circumstances. His Sundays were unfailingly the same: a modest breakfast, followed by recipe planning and making shopping lists. Then he would go to the farmers' market to buy provisions for the week, followed by a stop at Fairway to pick up any outstanding items. James would then spend the rest of the day cooking a big Sunday meal and would sometimes bake homemade sourdough bread. He would put on one of his favorite jazz records, open a bottle of wine, and lose himself in the kitchen. He wore one of his favorite white button-down shirts with the sleeves rolled up to his elbows, his forearm muscles twitching as he swiftly chopped and minced the fresh vegetables and herbs. He would show off, talking to her about knife skills and cooking techniques, but all she could ever pay attention to were the veins that traveled down his forearms, onto his hands, terminating at his fingers.

She slinked over to the island that separated the living room from the small galley kitchen and climbed up onto one of the barstools.

"Nice shirt," he said, as he handed her a cup of coffee.

"Oh, this old thing?" She winked at him and took a second to roll up the sleeves of his white button-down shirt that fit like a dress on her petite frame. She liked wearing his clothes; they felt safe somehow, as though they carried his love and devotion in every thread.

"Do you want to come to the market with me this morning?" he asked.

"Sure. Can I shower first?"

"Of course. Just remember, I like to go ahead of the midmorning rush, you know, when all the yoga moms are there with their kids zooming around on scooters."

"Okay," she said, taking a sip of her coffee.

He gave her an urgent glance.

"Oh, like now?"

"Yeah, now." The man was punctual.

IT WAS A beautiful day in the city, the sky a dark blue without a cloud in sight. The market was in one of the most dynamic crossroads in the city: a lush park filled with buskers, chess players, commuters dashing for trains, all framed by bars and restaurants. On the weekends, one of the city's best farmers' markets popped up in Union Square, a market that drew the best growers and purveyors from all over the tristate area. James liked to talk to the vendors about what was in season, making sure that he bought the freshest produce there. Cassie always felt like the produce was overpriced and made everything too precious to eat, but he enjoyed it.

James was talking to an artisanal grain vendor, and Cassie slipped off, folding into the crowd. The mass of people moved through the market at a leisurely pace, past the pastries, the meat vendors, the fresh vegetables from upstate, and finally reached the floral section. Cassie picked out a bouquet of pale pink peonies and paid for them with a crisp twenty-dollar bill. She touched their soft petals, appreciating their fleeting beauty. James walked up behind her, startling her.

"Peonies, huh?"

"Yeah," she said, pushing them into her face. "Aren't they beautiful?"

"You know I don't like the flowers here," said James, typing into his phone.

"They aren't for you," said Cassie, defiantly.

James stopped typing and looked up. He put his phone in his pocket and wrapped his arms around the small of her waist. "I know. They just don't compare to the wildflowers that grow on the hills surrounding Rome. The air is perfumed with jasmine— it's enchanting. I've been thinking about our conversation the other night, and I think we should rent a flat in Rome for a few weeks. There are more than a few things I've been meaning to show you, and Italy seems like the ideal place."

Cassie jumped up into his arms, causing him to drop his tote bags loaded with groceries. "I would absolutely love that," she said, and kissed him.

Maybe someone really could find everything they needed right here at the farmers' market.

4

Cassie had just arrived at work and was settling into her cubicle. She added fresh water to the peonies she'd bought the day before and positioned the silver vase in the corner of her desk. The flowers were a reminder that she needed to do more for herself, starting today. She went into the kitchen to fill up her water bottle, relieved that she had made it in before the majority of the office.

Leaning up against a cabinet, waiting for water to boil, was Ruby. She was an avid tea drinker and could usually be found in the kitchen hovering near the electric kettle while scrolling through her phone.

"I wish this kettle would boil faster," said Ruby, not looking up. "I have so much shit to do today." Suddenly, she stopped scrolling and pointed the screen toward Cassie's face. "Did you see this new restaurant that opened a few blocks from here? We should go for a drink after work one day."

"That would be fun," said Cassie, half lying. She liked being invited for after-work drinks but rarely went and even more rarely stayed for more than one drink. She would usually stay at her desk for an extra hour after the group left for the bar, relishing the chance to get *a little bit more* work done. That said, she invariably had fun when it was just her and Ruby—there was no one else in the office she wanted to be friends with.

Ruby was a savvy young woman who was smart, funny, confident, and cultured. She frequented the latest hotspots and nightclubs. She was consistently dressed sharply and made it look effortless: tailored suits at the office, black skinny jeans with silk blouses on the weekends, oh-so-short sequined black dresses on nights out, and without exception, Louboutins. She loved that pop of red, a signifier of success and even more ambition. She, too, had gone to good schools and landed her dream job, but she didn't have the same level of underlying anxiety as Cassie. She made everything look easy, from her cases to writing articles, all the while impressing the old men upstairs. Competition aside, Cassie loved spending time with her outside the office. She made Cassie feel like she wasn't so different, that she too could be an "it girl," the kind of woman who might make it into the *New York Times* style section, who could stay up late drinking martinis in speakeasy-style bars and still kick ass at the office the next morning.

"How are things going with James?" Ruby asked, dunking her tea bag into a mug.

"Good . . . At least I think so."

"Things are starting to get serious, no?" Ruby seemed to ask the same question every month or so. "When is he going to pop the question?" *Ruby* was not the kind of girl to get engaged—she felt too empowered when she started dating someone new.

Cassie laughed. "Not any time soon."

"I get the impression that he's from money," said Ruby.

Cassie would consider the comment rude coming from anyone else, but Ruby was Ruby.

"Why do you say that?"

"It just seems like he's never worried about money."

"Well, he *is* an accountant," said Cassie.

"Like I said. He's got it under control. Great marriage material." Ruby flexed an all-knowing smile over her cup of tea.

"Whatever you say. I have to get back to my desk."

WHEN CASSIE REACHED her cubicle, she clicked on her phone and was surprised to see four missed calls from an unknown number. Her heart raced with anxiety.

She dialed the number.

"New York General," said the voice on the other end of the line.

"Hi, I had four missed calls from this number. My name is Cassie Brooks. I believe someone was trying to reach me?"

"Hold please."

Cassie's stomach turned. She felt her palms sweating.

"ER," another voice answered.

"Hi, this is Cassie Brooks. I had a few missed calls from this number."

"Ah, yes, we've been trying to reach you. Do you know James Colwell? You were listed as his next of kin."

"Yes." Cassie's stomach dropped. "He's my boyfri—fiancé."

She didn't know why she lied. They weren't engaged, they were nowhere near getting engaged, but she thought it would help avoid questions, especially because James didn't have any immediate family.

"We have some unfortunate news for you, Ms. Brooks. Your fiancé was in a car accident this morning and has died. His taxi was involved in a collision."

She already knew—he hadn't been wearing a seatbelt in the taxi. He never did.

"We did everything we could. We tried to resuscitate him, but unfortunately, we were too late."

Cassie felt like she had been punched in the gut, hard and fast, her body ripped in two. She crumpled onto the floor, feeling the polyester carpet under her fingers with an acute specificity, rough and plasticky. A high-pitched ringing surrounded her like a thick cloud, drowning out the chatter of the office beyond her cubicle. She felt strangely light, disconnected from the earth, and almost like her head was full of helium, floating untethered from her body. *I was just with him yesterday*, she thought. *This can't be real.*

"Hello?" said the voice on the phone. "Ms. Brooks?"

She picked up the phone again, slowly, almost expecting to hear different news from the nurse.

"Yes, hello?"

"My condolences, Ms. Brooks."

"Thank you," she said quietly. "What now?"

"We need you to come in."

5

Cassie once believed that she had a magical power—she was able to handle stress better than most people. In fact, she performed *better* under stress. There was something about the pressure, the way she felt it tighten around her like a boa constrictor, that helped her focus. It was the force that got her through grad school, helped her concentrate during finals and get straight As. It was a skill that had helped her ascend at her law firm—a tailwind that lifted her through the late nights, the deadlines, and the constant degrading comments from her firm's leadership.

In the following weeks, she felt that same tailwind as she scheduled James's funeral, wrote his obituary, managed all the phone calls from his friends and acquaintances. It was all a blur; she was so focused on the minutiae, she often lost herself in them.

It was surreal that James was gone, and sometimes it felt like he was just on a work trip, not dead. After the accident, Cassie would stand in the shower letting the water run over her body, thinking about how he had just been there, every day adding to the tally of days without him. *Death*, she thought, *is an immovable force.*

While she had been too young to remember many of the details from her mother's funeral, she vividly recalled the world feeling suddenly cold and lonely, as though all the warmth from the earth had escaped. After that, she had a hard time trusting people, never wanting to get too close to anyone out of fear that they too would leave her.

Every day, she was reminded of the new void in her life through phone calls, messages, and letters from James's friends and distant family. Cassie spent hours listening to them grieve—how they missed him, how much he meant to their lives—but it was rare that anyone asked Cassie how *she* was doing.

David, James's best friend, was having an incredibly difficult time with James's passing. They had gone to college together and been roommates for a few years. David was a typical finance bro; he'd graduated from Wharton and landed an investment banking job at Morgan Stanley right out of college. After just a few years he was making more money than he could spend, and he validated his entire existence with how he spent money: ski vacations in Aspen, beach trips to Turks and Caicos, weekends in the Hamptons. Despite his braggadocio, he was an incredibly emotional man who was completely gutted when his best friend died. His way of coping was to call Cassie every day, clearly intoxicated, retelling his favorite stories. Some Cassie had heard, but many she hadn't, so she let him talk for hours on end, quietly listening to him twist and turn through his memories. David would be drinking throughout the conversations, and she would pour herself a glass of wine too—it made it easier to handle.

"There was this one time, we went to Daniel and had a midnight dinner that was something like eight courses. It was so extravagant—basil-fed snails, foie gras, and endless bottles of wine. The chef came and sat at our table for dessert and cognac. James was really the best guy. I miss him. You know," he said, meandering, "I wondered all the time why you two never moved in together. It seemed like the natural next step."

"I have a very traditional family; they wouldn't have approved," Cassie lied. In truth, she and James hadn't seriously talked about moving in together yet, and in truth, she still didn't feel ready. They had still been dancing around each other—each trying to make space in their life for the other while trying to maintain their independence.

She was at that age when all her friends were getting married off one by one and starting to have kids. Once there was a baby in the picture, her girlfriends would move to the suburbs and fall into their family vortex. It was natural, she told herself, but over time she felt like she was the only one who wasn't married, who didn't have kids, and was still in the city. After James died, a few of her girlfriends from college and law school called to check on her, and a few came to the funeral. They came to the reception, lasagnas in hand, for a few hours. Hugs and pleasantries were exchanged, but before long they hurried back to Grand Central Station so they could return to their families just in time for soccer practice, a dance recital, or whatever.

Cassie was surprised by how many people came to the funeral, so many of whom she didn't know. She recognized a few of James's coworkers, some old friends, but the event soon became a blur of handshakes and hugs.

"Thank you so much for coming," she said on repeat, barely hearing herself anymore. "James would have appreciated you coming." Hug. She felt her shoulders raise, as though her spine and shoulders could protect her.

"Yes, he was such a smart man, it's such a tremendous loss," they said, while her hands were squeezed in an attempt to convey comfort and solace. She tried to grab trays of muffins or appetizers to help defend her from the onslaught of physical contact—it felt so performative.

"He will be missed," people would say as they passed by her in the hallway.

But she knew everyone in the room was talking about her, and it made her terrifically uncomfortable.

THERE IS A funny thing that happens when a young woman loses her partner—society forces her to assume the identity of her dead lover. She is no longer an independent woman with her whole life and career ahead of her; she is "Cassie, girlfriend of James Colwell, who died tragically." She is defined by her lover's death. Forever.

IT HAD BEEN a few weeks since the funeral, and David was on the phone again. He called at least once a week to "check on her," but really, she knew that he just wanted to talk about himself. She tolerated it because she was so lonely, and she found him comforting. He wasn't James, but at least he was consistent.

"I just can't believe he's gone," David said, as he did every time. "I swear, it still feels like he's going to walk through the door, and everything will go back to normal."

Cassie was quiet on the other end. She poured herself a large glass of wine and sank into her sofa, sipping quietly while she listened to David talk.

"Have you gone to his apartment yet?" David asked. "You know there are a few things I would like to have."

"I know, David." Cassie felt her entire body clench. She had been avoiding going into James's apartment. "I'm not quite ready."

"I'll go with you. Let me go with you, Cassie."

"No, this is something I need to do alone." She took another sip of wine.

Because James owned his apartment outright, Cassie had the luxury of time and was not being rushed to empty it by the end of the month. That said, she was hyper aware of the building fees, insurance fees, and other bills that were starting to pile up. It needed to be dealt with. She was dreading it. Not only did it feel like an enormous task, but she knew that once she cracked that door open, the feelings would come down on her like an avalanche. She poured another glass of wine.

"Well, the apartment is yours now," said David. "He left it to you."

"It was a complete surprise," said Cassie, wondering if David was bitter about the will.

"I think he assumed you guys would be married in a few years," he opined.

"Well, he never asked," she said, feeling herself become a little resentful. Angry that she had to deal with all the logistics. Furious at James for dying.

"Are you going to move in?" asked David.

"I don't know if I can. There are too many memories there."

The line went silent, and she could hear him taking a sip of whiskey, the ice clinking against the sides of the glass as he drank.

"Cassie, I would be so lucky to meet a girl like you."

"You'll meet someone, David. You just need to stop dating those models."

"I like beautiful women. What can I say?" He was quiet for a second. "But you—you're special."

"Okay, David." Cassie already felt uncomfortable. "I've gotta go. We'll talk soon."

She hung up and thought to herself, *What the fuck was that?*

6

It was Saturday, and Cassie had already run her usual five-mile route, knowing that she would need the endorphins to help her get through the day. She found herself standing at James's door, still sweating despite her thirty-minute cold shower. It took a few minutes to raise her hand to put the key into the lock, the sound of which sent chills down her spine and made her entire body feel cold. She took a deep breath, turned the key, and pushed the door open.

The door creaked in a familiar way, but it felt drastically different this time. She half expected to hear Miles Davis on the surround sound and for James to come out of the bedroom, but instead there was silence. She closed the door behind her and let herself adjust to the space, hearing the subtle sounds of the building: the radiators, the neighbors' TV, the sound of the city outside.

James's plants were slumped over, looking thirsty and desparate. As she moved through the apartment, she scooped them up and placed them in the sink for a drink of water. She ran her fingers over the kitchen counter, remembering their nights together cooking, drinking wine, listening to music. James loved jazz and would tell Cassie about his favorite musicians—conversations that never stayed in her head. Now she regretted that she couldn't remember, that she hadn't cherished those little day-to-day moments more. She felt a lump growing in her throat and a piercing pain in her chest. Tears welled in her eyes.

James loved his apartment; it was his sanctuary. He was a private man, and she'd felt honored to be welcomed into his home. James had lost his parents at a young age too; it was something they bonded over early on. He managed his grief through organization, keeping his apartment as tidy as his bookkeeping. In so many ways, he was a natural accountant. Always taking stock, always documenting. He loved keeping track of small details—he even documented how much his plants grew every month.

She knew that he had inherited enough money to buy his apartment after his parents passed, but they never discussed it in detail. She felt awkward asking how much he'd received, and he never brought it up. He was like that—he never offered up information unless she asked him directly, often a few times. When James felt like Cassie was asking too many questions, he would pivot and make impromptu plans for them to do something—a concert at the Bowery Ballroom, a bike ride in Central Park, a walk through the Met, anything to divert the conversation. It was in those moments when Cassie felt closest to him, when they were out and about, distracted by New York City. He really knew how to make the time they were together count. Typically, he was so guarded, and it was one of the things about their relationship that made her doubt how close they *could* become. She had hoped that he would eventually become more transparent, but now he would never have the chance.

CASSIE SPENT A few hours just being in the apartment, sitting in James's favorite reading chair, tracing his footsteps through his morning routine. She found herself walking in the same pattern in his apartment over and over again, the way one rubs worry beads; it was repetitive and soothing.

The emptiness was heavy, the silence deafening. His death still felt surreal, and she had to keep reminding herself that this was her new reality. Her mind slipped every few minutes—almost as if she were in an alternate reality—and she would feel like nothing had changed. That she was just waiting for him to come back from buying a carton of milk. Then she would come across something—a photo, a pen from one of his favorite restaurants, or the cup of coffee that had been left in the sink—a cup that had never gotten washed—and she would fall back to reality.

It was five o'clock in the morning when Cassie woke up, stiff and cold. She had fallen asleep on James's couch and could barely remember what had happened the day before. Her grief felt like a thick cloud—she could barely think, had no concept of time, no appetite, no desire to do anything. She pulled a blanket over herself and turned back into the cushions.

Around noon, Cassie finally made it off the couch and into the kitchen. She boiled some water and made herself a cup of sencha green tea, not wanting to touch the coffee pot that was last used by James on the day he died. The grounds inside were probably moldy, but she didn't dare clean it. There was still a trace of him.

Cassie lifted the mug to her face, gently blowing on the surface of the liquid as she paced the kitchen. A waft of grassy tea hit her nose, a subtle note of citrus lingered, and she felt herself start to wake up a little bit—at least enough to function. She knew today was the day; she had to start cleaning the apartment out, prepare it to go on the market. Cassie had set a deadline for herself—she knew it was the only way it was ever going to get done. Three weeks, she told herself. *Three weeks.*

She found a box of crackers in the pantry and, upon opening it, realized how hungry she was. She hadn't eaten since the day before and was feeling sunken and dehydrated. Surprisingly, there were still some ready-to-cook meals in a cabinet—instant curry that just needed to be double boiled. James hated buying prepackaged meals, but he had them on hand for emergencies— hurricanes and snowstorms and the like. It had seemed inhumane to him to ask deliverymen to brave a blizzard for an order of tikka masala.

Cassie poked around for anything to make her bag of curry seem more appealing. She cooked a pot of long grain rice and topped some garbanzo beans with dried herbs that she scavenged from a spice rack. From the corner of her eye, she saw the wine cabinet and pulled out a bottle of pinot noir from Oregon. It was one of his favorites, and a wine he usually served when they ordered Indian food—real Indian food, not curry served from a pouch.

Cassie returned to the sofa, sat cross-legged, and slowly began to eat, letting the warmth of the food radiate through her body. After a few minutes, she started to feel better, connected to the earth again. She took a sip from her glass and knew the moment she had been dreading was upon her. It was time to start packing up James's belongings.

What did David want again? A baseball mitt? David and James used to play baseball on the weekends, retreating for hours at a time to the park and then to a favorite sports bar for postgame beers. She didn't even know where James would have put stuff like that—nostalgic objects and keepsakes.

She walked into James's room and opened his closet. There were the pieces of his uniform: five navy blue work jackets, tan trousers wrapped in bags from the dry cleaners, and stacks of white shirts. She gently fingered the cuff of one of his jackets, bringing it to her face. It still smelled of him, of fresh laundry and Old Spice. The scent of him—a haunting, visceral reminder of his absence—brought back the tight knot deep in her throat.

At the top of the closet were a few boxes, the white ones available from the Container Store. She thought it was funny that he loved organizing bins—but he claimed that being organized helped calm him. *It quiets the brain*, she could hear him say. *Why should I spend time thinking about the objects in my house, or what I have to wear? I can use that energy to focus on other things.* He was so efficient, it was annoying. She laughed as the tears began to fall.

The boxes were labeled neatly, using stick-on labels and all-caps script written in Sharpie. She pulled one of the boxes labeled BASEBALL off the shelf. In it, she found old baseball caps and a cigar box filled with baseball cards, but no glove. She put the box aside for David. She pulled down another box labeled NOTEBOOKS, filled with navy blue Moleskine notebooks that were all the same size, organized chronologically, with dates carefully written on each cover. Just looking at the box made her miss James, her chest tightening—he was habitually methodical, so precise. She tucked the box next to the other one, lining them up against the wall.

Cassie reached up for the next box, which was unlabeled. It

was so full, some of its contents fell out as she tipped it off the shelf. The box was filled with a dozen or so gallon-size Ziploc bags, each marked with a different name: Andy Folsom, John Davis, Dr. Paul Gardner . . . None of the names were familiar. She opened the bag that had fallen on the floor—John Davis—and inside she found a wig, two tan ties, a box of colored contact lenses, and another Ziploc bag. Her heart racing, she opened the second bag, dumping the contents onto the bed. Out fell a credit card with the name John Davis on it and a New York State driver's license for a John Davis with James's photo.

7

Cassie looked down at the bed and the pile of disguises laid out in front of her. There were ten different aliases, complete with hairpieces, photos, makeup, receipts, credit cards, and forms of identification—James's face with a different name each time. The IDs were clearly fakes, but pretty good ones. She looked more closely at some of the receipts; they were for lavish dinners—$645.17 at Per Se and $849.20 at Masa, restaurants she knew only by reputation. She picked up a plane ticket from one of the boxes and recognized the date. James had flown to Los Angeles a few weeks before his death, but he had told her that he would be at a financial summit in Cincinnati. She remembered, because it was a long weekend, and she had wanted to go to the beach with him before she got called into the office.

The bottom of the box was lined with cash, ten thousand dollars in one-hundred-dollar bills. There were a few money clips that each had five hundred dollars in them—folded in the same way that James tucked his bills into the gold clip she'd bought for him a few years ago. There was no doubt he had folded those bills, no doubt that he was the one who had organized the box.

There was a high-pitched ringing in her ears, the same one as when she received the call from the hospital. Her adrenaline was surging, and she paced back and forth in the bedroom.

What was going on?

Was he a spy?

Was he a drug dealer?

Who was James?

Who in the *fuck* was this man?

CASSIE'S STOMACH RUMBLED, and with it came a wave of anger. She was so confused and frustrated; she didn't know what to do with herself. *She had to get out of there.*

Cassie walked down the street to Olivia's Osteria, knowing it would inevitably cause a lot of raw feelings, but she needed familiarity, some element of comfort. Standing outside the restaurant, she heard the familiar buzz of a place she loved, smelled the aromas of their most famous dishes, and sensed a roomful of people oblivious to her pain.

Cassie walked in the door and made eye contact with Olivia, who was across the restaurant. Olivia sat a group of four at a table in the corner, dropped the menus, and ran back toward the door where Cassie stood. She wrapped her arms around Cassie and, with one arm around her shoulder, ushered her to the bar.

"How are you holding up, darling? We haven't seen you since the funeral."

Cassie felt her eyes well up again, and then the tears rolled down her cheeks. She couldn't get any words past the pinch in her throat.

"Don't worry, honey," Olivia said, holding on to her hand. "It will be okay. Are you hungry?"

Cassie nodded, wiping the tears from her cheeks.

"Okay, you sit down. I'll send some things over." Olivia dashed off into the kitchen.

Within a few minutes, there was a glass of her favorite rosé in front of her and a bowl of mussels cooked in Vermentino white wine—one of her favorite dishes. Olivia came over with a basket of fresh bread. "Hopefully, this will help a bit," she said, pausing a moment as the busy restaurant swirled around her. "Eat up. I'll be back." Olivia knocked on the bar top—something she habitually did when she dropped off food and had to rush away to help another table.

Cassie looked down at the bowl, feeling a sense of calm for the first moment in a long while. How many times had she eaten these mussels? Today was the first time she would eat this meal without James. She took a bite, and yes, it was helping. Each bite was better than the last; somehow more savory and delicious than she remembered.

She finished the mussels and started working on the broth—her favorite part. She used the shell of one of the largest bivalves as a spoon, scooping the broth into her mouth, savoring the intensity of each sip, while watching the small beads of glistening olive oil dance across the surface of the stock. Usually, Cassie let James eat all the bread; he liked to place the bread in the liquid, leaving it there for a few minutes until it was drenched with broth and saturated with its flavor. Tonight, the bread basket sat on the bar untouched.

Around ten, the restaurant started to empty out, transforming into a calm, enchanting scene. There were just a few people remaining in the dining room, *Exile on Main St.* played on the speakers, and each table glowed with candlelight and a small bouquet of white flowers. Olivia came by to refill Cassie's wineglass and sat down next to her.

"Goodness, what a night," she said, as she poured herself a

giant glass of wine. "I've earned this. Now, tell me how you're doing."

"Ugh, Olivia, it's tough. I'm not going to lie." Cassie felt herself sink under her own body weight. "I'm a strong person, but nothing has taken as much out of me as this. I miss him so much, every second of every day, and there are these waves of the most intense sadness that bring me to my knees. I finally went back to his apartment. It was like a time capsule, but in the worst way—a dirty coffee cup in the sink, his gym bag full of unwashed clothes. It felt like he'd gone out to get pizza and might walk through the door at any second. But of course he didn't. I've cried more in the last few days than I have since he died, and I just feel—destroyed." Cassie felt the tears behind her eyes again, a sensation that was becoming all too familiar. She rested her forehead on the bar, defeated. It was easier when she felt nothing.

Olivia rested her hand on top of Cassie's head, giving her a moment to gather herself. Cassie looked up, wiped the tears from her eyes, and managed to contort her face into a weak smile.

"The worst part about all of this is that I feel so *deceived*. It's one thing to lose your fiancé—it's another to realize you never knew him at all."

"What do you mean?" asked Olivia.

Cassie paused and considered what it would mean to share this secret with someone else. She met Olivia's eyes and felt trust for the first time in months. She couldn't stop herself—she leaned in and spoke in a hushed tone. "It's bizarre! I've been going through his apartment and there's all this *stuff*—wigs, credit cards under other names, costumes. It's as though he was living another life. *Many other lives*. I thought I knew everything about him, but clearly something else—something very, very dark—was going on. I found plane tickets, and the stubs correlated to dates when he was supposed to be in Cincinnati for financial conferences, but instead he was in London, Milan, Los Angeles. It's like I never knew him at all."

Olivia looked down at her glass of wine and spun it slowly a few times. The silence hung in the air uncomfortably. She took a long sip, downing about half of the glass's contents.

Cassie couldn't believe it. A wave of distrust rolled over her.

"Cassie," Olivia said, putting her glass of wine down on the bar, "follow me."

Olivia led them into the back of the restaurant and through a narrow passageway that opened into the kitchen, which was now quiet at the end of service. She stopped at the end of the corridor and turned around, blocking the entry to the kitchen. She looked at Cassie and smiled.

"What?" asked Cassie, confused.

"Look." Olivia pointed to the wall. "Notice anything?"

Cassie was standing in front of a corkboard covered in an array of passport-size photos of men and women from the past twenty years or so. Some were headshots, but some were printed from security cameras or grainy cell phone images. Underneath were handwritten names, dates, and notes with dishes, drinks, and personal habits. In some cases, there were multiple images of the same person dressed in different disguises: large hats, wigs, or different styles of clothing. The team at Olivia's Osteria had clearly been doing their homework. Cassie looked closer. There in the middle of the poster was a small photo of a man wearing a curly wig and a pair of thick horn-rimmed glasses she recognized from his apartment. It was James in disguise.

"WHAT IS THIS?" Cassie exclaimed, her heart racing. She felt her hands shaking violently and propped herself up against the wall. "Is this where you track people who dine and dash? We always pay—and tip!"

"No," Olivia said with a laugh. "James was a food critic, and not just *any* food critic, but one of the most influential restaurant critics in the industry. He redefined how restaurants are critically reviewed: before, diners relied on reviews from outlets like the *New York Times,* but James made everything available on social media—sometimes writing in real time, inviting his followers into every meal, bite by bite."

"Wait—James was the New York Secret Diner? *The New York Secret Diner?*"

She knew the account. Everyone followed @NewYorkSecret Diner, but no one knew who was behind it. His reviews could make or break restaurants; they had the ability to turn chefs into millionaires or put them out of business. Every few months, the *New York Post* would put out a story with a different theory about who was behind the account: one month it was a Yankees player, then a group of K-pop fans, and once it was the mayor. There was a popular hashtag, #NYsecretdineris, that people would use to post photos of likely suspects. Without fail, whenever a new review was posted, it was all New Yorkers could talk about, reveling in the cutthroat critiques and savoring the detailed descriptions of bucket-list meals that cost the equivalent of a month's rent. She, too, looked forward to the reviews, usually saving them for the train, when she would stand shoulder to shoulder with other New Yorkers, everyone bouncing off one another as the train traveled deep underground to the next station. She enjoyed looking over at other people's phones to see them reading the same posts, taking in each image. Food porn is, after all, the best porn.

"Yes!" said Olivia, putting her hands on Cassie's shoulders. "He didn't have those things you saw in his apartment for nefarious reasons—he was one of the most important restaurant critics in New York. He used disguises so he could dine without special treatment; it was the only way he could fairly judge a restaurant. A little trick he learned from his mentor, who was a critic for the *Times*."

Cassie felt her body crumple under her. Suddenly she was sitting on a sticky, squishy black kitchen mat, but the revelation of James's secret was a release both physically and emotionally. She felt a wave of elation that he wasn't a gunrunner, thief, trafficker, or any other kind of made-for-TV bad guy. But . . . he was a *food critic*?

"Come on, those mats haven't been washed down yet tonight— they're disgusting," Olivia said, and pulled Cassie up by the arm. "Back to the wine."

Cassie followed obediently and picked up her glass that was waiting patiently for her on the bar top. She felt slightly lighter. She laughed, quietly and under her breath, surprising herself. "Okay, what else do you know about all this?"

"A few years ago, he came in to review our restaurant, but we knew it was him. I didn't want to humiliate him, so I was very subtle about it. I just sent a few extra dishes his way, enough for him to realize the jig was up. He was angry at the time, but later he was able to joke about it with me." Olivia ran her fingers through her black bob, which ended at her chin, making her sharp jawline look even more angular. At one time, Olivia probably could have been a model; she was tall, thin, and had piercing blue eyes that sparkled when she got excited. "He hadn't yet learned how to move through the world in costume now that people were looking for him, so we coached him on how to make his disguises better, what to order, what questions to ask to learn more about how a restaurant is run. I even had an actor friend come by one day to coach him on his characters—it was so much fun. I can't believe you didn't know. You were all he ever talked about. He was so smitten with you; I was sure you knew."

Olivia poured two more glasses, trying to compensate for Cassie's silence.

"You know," she continued, "sometimes I was invited to go with him for a review. He would give me a character, and I would have to create a costume and a persona to accompany his direction. It was *theater*! My favorite was the time I dressed up as a frumpy older woman and we went to Per Se. That meal was flawless! Course after course of the most incredible food—a perfect crescendo from vegetables to fish to meat to dessert. It was like a symphony." Olivia had her eyes closed and was lost in memory. "It was one of the best meals of my life."

"I wish I could have experienced it," Cassie said, playing with the stem of her wineglass. Grief. Happiness. Panic. Relief. Now *jealousy*. She couldn't even imagine what emotion could be next.

8

The next morning, Cassie woke up with a splitting headache. She was rarely hungover; usually she wouldn't let herself drink enough, but last night had been different. She threw herself in the shower and got dressed. Navy trousers, a white blouse, and a navy blazer. She was probably overdressed for a desk day, but it helped motivate her—a trick she learned in grad school, especially on those days when staying in bed seemed like the best option.

At work, Cassie walked out of the elevator and into the office, trying to slip in silently. She sat down at her desk and turned on her computer. Before she could sip her coffee, a head popped into her cubicle.

"Hiya." It was Ruby. "How are you feeling today?"

Ruby was very good about checking in with Cassie.

"Meh," Cassie replied, feeling guilty and cranky.

Before she knew it, Ruby was sitting in the empty chair in her cubicle—the one usually reserved for her purse, coat, or anything else that could block someone from sitting there. She preferred to talk about personal things outside of the office, but today, she really needed a friend.

She leaned closer to Ruby and quickly blurted, "Apparently, James was living a double life."

"Whhaaaattttttt?! An affair?"

Cassie caught herself—this was James's biggest secret, something he didn't even trust her with. But it was burning inside her. "No, he was @NewYorkSecretDiner. I found his disguises, credit cards, stacks of cash in his apartment, and Olivia from Olivia's Osteria confirmed that he'd been running the account for years."

Ruby sat mouth agape. "Are. You. Serious?"

"Yes, and I've been having so many feelings about it. I feel relieved that he wasn't a criminal of some sort, but also mad and sad that he was living this whole other life that he never told me about. And—it was an awesome life. He ate in all these incredible restaurants, had amazing experiences, and didn't want to include me."

"Cass, you're not even that interested in food. You're more yourself in your spin classes than you are at a twelve-course dinner."

"Well, maybe because I've never *had* a twelve-course dinner. I've never had the chance to experience any of these things because I was never invited. And it makes me even angrier because I worked so hard through law school and then here at the firm— all I've done is work. I've never felt like I had time or money to experience lavish dinners." Cassie was silent for a moment. "I just wish I could have been invited. I think I would have enjoyed it."

Ruby looked down at her feet and pulled her lips into a frown. "Yeah, it was truly shitty that he didn't invite you, especially considering how frequently he was eating out. Critics must eat out, what, every night? I don't know how they do it . . ."

"Me either," said Cassie, following the unspoken part of the conversation. Like most women she knew in New York, was obsessed with her dress size and found it to be just as defining as her name or her profession. She found it frustrating that society made it seem that for women to be successful they had to "have it all"—a great job, kids, a perfect husband, a home featured in *Architectural Digest*, and a toned twenty-six-inch waist prominently displayed on social media.

"But I wonder what it would be like to do a job like that . . ."

"Well, you know," Ruby said, "@NewYorkSecretDiner *was* a secret account. No one knew who was running it. If you really want a job 'like that,' why couldn't you just start posting? Take yourself out to dinner and copy his technique."

It was an insane idea. "That's the craziest thing you've ever said, Ruby. I could never violate his privacy like that. Besides, I know nothing about food or fine dining, and I don't have access to the account. I just found out it was him last night!"

"You have his phone, don't you?"

Ruby was right. Cassie had James's phone; all she needed to do was figure out how to hack into it.

"He's a guy. He can't be that hard to impersonate," said Ruby.

CASSIE WAITED UNTIL five fifteen, the earliest she could possibly leave her desk without raising eyebrows. She rushed through the subway in what seemed like the longest commute of all time, finally arriving at James's block just as rush hour segued into the evening dinner surge.

Inside his apartment, the dreaded white plastic bins were there to greet her. They were neatly filled, organized into personal items, childhood items, and work items. She laughed at the "work items" bin—was it possible that he wasn't *ever* an accountant?

After a few moments of searching, she found what she was looking for—the Ziploc bag from the hospital that contained his phone, wallet, and keys.

She opened the bag, acutely aware that it contained air from the day he died, and pulled out the items, arranging them on the table. She plugged in the phone and paced impatiently while it crawled toward a fifteen-percent charge. Then she hit the power button and audibly exhaled when the phone lit up as it turned on.

Truthfully, Cassie wasn't the suspicious type and had never had any reason to snoop through her boyfriend's phone—but she was on a mission to find the truth about what he had been up to. Heart racing, she ran through a few options for the pin number: the address to his building, the last four digits of his phone number, and then his birthday. She was in.

Cassie carefully swiped through the home screens, unsure of where to start. He had organized all the apps into categories, which made it surprisingly difficult to navigate.

She found the Instagram app and clicked on the pink-and-orange icon. Notifications started pouring in, and she watched the numbers in the little heart icon that indicated likes and comments whiz from 124 to 267,569 in a split second. That was *a lot* of likes. Carefully, she scrolled through, looking first at his feed and confirming that yes, he was in fact @NewYorkSecretDiner, and then at the accounts he followed—all major restaurants and the accounts of chefs from all over the world.

Swiping left, Cassie accessed the direct messages within the app, where there were thousands of unread messages. Notes from fans, people asking for tips, and invitations from chefs brave enough to risk a scathing review, because a complimentary review from @NewYorkSecretDiner was a Midas touch for a new restaurant. Slowly scrolling through the comments, she got a sense of the incredible power that James wielded; it was strange that the success of so many businesses relied on one man who hid behind a technological veil. Cassie couldn't even imagine the amount of work and research James must have done for years so that he would be able to critique such a wide range of restaurants—she barely knew a roux from a ravioli.

Cassie toggled over to his note-keeping app and found hundreds if not thousands of notes, all organized by date and geo-tagged. She discovered lists of restaurants he wanted to visit, links to articles about chefs and new restaurant openings, and image folders for each meal—simple overhead shots of each dish—images she remembered seeing on the account's feed just a few months ago.

Within the notes, she could hear James's voice in the writing that she knew so well from the @NewYorkSecretDiner account. It was now obvious that he had dedicated a significant amount of time to this every day, studying the culinary world, needing to understand even the most subtle of nuances. Had he really been watching baseball games on his phone, or had he been researching the next up-and-coming restauranteur about to break onto the scene? Had he been mindlessly scrolling through Instagram, or had he been chatting with fellow critics and chefs?

The questions started flooding her mind again. Had James even been an accountant year-round, or had he just worked tax season? She had never thought to question how much money he said he made, but suddenly she suspected his lifestyle might have been funded by more than desk work.

She looked up from his phone and across the room at a row of the navy blue notebooks. She pulled one down, cracked open the cover, and out fell a menu from Gramercy Tavern.

February 2, 2019—Gramercy Tavern

Diner—"Charles"
Interior: A hybrid of European and American sensibilities, dark woods mixed with crisp white linens and strategically placed artwork, albeit a bit predictable. Feels overly "homey." A beautiful flow from the entry to the day-lit bar to the impeccably dimly lit dining rooms, each opening up a new world one after another. There is not a bad seat in the house; each table is well considered and articulated with flattering lighting and artwork, finished off with a bouquet of seasonal flowers.

1. Old Fashioned made with overproof bourbon and lots of bitters—beautifully presented with a clear king cube and a twist of orange.

2. Roasted Oysters with smoked butter, Meyer lemon, and microgreens—fantastic combination of the flavors of brine, brown butter, and the brightness of the lemon. Greens superfluous, perhaps better with delicately chopped chives.

3. Beef Tartare with Quail Egg—1 cm cubes. Mixed tableside with quail eggs, greens, oil, salt + pepper. Served with crispy thin toast, needs more toast.

4. Duck Meatloaf with seasonal peas, peppers, and chimichurri—gamey, a tad overcooked, but well-

balanced mix of fat, cut with the spicy acid of the
chimichurri. Caramelized, crispy edges.

5. Beignets for dessert—reminds me of New Orleans but
with the freshness of blueberries and passion fruit
ice cream. Micro basil. Thrilled they weren't served
with powdered sugar.

Cassie felt her stomach rumble. His notes were detailed enough
to evoke a memory of the meal itself—enough to help write a review, which would inevitably be even more specific. The journal
was filled with detailed notes from hundreds of meals, supple-
mented with menus, receipts, cocktail napkins, maps, clippings
of other restaurant reviews, chef profiles, business cards, and
other memorabilia. In all, there were about six years of journals,
all tracking his journey from accountant to secret food critic. It
was all there—meticulous reporting of every restaurant he had
visited and where he wanted to go next.

She picked up another one of the books, flipped through it,
and saw her name flash on a page. She hadn't realized that he
used these books as personal journals too.

Tonight's dinner was exemplary, a pop-up dinner set in
a private brownstone in the West Village. The dining
room was lavishly adorned with autumnal branches and
gigantic candelabras filling the room with a romantic,
flickering glow. I wish Cassie had been there, that
I could have shared it with her. It seems foolish to
experience so much decadence alone, without the

people I care about the most. What's the point? I should tell her. How do I tell her?

The last thing I would want is for her to find out that I've been lying to her all this time and to assume that there are more lies. One lie can completely corrupt a relationship—how can you build trust after that? Would she ever believe me again? Would she understand? She's a lawyer, her instinct is to be defensive, it would probably push her away.

Cassie let the journal fall into her lap. She felt the tears start to roll down her cheeks again, salty and bittersweet.

9

CASSIE: Hey, are you up?

RUBY: Sure am.

CASSIE: I got into his phone.

RUBY: And?

CASSIE: It's all true. He was @NewYorkSecretDiner, and he was going to restaurants in character. He has journals, notes, and clippings about all kinds of restaurants in New York, and all over the world. It's truly impressive.

RUBY: Wow. James. Full of surprises, that one.

CASSIE: I know, right?

RUBY: And wouldn't it be delicious if his next persona was a woman?

CASSIE: I don't know, Ru, it's becoming more and more clear that it was important to him that he remained secret. It's like this account was the one thing he was truly passionate about in life.

RUBY: Other than you?

CASSIE: 💔

RUBY: I always told you that he was obsessed with you.

CASSIE: 💔 💔 💔 BRB, crying.

RUBY: Unpopular opinion here, but maybe he left all those things for you to find? Maybe this is his way of inviting you along?

CASSIE: No, this was HIS thing. And he guarded the secrecy of this account with his life. He never even told me about it!

RUBY: If you think about it—who would know? If his identity was such a closely guarded secret, who would ever figure it out?

CASSIE: You have a point there. But why do you want me to do this so badly?

RUBY: I think it could be good for you—it could be good to do something other than law for once. You can get a bit myopic, sweetie. Think of it as a palate cleanser.

CASSIE: I don't know what you're talking about. 😂

RUBY: Miss Tunnel Vision, herself!

CASSIE: Okay, okay, I get your point.

RUBY: All I'm saying is that maybe you can have some fun for once—that's all.

CASSIE: You're a terrible influence.

RUBY: And your #1 fan. Love you, mean it!

Cassie woke up, her neck stiff from falling asleep on the sofa. On the coffee table was a mess of notebooks, an empty wineglass, and three cell phones strewn about—James's phone, her work phone, and her personal phone. Groggy, she got up and stumbled into the kitchen, where she filled a glass with water, letting the cold liquid refresh her. She settled back onto the sofa, reaching for her phone, yearning for a few minutes of mindless scrolling to let her brain unwind.

She scrolled, looking at the stylized images of beautiful people on exotic getaways, everything staged and curated. She zoomed past the ads, beautiful plates of food, incredible sunset scenes, flawless homes, double-tapping whenever something pleased her.

In her haze of fatigue and loneliness, she convinced herself that it made sense to log into his account—just to keep tabs. She found a .txt document on his phone with all his passwords, instantly giving her access to all his accounts, from email to social media. She told herself that it was honorable to monitor for any trolls or negative comments, especially since @NewYork SecretDiner had practically vanished, and his followers were starting to send messages wondering where he went. She felt like she had to protect his legacy, especially now that she knew about @NewYorkSecretDiner. Cassie added the account to her personal Instagram feed on her phone—using his phone felt like too much of a violation of privacy.

DUTIFULLY, CASSIE RODE the subway to work and plugged away at her work responsibilities, although her mind was elsewhere. Every half hour she would check her phone, scrolling through the @NewYorkSecretDiner feed, letting herself feel a little closer to James, if only for a fleeting second. Finally, it was five thirty, and she slipped out the door, eager to get back to James's apartment.

After a few hours of sorting clothes to send to Goodwill,

she flopped onto the couch, retreating into the comfort of her phone. Photos of stylized cocktails zoomed by, along with picturesque scenes from architectural restaurants, impromptu snapshots of boba teas, beautiful people sharing selfies—vignettes of Instagram-perfect lives, all carefully curated for public consumption. Nonetheless, Cassie indulged and took comfort in it.

One image stood out to her, a scene from a downtown restaurant, the light coming through the window and landing on a vibrantly hued grapefruit and radicchio salad.

"Gorgeous," Cassie commented, adding a white heart emoji.

She kept scrolling, but something felt . . . strange. She toggled over to the home screen, and her stomach sank. She was in the @NewYorkSecretDiner account. She had responded as @New YorkSecretDiner. She had liked *so many* photos as @NewYork SecretDiner.

Her palms started to sweat, and her stomach turned—she was horrified. She had responded as James. Panicking, she toggled over to the settings, shocked to see how many photos she had liked in what seemed like only a few minutes.

And then the DMs started.

"You're back!" said one, followed by a string of food and cooking emojis. "Where have you been?"

"Does this mean @NewYorkSecretDiner is back in action?" said another.

"Anxiously awaiting your next review," said another.

Then she got a notification. Another account had posted "Has @NewYorkSecretDiner returned from hibernation? New activity, with @NewYorkSecretDiner liking several posts this evening." Accompanied by a screenshot of a post liked by the account.

She felt sick. Cassie fell back into the couch, her heart racing. She had to talk to someone.

"Hello?"

"Ruby, it's Cassie. I fucked up. OMG, I fucked up. Shit shit shit shit shit."

"Slow down—what happened?" asked Ruby.

"I accidentally liked posts with James's account. The internet thinks he's alive."

"Wait, what?" asked Ruby. "James's account?"

"Yes, James's account." Cassie started pacing back and forth frantically, adrenaline and fear surging through her body. "I logged into his account on my phone," she confessed.

"Well, this escalated quickly."

"Ruby, come on—this is *serious*."

"Is it?" Sometimes Ruby was infuriatingly blasé.

"Yes. And there are screenshots—fan accounts that somehow track his activity. And people are asking where he's been, asking why he went AWOL."

"Um, that's scary," said Ruby. "That's like the fan accounts that track activity on celeb accounts. It's really crazy that people were tracking *his* account."

"Tell me about it. Shit. What do I do?"

Ruby didn't respond.

"Ruby? Are you still there?"

"Yes, I'm thinking." Ruby paused, and Cassie could hear her fingernails tapping in the background. "Does it matter? Okay, so, worst case, only a handful of people knew that James was the Secret Diner, and while they might be freaked out, did they know enough about how he worked to know that he worked alone? Would they have known if he brought in a team of some sort?"

"I'm not sure," said Cassie. "I know of at least one person who went to review restaurants with him. I just read that he wanted to tell me about the account, he wanted me to be able to go with him, but he was nervous about how I would react to his lie."

"So, let me ask the question: If he was still alive, would you want to go with him?"

"Of course, I would have loved to have been included. I'm quite irritated that he *didn't* invite me, that he kept it all a secret."

"It's no longer a secret, Cass. Now it's up to you what you want to do with this information."

After hanging up with Ruby, Cassie was suddenly consumed by hunger. She had to get out of the apartment. Cassie grabbed her coat, tucked her phone into her bag, and headed down the street to Olivia's. It was a busy night, and even from the street, she could see how full the restaurant was. Couples leaned close together over the tabletops, faces lit by the soft glow of a single candle; a family of six occupied the window banquette, multiple generations sharing stories and passing appetizers of creamy burrata with cherry tomatoes and fried calamari around the table.

Olivia waved her in and pointed at their—her—favorite corner seat at the bar. Cassie squeezed past the crowd waiting for a table, comforted by the bustling service. Just as she sat down, Olivia placed a glass of sparkling rosé in front of her.

"You must try this, it's my new favorite rosé. It's called the Callie from Un Femme Wines. I'm obsessed," she added, before knocking once on the bar and running off again to help another table. There was a unique energy to a busy restaurant: the hum of conversation, the volume of the music that forced people to talk just more closely, and the constant motion of servers, bussers, and the kitchen working busily through the dinnertime rush.

Cassie looked down at the menu, wanting to try something different, something that wasn't part of James's usual order. She wanted something warm and fortifying.

Olivia was in front of her again; the woman moved incredibly quickly during service.

"Pappardelle ai Funghi, please."

Olivia raised her eyebrows, and Cassie smiled at her, taking a sip of the crisp rosé that reminded her of fresh raspberries.

THE HANDMADE INCH-WIDE pasta coiled around the bottom of the bowl, topped with a simple sauce of sautéed mushrooms, olive oil, and garlic, garnished with chopped parsley, lemon zest, and grated Parmigiano Reggiano, the aroma nutty and welcoming. She looked down at the bowl and then back toward the kitchen. Someone had spent hours making the noodles from eggs and flour, while someone else had cut and prepared the mushrooms, and another person had cooked it all together right before it was served. Each element of the dish was a decision that someone thought about carefully. Realizing this, she decided she was going to let herself eat—really *eat* and enjoy—savoring every bite out of gratitude for all the hard work that had gone into her meal.

She pulled out her phone and positioned the camera above the dish and snapped a photo. She was a little embarrassed, but no one was looking at her anyway. She studied the image on her screen and pulled her cheeks into a frown. It was a dark blob with even darker spots where the mushrooms were supposed to be. Maybe the flash would help. She tried again, this time blasting the plate with artificial light. Now she was *really* embarrassed—she instantly felt guilty for disrupting the candlelit glow of the restaurant. She looked at the image. It was even worse—the beautiful plate of pasta looked almost like plastic, the flash calling attention to the oil and the shininess of the plate.

Giving up, she picked up her fork and spun one of the wide noodles around its tines until she had a good bite of mushrooms, noodles, and cheese. Bringing it to her mouth, she could smell the woodiness of the mushrooms, complimented by the tanginess of fresh Parmesan cheese. Her first bite melted in her mouth, soft and warm, a flavorful layering of starchy noodle, nutty mushrooms caramelized in oil, and the brightness of salt and lemon zest. She closed her eyes and let herself experience the bite of food—it was like she was tasting for the first time.

As she was finishing the dish, Olivia made her way over. The restaurant was winding down for the night, and she finally had some time to come over and chat.

"Don't you ever flash your dish in my restaurant again," joked Olivia. As if one in five patrons *wasn't* posting pics of the restaurant's beautiful dishes. She placed a panna cotta drizzled with homemade rhubarb compote in front of Cassie, with two spoons. "What were you doing, anyway?"

"I guess I felt inspired. The food is so beautiful here."

"You're starting to sound like James," Olivia quipped, taking a bite of panna cotta.

"Maybe that's not a bad thing," Cassie said.

10

The next morning, Cassie was at her desk when Ruby popped into her cubicle, leaning against the entry. "How are you doing today, sunshine?"

"I'm good!"

"Wow—I haven't heard that in a while. Feeling better than last night?"

"Yes, I guess," said Cassie. She leaned in closer to Ruby, and, after looking around, she whispered, "Last night . . . I took photos of my food." Cassie brought her hands up over her eyes. "I was so embarrassed, but it was kind of fun. It was nice to have a reason to pay attention. And you know, when you really study what is put in front of you, there's a different kind of appreciation. The little details matter—someone in the kitchen thinks about every little thing, why each ingredient is used. It makes me think about the conversations I would have with James; it's almost like I can hear his voice in my head again. So much was coming back to me. It was kind of supernatural."

"See, I think James knew you would enjoy the culinary arts— you just needed a little push to get into it. Maybe this is a way to connect with him again."

"Maybe," said Cassie. "I miss him."

"You will always miss him. Try not to take it so seriously,

Cass. Insta accounts come and go all the time. People start these things and abandon them for a million reasons. No one is going to think that there is anything weird happening. I doubt anyone will even notice. And if they do, you can just say that there was a team of people, and you were on that team. Try to have fun with it—you deserve it. If this is something that is bringing you joy and something that helps make the pain more manageable, then do it. Fuck what anyone else thinks."

"So, what now?"

"Want to go to dinner tonight?"

"Sure, that sounds like fun," said Cassie, perking up.

"Okay, but you have to find the restaurant." Ruby spun on her heels and headed back to her desk, giving Cassie a wink as she did.

AT SIX O'CLOCK on the dot, Cassie and Ruby met in front of the elevator. They were both in navy suits, not exactly dressed to go to a hip downtown restaurant. Perhaps, Cassie supposed, it was best to think of their outfits as a clever disguise?

"Where are we headed?" Ruby asked.

"This spot is called Ukita Sushi. The internet tells me it's a new hotspot near Saint Marks."

"Do you know anything about it?" asked Ruby, smiling.

"No, I just went by the number of stars on the review, and the number of dollar signs when you look it up."

"Okay." Ruby laughed. "Next time, maybe you should read a little bit more. Lead the way," she said, motioning for Cassie to enter the elevator in front of her.

They popped out of the subway at Astor Place, a bustling intersection located near multiple universities. The air was filled with the smell of street food: shawarma restaurants and Japanese yakitori spots. Cassie loved the convergence of cultures in the neighborhood; it was the kind of place where you would find college students, New York City's old guard, young professionals, and well-heeled new-money types who preferred to live downtown because it had more "soul." She and Ruby cut east, making their way to Second Avenue, a strip where new restaurants frequently opened—the rent was still cheap and the area had the same energy as "old New York," complete with dive bars and late-night clubs that opened after midnight.

The restaurant was austere on the outside—simple black wood planks and a tiny stainless-steel sign that announced its location. They walked through the door and into a small foyer framed by black-and-white Japanese tapestries that hung from the ceiling.

"How many?" asked the hostess, almost in a whisper.

"Two for dinner," said Cassie, hoping they could get in without a reservation. It was a Wednesday.

"Sushi counter or table?"

Cassie looked at Ruby with a blank expression.

"Sushi counter," said Ruby, stepping in.

"Follow me," said the hostess, grabbing two small menus from the hostess stand.

Cassie and Ruby took their seats at the sushi bar, sitting eye level with freshly cut slabs of tuna, octopus, yellowtail, snapper, and other types of fish that were unrecognizable. Cassie looked down at the menu in front of her, which listed just three things:

Omakase—Small
Omakase—Large
Sake Pairing

"Ummmmm . . ." Cassie looked up at Ruby, slightly freaking out. She had no idea what any of this meant.

"Omakase, large, for both of us," Ruby said to the chef, "with the sake pairing. And hot tea." She turned to Cassie and with a grin on her face said, "You brought one of those stacks of bills, right?"

Within moments, the waitress brought over two glasses of crisp, chilled sake that tasted like Asian pears and Meyer lemons. Cassie watched the chef behind the counter carefully slicing fish, pressing it into a ball of sushi rice, and finishing it off with a swipe of soy glaze. As though in one fluid motion, a jewellike piece of sushi landed on the small wooden plate in front of her.

The chef leaned toward the two women. "Kampachi, also known as amberjack."

Cassie looked at Ruby, puzzled. There were no utensils. How was she supposed to eat this?

Ruby gracefully picked up the piece of sushi, delicately pinching it between her thumb and forefinger, and popped it into her mouth. Cassie followed her lead and ate it in one bite, even though it felt too big, almost gratuitous. She tasted the sweetness of the rice, mixed with the salinity of the fish, which had been finished with yuzu soy. Her eyes closed in bliss as she leaned back in her chair to slowly chew. For a moment, she was transported. She had never tasted anything like this, certainly not from the sushi restaurants she usually frequented, the ones that specialized in spicy tuna rolls. This was another level, the piece of fish like a work of art.

"Kasugo, red sea bream, with pickled plum," the chef said. Before her appeared a beautiful piece of orange-hued fish accompanied by delicately sliced fruit. Cassie pulled out her phone and took a photo—not great, but better than the ones she'd taken the night before. The chef looked down at her and smiled patroniz-ingly; this was clearly a hotspot for food bloggers in search of sushi porn. She was slightly embarrassed, but she desperately wanted to remember the details from the meal. She reached out to pick up the piece in front of her—it had been slightly seared and had the most delightful flavor of salt and smoke that was cut by the sweetness of the pickled plum.

A new sake was served, this one white and creamy—an un-filtered nigori sake that tasted of jasmine, orange blossom, and vanilla.

King salmon with smoked soy sauce was followed by a bite of sea bass topped with a dollop of lime foam and sea salt. Fatty tuna was followed by an even fattier tuna, each delightfully buoyant and yet like velvet on her tongue. And then a mysteri-ous dark yellow paste arrived, wrapped in a column of seaweed.

"Uni!" gasped Ruby.

"What in the world is uni?"

"Sea urchin—it's a delicacy." Ruby swiftly ate the bite and moaned shamelessly, her eyes closed.

Cassie hesitantly popped the food into her mouth—it was strangely creamy and coated her tongue with the tropical flavor of mango, in stark contrast to the crunchy, salty seaweed. It was, without a doubt, simply delightful.

"Ugh, I forgot to take a picture!" said Cassie, waking up from her uni trance.

"Live a little!" exclaimed Ruby. "You are too hard on yourself—not everything needs to be the pursuit of perfection."

The next sake was a chilled Junmai Daiginjo that smelled of ripe melon and sea salt, served in thimble-like glasses. Ruby raised her cup.

"To you, my dear Cass, and to letting go."

They clinked glasses. *To letting go.*

The sake wrapped around Cassie's tongue—sweet with the flavors of pear, cantaloupe, and black pepper. It was both velvety and acidic, and she wished the glass was bigger. Cassie was feeling the buzz of the alcohol, and she enjoyed feeling the stress of life leave her, even just for these couple of hours.

"I'm thinking about posting this dinner on the account," confessed Cassie.

"Well, that's obvious. I've never seen you take photos of your food before."

"There's not much to document in a midtown salad," said Cassie, rolling her eyes.

"Very true," said Ruby with a sigh. "I'm just glad you're finally listening to me."

"It could be fun, having a reason to go out and eat in fancy restaurants. Plus, the DMs are basically a road map to all the new restaurants in town. Pretty much every chef that is opening a new spot invited James in."

"Ah, yes! You can *write* the reviews that cause all the two-hour wait times. I'm in!"

"Besides, a woman would be the best disguise of all," Cassie said, and laughed. She picked up the last piece of sushi in front of her—a rectangular block of cooked egg—tamago. It was sweet and tasted like custard.

"I love that," Ruby chirped. "I once read on Reddit that so many people assume that @NewYorkSecretDiner is a man. You follow r/WhoIsNewYorkSecretDiner, right?"

"Isn't Reddit just for trolls?" Cassie asked.

"Oh, Cass, you have so much to learn. Speaking of which, did you know that sushi chefs in Japan spend something like ten years learning how to make tamago?" said Ruby. "It's the only thing they make until they have perfected it, and only then are they able to start making sushi."

"Still sounds more fun than law school," quipped Cassie.

"Isn't that the truth."

THAT NIGHT, CASSIE sat down in front of her laptop and typed out her recollections of the meal. She tried to remember the feeling of each piece of fish on her palate, how each texture was different, and any flavors that came to mind. She couldn't get over how the sea urchin had tasted like tropical fruit—no—like a creamy tart *topped* with ripe mango slices. She spent a great deal of time trying to find the words to describe the fresh wasabi, which was completely different from the store-bought wasabi paste she was used to. It reminded her of minced cucumber, icy and refreshing on her tongue, with the spicy kick of horseradish.

It was almost as though she could hear James, his comforting low voice, methodically talking through the meal, just like he did every time they went out to eat. Was he going over his tasting notes in the moment? Looking back, she realized that he would explain the subtleties of cooking techniques and why the dish worked as a whole. If only she had realized what he was doing and had paid more attention. The thought of it made her ache, as though she could feel the presence of his absence. Today, it brought on a new dimension of grief, a longing for what had been there all along, right under her nose.

She knew she would have to find a way to mimic James's writing if she was going to pull this off—it would have to seem like

@NewYorkSecretDiner had just taken a long vacation or some-thing. James's voice was such a big part of the account—it was so confident. Within a single caption, he had the ability to make someone feel as if they were sitting in the restaurant with him, offering glowing praise or devastating pans at the same time. She found notes in one of his journals about an omakase meal in a sushi restaurant in Los Angeles—his notes were so brief, almost perfunctory, but they were something to model *her* review on.

> Ukita Sushi in the East Village is a hushed omakase-style sushi bar that is reminiscent of those in Japan, where each piece of fish is presented individually. The $225 meal started with pieces of sushi that were light and tasted of the sea, with a crescendo to richer, fattier fish. A sake pairing beautifully complemented each dish, with the pronounced flavors of soy, yuzu, smoke, and sea salt. The only thing disappointing about Ukita Sushi was how fast the meal seemed. I found myself wanting more time between each bite; however, those extra moments would have been impossible to enjoy with the pressure of the crowd waiting outside.

Not terrible, but certainly not worthy of publishing. Besides, she'd failed to capture the entire meal, something @NewYork SecretDiner did without fail—a photograph of every single dish was always posted with every review.

The one picture Cassie remembered to take looked awful, and it frustrated her—she used to be good at photography! There was something missing. She pulled out the Ziploc bag filled with

James's personal items from the hospital, and in it was a pocket-size camera and a small black-and-white cube. On its side was a switch—it was a tiny light!

She turned on the camera and found images of what was, without a doubt, his last meal. White tablecloths, multiple settings of silverware, and precious compositions of food on stacks of multiple cascading decorative chargers. As to be expected, the whole meal was meticulously documented, from the exquisite bread basket to the silver tray that held the check at the end of the meal. She felt grateful that he'd had an impeccable final dinner.

11

The next day at work, Cassie did the bare minimum. She filed the cases that needed to be filed and spent the rest of her day studying the @NewYorkSecretDiner account, paying close attention to the tone of each review and the angles of the photographs, trying to dissect where the light was positioned so that she could re-create the same look. She watched YouTube videos to learn how to use the camera and wirelessly transfer the images from the camera to her phone. She studied food blogger videos on how to create "ultimate food porn" images: sandwiches cut in half with cheese stretched and oozing between the two pieces, ice cream cones held up against a painted brick wall, and gluttonous spreads of too much food for even a large group of people to consume. James's photos were consistently simple—they showed each dish in a casual, elegant way that was more utilitarian than anything. He was just trying to document the meal, not make it into anything else. Sometimes he shot dishes from above, abstracting the plating into colors and patterns, but most often, the photo was from his vantage point, describing the scene as a diner: fork, knife, spoon, wineglass, water glass, all surrounding the plate of whatever he was about to consume.

Cassie needed practice.

She left work early and headed to the Strand, this time flying through the store, picking up a book on food photography—*Delicious Light*—and a few cookbooks—*The Basics of French Cuisine* and *Rustic Italian Cooking*—and a monograph by a famous chef that was filled with the most beautiful images of food she had ever seen. It was research, she told herself; she had to learn from the best.

That night, she ordered dinner from a neighborhood bistro, making sure to order a starter, a main, and a dessert. She ripped open the takeout bags and plated the food on her modest white ceramic plates that could never mimic a fine-dining experience. She set the table, poured a glass of ice water, a glass of wine, and scattered a few candles around, dimming the lights to emulate the ambiance of a restaurant. Holding the cube light in her left hand and the camera in her right, she was able to illuminate each dish from above and at a slight angle, like James's pictures. Through the lens of her camera, the salad looked bright and appetizing, but the salmon looked shiny and fake. She moved the light back and was able to reduce the glare. Not award-winning, but better than before, and certainly better than a cell phone image.

12

"Get in, loser, we're going to lunch." Cassie held the elevator door open for Ruby. "I've booked us a table at the Modern."

"I'm really starting to like this new girl Cassie," quipped Ruby. "She really knows her way around town."

The two women rounded the corner onto Fifty-Third, entering the restaurant through a dark tunnel that opened onto a beautifully day-lit space outfitted with black-and-chrome furniture from another era. The hostess led them through a mirrored bar, past a row of diaphanous screens, and into an atrium with high ceilings that looked out over the museum's courtyard. Tall floral arrangements drew Cassie's eyes up, following the marching rhythm of the aluminum mullions that carried up the building. She and Ruby were seated at a two-top next to the glass, and within moments a server was at their table.

"Anything to start with today?" asked the server. "Champagne?"

Cassie looked at Ruby. "One glass can't hurt, right?" She turned to the server. "That sounds delightful."

"What has gotten into you?" asked Ruby.

"I'm going to do my first review," said Cassie, leaning forward. "I found his photo setup, and I've been studying his captions. I think I can do this!"

"Bollinger Blanc de Blanc," said the server, presenting the bottle to Cassie. "It's our recommended champagne by the glass." She poured a small taste into Cassie's wineglass.

Cassie picked up the glass and smelled the wine, then took a small sip. It had more flavor than any champagne she'd had before—it was full and round, tasted of toasted brioche and cooked pears topped with cream. Her eyes widened. "That is delicious." The two glasses were filled, and they immediately clinked them together.

Cassie looked down at the menu—it was straightforward and clearly seasonal.

"We should divide and conquer," said Cassie, as though she had done this before. "I'll get the oysters. You get the sturgeon to start, and then one of us should order the ricotta gnudi and the other, the roast chicken. And we must order the chocolate tart with cardamom."

"Fire away," confirmed Ruby, smiling with pride.

Each dish was more beautiful than the last. The oysters arrived on the half shell and served with vibrant, almost sour kumquat mignonette, the combination of which was bright and briny and almost candy-like. *Click.* The sturgeon was smoked and came on a bed of gem lettuce covered in a thin layer of creamy sliced avocado, which balanced the flavors of the smoky fish. *Click.* The ricotta gnudi were pillows of ricotta covered in flour, boiled and served over baked summer squash and drizzled with a miso sauce. *Click.* The roasted half chicken came spatchcocked alongside blackened peppers and hen of the woods mushrooms that were lightly baked until soft. *Click.* They finished the meal with the chocolate tart, creamy and decadent, with the unexpected spice of green cardamom. *Click.*

At the end, Cassie ordered another glass of champagne. "I'm not going back to the office."

"Good for you, Cass. Unfortunately, I have a case next week, so I have to go back. Enjoy, and let's talk tomorrow. I'm proud of you."

CASSIE TOOK THE subway home and rushed in the door, stripping off her coat and dropping her bag on the entry table. She collapsed onto the sofa, slightly buzzed. She pulled out the phone and the camera and, recalling the instructions, transferred the images from the camera directly onto her phone. They weren't half bad, but she knew full well that the restaurant's day-lit table was the defining factor that made the photos so good.

She opened her computer and pulled up a few of James's old posts—giving them one last study before she started building hers: the sequence of images and, most important, the captions. If she was going to pull this off, it had to sound like the same person. She had to sound like James.

Lunch at the Modern

It is a privilege to dine at the Modern, elbow to elbow with some of New York City's most prominent movers and shakers. The meal is rigidly seasonal, an unsurprising choice from Chef Thomas Allan. Starting with fresh oysters topped with kumquat mignonette, both delightful and refreshing, paired beautifully with a glass of Blanc de Blanc champagne. Gem lettuce topped with avocado and smoked sturgeon was delicious but arrived limp on the plate. Handmade gnudi transports the diner to Italy, where the pillows of ricotta are just as Nonna would make—light and dangerously delicious, surrounded by autumnal squash. The roast chicken was lovely, especially when served with maitake mushrooms and blackened peppers. We concluded with dessert—a chocolate and cardamom tart that was reminiscent of the Middle Eastern shops found on Atlantic Avenue, where the aroma of ground spices hangs in the air. All in all, the meal was quite delightful if lacking imagination and surprise, but a powerful lunch nonetheless.

Review: ✎✎✎ (of five)

#NYSecretDiner

Once the post was built and the photos were in place, she closed her eyes and clicked the Share button. She threw the phone onto the coffee table, exhausted.

Cassie got up, walked around the apartment, and circled back to the phone. It had only been a matter of seconds, but she couldn't take the suspense. She opened the app and saw hundreds of likes pouring in—and seemingly just as many comments:

Welcome back!

Put me on the waiting list.

"Well, this is fun," Cassie said to herself.

A FEW HOURS later, Cassie opened the app and started scrolling through the notifications. The response was overwhelming—was she supposed to respond to every person? This was nothing like the kind of traffic she received on her personal account, where she had 147 followers. No wonder James was on his phone all the time.

Cassie swiped over to the DMs, and there were hundreds of messages from his followers, which were mostly complimentary.

@FABFOODIE3742
We've missed you, NYSD! We were starting to get worried. It's not like you to be silent for so long.

@EATINGMYWAYTHROUGHNYC
I love the Modern. Thrilled to hear you had a great experience there.

@DAVIDMAKESMONEY
Who is posting this?

Cassie was surprised to see David's handle pop up in the DMs, but then again, he was a self-proclaimed gastronome, so it tracked that he followed @NewYorkSecretDiner. She read the message again, and her heart started to race. Could he have known that it was James's account? She marked the message as unread and ignored it, unsure how to respond.

More messages came in: notes from other reviewers, chefs, restaurant owners, PR people. There were so many invitations—to restaurant openings, chefs' tasting events, private dinners—that it was overwhelming. Cassie scrolled back to earlier DMs to see how James would respond to his messages. He must have had a system to remain anonymous.

@BLACKENEDRESTAURANTNYC
Hello! We would love to host you at the opening of Blackened, a new wood-fired restaurant. Would you be interested in joining us for dinner?

> **@NEWYORKSECRETDINER**
> Thank you so much for reaching out. I prefer to make my own dinner reservations, but I will add Blackened to my list of restaurants to visit.

She kept scrolling.

@CHEFSKNIFEPR
Good morning. We are hosting a small tasting event with Chef Veit next Tuesday. It will be a very exclusive event. Might you be interested in joining?

> **@NEWYORKSECRETDINER**
> It is a privilege to be invited, thank you. I am unable to attend, but might I recommend Joshua Delmonico, a writer from the Brooklyn Foodie magazine?

She recognized the name, Joshua Delmonico, whom James had styled with an inky black wig that made him look Italian. Suddenly, she understood. He recommended another writer when, in fact, he was said writer using an alias. People used pen names all the time to write books—and apparently to review restaurants. She picked up his phone and toggled over to his Gmail and found email addresses that corresponded to all his aliases. It was so simple.

Cassie decided that she needed some ground rules. She could only go to events that were close to her office, so that if she got called in, she could drop everything and rush back to her desk. She would always use an alias, and she would only accept dinners. Except on weekends. She could do lunches on weekends.

An invitation for an event at Boucher caught her eye. It was a new minimalist restaurant in the Meatpacking District that was quickly becoming a hotspot. One of those gigantic, theater-like restaurants that catered to the fashion scene. From what she could tell by the photos of the interior, it was a beautiful space: dark, moody, a place where she could attend the event and remain somewhat anonymous.

She grabbed her phone, toggled over to Gmail, and created a new account. Ayla Ashley. *Her* new alias.

13

On Monday Cassie left work at five fifteen again. She slipped past the receptionist, avoiding any of the firm's top brass. She didn't enjoy feeling like she was sneaking around, but she felt a powerful, magnetic pull to this new world that she had recently discovered. Law was starting to make her feel hollow, and she desperately wanted to feel a connection to a community where people were inspired to be creative instead of destructive.

In the subway heading downtown, Cassie touched up her makeup and traded her suit jacket for a black cardigan accented with black beads that she had found in a vintage shop a few years ago. Moments before the train reached her stop, she swapped her modest work slides for a pair of classic black pumps, to make herself look less like a lawyer. She was ready.

Outside the restaurant, there was a pair of women holding clipboards. Oh no, she thought. She wasn't expecting to have to talk to anyone official. She sheepishly walked over to the door and quietly said, "Ayla Ashley, I'm here for the event." Miraculously, without much conversation, the women opened the door and welcomed her into the restaurant.

"Follow me," one of the clipboards said.

Cassie followed the woman through the restaurant, snaking past the glittering bar, screened banquettes with beautiful people behind, and into the raucous kitchen. Then through another door and into an exquisite dining room lined with undulating gold walls, with a monumental burl wood dining table in the center.

Another woman handed Cassie a half-size Hendrick's martini with a cucumber garnish. "Ayla, right? Welcome. We have quite a night lined up for you. There is a preview of Chef's new tasting menu. It's fifteen courses. I hope you're hungry." She led Cassie over to her seat, marked with an inscribed name card. Her new name looked so pretty in calligraphy.

On her right was an older gentleman in a tweed blazer, elbows well-worn, and with slightly crooked glasses. On her left was a smartly dressed woman with a short bob reminiscent of a 1920s flapper. Both pulled out notebooks and pens, visibly ready to review.

The meal started with a glass of French Burgundy and an amuse-bouche of smoked trout roe on a piece of buttered crisped bread and topped with thin, precisely cut chives. Cassie pulled out her little light and held it up above the dish. Using her other hand, she snapped a few quick photos, trying to be discreet. Mr. Tweed wasn't taking images, nor was Fashionable Bob.

She put the bite in her mouth, feeling each little sphere pop to reveal its creamy, briny liquid center, exploding with flavor. She took a sip of the wine, bright and acidic, just enough to cut through the thickness of the roe that remained in her mouth.

The next dish arrived in a beautiful conical bowl: grilled peas and Parmesan topped with sweet pea flowers. The room started to grow louder as the dinner guests relaxed into the meal. There was a buzz of chatter and the comforting pings of cutlery hitting plates. She looked around the table, adorned with beautiful florals and tall, flickering candelabras. Everyone in this room was truly enjoying the moment. And so was she.

Buzzzzzzzzz.

Cassie's phone lit up with a notification. *Seriously?* she thought as she pulled her phone into her lap to read the message.

> Merger just closed. We start tonight on the Meyer deal.

Shit.

Cassie felt a lump grow in her throat and that familiar rush of anxiety surge through her body. Her heart started racing, and her stomach churned—it was a feeling she knew all too well. The last thing in the world she wanted to do was go into the office. She felt a rush of anger—at her job, at her sense of obligation, at *herself* for invariably doing the "right thing," the "disciplined thing."

Almost as if someone else was guiding her, she stood up, walked over to one of the members of the PR team, and told them that she had to leave. There was a family emergency, she lied. She gave her thanks, holding back tears, sad to leave this beautiful candlelit room and its delights.

She walked slowly back through the restaurant, feeling defeated. Outside, her hand hailed a taxi, which took her uptown, back to her office.

CASSIE THREW HER bag down onto the chair next to her desk, angry to find herself back in the office already. She had only been gone for a few hours. It was *inhumane.*

The team was starting to congregate in the library, each face more sullen than the next. Across the table was Ruby, who had clearly been on a date and was especially irritated to be called in. After a short debrief, the lead lawyers left the room, leaving the younger staff to do the actual work. The room started to clear, and Cassie looked at Ruby, who rolled her eyes dramatically before getting up and heading back to work.

Cassie grabbed the books she needed from the library and dragged herself back to her desk. She sat down at her computer but was distracted. She kept thinking about that amazing meal—the kind of meal she had perpetually dreamed of, and she wanted more of it.

AROUND 3:00 A.M., Cassie decided to head home. Sitting in the back of a car, she scrolled mindlessly, occasionally taking a moment to look at a photo of a beautiful landscape or plating porn. She noticed there were quite a few DMs that had come in over the past few hours and toggled over to the inbox. One note popped out at her. The icon was bright red with a white capital V—the Viand Awards.

Dear New York Secret Diner,

Congratulations again on winning the Viand Award for short-form cuisine writing. It was unfortunate that you were unable to attend the awards ceremony last month. We were very much looking forward to meeting.

We are reaching out again to invite you to be a secret reviewer for the Viand Awards, the world's preeminent restaurant ranking institution. We will be embarking on an all-expenses-paid European tour of a selection of the world's best restaurants, starting in Paris, France. Your affiliation with our website can remain anonymous, and your reviews will be entered into the judging for next year's restaurant rankings. We are offering a flat-rate one-month stipend for the judge's seat. Only people who have won a Viand award in the past are invited on the trip, and we are thrilled to extend the invitation to you this year. If you are interested in attending, please reply as soon as possible.

Regards,
The Viand Committee

Cassie was shaking—it was an invitation to go to Europe. *Wouldn't that be spectacular?*

Her mind was already racing, and she could envision herself in a smart black suit, sitting at a table with white linens, enjoying an elaborate meal at a table for one. Perhaps she would wear a big, theatrical hat like Gael Greene, playing the part of a society swan. She felt so desperate to take a break from Stevens & Sweeney that the idea of disappearing into someone else's life was incredibly tempting, especially when that life involved a trip to Europe.

14

The next morning, Cassie couldn't wait to tell Ruby about the message. She got to work early and bounded over to Ruby's desk, two matcha lattes in hand.

"You are not going to believe what just happened." Cassie handed over a paper cup.

"I saw you posted your review of the Modern," Ruby said. "Nicely done." She was perpetually supportive.

"Yes—and last night, I was going through the DMs, and I found an invitation for a four-week trip to Europe from *the Viand Awards*!"

"Seriously?"

"I'm not kidding. Do you want to see the message?"

"That's a *thing*?"

"I guess so. I have been wondering how James was able to visit all those incredible places. I guess they were organized for him."

"That adds up. You know, I once listened to a podcast about a tequila brand ambassador whose job was to host writers and VIPs in Mexico. It was funny, his job was part entertainer, part educator, part problem solver."

"Stay focused, Ruby," Cassie quipped.

"Sorry—I digress. The real question is, how do *you* get to go?"

"I can't, you know that. I have a job," said Cassie, ever the good girl.

"You are the keeper of the account; you *are* @NewYorkSecret-Diner now. James is gone, but, honey, you're still here, and if working in a law firm isn't making you happy, you better find something that does. James died unexpectedly, and so could any of us, so go live your life. Get on that plane!"

"I've invested too much in becoming a lawyer." Cassie sighed, defeated. "I can't quit."

"It's your life, Cass." Ruby shrugged and looked back at her computer. "You could ask for a sabbatical—you would be able to take a few months off and still have a job when you come back. The old-timers do it all the time. Besides, if you want to quit while you're on sabbatical, you can always do that too."

"I guess that's true."

"So, what did the message say? *Exactly?*"

"Just that he won a writing award. It seems like the prize was a seat on the trip?"

"Did they know that it was him—as in, James?"

"I don't think so. There wasn't a lot in the message, but they addressed the note to his Instagram handle, and mentioned that he missed the awards ceremony."

"So, @NewYorkSecretDiner could be anyone, right?"

"Presumably."

"I think you should figure out how to get on that trip."

"Maybe you should do it," Cassie said, deflecting.

"Ha! That would be hilarious. Maybe if it was a press trip for Balenciaga! I'm no foodie!"

"Neither am I," Cassie said.

"But you kind of are. You and James used to go out to eat all the time. Plus, don't you have his notebooks? Those could be helpful, no?"

"But what about work?"

"Cass, when are you going to stop using this place as an excuse? Life doesn't happen in your cubicle. It happens outside these damn walls."

Cassie walked back to her desk and sat down. She turned her computer on and looked at the stack of paperwork piled in front of her. Ruby was right. Law didn't make her happy; it made her miserable. Her career had become an obligation—there was no joy anymore.

"Cassie, you're late," her manager bellowed from halfway down the hall, startling her. "I need that paperwork for the Michelin account—where is it?"

"I've been working on the Meyer merger—I was here all night."

"So you're telling me you're unprepared," he said, looking down at his watch.

At this point, she was used to taking abuse from the higher-ups at the company, who used the power of their positions to wield control and cause fear, firing onslaughts of insults and blame. It was not a productive leadership tactic, and she could feel its destructive implications: insomnia, depression, debilitating anxiety. Cassie's hands started to shake again, a warning sign of a panic attack to come.

"Um—"

"Seems so. Well, then, you're off the account," he said before storming back to his corner office.

Cassie stared at the wall, aghast. She had spent the past two years working on the Michelin case, logging hours on weekends and holidays. She had invested so much of herself in it, believing that it would be the account that would get her the next promotion, one step closer to making partner. And now the case was being taken from her, surely to be handed over to a junior lawyer. All of her hard work would amount to *nothing*.

She felt the blood draining from her body. What was it all for? Why was she working so hard? She rarely saw her friends, her boyfriend was dead, all she had was her work, and look how quickly that could be taken away.

This career doesn't love you back, Cass, she thought to herself, dropping her head into her hands. She felt the tears start to roll down her cheeks, salty when they touched her lips. *You can't do this anymore*, she thought. *You can't do this to yourself anymore*.

It was time to try something new. She wanted to be happy. Soon.

She looked at her phone, sitting next to her keyboard. She picked it up and scrolled through the DMs until she found the message from the Viand Awards.

> Hello—thanks so much for the invitation. I would be honored to attend. When do we leave?
> NYSD

And with that, Cassie turned back to her computer and typed out a letter requesting two months off. She hit print and headed straight for HR.

15

At two o'clock on the dot, a black car pulled up in front of Cassie's apartment building, her name on a piece of paper in the window, crudely penned with a thick, black marker. It had been three weeks since she received the message from Viand, which felt like a whirlwind as she was getting ready: packing, lining up plant sitters, and wrapping up the last outstanding items at work.

The driver loaded her bags, and Cassie crawled into the back seat, buckling her seatbelt with an audible *click*. A pang of irony hit her deep in her throat. She wished James was here and that they were setting out on a great adventure together. Instead, she glanced over at the empty seat next to her and felt a wave of loneliness wash over her. She looked out the window at her building for one last glance as the driver pulled into the street, turned the corner, and drove toward the airport.

CASSIE PASSED THROUGH the airport doors and into the buzzing lobby, looking for Kelly, who headed up public relations for the Viand Awards. Far in the distance, she saw a petite blond woman dressed in black who also seemed like she was looking for someone. Cassie moved in her direction, navigating families toting tired kids, veteran fliers with their impossibly small suitcases and wrinkle-proof business attire, and couples taking longer-term trips with carts loaded with enormous bags.

"Kelly?" Cassie asked as she approached.

"Yes! Cassie, it's so nice to finally meet you!" said Kelly, reaching out her hand. "I'm such a huge fan of your work. Everyone *lives* for your reviews!" Kelly caught herself, obviously remembering their conversation. "But as we discussed, no one else on the trip needs to know that you are the New York Secret Diner. It will be our little secret," she said with a wink.

Cassie looked at the floor. There it was—the big lie was now out in the open, and it made her uneasy. She was never good at lying, but now she had to. "Thank you, I appreciate that. The anonymity is important to me."

"Everyone will be reviewing for the Viand restaurant rankings, and that's all you need to say."

Cassie nodded. She had spent the last three weeks spinning anxiously on exactly how she was going to keep everything a secret. But last week, she finally had a phone conversation with Kelly at length about her hesitancy to reveal who was behind the account that made her feel so much better. The last thing she wanted to do was to strip the mystery from the account, knowing that it was part of what the readers and the internet loved. Somehow, it was just as intriguing as the food porn. Besides, James had wanted it to be anonymous, and she surely didn't deserve any credit.

"And congratulations on the award! You must be so proud!"

"Yes, it came as a complete surprise," Cassie said uncomfortably.

"I absolutely loved the piece you submitted for the culinary writing awards. I think you're going to do so well on this trip.

We're always looking for fresh talent. It's a great group of people—they're award winners from previous years. Our group is flying in from all over the world, and I'm sure it will be great fun to compare notes from all your travels."

"Of—of course," she stammered, not sure how she felt about this new information. Could they have known James? Would they be able to tell that she wasn't the same writer who submitted the story for the award?

Kelly handed her a folder with a detailed itinerary that laid out every stop of the trip. Cassie eagerly flipped through the materials. This was going to be the trip of a lifetime—she just had to make it through without blowing her cover.

"We just need to get you checked in," Kelly said, leading her toward the group check-in counter.

"Passport, please," the agent said.

Cassie handed her passport to the agent and put her bag on the scale. It was tagged and made its way down the conveyor belt and into the bowels of the airport, on its way to Paris.

"Here's your ticket," said the agent. "Have a nice flight."

"You too," said Cassie, then cringed at her mistake.

"Come on," said Kelly. "Let's go check out the TWA Hotel bar. We're meeting Ben there."

CASSIE FOLLOWED KELLY through the terminal, onto the airport train, and down a narrow, white, portal-like corridor with bright red carpets that rose in a gradual arch and then sloped back down again. When they came out of the tunnel, Cassie looked up and saw the expanse of space around her—the historic TWA terminal, freshly renovated into a destination hotel, bringing the building back to its 1960s glory. She remembered the building from old art history books and from the movies, but it was even more impressive in person. She looked around, letting her eyes feast on the dynamic features of the space: the curving concrete that mimicked flight paths, the crimson seating areas sunk into the floor, making the soaring ceiling seem even higher, and the iconic, bulbous flight board that now served as a cocktail menu. The terminal reminded her of a cathedral rising toward the sky, inspiring awe in those below.

"You're going to love Ben. He's a delight to travel with," Kelly said as they made their way over to the café. She spotted a man sitting across the room, waved, and started walking more quickly in his direction.

It dawned on Cassie that everyone on this trip probably knew each other, everyone except her. And it was going to be more difficult than she'd thought to convince a group of veterans that she was a legitimate food writer. She swallowed hard and smiled at the man standing in front of her. He was Asian, medium height, with longish hair and a warm, inviting face that exuded confidence. He stood and extended a hand to Cassie. "So nice to meet you. I'm Ben."

Ben was clearly someone who knew how to travel. His suitcase, a sleek metal Rimowa, was half the size of hers, and made her clunky old roller bag look paltry in comparison. For his carry-on, he had a small backpack, and he was wearing an athleisure suit accented with an emerald-green silk scarf that caught the light beautifully.

"How was your flight?" asked Kelly, as they all took a seat.

"Just fine," he said. "I slept most of the way. I only woke up for late-night ramen on the flight. ANA has incredible service in business. I'm just coming in from Tokyo," he added, now looking at Cassie. "I was on assignment for *Traveler*."

Of course he was.

"The flight itinerary was rather circuitous," Ben continued, "but you know what it's like lining these trips up back-to-back. I'll take any flight that gets me there," he said with a laugh.

"I love the Rimowa," Kelly commented, running a finger over the top of the striated silver bag.

"I just wrote a feature on the brand for *Traveler*. They sent me a set to review."

"Please tell me you brought both of them," Kelly said in jest.

"Of course I did! They sent me a trunk, and it's the best piece of luggage I've ever owned. I've been on the road for three weeks, and it's a *lifesaver*. Melbourne, Fiji, Tokyo, and now Europe. But don't worry, Kel, I remembered to pack my tux."

Tux? Cassie's mind started to race. What in the world could they need formal attire for? She hadn't brought anything dressy, and she was now regretting not reading the itinerary that Kelly sent the week before in detail before she packed. Once again, she had let her damn job take over her life.

"How much time do we have before our flight?" asked Ben.

"We have quite a bit of time. I had Cassie come to the airport early so you two could meet. Shall we have a glass of champagne?"

"Naturally," said Ben, "and some duck croquettes." He let out a childlike giggle that was pure joy. "They are my favorite here."

"I love that you have a favorite dish at the airport," said Kelly.

"I basically live in airports these days. I have favorite spots in all of them. I could write an airport guide at this point with all the chicest spots."

"I would buy that book. Okay, it's champagne o'clock."

Kelly called the waitress over and fired off the order: "One bottle of Beaumont des Crayères, duck croquettes, crispy salmon sushi, and a black truffle pizza." She shut the menu and turned back to Ben and Cassie. "We don't want anyone going hungry, now, do we?"

Within moments, three champagne tulip glasses were placed on the table, and the waiter came over to present the label to Kelly. She nodded, the bottle was opened, and she tasted the wine before the server poured a glass each for Cassie and Ben.

"To our amazing adventure," said Kelly.

Cassie took a sip of her champagne, feeling the bubbles dance as they went down her throat. She took another sip and started to relax.

"So, Cassie, who do you write for?" asked Ben, leaning back into the powder blue, sculptural chair.

Cassie felt her whole body tense up again, negating the half a glass of wine that she had already downed. But if there was one thing Cassie knew, it was how to perform well under stress. She took a deep breath while pretending to nose her glass of wine.

"I freelance," she said succinctly.

She needed to get her story straight—and fast. This wasn't the last time she was going to be asked this question, and she needed to be more prepared. So she deflected. "And yourself?" she asked, knowing that people usually loved to talk about themselves more than anything.

"I'm a freelance writer, mostly food and travel. I've done everything from writing to editing to social media, but I'm happy being on the go these days. You can find me on socials as @flyfoodiefly. I'm just starting to dabble with TikTok, and it's fun." Ben leaned forward to pick up a piece of sushi, popping it into his mouth and chewing while he took a swig of champagne.

"Dabble? You have like five hundred thousand followers," Kelly said. "You're kind of a big deal."

"Hilariously, those numbers are small these days. It seems like the success marker now is over a million. But it's so easy to have content go viral, especially compared to the other apps. The crazier and weirder it is, the more people want to watch it. It's really wild."

Cassie was flabbergasted. She knew that TikTok was a big deal, but she hadn't realized just how powerful a platform it was. Even more daunting was the idea of building a new following on a different app—she didn't even know how to handle James's account with its 1.2 million followers.

"Are you on TikTok?" asked Ben, cutting open a duck croquette.

"No, not yet," she answered. Another social media channel was the last thing Cassie needed. She felt like she barely knew herself since James died.

Ben fell back into his chair. "Oh my god, these are amazing." He lifted the plate of croquettes and passed it to Cassie. "Make sure you get some of the fig butter."

Cassie speared one of the fried balls and placed it on her plate, along with a scoop of the dark brown paste. They looked simple enough, like any bar food. When she cut it open, though, it erupted with steam, gooey Gruyère cheese, and shredded duck meat. She cut it into quarters, rationed out the fig butter for each piece, and took a bite. Salty and crunchy, the meat sweet and savory—and Ben was right. That fig butter—the creative addition of fat and sweet jammy fruit, punctuated with large crystals of crunchy sea salt—made the dish sing.

"It's the holy trinity of sugar, fat, and salt," Ben said, and took a drink of champagne.

The pizza arrived just as the group polished off the last croquette, filling the air with wafts of nutty truffles.

"Some say that truffles taste like the forest floor, but *some* say they taste like the human body," said Kelly, as she stabbed an egg yolk, releasing a thick yellow goo all over the pizza. She pulled a piece onto her plate.

"Oh yeah, I wrote a story on this," said Ben. "Feet, body odor . . . sex. Truffles have a particular form of stink that attracts people in an animalistic way—it's what explains why people will pay so much money for even the slightest hint of truffle."

Cassie pulled a slice of truffle from the pie and put it on her tongue. Certainly nutty, cool, crunchy . . . but sex? She didn't get it. She shrugged and took another bite.

"I think you need more butter and cheese; cheese famously helps me get in the mood," Ben said with a laugh, pulsing his eyebrows up and down.

Cassie and Kelly laughed and agreed.

"We should probably make our way to the gate," said Kelly, handing her credit card to the passing waitress.

Cassie fumbled to get her wallet from her bag. "How much was it?"

"Not to worry," said Kelly.

"Oh, is this your first review trip?" said Ben, mouth agape and glass in hand.

"Yes. Is it that obvious?" Cassie asked, feeling her face warming with embarrassment. "But I've done similar trips for other teams," she lied.

"Oh, sweetie. You're a Viand virgin. That's *adorable*." Ben laughed, then emptied the contents of his glass into his mouth. "Don't worry, we're going to have the most amazing time."

CASSIE AND BEN followed Kelly through the airport, chitchatting along the way. They breezed through security and made their way to the gate, where their flight was about to board.

"Come on," said Kelly, pushing her way into one of the lines. Cassie thought it was strange that they were boarding the flight before everyone else—maybe because they were booked on a group ticket? She paid it no mind and continued to talk with Ben, who was deep into a story about his last trip to Singapore and the amazing street food he ate there.

Cassie and Ben continued to follow Kelly to their seats. Cassie presumed they were all sitting together. Suddenly Kelly stopped.

"Cassie, I think this is you, and Ben has the window seat across the way, and I'm over here," she said while gesturing toward a generously sized lay-flat business-class seat in the middle row. "You take the window seat; it should have been booked that way."

"There must be a mistake," said Cassie.

"No mistake," said Kelly, handing Cassie her ticket. There it was: 10A, in ink. She slid into the podlike seat, stashing her bag in the cubby in front of her. She was searching for the parts of her seatbelt when she looked up to find the flight attendant standing next to her.

"Good evening, Ms. Brooks. Would you like water, juice, or champagne?"

There was no question. "Champagne, please."

Cassie glanced over to Ben, seated in 10F, and he raised his glass to her and blew a kissy face, like he was posing for a photo. Cassie raised her glass in return and took a sip, overwhelmed with excitement.

She poked around the pod, hitting buttons and pushing levers, trying to understand how to operate the seat without giving away another secret: she had never flown business class before. She looked across the airplane and saw Ben, with a sheet mask on his face, his phone extended at arm's length, talking to the camera. She laughed. He looked like a ridiculous horror movie character, but he clearly knew what he was doing. She wished she had that much confidence.

Cassie pulled her phone out of her bag and checked it in the last moments before the flight attendants closed the doors. She had an underlying anxiety, not only because she was flying across the Atlantic, but also because she had nothing to do. For the first time in a long time, she didn't have a stack of documents to review, an article to write, or a case to prepare. Now there was nothing.

Her phone buzzed, and she felt that familiar pulse of stress, the kind she thrived on.

> RUBY: Safe travels. I hope you have the most amazing trip.

Cassie sighed audibly; she was relieved it wasn't someone from her firm trying to get her to come back.

> RUBY: I'll miss you terribly when you're gone. At least I'll have the dinosaurs to keep me company.

It was Ruby's classic dig at the older partners.

> CASSIE: Thanks. I'm a ball of nervous energy. I've never felt like more of a fraud.

RUBY: Fake it till you make it. You've got this. 😘

CASSIE: I'm terrified I'll get found out. That the other people will know I'm not supposed to be here.

RUBY: Just stay ahead of it. Don't give them reasons to doubt you. It's just like the courtroom.

CASSIE: I just want to make James proud.

RUBY: I know you do. And you will. Seriously. You're beautiful! You're amazing! You're brilliant! Everyone loves you!

Ruby's last saccharine message was an inside joke that centered around a hideous bowl that Ruby had given Cassie the previous Christmas, inscribed with those exact manifestations. It was bright yellow, and didn't match anything in her apartment, but she wouldn't give it up for anything. Every time Ruby repeated the words to her, she felt stronger and more confident.

CASSIE: Love you, mean it. I'll text you when we land. 🩶

Her mind started to spin uncontrollably. Would James have approved, or would he have been horrified? Would he have preferred for her to stay at her job, sad and unsatisfied? She knew he wanted to share the meals with her, but would he have approved of her taking over his life? The plane started to pull back from the gate. It was too late to doubt her decision now.

CASSIE WOKE UP in a daze, and she had completely forgotten where she was. The lights in the cabin were gradually becoming brighter as though to simulate daylight, and clinking sounds of breakfast service filled the plane.

The captain announced that they would be landing within the hour, and Cassie jumped up to use the bathroom and fix herself up. On her way she passed Kelly, who was miraculously still asleep, mask on, oblivious to the commotion around her.

"Kelly takes sleeping pills on long hauls, and she doesn't eat until noon. No matter the time zone," said Ben from behind her.

Cassie started. "Where did you come from?" She had no idea what she looked like, and she frantically started running her fingers through her hair in a desperate attempt to make herself look more presentable.

"Oh, sorry. I didn't mean to surprise you. Don't mind me. I always try to walk around before we land—it helps get me ready to sprint faster to beat everyone to immigration."

Paris

16

Cassie felt tired and sticky, like she was covered in plastic. She was fatigued, but her adrenaline had kicked in thanks to the excitement of a whole month of food, wine, and travel.

The trio made their way through immigration, and while still in the terminal, Kelly led them toward the airline lounge. "We're going to meet the rest of the group here. We have a few hours until their arrival, so I figured we could freshen up, eat, send some emails."

"Freshen up?" asked Cassie.

Ben leaned over and whispered in her ear, "They have showers, and they're *luxxxx-uuuuur-ious*." Ben spun his suitcase around like it was a dance partner and winked at Cassie.

Showers in the airport? Already, this trip was *very different* from the last time Cassie was in Europe, backpacking in the summer between her junior and senior years of college. She'd lived on tubes of crackers, local cheeses, and cheap bottles of wine, occasionally indulging in a Nutella packet swiped from breakfast. She had stayed in hostels, slept on trains, and made conversation with strangers she would never see again, people from every land and language. Cassie envied the people who returned from their backpacking trips saying that it was the "best trip of their life" or the "best summer ever." She'd felt alone, like an outsider, existing on the fringes. The only time she felt like she could rest was in a quiet corner of an art museum, waiting for a train, eating a baguette with a sad lump of cheese in the park. What was supposed to be a glorious, life-changing experience was a lonely couple of months for Cassie.

THE LOUNGE WAS shiny and beautiful, and felt both chic and executive. Well-groomed travelers were nestled into overstuffed armchairs, tapping away on laptops or scrolling on their phones as they waited for their flights. There was a specific decorum in the lounge that the public areas did not have—a hush in the air, cut only by the clinking of plates and coffee cups, the hum of the coffee machine, and the occasional pop of a bottle of champagne.

"Seems early for a drink," said Cassie, as the group settled into a cluster of chairs that overlooked the tarmac.

"Ha—it's five o'clock somewhere," said Ben. "Besides, airports exist in their own time zone, and it's always happy hour. But first, let's get on the list for a shower. I hope there isn't a queue. Do you want me to sign you up?"

"Sure," she said, before falling into the armchair behind her, tired and feeling outside of her own body.

Ben came back after a few minutes with two coffees. "So how was your flight?"

"Decadent," said Cassie. "I slept so well." The flight had felt so special. It reminded her of the way travel used to be, when it was exotic and glamorous. Best of all, she had a feeling of *escape*— from New York and from the earth. Up there, no one could reach her, and for seven glorious hours she felt completely liberated.

Free from the anxiety of her job, from the memory of James, from the stress of the Monday-to-Friday grind. She could just be in the moment and enjoy what *she* needed, whether it was silence, a juicy rom-com, or another glass of wine.

"Your first time flying up front?" he asked. He already knew, and he didn't even let her answer. "It's the best. But flights from New York are almost too short. I try to skip breakfast when I cross the pond; it buys me an extra hour of sleep," said Ben, flexing his veteran traveler status.

Kelly came back to the table carrying a small plate of food and a latte. "Great flight, no?" She looked very well rested thanks to the Ambien.

"So, who else is on this trip?" Ben asked, before biting into a croissant.

"Rebecca Riggs and Eamon McLaren. Both are coming in from Los Angeles."

Cassie knew the name Rebecca Riggs; she was a famous cookbook author who was frequently featured on the morning shows and in cooking magazines. She was known for her approachable recipes that had surprising flavor combinations and that were easy for the at-home cook to prepare. James had a few of her books, and Cassie could see the cover in her mind: the beautiful woman with a silvery bob in a colorful jacket, oversize eyeglasses, and red lipstick, walking through the farmers' market carrying a basket of kale and a loaf of freshly baked bread. She was one of the chefs credited with bringing the farm-to-table movement into popularity, promoting locavore chefs who previously were ignored by the fine-dining establishment. Just thinking about her brought Cassie right back to James's kitchen: her sitting on a barstool, sipping wine, and flipping through the pages, one photo more beautifully colorful and opulently styled than the next, and James in the kitchen furiously chopping, with a focus that was nearly impossible to break. He loved cooking, and she loved watching him cook. Her stomach twisted, and she felt that pang of longing that she was starting to grow accustomed to.

The other name she did not know.

"Who is Eamon McLaren?"

"He is mostly known in the wine world," Kelly explained. "He's a notable winemaker and a sommelier. He writes for many wine publications and has a series of books published about regional wines."

"Sounds intimidating," said Cassie.

"Naw," Ben interjected. "He's also nice to look at."

Cassie's phone buzzed, and she felt a familiar wave of alarm and snapped into what she joked was her "panic pose": shoulders up, with her two thumbs positioned on her phone, ready to fire back a response. Why was her firm texting her now?

Lodestar Lounge: Your Shower Suite is ready. Please head to Suite 7, read the message. Cassie felt a wave of relief.

"That was fast," said Cassie. "Should I leave my bags here?"

"Take them with you," said Ben. "We're in the queue right after you."

"Okay, see you in a little while."

CASSIE WALKED DOWN a narrow, dim corridor that glittered with tiny starlike lights on the ceiling. She came to the end of the hall and pushed open the door, but, to her horror, there was a man in the shower, his face angled upward and buried in the stream of water. Cassie froze, unsure how to get this man out of her shower suite, and yet she couldn't help but notice his physique. He clearly worked out, and it showed in his hamstrings, his built chest, and his muscular arms. She couldn't look away as he reached up to rub his face and run his hands along the side of his head. His abs flexed, revealing the diagonal lines of his ribs, which seemed to be carved into his torso. Her face heated, and her heart raced. Cassie shut the door, careful not to let it slam.

Cassie looked down at her phone. *Suite 7.* She looked up—she had opened the door to Suite 8. *Shit. Shit. Shit,* she thought. *I'm such an idiot . . . but what a gorgeous man.*

THE SHOWER WAS hot and comforting and was everything she needed. Ben was right; airport showers were one of the true luxuries of international travel.

She took a little extra time to apply moisturizer and her makeup to compensate for the long flight. She dabbed on a little blush and some lipstick, just enough to feel like a coat of armor.

You've got this, Cass, she told herself. *Let them lead the way. You will figure it out as you go along.*

Her hands were still shaking, and her mind kept going back to her encounter with the naked man. Had he seen her? Surely not. She tried to push the thought out of her mind, but the smell from the shower kept bringing her back—bergamot and rosemary, and the sight of his hamstrings with small suds of soap falling down, tracing the lines of his muscles.

Cassie returned to the lounge, walking a little slower, enjoying not having anywhere she needed to be. From across the lounge, she saw him. The man from the shower was talking to Kelly and Ben. The man with the abs was Eamon.

"Everyone, this is Cassie Brooks," said Kelly. "This is her first Viand Awards trip, but she's a prolific reviewer, so please help show her the ropes. Cassie, meet Rebecca and Eamon. They are both veteran reviewers for us, and they should be able to help you along the way."

"Hello," said Cassie, her stomach turning with the mention of her "prolific" work. She raised her hand in a sheepish wave, avoiding eye contact with Eamon. He was even more handsome up close, despite the fact that he now had clothes on. Her mind was racing. *Did he see me? There's no way he could have seen me. His eyes were covered. He didn't see me. But what if he did see me?* She felt sick to her stomach with embarrassment.

"Hello," said Rebecca, extending her fragile, birdlike hand to Cassie. "Pleasure to meet you."

"The pleasure is all mine," she replied.

Cassie then turned to Eamon and smiled quickly as she shook his hand, her eyes darting around nervously. Eamon's hand, large as a baseball mitt, enveloped hers. He smiled warmly, his deep hazel eyes shimmering. "Pleasure to meet you. It's Cassie, right?" His hand held hers for a moment longer than normal, and his eyes moved over her quickly, as though he was trying to take her in as fast as possible. All she could think about was seeing him naked, the water running over his body. In a split second, she watched what she could have sworn was a smile flicker across his face, almost as though he had read her mind.

"Yes," said Cassie. She struggled to find words to respond. "Um, nice to meet you too." He was beautiful, there was no denying it. The kind of guy who could get whatever he wanted.

I have no right to be here, Cassie thought to herself as she sat down in a chair, feeling like a black sheep. She looked around at this intimidating group: an author she had admired for years and who had arguably helped changed the entire restaurant industry, a veteran travel writer who had been around the world many times over, and a fucking sommelier who she had now seen naked.

She was officially out of her league.

17

The group loaded into a sleek black Sprinter van that was waiting outside the airport. Cassie crawled into the back row and leaned her head against the window, feeling the chill of the glass against her dehydrated skin.

Once everyone was in their seats, Kelly stood up to address the group.

"Welcome, everyone. I'm delighted that you are all here as our guest judges for the Viand Awards finals. As you all know, the short list has already been established. Your visits will be the third and final visit for each restaurant, so your reviews will decide the final rankings and the winners of this year's awards. I have welcome packets for everyone with your assigned schedule and respective restaurants. We have included research days into the schedule, and you should use these for interviews, background research, whatever you deem helpful. Reservations have already been made for you and are included in your itinerary. You will also be given a credit card; you can charge all the meals you've been assigned to review onto that credit card. You will dine in pairs, and each of you will submit a review online. Secure log-in details are in your packet. Please note that all reviews must be uploaded within seventy-two hours, with no extensions. Warning: there are days that you will be asked to review more than one restaurant in a day, so plan accordingly."

"Don't eat too much?" Ben joked.

"Exactly. You're responsible for fairly judging each restaurant despite what else you've eaten that day."

This was going to require a whole new level of self-discipline, thought Cassie.

"Tonight, everyone has the night off, so rest up. Finish those outstanding assignments, catch up on sleep, but tomorrow we begin."

The group applauded, and Cassie looked out the window, watching the suburbs of Paris whiz by, feeling the knot of anxiety building again. It was suddenly apparent to her that she hadn't really thought this through—the nuances of exposing herself like this. It was one thing to be posting as @NewYorkSecretDiner on her phone; it was an entirely different thing to be sitting across the table from veterans of the food and restaurant industry, posing as an expert. If they ever found out the truth, she would surely be kicked off the trip and sued for fraud, which would be insignificant compared to the humiliation of being disbarred if anyone from Stevens & Sweeny ever caught wind of her lie. Who would ever hire her after that? And then what? Would she even be able to support herself anymore? She had about six months of savings in the bank, and she was using a chunk of it to make this trip happen. Would she have to sleep on Ruby's couch until she found a job, likely outside of her studied profession?

She took a deep breath and tried to calm down. She told herself that James too was a beginner at some point, trying to develop into the notable critic he ultimately became. Like Ruby had said, there was only one option: fake it till you make it.

THE VAN TURNED onto Avenue Montaigne and pulled up in front of a large building with curving art nouveau–style balconies, decorated with scarlet awnings above and overflowing baskets of bright red geraniums below.

The group tumbled out of the van, and every single person stared up in awe at the hotel.

"I've always wanted to stay here," said Rebecca, reaching her phone up to take a photo of the building.

Ben was already in influencer mode, shooting a video of the façade, and then a selfie, ending the video by giving a peace sign.

"Welcome to Plaza Athénée Paris," said a man wearing a black suit and white gloves who opened the colossal door for the group.

Cassie followed Kelly under an undulating glass-and-blackened-steel awning, also in the art nouveau style, through the grand double doors, and into the lobby of the hotel. It was a square room, with a circular colonnade in the center, each column decorated with a silver metal strap that held a large vase of white flowers with tropical greenery that reached toward the ceiling.

On the other side of the room, opposite the entry, was another archway, filled in by a set of glass-and-blackened-steel French doors. The glass transom mimicked the shape of the balconies on the exterior, while also being reminiscent of celebratory ribbons. Cassie wandered through the doors and found herself in a marble-lined gallery that extended through the hotel. Across the hall was a large room that was perhaps a ballroom at one point and was now a restaurant filled with bustling waiters in the middle of lunch service. She continued to walk down the hallway, stopping to look in the hotel's shop vitrines filled with multitiered diamond earrings and ornate, sparkling emerald necklaces instead of the typical tourist tchotchkes found in a usual hotel gift shop.

Cassie walked back to the lobby and found the group gathered in the rotunda, continuing to film and take photos, except Eamon, who had found a place to sit on the far side of the room, where he was leaning forward and reading on his phone. Cassie finally got a good look at him. His dirty-blond hair was both messy and somehow exquisitely coiffed. He had a pronounced profile, with strong eyebrows that made him look a little rough and full lips that made him seem vulnerable and tender. He was clearly a chameleon, someone who was so comfortable in his own skin that he could adapt to any situation. Even here, in a five-star hotel, he seemed like he belonged, despite the worn black Carhartt jacket, weathered dark-wash jeans, and beat-up boots. She wondered if he smelled like newly tanned leather and juniper—earthy, sweet, and slightly brutish—a thought that made the skin all over her body run hot and tingly.

Kelly called for everyone's attention and directed the group toward where Eamon was sitting. "Here are your room keys and welcome packets. Enjoy your free time, and we look forward to reading your reviews."

"Want to go explore?" Ben whispered in her ear.

Cassie was surprised that Ben had asked. "Yes, please."

"Okay, I'll meet you in the lobby in an hour. I love Paris so much."

18

"My god, this hotel is exquisite," Ben exclaimed as he walked toward her. "I've stayed in some pretty nice places, but this is next level."

"I can't really wrap my head around it," confessed Cassie.

"Have you seen the courtyard yet?" asked Ben, pulling her back into the hotel, down the diamond-flanked hallway, and out a set of double doors.

Cassie looked up, slack-jawed. All eight floors of the interior courtyard were covered in greenery: crawling vines that framed the arched windows, planter boxes filled with brilliant red flowers, large topiaries and old trees that visually connected the courtyard to the sky. Small red awnings gave the windows a warm glow, matching the crimson café umbrellas below.

"I could happily sit here all day," said Cassie.

"Gorgeous, isn't it? I think Elizabeth Taylor and Grace Kelly used to stay here, and now it's the epicenter of Paris Fashion Week."

Ben already had his phone out, filming the courtyard for his followers.

"I get the sense you're constantly filming," Cassie said, half as a question.

"Ugh, yes, the algorithm must be fed. But in all honesty, it's fun. I know that my followers really enjoy seeing the behind the scenes of events they would normally never be able to attend. It lets them live vicariously."

"You must be living quite the adventure if so many people want to watch."

"Obviously! You know, it's funny. Sometimes my followers like my content more when I'm at home just doing nothing. But they love to see the glamour too."

Cassie flashed to a fantasy of the kind of life she would want to showcase on social media—glittering parties and elegant, multicourse dinners. Trips to Australia and through South America, Cassie in pursuit of the next spectacular meal.

"I like to think that I'm in a kind of relationship with my followers," Ben continued. "They have needs—to learn, to be inspired, or to be entertained—and I need to meet those needs. If I don't, they will move on to someone else, and then I'll be punished by the algorithm," he said, holding the door open for her.

They passed back through the lobby, admiring the intricate chandeliers overhead and the statues that flanked the doorways, framed by art nouveau–style marble arches. Cassie looked down at the phone in her hand, questioning if she could maintain a relationship with hundreds of thousands of people online.

"That said," he added, "I truly believe that I'm opening a portal to another world for them. While most people are stuck in cubicles, bogged down with screaming kids and the mundane aspects of day-to-day life, I can offer an escape. I can provide a glimpse into another world—a luxurious world where the champagne never stops flowing."

"You're living a great story," she added, feeling a pang of jealousy. There was nothing she wanted more than to live her own great story.

"I do my best," he quipped.

"So how do you stay grounded, with all of this?" Cassie asked, gesturing at the surrounding scene.

"Well, I go home to my postage stamp of an apartment, I see my friends, I spend time with my family. I also try to give back. I volunteer—charity is a big part of who I am."

"Good for you. If every trip starts off like this, I can imagine how your sense of reality can get quickly distorted."

"Sure can," Ben said with a laugh. "At the end of the day, I'm just so grateful to be able to live this life. I love bringing stories to life, more than anything. It never ceases to amaze me how even a little bit of shine can be a game changer for these small businesses."

"Oh, you've got a heart of gold, huh?" Cassie said in jest.

"Go on," he joked, pretending to fan himself with his hand. "In all seriousness, it's our job to give these restaurants some national attention—just a mention can go a long way. It feels amazing when a little restaurant I loved makes the list. Part of me wants to keep the gems small and true to what they are when I first experienced them, but another part loves to see them blow up and become an international sensation. I guess you could say that it's my way of expressing gratitude."

"I'll say it again: heart of gold."

"Eh—I don't know about that. Come on," said Ben, gesturing outside. "I reserved bikes for us."

WAITING OUTSIDE THE hotel were two cherry red cruiser bikes with big wicker baskets on the front that matched the hue of the awnings on the hotel.

"How chic!" exclaimed Ben. "These are such a vibe!" He snapped a few photos and handed his phone to Cassie for her to take a few pictures of him posing on the bike in front of the hotel. "Okay, your turn," he said, gesturing for her to take his spot. "For the followers!" he shouted, making her laugh.

Ben led the way; he knew Paris well. They rode down Avenue Montaigne and along the Seine. Boats and open-roofed tourist barges crawled along the wide, tree-lined river, tourists taking photos as they passed by architectural monuments and under arched bridges. They cycled past groups of schoolchildren on their daily outings, past entwined lovers sitting on park benches, and past runners out for an afternoon jog. And then, suddenly, they were at the base of the Eiffel Tower, surrounded by tourists and vendors selling trinkets.

They took a few selfies and hopped back on their bikes and rode back across the Seine. They rode past the Musée de l'Homme, past the Pont Alexandre III bridge, cutting north to the Palais Garnier, and then down the Avenue de l'Opéra, landing in the courtyard of the Louvre, with its iconic glass pyramid designed by I. M. Pei—each location documented with quick snippets of video and selfies.

"Do you want to go inside?" Ben asked, casually straddling his bike and checking the messages on his phone. "The *Mona Lisa* would love to see you."

Cassie laughed. "I'm not in the mood for crowds. Let's keep going."

THEY RODE PAST the Musée d'Orsay, then cut south on the Rue du Bac, stopping in front of a picturesque shop front with gold inset arched windows and, above the door, large gold capital letters spelling out DEYROLLE.

"You have to see this place," said Ben, popping off his bike and leaning it against a bike rack. "It's a gem of a shop, and a little bit off the beaten path."

The shop had high ceilings painted seafoam green, with mint-hued walls framed with dark wood, and glass cabinets filled with wonderful displays of taxidermy tropical birds frozen midflight, crystals, luminescent butterflies, and deconstructed lobsters with their shells pulled apart to demonstrate their mobility. On one side of the room, full-size taxidermy polar bears stood on a gigantic glass vitrine filled with displays of fossils, and in the other, a frozen pride of lions sat on the floor in front of a window, next to a zebra, a giraffe, and an albino peacock presenting its feathers. Under each display was a prominent sign that read, "Pas de Photo," and underneath it, "No Photos," with an icon of a cell phone covered by a prominent red circle backslash symbol.

Ben pulled out his phone and snapped a selfie with a brown bear standing on its hind legs, its fur almost golden. Cassie audibly gasped. Ben fired a look at her and put his finger up to his lips, urging her to be silent. Cassie wandered up the creaking stairs and into a room full of insects: moths, bees, and displays of butterflies, their colorful wings shimmering in the light.

Suddenly Ben was next to her. "Isn't this place amazing?"

"Yes. It's mesmerizing."

"Whenever I'm in Paris, I come here and take a few photos with my 'friends.' My followers love it." He quickly showed her his phone, and on it was a photo of him with a baby elephant, eyes glazed and vacant, almost like a teddy bear's.

"I thought you were a foodie. Isn't this off . . . subject? I thought influencers were supposed to have a niche."

"Yeah, sure. But people want to have fun too. They are living *through* you—they want to feel like they're on the trip with you, and that you're the most fun person in the world to travel with. With me, we go to fabulous restaurants and bars, legendary shops, and meet beautiful people . . . and animals." He let out a big belly laugh and wrapped his arm around her, placing their faces directly in the frame of his camera.

"Smile!" he said, before taking a few more selfies. Ben locked his arm into the corner of hers and moved them toward the door. "Come on, there's so much more to see in Paris."

"Question," said Cassie, as they mounted the bright red bikes. "Do I need a formal dress? I overheard something about a tux."

"Did you not read the itinerary?" he said, his mouth open dramatically. "Rookie mistake. We're going to the Viand gala in Venice—the dress code is black tie. From everything I've heard, it seems like it's going to be quite the affair."

"Will it be anything like the awards ceremony they had in New York this year?"

"Oh, were you there? Funny we didn't meet."

"Yeah, funny," she choked out. "I was there to accept the award for short-form cuisine writing, but I had to leave early," she lied. "Family emergency. So back to the question—do I need a dress?"

"Yes, you absolutely do. And I know exactly where we should go to get you one."

CASSIE FOLLOWED BEN down Rue Rivoli, past a shimmering glass building that seemed to ripple with the movement of the street traffic, and pulled up in front of an art deco–style building adorned with orange-and-white floral tiles, "Samaritaine" emblazoned at the top in an ornamental font.

"You're going to lose your mind in this store, it's so gorgeous," said Ben as he locked up their bikes. "It is one of the oldest department stores in Paris, and they carry all the best brands. Lanvin, Acne, Bottega Veneta, Chloé . . ."

"Fantastic," she said, following him inside.

She looked up and let her eyes wander around the light-filled six-story atrium. The store had been built in the early twentieth century, and all the metal was covered in little rivets holding it all together: beams, joists, and the mint-colored balustrades that framed the galleria. Recently renovated, the store felt both modern and vintage at the same time. Peach and yellow hues complemented the ornate metal work, grounded by the gray-and-white inlay marble floor.

"Let's look at Givenchy," he said, practically running through the store.

"You're the fashionable one here," she said.

"That's obvious," he deadpanned in a way that if it wasn't so true would have been hurtful. She needed all the help she could get.

They climbed up another flight of stairs until they were in the Givenchy boutique, and Cassie was out of breath. Ben was already buried in the racks, pulling pieces for her to try on.

"What size are you?" he fired at her.

"Um, a six."

Ben flew around the floor, giving directions to the shopgirls. "This reminds me of when we had to do editorial pulls for the fashion magazines. We had such little time, but I *thrive* under pressure."

"Don't we all?" Cassie said, relating to the feeling.

While Ben shopped, Cassie roamed around the store, admiring the detailed beadwork and creative silhouettes, her fingers grazing over the silk and cashmere garments.

"Cass, I'm ready for you!" he said, hooking his arm with hers and leading her toward the dressing room. "I hope you don't mind, but I've pulled a few other things for you. I got the feeling that you might need a few other outfits."

Her face flushed pink, but she knew it was true.

Hanging in the dressing room were stacks of clothes—about six evening gowns, four blazers of different colors, tailored skirts, and a few professional-looking jumpsuits. Ben had grabbed great pieces for her style; everything was on the minimal side, timeless, but with a contemporary edge. She started with the dresses, eliminating a navy blue one because it reminded her of the office; a white one because she was entirely too clumsy to wear white to a food event; and a light pink one that felt too young. She tried on a vibrant red dress with architectural cutouts in the neckline. She stepped out into the lounge and did a spin for Ben.

"Yes, that is absolutely the one. You are a vision in red!" He stood up and circled her, checking the fit. "It's jersey, so it will pack well. Just don't cram your suitcase too full, and remember to steam it when we get to Venice."

"Noted," she said.

"It fits you impeccably. I'm proud I haven't lost my touch."

"You should be a stylist," said Cassie.

"Maybe one day when I'm sick of traveling. Although I doubt that will ever happen." He laughed, as though he knew himself all too well.

"Celebrity stylists travel with their clients all over the world, especially on press tours."

"You're so right. Wouldn't that be the dream?" he said as he dramatically steadied himself on a table covered in folded cashmere sweaters.

"I have no doubt you can make something like that happen."

"Now that I think about it, I know some people in the industry. I could make some calls and try to trail them so I could build up a résumé."

"I would hire you," she said honestly.

"You already have," he said, followed by an air kiss. "Okay, miss, back in the dressing room. I want to see more."

Cassie selected a smart black V-neck jumpsuit, a gorgeous black-and-silver skirt that would work well for lunches or dinners, and a stylish tailored gray wool blazer that had silver thread in the blend. Ben added a pair of strappy gold heels to go with the gown and sculptural gold earrings that brought the whole outfit together. When the saleswoman rang everything up, Cassie winced and pulled out her credit card. This wasn't how she envisioned spending her savings, but it had become abundantly clear that this purchase was more of a need than a want.

What else had she missed in that itinerary?

19

That was so much fun," said Ben. "A Parisian shopping spree was not on my bingo card for this trip, but, man, I'm so glad we did it."

"Fortunately for you, it was my credit card," she said, laughing. In truth, she thought it was great fun too, and she had never indulged in shopping like that before. "Maybe by the end, you can give me a complete makeover."

"If you're lucky," he said. "Getting hungry?"

"Sure. What do you have in mind?"

"There's a new hot bao place that opened in the eleventh arrondissement. It's not that long of a ride, and it's so beautiful out."

"Let's go," said Cassie, placing the large shopping bag in the wicker basket attached to the front of the bike.

AFTER A SHORT bike ride back along the Seine and up a wide, busy boulevard, they arrived at a modest dim sum restaurant.

"Dim sum? For dinner?" Cassie asked.

Ben laughed. "I can only have so much French food, and I know we're in for a long haul of fine dining. Sometimes I just need a taste of home, and this place is straight out of Hong Kong. I hope you don't mind."

"No, not at all," said Cassie. "How often do you come to Paris?" she asked.

"At least once a year. I used to come for fashion week when I was writing about menswear, but I've moved away from that. No one in fashion eats. It was depressing." He opened the door for her, welcoming her into the mint-colored restaurant with pink tables and mismatched teal chairs, red, industrial-looking light fixtures, and Chinese lanterns hung from the ceiling.

"That wouldn't be a good situation for us foodies," Cassie added.

"Ha! No. It was bad. I get too hangry to work in an industry like that."

A waitress came by and, without hesitation, Ben ordered. Moments later, she brought over two tall glasses of milky boba tea and a large bottle of Tsingtao beer. Ben filled two small bistro glasses slowly, not letting the foam rise too much. Cassie took a sip of the crisp beer, and before she could even realize, she had downed three-quarters of the glass.

"Wow, I guess I was thirsty," she said, laughing at herself.

"I'd say." Ben filled her glass again and signaled for the waitress. He ordered another bottle of beer and a large bottle of sparkling water. "I've heard the new luxury move is to have three beverages in front of you at all times." He laughed loudly. "Look, I can tell you're green, so just remember this tip: don't drink everything in front of you unless it's water. In which case, drink as much as you can. It's nearly impossible to taste accurately or remember details when you're drunk, and you can't keep eating if you're hungover, so drink tons of water. Especially sparkling water. I truly believe it's secretly hydrating—even if there is no science to it. But I digress. And remember the number one rule: if something is mediocre, don't eat it. Don't waste the space in your stomach or your mind."

"Noted," she said, opening the bottle of water and pouring two glasses. "How did you learn all of this?"

"Boots on the ground. Honestly, I've been on too many press trips, and I guess you could say I've learned through experience. I try to remind myself that our readers are spending their hard-earned money to go out and eat, and I owe them my time and respect. I take it very seriously. I'm always heartbroken if someone writes to me and tells me that they had a bad experience at a restaurant where I gave a good review. I feel like I've let my readers down and broken their trust. But truly, it's so difficult for writers to give an authentic review when you're wined and dined and free things are sent from the kitchen. Your average Joe, now, they get the real experience."

Cassie flashed back to James's closet full of disguises. She let herself fantasize for a moment about what it would have been like to go on a secret review mission with James. Maybe they would have dressed as an older couple, professors visiting from Chicago. They would have shared pictures of their fictional dogs with the waiters. That would have been sweet.

"How did you start writing about food and travel?" asked Cassie.

"One article at a time," said Ben, followed by his famous laugh. "I always wanted to be a writer, but I also wanted to see the world, so I started pitching travel editors. I would look up their names in the mastheads and email them. Sure, lots of emails bounced back and I got lots of rejections, but with time, my pitches were accepted. This life is not for everyone, but I love it. I work for myself, I get to set my own schedule, and I'm constantly seeing something new. I've thought about going in-house, but I don't think I would work well in an office. I'm too independent."

"I know what you mean," Cassie said. "I've had some really tough work situations." Then she remembered that technically she still worked at her firm, and her stomach sank with frustration.

Another bottle of Tsingtao was delivered to the table, and the glass shimmered green in the candlelight. Ben filled up their glasses, then raised his.

"To Paris," Ben toasted.

"To Paris. Thank you for bringing me here." Cassie let her body relax, and she draped her arm over the back of the chair. "I could get used to days like today."

"Viand is great because we get some downtime. It's not a death march like some trips, where they overbook the whole schedule," said Ben, followed by another laugh. "So, how did you start reviewing?"

"Well," said Cassie, slowly, "I kind of fell into it." She still didn't have a good story to explain how she got here, other than the fact that she was pretending to be James.

Mercifully, the waitress interrupted her, covering the table with round bamboo boxes filled with braised eggplant with fresh scallions, greens covered in a sticky brown garlic sauce, plump steamed buns filled with sweet pork, and siu mai, one of the restaurant's specialties. The waitress brought small blue-and-white plates, along with dipping dishes, chopsticks, and crunchy chili oil.

Ben stood up and declared, "The camera eats first," before wrapping a small handheld light in a napkin and holding it out to create a beautiful diffused light for his photos.

The two snapped into action, pulling out their cameras and

arranging plates and glasses of tea just so to make the scene come alive in the photos. Ben scanned the table with his phone, capturing a scenic video, and then focused on still images.

"Cassie, will you reach for a dumpling?" Ben directed. "Oh yeah, that's great—I love hands in overhead shots. It makes the whole scene come alive."

After modeling the chopsticks, Cassie focused her camera on the gossamer edges of the dumplings, their skin light and translucent. Once in a while, she would catch the aroma of the dumplings, tempting her with their sweet and savory smells, but she continued to shoot until Ben was finished.

"Okay, I'm done," he proclaimed, sticking his camera in his bag. He picked up his chopsticks and scooped up one of the dumplings, bringing it up to his eye level, inspecting it closely.

"Aren't they happy?" he asked, before popping the dumpling into his mouth.

"The happiest," confirmed Cassie.

She watched as Ben picked up one of the spherical dumplings ever so carefully with his chopsticks and placed it on a blue ceramic soup spoon. He dressed it with scallion sauce, and then brought the spoon to his lips, taking a small bite, sucking out the broth. Next, he spooned the chili crunch on and chased the dumpling into his mouth using his chopsticks. He sat chewing, eyes closed, lost in the moment.

After a minute, he opened his eyes, sighed, and took a sip of beer. He looked so content, so happy. This meal was transporting him.

"You sure love these dumplings," said Cassie.

"They remind me of home. Food is so powerful; the aromas

and flavors tap into a part of your brain that contains visceral memories. I think it's incredible how food is a kind of time machine, a vessel that can move us through space and time instantly. Really, it's our brains—we're essentially hallucinating when we taste familiar flavors."

His words hung in the air. Ben had so much respect for food, how it was made, and the power it had over people. She took a soup dumpling and mimicked how Ben ate his, enjoying the salty, savory broth as it ran down her throat, followed by the fatty pork and bright scallions wrapped in the silky, almost diaphanous pastry.

"That's such a nice way to think about it," she said. "Can I ask you a question?"

"Sure," he said, mouth full.

"You've reviewed—what—thousands of restaurants—how do you remember all the details? The restaurants, the cities, the chefs, the ingredients. I'm still pretty new at this, and I'm interested in learning other people's methods."

"Oh yeah, it's a lot. Especially after so many years. For the first few years, the memories were pretty clear, but those recollections have faded—I blame all the cocktails," he joked. "But seriously, I keep notes. I take photos of menus, I write down memories in my note-keeping app, but honestly, the photos of the plates are the most important. Once I see the image, I can instantly remember the dish, what it tasted like, how it made me feel. But who knows? Maybe as I get older, I won't be able to do that. What about you?"

"Journals," Cassie lied, remembering James's bookshelves stacked with his notebooks. "I have them organized chronologically."

"That sounds ambitious and academic," said Ben, picking up a piece of eggplant, charred and glistening with sweet glaze. "And heavy."

"Maybe, but it's the way I've always worked," she said, extending James's truth to herself. It was true that she preferred paper notebooks over digital tablets and felt like it was the best way for her to stay organized. It was one of the things that she and James had in common, a love for tangible mediums. "I prefer print. I like reading real books, I like taking notes on paper, I like having physical evidence, I guess."

"You're one of *those*, huh?"

"Whatever that means," she said, and laughed.

"So, what are you most excited about for the trip?" Ben asked.

"I'm not sure. My plan is to let the next four weeks wash over me. Let life happen. I'm trying this new thing where I don't try to control everything."

"That explains why you didn't read the itinerary. I'm shook that you didn't even scan it, just to see the restaurants on the list. Weren't you the least bit curious?" he asked.

In truth, she wouldn't have been able to tell the difference between a neighborhood bistro and a starred restaurant on paper. "I was only invited three weeks ago, so it's been a bit of a whirlwind. I'm probably filling in for someone who couldn't make it."

"That doesn't matter. You're here now. The good news is that these trips are great because you can just go with the flow. I, however, like to build out my own itineraries with a story in mind, so I've already added more reservations to the itinerary."

"Ambitious," Cassie added.

"What can I say? It's just the way I am." He paused and took a sip of beer, then looked directly at her, almost suspiciously. "I get the feeling that you're running away from something."

"Maybe," she said, feeling exposed, "but what if I'm also running toward something?"

"Ha. Like what?"

"Let's just say that I'm ready for something new in my life—a seismic shift."

Cassie looked down at her plate. She felt tired, full, and ready to sleep. She yawned and leaned back in the banquette.

"Nope, no drooping. We have one more stop."

The waitress cleared the table and brought the check. Cassie and Ben split the bill, their credit cards clinking onto the red tin tray one after the other. Like old friends.

"So, where are you dragging me now?"

"A cool cocktail bar hidden deep below the streets of Paris. It's for my *Traveler* story."

Cassie's curiosity was piqued. "Okay, but only one drink."

Once the checks were signed, Cassie followed Ben toward the door. But instead of walking out onto the street, he took a hard left past the kitchen and knocked on an unmarked door, which opened onto a rough concrete staircase, and descended into the basement. They followed a trail of votive candles down the stairs and into an exposed concrete room with a glittering stainless-steel bar on the far end and a shimmering silver ceiling that looked exactly like water. Around it was what looked like the walls of a pool . . . and a pool ladder . . . and a black-and-white-striped diving board . . . on the ceiling.

"Welcome to Argent Piscine," said Ben, pointing to the inverted swimming pool above them. "I've been dying to see this bar—it just opened."

Cassie felt her jaw release, and she studied how the molded silver panels mimicked the movement of water, reflecting shimmering light throughout the dimly lit space. It was calming, tranquil, and incredibly exciting at the same time.

"I feel like I'm in a piece of art."

"You are," said the bartender, as he placed two menus in front of them. "Bonjour, I'm Niko."

"Bonjour, Niko," said Ben. "What should we drink tonight?"

"Our menu is inspired by the Asian pantry: matcha, gochujang, miso—things like that. What kind of cocktails do you typically enjoy?"

"Something opinionated," Ben said confidently, while perusing the menu. "I'll have the L'année du Tigre."

Niko and Ben looked at Cassie.

"How about an espresso martini?" Cassie said, feeling exhausted from traveling and riding a bike all over the city. She needed something to help her stay awake, especially for the bike ride back to the hotel.

"Coming right up."

Cassie watched the bartender as he worked, moving quickly behind the bar, pouring ingredients into shaker tins, his fingers twirling around a jigger as he worked. He scooped the ice and poured it into a silver cocktail shaker that reflected the candlelight of the room, and then closed the tin with a loud thud. He lifted one of his elbows high above his head and proceeded to shake, starting off slowly and gradually speeding up with mechanical precision. The sound was loud and invigorating, and she felt herself sit up a little bit taller on her perch at the bar.

He placed a cocktail coupe in front of Cassie, then whacked the shaker on his elbow, cracking it open, and strained the brown liquid into the glass until it turned into a thick layer of foam on the surface of the drink.

"Un espresso martini, madame," he said, gently pushing the drink toward her.

"Merci," said Cassie, bringing the drink to her lips. She took a sip—it was cold, with the flavor of sweet coffee and alcohol. It was exactly what she needed, and she felt the first jolt of coffee in her system.

"I'm kind of nervous about tomorrow," she confessed to Ben.

"Oh, don't be, it's like any other restaurant review. And it's Paris—it will be delicious. There are no bad restaurants on the list. Do you know how many writers would die to be on this trip?" asked Ben, unknowingly rubbing salt in the wound.

"Many," she said, then took a large sip of her martini. "I'm sure." She wondered if he could see her anxiety.

"What do you want to get out of the trip?" he asked.

"Clarity, I guess. I feel like my compass is spinning, and I don't know which way is north—you know, what path I want to take next. You?"

"Same thing as always—more opportunities to do what I love," he said.

"That's really the thing, huh?" she said, then added, "Doing what you love?"

"I think so. I'd rather do this and be happy than be chained to a desk all day."

"I'm sure that makes some people happy too," she said, almost trying to justify her life in New York.

"Sure, but I'm not those people," he concluded, before finishing his cocktail. "We should probably get going. We have a bit of a ride back to the hotel. Thanks for indulging me. Today was so much fun."

They paid their tabs and headed toward the door.

"Thank *you*, Ben. I really appreciate your help."

"You're so welcome! I'm glad you're here. You're not like the other writers who are usually on these trips. You have a different perspective that is really refreshing."

20

The next morning, Cassie woke up groggy and was shocked to discover that it was already ten thirty. She was disoriented and surprised to find herself in such a glamorous hotel room. Out of habit, she reached for her phone, scrolling through her camera roll, looking at the photos from the day before. She scrolled through Instagram first on her personal account and then on the @NewYorkSecretDiner account, where there were over three hundred new comments and more direct messages than she could count. Some people asked for restaurant recommendations, some wondered what the next review would be, and others commented on her last posts from when she was in New York.

She thought about posting a few images from the bao restaurant with a quippy caption about the New York Secret Diner being on holiday, something that would make it clear that it wasn't a *review*, per se. But she couldn't square that circle. Would a restaurant critic ever really be on vacation? Wouldn't they seek out the best restaurants, wherever they were?

Surely Ben and the others knew the @NewYorkSecretDiner account and would quickly realize that she was the one posting. Cassie played it all out in her head: being called a liar, a fraud, and being sent home while still in the first city. Her colleagues at work would question why she was home so soon and what had happened to the plans for her sabbatical. It was too mortifying to think about. And besides, she felt deep and intense loyalty to James and that she should keep the account secret.

Instagram had never come naturally to her; she was always hesitant to let her colleagues know what she did in her spare time. She also knew that this trip would be too amazing not to post, but her personal account didn't feel like the right forum. She still didn't want people from work to know where she was, and she couldn't bear to imagine what they would think about her becoming a food critic. Surely they would consider her to be a failure. She needed a new account.

@EatPostLike

In pursuit of all things delicious.

She uploaded a few photos from the day before, noted with geotags, and short but tasty captions. She then uploaded a black-and-white profile photo of herself wearing a large sun hat, making her face dark and unrecognizable, just like Gael Greene. The photo was cryptic enough to give her an aura of mystery, but it also had the air of a woman who should be staying at the Plaza Athénée and eating at all the starred restaurants Europe had to offer. It could be mysterious without being *completely* anonymous; after all, her travel companions would be with her, and would likely put two and two together.

Feeling good about her new digital incarnation, she threw the phone on the bed and walked into the marble bathroom to shower.

AFTER WHAT FELT like an irresponsible amount of time standing under the stream of water, Cassie sat on the bed, wrapped in a hotel robe with a towel twisted on top of her head. She studied the itinerary—her first review was the next day, which gave her more than twenty-four hours to google her dinner companion, the renowned Rebecca Riggs.

Cassie pulled her computer onto her lap and settled in to do research. She had a whole, delicious day to read up on Paris, and to learn as much as she could about Rebecca. She scanned the images of Rebecca's books, studied the press photos from glittering New York parties, and read through her reviews. She was the definition of establishment; she had been in the food industry for decades, knew the most important chefs, wrote for a long list of major publications, and had a series of her own books, all of which were *New York Times* bestsellers. This woman was a force, and Cassie was excited to learn as much as she could from her.

21

The next day, Cassie came down to the lobby at exactly five o'clock, where she found Rebecca sitting on a bench across from the reception desk, waiting for Cassie.

"Are you ready?" asked Cassie, excited for the first official meal of the trip.

"I am," said Rebecca, and popped up out of her seat. "There's a car waiting for us," she said as she walked toward the door. Rebecca was wearing a modest black dress with a silver Chico's jacket that complemented her silvery hair, her outfit completed with a pair of black-and-white Parisian-looking ballet flats. Black, thick-framed cat-eye glasses punctuated the look, but her bright cherry red lipstick made it iconic. She walked with the confidence of a woman who had achieved everything she wanted in life, and while still a beautiful woman, Cassie could see that in her younger years, Rebecca had been drop-dead gorgeous.

Cassie was wearing her new black jumpsuit that she'd gotten the day before, accessorized with a vibrant pink silk scarf that had been her mother's. Although it didn't smell of her perfume anymore, she could still feel her mother's presence when she wore it. Sometimes she thought of it as a protective cape, a magical garment that warded off negativity, making her feel just a little stronger.

Outside, a sleek black town car pulled up, and the bellmen opened the two rear doors for Cassie and Rebecca, who slid into the back seat.

"This is fancy," Cassie said, running her finger along the burl wood trim on the interior.

"The hotel has a fleet," Rebecca said. She leaned back and sighed. "It's so chic. I never get over these trips. They're like a dream."

"You've been on a lot of these trips?" asked Cassie, while buckling her seatbelt.

"I try to do this trip every year when I can. Sometimes in Europe, sometimes in Asia, wherever they want to send me. It's always a highlight."

"Wow, I feel incredibly lucky to be on this *one* trip," said Cassie, feeling her youth and inexperience.

"Well, honey, do a good job, and before you know it, you'll be celebrating your twentieth anniversary with the Viand Awards. The trick is to always be on time, be polite, and don't forget to enjoy yourself."

"Sage advice," said Cassie, growing even more excited. Could she really do this for twenty years? Was there a way to support herself as a restaurant critic? She wanted more than anything to quit Stevens & Sweeney and never look back.

"Looks like we're here," said Rebecca, tapping on the window with her sunglasses, clutched neatly in her left hand.

The car pulled up on Quai Jacques Chirac, and Cassie was surprised to find herself under the Eiffel Tower once again. They walked past the street vendors selling selfie sticks and flying UFO toys before stopping in front of the south pillar. Cassie pointed her camera up toward the underside of the tower, with its impressive bridge-like structure exposed to the crowds below.

Cassie walked quickly to catch up to Rebecca, who was now standing under a round brown awning that marked the entrance of the restaurant.

"Is this the right place?" said Cassie, a little confused.

"Yes," said Rebecca, gesturing to the lettering on the awning that read "Le Jules Verne."

"Come on," said Rebecca, as she walked up the stairs and into the compact lobby, which was adorned with black-and-white photographs and two bronze busts, one of Gustave Eiffel, the architect of the eponymous tower, and the other of Jules Verne, the French novelist and poet who was well known for advocating for scientific and industrial progress. Cassie pulled out her phone while they waited for the elevator.

> **CASSIE:** Have you ever heard of Le Jules Verne?

> **RUBY:** Holy shit, is that where you're eating tonight? I've always wanted to go there. Preferably with a handsome man who has a box of diamonds in his pocket.

> **CASSIE:** Am I the only person on the planet who doesn't know what this place is?

> **RUBY:** That would not surprise me. Well, sweetie, you're about to find out. I need minute by minute updates.

CASSIE: @EatPostLike

RUBY: Oh, is this the new Cassie?

CASSIE: ⭐

RUBY: Following!

"BONSOIR, BIENVENUE AU Jules Verne," said the elevator attendant, holding the door open for them to enter. Cassie followed Rebecca in as her heart began to race, her mind spiraling. She should've been researching this clearly legendary restaurant, not Rebecca. How could she have squandered her time so foolishly? How did she not know about this restaurant?

No one knows but you—and Ruby, she thought to herself, taking a deep breath. *This is in your head.*

The doors shut, and the elevator slowly ascended up the leg of the tower. Cassie looked up and could see that they were traveling *within* one of the pillars of the Eiffel Tower, the structure held together by tiny rivets and the sweat of thousands of men. She pulled out her phone and took a quick video as they moved past the first observation deck and on to a second, where the elevator stopped, opening its doors onto the dining room.

Cassie and Rebecca stepped off the elevator and gasped, in awe of the pristine dining room. Cassie panned the room with her camera, trying desperately to capture the beauty of the restaurant.

"Oh, they've renovated!" exclaimed Rebecca. Clearly, she had been here before.

The room was not terribly tall, and Cassie's eyes were drawn to the perimeter of glass windows that wrapped around the restaurant, framing the expansive views of Paris. From their vantage point, she could read the radial organization of Paris, its boulevards darting across the city, connecting neighborhood to neighborhood. She noticed that she was slowly floating toward the glass, past the beautifully curved white banquettes and carefully set tables with glittering wineglasses on top. She took in the view of Paris from here, from this perspective of privilege, looking out over the beautiful parks and the immaculate buildings.

"Beautiful, isn't it?" asked someone from behind her. "I'm Claude. Can I take you to your table?"

Cassie blushed. "Of course," she said, slipping her phone into her bag.

"We have you at one of our best tables this evening," Claude said as they walked to the other side of the restaurant. He pulled out her chair, and as Cassie sat, another waiter draped a napkin over her lap.

"Merci," she said quietly.

They were seated at a table next to the window and centered on the restaurant, the structure of the tower forming a V on either side of them. There were no other tables seated yet, and it felt special to have such a place to oneself, if only for a moment.

"I hope you don't mind that I requested such an early reservation," said Rebecca. "I just love being the first one here."

"Why is that?" asked Cassie.

"Well, first of all, look at this view. It's spectacular, and I want to spend as much time with it as possible. Sure, it's enchanting at night too, but I particularly love it before dusk. It is such a magnificent way to see Paris." She gestured to the window, where the view extended for miles, through the suburbs and out into the countryside.

"I think you're a very smart woman," said Cassie, honestly.

"Second, I love to see the calm before the storm. The staff is still polishing and doing last-minute preparations for service, the kitchen isn't inundated yet—not that you would be able to tell in a restaurant of this caliber—and you get just a few extra minutes of time with your server. I always like to get to know them a little bit—it makes the whole experience more human, if you know what I mean." Rebecca smiled warmly and took a sip of her ice water.

"Don't they know who you are?" Cassie asked.

"Of course they do! But they don't know what I'm here for." The comment must have reminded Rebecca why they were there, because she started scanning the table, looking for water marks on the silverware, misaligned place settings, or any other defect that might catch her eye.

"Good evening, welcome back to Le Jules Verne, Ms. Riggs," said their waiter, addressing Rebecca directly. "We're thrilled to have you join us again. I'm Claude, and I will be your server this evening. Tonight's menu is called Extraordinary Voyages and is inspired by the work of Monsieur Verne. Will you be having the seven-course or the five-course menu?"

"Seven," said Rebecca. "And the wine pairings for me."

"Moi aussi," said Cassie, dusting off her very basic French.

"Brilliant," he said. "I will be back shortly."

Rebecca leaned in and said, "The price is negligible between the five- and seven-course options, don't you think?"

"Certainly," said Cassie, who made a mental note to double-check the prices when she got back in front of her computer. "Besides, we don't want to miss anything, do we?"

A few moments later, the waiter returned to their table and poured them each a glass of champagne. Then a small plate arrived, a single round pastry on it.

"Gougère, with warm brie and crushed pistachios," said the waiter in a low, hushed tone.

Cassie snapped a few photos, feeling embarrassed that she was photographing her food in such an exquisite restaurant. She looked over, and the waiter smiled at her in a way that told her that everyone photographed their food here.

She picked up the tiny pastry and popped it into her mouth, letting the warm cheese melt her whole body. It was sweet, a little salty, with the earthy umami of the cheese and a slight crunch from the nuts. She jotted down a few notes in her notebook and noticed that Rebecca was quietly dictating—was she using a microphone? She was very subtle; the waiters would assume that the two women were engrossed in conversation, not verbally taking notes.

Cassie took a sip of champagne and looked out the window again, lost in the view. She found herself thinking about James. He would have loved it there: the restaurant team that operated like a well-oiled machine, the understated but elevated interior design, and the food, the first bite forecasting just how incredible the rest of the meal was going to be. She let herself fantasize for a second—visualizing him walking through the restaurant in his tuxedo, the satin lapels glistening in the evening sunlight. Before she could let her mind wander too far, the next dish arrived.

It was presented on a bulbous white ceramic plate, with a spherical white mass in the middle that was dusted with a green powder.

"Crab," said the waiter, "served with iced consommé, caviar, and a Granny Smith zephyr, paired with a 2013 Puligny-Montrachet premier Cru Sous le Puits from Domaine Jean-Claude Bachelet."

Cassie cut into the white sphere, which cracked under her knife, surprising her. It was a meringue. She took a small bite, letting the flavors spread over her tongue, tasting hints of salty curry. She scribbled a few notes when no one was looking, then picked up her camera again, examining the dish through her lens.

"This is exquisite," said Rebecca, using her fork to probe all the different elements of the dish and taste them separately.

By this time, more people had entered the restaurant, and the room started to hum as service picked up. The patrons were mostly couples, but there were also a handful of small groups excited for a notable evening, one that most of them had traveled extensively for.

"This is the meal of a lifetime for so many of these people," Rebecca said. "They have been looking forward to it for so long. *This* is why I take my job so seriously. If I give a positive review, these people depend on it. They expect quality. I would absolutely hate to let them down."

Cassie wondered what she could bring to the table that was different, how she could make her restaurant reviews more relatable to readers, somehow providing more value to them.

"I agree," said Cassie, her eyes habitually drifting toward the window.

"It's hard to stop looking," Rebecca said. "But there's more to see inside. I bet we see—what? Three engagements here tonight? What do you think?"

"Eh, maybe four?" said Cassie, wondering what else this woman had seen over the decades of her career.

"I fell in love here once," Rebecca continued, her voice softening. "It's so easy to fall in love in Paris."

"Who was he?"

"He was an English businessman; I think he used to work with Russian oligarchs."

"That sounds shady," said Cassie, cringing.

"Yeah, it probably was. But he was terrific fun. We ate at sweet neighborhood Parisian restaurants, danced in late-night clubs, strolled through the Louvre hand in hand, and stayed in bed until noon. It was a beautiful tryst, and I'm so grateful for those memories."

"So, what happened?" Cassie reached for her glass of Chardonnay, still half full.

"Oh, it fizzled out. I think he might have been married, and I had to get back to California to work on my next book."

"Work," Cassie emphasized, relating to the feeling of sacrificing all too much for her career.

"I'm a workaholic. It's my fatal flaw." Rebecca shrugged and emptied her glass of wine into her mouth.

The next dish was served: a white bowl filled with white bubbling foam and a black circle of caviar topped with a leaf of parsley. "Potage crème dubarry served with leek and caviar."

Cassie tried Rebecca's tasting method and determined it was indeed helpful to taste each component separately before trying them together. Maybe it would help her better understand what each thing was and why it was on the plate.

"Were you ever married?" asked Cassie, once she knew Rebecca was finished dictating into her mic.

"I was, a few times. But I always felt too . . . tied down."

"Sounds familiar," said Cassie.

"Oh, I sense some drama," said Rebecca, leaning forward.

"It was more sad than dramatic, but yeah. I wasn't a great partner. James, well, he was wonderful. The more I think about it now, I think I took him for granted. I had a hard time appreciating how he expressed love and affection when we were in the moment."

"The most important partnership is with yourself," said Rebecca, with a new twinkle in her eye. "At least that's what I tell myself through every divorce. But you're too young for that, honey."

"Do you ever get lonely?"

"I do. But at the end of the day, I'm too much of a rebel. Hello, Claude," she said to the waiter, who had interrupted her train of thought when he arrived at the table. She clearly loved attractive men, and whenever Claude approached, something changed in her, and she seemed to glow, radiating her beauty outward.

"Are you ready for your next dish?" asked Claude.

"We are," said Rebecca, her face beaming at the young, handsome waiter.

"Langoustine ravioli served with Parmesan cream and a fine beetroot gelée," said Claude as both plates were served at exactly the same moment. "Would you care for shaved white truffle?" he asked, holding out a white mass and a polished silver grater.

The two women both nodded, and Claude proceeded to shave the truffle directly onto their plates, the white flakes falling gently like snow.

THE NEXT DISH was a piece of cod cooked with bottarga—cured fish roe—lobster coral, and a spicy jus, followed by the farmhouse chicken, served with wine sauce and wild mushrooms. The chicken didn't look like a chicken at all—it had been deboned and shaped into a thin cone that resembled a parsnip, a culinary trompe l'oeil.

They both had a line of six glasses of wine in front of them, each glass with a few sips left. It was such a shame to leave anything in the glass, but she heeded Ben's advice not to drink everything, now seeing why it was such an important rule.

Across the restaurant, a group erupted into applause, and Cassie looked over to see a couple kissing.

"That's one," said Rebecca, without looking over her shoulder.

"Are we ready for dessert?" said Claude, who was scraping the tablecloth to remove any crumbs.

"We are," said Cassie excitedly.

"First, there is a chestnut puff pastry, followed by a chocolate biscuit with bitter chocolate and buckwheat ice cream."

As she ate, Cassie could hear Rebecca dictating into the sleeve of her jacket, describing the flavors of the nutty cream, chocolate, and butter with a touch of salt. Once Rebecca stopped talking, Cassie realized she had eaten the entire thing, scraping the remaining cream off the plate and onto her fork.

"You liked that one, huh?" said Rebecca, before taking a sip of wine. Across the room, applause broke out again.

"That's two," said Cassie.

"Can you imagine getting engaged here? How romantic," Rebecca said, swooning.

I can, thought Cassie, as she looked out over Paris, the sun starting to set over the city, her mind focused on James. She was confident he would have loved this Paris and especially the Jules Verne. Maybe this is where he would have proposed to her? She longed to go back in time, so they could have more afternoons lying on blankets in the park, days spent wandering around museums, and evenings exploring the city's restaurants and their extensive wine lists. Most of all, she wished that they had followed through and booked the trips they talked about—who knows what could have happened between them.

The plates were cleared, and to Cassie's surprise, a second dessert arrived: an architectural chocolate tart made from thin chocolate crust filled with cream and dusted with shaved chocolate that oozed over the plate when she cut into it. She took a few bites, enjoying the sweet flavors of chocolate and cream, leaving the rest on the plate.

"All finished?" Claude asked when he came to clear the table.

"Oh, yes. Everything was delicious," said Rebecca.

"Thank you for joining us this evening, here at the top of the world," he said before placing the check on the table.

Simultaneously, Cassie and Rebecca dropped their credit cards onto the silver tray and then turned to take in the view for a few more moments.

"I guess there were only two tonight," said Rebecca. "We were both wrong." She gave Cassie a smile and looked out over the city. The sun had gone down, and the lights of Paris were twinkling. And then, at the top of the hour, the tower itself exploded with tiny flashbulbs, illuminating the restaurant with flickers of light.

"Are you enjoying the light show?" asked Claude when he returned to the table. "Did you know that it took twenty-five mountain climbers five months to install all the light bulbs?"

"Were you one of them?" Rebecca asked flirtatiously.

"Maybe I was," he retorted. "How was your evening?"

"Delightful as always, Claude. I'm so glad I was able to bring my niece and share this incredible restaurant with her."

Cassie felt her cheeks go hot. *Niece.* She was pretend family. She must not have humiliated herself too much.

22

Back in her room, Cassie sat down at her laptop. She yawned and made herself a cup of tea, trying to settle in to write her review. The white of the page was daunting. She found herself getting up for every reason—she had to go to the bathroom, she needed the cord to her camera, her phone should be charged. She uploaded the photos, giving them a quick edit, once again stalling the writing process.

Finally, around 10:00 p.m., she started writing.

She decided that maybe the best way to conquer these reviews was to write them *to* James—kind of like a love letter. It felt more honest that way. She could include him and didn't feel like she was trying to impersonate him.

Early Dinner at the Jules Verne, Paris

Oh, how I wish you could have joined me for dinner this evening at the Jules Verne, the iconic Parisian restaurant where I had a vision of you: handsome, and dressed in a dapper suit. Us, celebrating our twentieth anniversary, our hair silvery with age and our hearts still intertwined.

Did you know that people travel from all over the world to dine 123 meters above the streets of Paris? You would have loved the views of the city, the focus of the team, the wines, and the food, which was immaculate. Chef Frédéric Anton prepared a culinary concept simply titled "Extraordinary Voyages" that draws inspiration from the land and sea. The highlights were the langoustine ravioli, wrapped in a vibrant pink beetroot gelée, the farmhouse chicken with nutty mushrooms, and the three rounds of dessert that included a chocolate tart and two jewellike petit fours. While minimal, it is clear that the team at the Jules Verne spends many days preparing the components for each dish, which are then brought together in the kitchen and beautifully presented—that is, if you can keep your eyes on your plate and away from the breathtaking city views that surround.

Wish you were here.

#EatPostLike

She edited a set of photos and hit Post, before toggling over to the @NewYorkSecretDiner account, where she shared her post in the stories. No one would catch on to a reshare, and besides, she needed the boost of engagement. She was satisfied with her review. Next, she had to complete the Viand Awards questionnaire, marking twenty out of twenty on most of the five categories and writing out a formal review for the team.

```
Quality of Ingredients—20
Mastery of Culinary Techniques—20
Harmony of Flavors—19
Uniqueness of Perspective—18
Consistency—20
```

If all the restaurants were this good, it would be increasingly difficult to discern what restaurant was better than another—it would surely come down to subtleties.

It was three in the morning when she finally finished, crawling under the three-thousand-thread-count sheets, excited to sleep. But first, she checked the itinerary for the next day. She was scheduled to go to Reims with Eamon, the prospect of which made her stomach turn nervously. They hadn't spoken since the airport, but the mention of his name made her mind flash back to the lounge. Him in the shower. Soap suds. And those soft hazel eyes that seemed to pierce right through her thoughts when they finally met hers.

23

The next morning, Cassie woke up around nine and was feeling the late night before. She packed her bag quickly, albeit sloppily, but she made sure that all her belongings and new purchases were tucked into her suitcase.

Downstairs, Ben was halfway through breakfast, but he invited her to sit down with him.

"How was your dinner last night?" she asked.

"Exquisite," he said. "We went to Ledoyen, and it was just *beyond*. Where did you go?"

"The Jules Verne."

Ben dramatically fell back in his chair, swooning. "How *divine*," he said, once he pulled himself upright. "You're so lucky—well, we all are. So what's on your schedule for today?"

"I'm going to the Restaurant Le Parc at the Domaine Les Crayères, with Eamon. Apparently, it's out of town and we're staying the night there."

"Lucky you," said Ben, his eyes sparkling with delight. "I've heard such wonderful things."

It was another restaurant she had never heard of. "I'm pretty nervous, to be honest."

"You need to relax. What's there to be nervous about?" he

asked. "It's going to be wonderful. What time do you need to leave the hotel?" Ben smeared a fluffy croissant with butter.

"In an hour, which is sooner than I'd like."

"Are you packed? Sit down and have a bite. It will calm your nerves. Besides, there's seriously nothing to be nervous about—Le Parc is supposed to be magnificent."

Reims

24

Cassie came down the elevator with her bags at eleven on the dot. She found Eamon waiting in the lobby, black Persol sunglasses on, looking at his phone. The light was coming into the lobby from behind him, illuminating his silhouette and making the curls of his hair glow in the sunlight. His features were sharp and looked like they had been chiseled out of stone; especially his cheekbones, which caught the light of the atrium on his freshly shaven skin.

"Hello," she said timidly.

"Ready to go?"

"Ready as I'll ever be." Cassie swallowed hard and moved toward the door, her suitcase trailing behind her.

They loaded into the car, Cassie and Eamon in the back seat, and drove through the city, winding through midday traffic. They whizzed past the Place de la Concorde, the monumental obelisk that stands just north of the Seine, and past the Palais Garnier, the gilded opera house with its wide, oxidized copper roof, and finally arrived at the Gare de l'Est railway station.

Cassie trotted behind Eamon, who was walking at a quick pace, parting the crowds in front of him. He stopped in front of the announcement board and stared, waiting for their track to be assigned.

"This could take a while. Coffee?" he asked, looking down at his watch before gesturing toward a small café in the middle of the station.

"Sure," said Cassie, desperate for more caffeine after her late night. She needed to find a more sustainable sleep schedule if she was going to be on her game for the entirety of the trip.

While they walked, Cassie looked around the main hall, capped by an enormous skylight, large arches flanking either end. On the far wall was a beautiful semicircular window that fanned around a clock like the plumes of a peacock.

Eamon ducked into the café and ordered two coffees in flawless French. It was now obvious that everyone on the trip spoke French except for her, and the realization made her cringe with inadequacy. He paid, then handed the cup to Cassie. "Don't expect much," he said. "The coffee in train stations is usually terrible."

Cassie took a small sip, not wanting to burn her tongue. "Confirmed—it's barely drinkable," she said, earning a small smile from Eamon.

They sat down at a table, and Eamon took off his sunglasses and locked his big, doe-like hazel eyes on hers. She took a moment to study his strong brow, the hairs of his eyebrows borderline feral. He blew on the surface of the coffee, making his lips look even more pillowy, and she wondered for a second what they tasted like, before she shook the thought out of her mind.

"So, Cassie, tell me about yourself," he said.

"What do you want to know?" she said.

"Well, most of the Viand reviewers know each other, but you're new. Tell me about what you do."

"Is this a job interview? From what I understand, I already have the job."

He laughed, caught off guard. "It's true. I'm just curious. It's such a small group, and many of us are industry people who have known each other for a long time, but I don't know anyone who knows you."

"You've asked around?"

"Maybe," he said, his face breaking into another smile.

"Well, you can call off your goons. I'm a writer." It felt good to say something that felt true-ish. At least for the moment.

An announcement started over the loudspeaker, calling out a train arrival.

"That's us," said Cassie, jumping out of her seat, relieved that she had an excuse to avoid the interrogation, and dumping her half-full coffee into the trash. "It was terrible anyway."

THEY BOARDED THE train and shuffled into their seats in the first-class car. Cassie took the window seat and Eamon the aisle seat across from her, so they were facing each other, with a small table in between.

"So, how did you start working with the Viand Awards?" Cassie asked after they were both settled in.

"I've worked in the wine industry for about fifteen years, and I've helped build a few wine programs around the country—the United States, that is. I developed some relationships, both with restauranteurs and with the press, and I was asked to start writing about wine. Naturally, the focus slowly shifted, and I started writing about wine at restaurants, and then about the restaurants themselves. It's a nice thing to do along with consulting."

"What do you consult on?"

"Wine."

Duh, Cassie thought to herself, hearing the deafening sound of silence as she tried to find something else to ask, something to pivot the conversation.

"What do you love about the wine industry?"

"Good question," he said, shifting around in his seat. "There's so much diversity, from collector bottles to canned wine. There's literally a product for every single type of consumer. But more than that, wine tells a story—it speaks to a place, a specific time, and the people who made it. It's extremely labor intensive to make wine, which is such a critical part of the story but is easily forgotten by consumers. I swear, some people think it grows in a bottle."

The conductor came through to check their tickets, and Eamon smiled warmly at the petite blonde. Cassie found herself becoming acutely aware of how he was looking at the conductor, and she wondered if this was how he interacted with everyone or if it was just women. Was this a twinge of jealousy?

"Bonjour," he said, his voice softening a little.

The conductor returned the smile and the greeting— "Bonjour"—taking a bit of extra time to punch his ticket and make small talk.

After the conductor moved on, Cassie stared blankly at Eamon and said nothing.

"What? I'm just being friendly," he said. "Plus, if I can be nice to someone and make their day just a little better, what is the harm in that? It doesn't cost me anything to make someone feel good. Why wouldn't I do it?"

He had a point. Cassie looked out the window and watched the landscape speed past, changing from the city center to the suburbs and finally into the surrounding countryside, with rows of vineyards whizzing by on either side of the train.

Her stomach dropped with realization. They were heading to wine country, she a complete newbie and Eamon probably one of the preeminent experts on wine in the United States. For a moment, she thought she might be able to just jump off the train and disappear into the countryside, saving herself from embarrassment.

"Have you been here before?" she asked.

"Where?"

"Re-i—" She didn't even know how to pronounce the name of the city where they were headed. She felt herself wishing she could go back in time and study French instead of Spanish.

He cut her off. "Reims? Yes, of course. It's a frequent stop on any Champagne tour."

She felt herself shrivel. They were headed to the Champagne region. She should have known that. She should have looked that up. She used to be so good at doing research, preparing for her job, and now—this was the last time she would go into a review unprepared, she vowed to herself.

Cassie turned to her phone, trying to resist the urge to Google binge for the rest of the trip. She opened Instagram, checking the stats on her post from the evening before. To her surprise, the post had done well. It had a high number of likes, and she had a few thousand new followers thanks to the @NewYorkSecret-Diner boost. She switched accounts, scrolling through the DMs, and her stomach sank.

@JERSEYGIRL78

When did this turn into an aggregator account?

@BURGERSOVERBROS

Now this is some bourgeois bullshit.

@ANTONIOCOOKS
Plating Porrrnnnnn.

@DAILYAMY
Beautiful photos, but some details
on the meal would be helpful.

@BARRYINTHEKITCHEN
What the hell is this?

@CANTINA14522
I don't need a love letter; I just want to
know what's in the consommé.

@KHYTALKSTRASH
Where is @NewYorkSecretDiner? We
don't want other people's posts!

And one more comment, that upset her so much that she
switched her phone to silent mode, desperate for a mental break
from the incessant buzzing:

@DAVIDMAKESMONEY
👀

Her heart sank. She tried to do something different—something
creative—and failed completely. More alarming—was David on to
the fact that she was in James's account? She brushed it off. What
could he do anyway? She threw her phone into her bag, crossed her
arms, and retreated into the view of the landscape speeding by.

A CAR PICKED them up from the station. The driver took a few extra minutes to drive around the city while he pointed out some of the main attractions along the way—Notre-Dame de Reims, La Porte de Mars, and the Place Drouet-d'Erlon—before turning onto roads that were lined with grape vines growing in neat rows.

The driver slowed down and turned onto a gravel drive before passing through an iron gate. In front of them was the hotel, a stately three-story château that belonged to a very well-off family at one point in time. Once inside, they were greeted by a receptionist.

"Bonjour, Ms. Brooks. Welcome to Domaine Les Crayères. We have you in one of our Prestige rooms, which overlooks the park. Dinner starts at eight o'clock. Do you have any allergies we need to be aware of?"

"None," she said, letting her eyes wander around the beautiful lobby. She was handed a brass skeleton key on a heavy, blue silk tassel. She walked up a grand staircase and through the small corridors of the hotel, eventually coming to her suite, which was the size of a Manhattan apartment, lined with ornate blue-and-gold wallpaper. Cassie flopped onto the princess-style bed and stared up at the butter-colored ceiling. She felt tired, but she had a few hours before dinner, and she was going to make the most of it.

25

Cassie circled around David's comment, spinning through different fictional scenarios. What was he trying to prove? She decided to go for a run so that she could clear her mind. She laced up her running shoes, then locked her door and headed downstairs, leaving the key at the front desk. She stepped outside, feeling the familiar adrenaline rush she always had before a run. She needed to get out of there, and hopefully get rid of some of her frustration.

After the first mile, her body began to relax, and she was finally able to run with ease. As she ran through the empty roads lined with row after row of grape vines, she let her mind wander, but she kept coming back to how small she felt after reading all those comments. It was just social media! It was supposed to be easy! How could social media be so hard? Who was she kidding? She was a *lawyer*, not a food critic.

But more than that, she felt like a liar. She *was* a liar. She was trying to convince all these people that she was a top-tier restaurant critic who deserved to be on this trip, but the reality was that she had no place being there. *Why did I even let myself come on this trip?*

At this point, she was starting to hyperventilate, so she stopped and bent over, staring at the gravel between her feet.

She was wheezing, desperately trying to suck oxygen into her lungs. The tears started to stream down her cheeks, and then she broke down entirely, loudly sobbing in the quiet of the countryside.

"Hello?"

"Ruby? It's Cassie."

"Hiiiii, are you having the most amazing time? Where are you? You never sent me photos from last night."

Cassie could hear the coffee maker in the background. Ruby was in the break room at the office.

"Um—" Cassie could feel her throat tightening, and then she started crying again.

"Aw, honey, what's wrong?"

"I just don't think I can do this, Ruby; I feel like a complete fraud. If they find out that I lied to get here—I'm finished. I don't know how to do this. There are too many details. I don't even know what I'm supposed to be *faking*. I should just come home. This feels *wrong*."

"Slow down, Cass. Take a deep breath. You're a smart person, and you're learning. It's just like being a junior attorney—just nod your head and figure it out as you go. Be yourself, and *trust* in yourself. There are plenty of restaurant critics out there who aren't as smart as you are."

"But I'm not even a real critic," she spat out.

"That's okay. You're going to figure this out. Just lie low, pay attention, be a sponge, and take in as much as you can. You'll be okay. It's just like your first year in the office. Remember how awful *that* was?"

Cassie laughed, half coughing and crying. "I'd prefer not to."

"Look, you've been in a profession that has trained you to think that you're not good at anything. You've been beaten down. But this is a chance for you to change that and do something different."

"I'm not even sure what I want at this point."

"Which is *why* you're on this trip. Look, this is the opportunity of a lifetime. You can do this. Just relax, and you'll figure out the details. You always do. There's nothing you love more than a good challenge."

"That's the thing, Ruby, I'm forgetting to do even the dumb stuff, like researching where I'm going. I've been going in blind and embarrassing myself."

"Well, stop doing *that*. Build better habits for yourself. You'd never go into the courtroom unprepared. Why are you going into this ill-equipped?"

"I guess I didn't realize that I needed to *be* prepared."

"See, you're learning. Do your homework, and you'll be fine. You're a smart girl."

"I wish you were here."

"Trust me, I wish I was there too. You wouldn't believe the bullshit that's going on this week. I won't get into it; it will send you into a rage."

"Ha, yeah, probably better that I don't know. Thanks for taking my call. I really appreciate it."

"Anytime, babe. Now go get 'em."

RETURNING TO THE hotel, Cassie felt better and was determined to spend the rest of the afternoon doing her due diligence on the restaurant she was assigned to review. She grabbed her key and was crossing through the lobby while looking down at her phone, checking her email at the same time. It was strange not having the usual barrage of emails from work, but there were still things to tend to: bills and emails from friends checking in on her, including one from David that she left unread. She really didn't have the time or patience for a walk down memory lane with him today. She toggled over to Instagram, and as soon as she started scrolling, she noticed she was about to walk into something—or someone.

Eamon.

Cassie jumped, startled that he was so close and she hadn't even noticed.

"I was wondering when you were going to see me standing here," he said, smiling and holding his ground.

"Oh my god, I'm so sorry. I didn't see you. I was just checking my— You know what, it doesn't matter." She noticed that they were still standing very close together, almost touching, and she took a step back, suddenly aware that she was still sweating.

"You're lucky you've never been hit by a car walking and texting like that."

"Ugh, I know. It's the New Yorker in me. Always working," she joked, nervously. She pulled down the brim of her hat to conceal her makeup-less face. "I should go take a shower," she said, trying to step around him to get to the staircase that led up to her room, but he stepped in front of her to capture her attention.

"Before you go, I set up a wine tasting at seven. You're welcome to join if you would like to. We'll be on the back patio."

"Um. Sure. That sounds nice. See you then."

Shit. She only had a few hours to shower, get dressed, and read as much about this place as she possibly could.

CASSIE STARTED WITH the basics: the hotel's website that told the history of the building, the architect, and the previous owners, and listed bios for the current chef, director, maître d', and sommelier. She spent some extra time studying the chef, analyzing his ethos about raw ingredients, how he wanted to build a relationship between the place and the food with his cooking. She took note that his menu was built around the freshest ingredients available, and the dishes changed daily, making it impossible to anticipate exactly what would be served.

After she read all the reviews she could find online, she dug through her bag to find one of James's journals that she had tucked into her suitcase at the last minute. She flipped through it, trying to find something on France, specifically on the Champagne region.

The notebooks were organized by country, starting with the capital city, where he would list out notable restaurants, chefs, and hotels, then supplement each section with traditional, regional recipes, local delicacies, and other notes scribbled in the margins. She flipped past his entries on Paris, now seeing an entire page dedicated to the Jules Verne, past the sections on Lyon, Provence, and Gascony, before coming to his section on the Champagne region.

A week in Champagne: Aÿ-Champagne, Fleury-la-Rivière, Épernay, Baconnes, and Reims. Tour large Champagne houses and small growers, as to understand champagne

production and how chefs use it for inspiration.
Close look at terroir-driven cuisine that mirrors wine
production: soil, water, grape varietals, chalk.
Time? How does the idea of time influence the
cooking? Agricultural cycles of the vines, fermentation,
maturation time on lees: 15 months to 3 years.
Could be a good trip for Cassie.

Café du Palais—traditional
Racine—French-Japanese—vegetables, 15 seats per
  seating
L'Assiette Champenoise—*** sustainable
Domaine Les Crayères—must visit

Tucked into the pages was a newspaper cutting on Les Crayères, which reviewed the restaurant, highlighting the current chef. It had clearly excited James; there were blocks of underlined text, quotes from the chef, and revelations on the quality of service within the restaurant. Scribbled in the margins were notes from James: *raw materials—Champagne: clay, vines, shoots, leaves.*

Next, Cassie spent some time on Instagram studying successful posts and videos from other creators that she could try to emulate. She needed to create a voice for herself, something that felt like her own. The past forty-eight hours had validated what she already knew: a strong Instagram account would open doors and help her build a new career. James had built his following in the early days of Instagram, when it was primarily a photo sharing app. The current version relied heavily on video reels that were set to music and had an incredible way of bringing a scene to life. She clicked through her favorite travel accounts and studied the reels, taking note of their camera angles, hooks, transitions, subject matter, and captions. If she could master reels, her account would surely grow quickly, and with it, she could earn even more opportunities.

26

At seven o'clock sharp, Cassie descended the stairs of the hotel, dressed in a tight-fitting black dress with a black blazer, classic black high heels, and the sculptural gold earrings she'd bought in Paris. She'd finished off her look with two sharp lines of liquid eyeliner above each eye and a swipe of bright red lipstick, inspired by Rebecca's style from the night before.

Through the glass doors she could see Eamon sitting out on the patio, tapping on his phone. He was wearing a fitted gray suit and a white button-down shirt with a thin black tie, adorned with a matte black tie clip. He had just showered; his hair was still wet and gelled into a casual blond wave, which in combination with his black rock and roll–style sunglasses made him look undeniably cool. She took a deep breath, pushed her shoulders back, and stepped out onto the patio, which was flooded with the early evening light. She pulled her large cat-eye sunglasses out of her bag and walked across the patio, careful not to trip on the loose gravel beneath her feet.

"Hello," she said, approaching the table, but before she could get too close, Eamon hopped up and pulled a chair out for her. "Th-thank you," she stammered. "You didn't have to do that."

"Once in hospitality, always in hospitality," he said with a shrug, masking his manners as an occupational hazard. "You clean up well," he added, before sitting down in his chair. "How was your downtime?"

"Productive," she answered, then deflected immediately: "What a gorgeous spot."

"It truly is. I'm always so thrilled when I'm assigned to review Les Crayères. Have you been here before?"

Wasn't it obvious? "No, I haven't. How many times have you been here?"

"Quite a few. How many times, exactly? I'm not completely sure. There was one time we came here with a private client who was building their cellar, and oh, man, did we drink some amazing wine. They brought out the most incredible vintages from the last century, including a 1951 Bollinger R.D. made from pre-phylloxera vines. I can still taste the seared foie gras paired with an impeccable 1978 Chateau d'Yquem." He paused, letting the memory carry him away for a second. "It was . . . sublime."

Cassie tapped a few notes into her phone to look up later:

Pre-fau-lix-ara? Vines.
Yakemme?

"So, tell me more about this tasting," she said.

"It's informal. The sommelier is a friend of mine, and he's going to set up a tasting of a few bottles of champagne."

Cassie wasn't surprised. Eamon gave the impression of being the kind of guy who knew someone at every restaurant around the world. He was magnetic, and people seemed to adore him. What was not to like? He was handsome, charismatic, and friendly to everyone—bellboys, coffee attendants, conductors.

For just a moment Cassie wished she was a little bit more like Eamon and less like . . . herself.

He continued: "And it was an excuse to get you to come down and have a drink with me before dinner."

Her face flushed, and she smiled, unsure how to respond. "Lucky for you, it doesn't take much for me to drink champagne," she finally spat out, and she reminded herself of Ben's rules about drinking too much, knowing full well that they were likely going to have a wine pairing with dinner.

A few moments later, the sommelier came out with a tray of glasses and three bottles of champagne. "Bonsoir, je m'appelle Marc."

"Bonsoir," said Cassie. Her French was clunky and Americanized. "Je m'appelle Cassie."

"Welcome to Domaine Les Crayères. We have quite a special evening lined up for you."

"I cannot wait," said Cassie.

She was ready. She had studied everything she could in a short few hours, analyzing previous dishes found in articles and blog posts, scouring geotags on Instagram for images and videos, with the goal of being as prepared as possible.

Marc smiled at her; he was warm and welcoming. "Where are you from, mademoiselle?"

"New York. Manhattan."

Eamon looked up and seemed a little surprised.

"Eamon, are you still in New York?" asked Marc.

"I am," he said, "but it's a slum compared to France."

"Oui, we must get you here more often."

"I try . . . I try," he said with a laugh. "So, what do you have for us?"

"We have three rare vintages I would like to share with you. I've been saving them for some very special VIPs." He winked at Cassie. "Will you be joining us for some champagne?" he asked her.

"You don't come to Champagne to drink water, do you?" said Cassie, recalling a line from one of the blog posts she'd read in her research blitzkrieg.

Marc laughed. "No. You don't."

Cassie blushed slightly, smiled, and felt her armor come down a notch. She took a moment to snap a few photos and capture a few quick videos of the green lawn with the sunset beyond and the beautiful estate.

"The first bottle is a Dom Ruinart Blanc de Blancs from 2010." Marc pulled back the metal foil on the top of the bottle and unwound the cage. He then covered the top of the bottle with a white cloth and with a quiet *pffftt* slid the cork out of the bottle.

"Well done, my friend," said Eamon.

"This is my *job*," joked Marc.

He poured some of the champagne into his glass, gave it a quick swirl, and slid the liquid into his mouth. "Magnifique." Marc then poured the wine into the glass in front of Cassie and then the glass in front of Eamon.

Cassie turned her lens to the glass, now filled with the straw-colored wine, and she captured a few short clips of the bubbles as they danced their way to the top of the glass. Then, she brought the glass up to her nose, smelling the layers of aromas from glazed apple to cooked quince. She took a sip and let the wine coat her tongue, enjoying the effervescence and the flavors of apricot, roasted hazelnut, and a gingery pastry with Meyer lemon on the end.

"This is beautiful," she said. "Thank you. I heard you helped design the stemware. I love that you've designed a glass specifically for older vintages."

Eamon was taking notes but suddenly stopped. He looked up at her, surprised.

"Oui," said Marc. "It took quite a few years to get it right, but I'm very proud of the shape of these glasses. It helps emphasize the aromatics of the wine, without sacrificing the verticality of the bubble."

"They are beautiful," said Cassie, holding up the bulbous glass to take a better look at it. "Tell me more about the collection of wines on the property."

"We have more than nine hundred different types of champagne in our cellars, which does not include the other still wines we have. I would venture to say we have one of the best wine cellars in the region."

"And yet there's a corking fee on the menu? Who would need to bring their own bottles?" she asked. "Seems like you have everything under the sun."

"Collectors looking to show off," Eamon opined.

"Exactly," said Marc. "I've opened some truly remarkable bottles over the years. Eamon, you were here for some of those bottles. Wasn't that a crazy night?"

"Very. Epic, legendary, *iconic*," Eamon added, before turning his attention to the next bottle of wine. "So, what do you have in your hand, Marc?"

"Eamon, you are going to love this one. It is Armand De Brignac Brut Rosé. Fifty percent Pinot Noir, forty percent Pinot Meunier, and ten percent Chardonnay."

The bottle itself was mesmerizing: pink and mirrored, with

an emblem of a spade on the front. Marc poured the wine into her glass, drawing attention to the color as it left the bottle. The wine was a pinkish copper color and shone brilliantly in the sunlight, the tiny bubbles dancing their way to the surface of the liquid. Cassie loved tasting through the different layers of flavor of the wine, each one revealing itself as the liquid moved over her tongue and down her throat.

"Wow," she said after taking a first sip. "That is wild," she said, sticking her nose back into the glass. "I'm getting so much spice, but also summer berries, almond brioche, and, what is that, red currant?"

"We should hire you to write tasting notes," Marc joked, pouring himself a small taste of the wine. "I have one more selection to pour for you this evening before I head back to the dining room for service." Marc peeled the foil off the third bottle of wine. "I really hope you enjoy this. It's Dom Perignon, a very rare bottle, one we acquired from a neighboring cellar. Just for fun, we're going to make this one a pop quiz—you must tell me the vintage."

The wine was darker in color than the others, almost the hue of straw, and seemed a little . . . flat.

Cassie nosed the wine and smelled the familiar flavors of fruit and brioche, and it did have a slight effervescence to it.

Eamon nosed the glass, almost cupping his nose entirely. "Oh my," he said. "This is pretty old." He kept sniffing and guessed, "I don't know. Maybe the eighties? Late eighties? I know that nineteen eighty-eight was a good vintage across France."

"Impressionnant, tu as raison. Nineteen eighty-eight," said Marc. "Bien joué. You haven't lost your touch, Eamon. Enjoy—I will see you inside when you're ready for dinner."

He smiled and left them with their multiple glasses of wine.

"Well, this is a treat," said Cassie. "Thank you for inviting me."

"Of course," said Eamon, one arm draped over the back of his chair, his body completely relaxed. He was gazing out over the gardens, appreciating the manicured view in front of him. "I didn't realize you knew anything about Champagne."

"I don't," she said, and raised her glass to take another sip.

GOLDEN HOUR WAS beginning to settle in, and Cassie was enjoying the feeling of the warm sun on her skin. She looked out over the green lawn, which reached out from the patio to the perimeter of trees that gave way to a view of the landscape beyond. It was a beautiful estate. She took a deep breath, filling her lungs with the fresh air.

"Not bad, huh?" said Eamon.

"Not at all. Question—does *everyone* here know who you are?"

"Pretty much."

"So much for anonymous reviewing," she quipped, suddenly realizing how well known these three writers were, and that this was their scene.

"If there's one thing I know about this restaurant it is that everyone who comes here is considered a VIP. The service would be the same no matter who you are. But let me be clear: they don't know that we are on assignment, so they have no idea that this meal is on the record."

"But how do you know if you're accurately evaluating the service if they know you? Wouldn't it be better if you—we—were all incognito?"

"Ha. Sounds like you got pulled into this life because of the myth of the restaurant critic. You want intrigue? Okay, we'll be honeymooners tonight. How about that?" he said with a flirta-tious wink that sent a current of electricity up Cassie's spine.

"From Dallas. Big oil money," she added, masking her voice with a faux southern accent.

"You've got it now. We were just in Lake Como, and we're in the second week of our trip," he piled on.

"Naturally," she said, wondering what a honeymoon in Lake Como would be like with Eamon.

"Honestly, though, it's incredibly difficult to be an anony-mous critic these days, because we all have such large digital footprints. Hell, there is even a photo of Pete Wells on the inter-net. And on top of that, you must create unique email addresses in order to make reservations, have multiple credit cards under other names in order to pay—it's so much work. There is already a lot of work that goes into this job: the research, talking to chefs, fact-checking, not to mention the writing and editing. I com-mend people who do the whole undercover thing, but it's more than I can handle."

"So, what else do you look for, other than the quality of the food?"

"I like to look for some of the intangibles that make din-ing in a restaurant so transcendent—what makes it a unique experience. Storytelling, cultural elements that are woven in, craft, discipline, hospitality—it's all part of it, and sometimes it can be the little things that push a restaurant over the top. I also make a point of observing the room around me to see how other guests are reacting. You can usually tell if another table is having a bad experience or if the team is providing ex-ceptional hospitality. At the end of the day, great restaurants must deliver an exceptional product and experience to all their guests, so the table next to mine is just as important as what is happening right in front of me."

"I guess everyone has their style," Cassie added.

"It's true, and I've found that different people look for different things. There are some who always look for the flaws, tiny inconsistencies, and the cracks in the system. I, however, believe that restaurants are art, and with that comes so much more than just perfection."

"What's that?"

"Humanity."

27

Cassie followed the host to their table, passing by the neo-classical columns that marched around the room, framing floor-to-ceiling glass French doors and ornate carved fireplaces with oil paintings hung above. They passed under a large oak arch, and into a small glass bay that protruded into the garden, capped by a glass dome trimmed with sheer curtains. A single crystal chandelier hung over the table that glowed in the summer's evening light.

Once they were seated, Cassie leaned toward Eamon and said, "I feel like I'm dining in a museum."

"That's because you basically are," Eamon whispered in return. "This place has major historical significance, at least in the wine industry."

Cassie took a moment to look over the menu, making notes about the ingredients she didn't recognize. At the very least, by the end of this trip, she would have a thorough understanding of European cuisine.

"Are you enjoying yourself?" Eamon asked.

Cassie paused. It was a strange question to ask about a dinner set up by a corporate institution. "Yes, of course," she said, not sure where the conversation was going.

"Good. That's the first rule of this game. Well, technically, the third. Be on time, be polite, and don't forget to enjoy yourself."

"Wait. That's *exactly* what Rebecca told me."

He laughed. "Yep, that's the advice she gave me a few years ago. It's worked out well so far."

"She's a wise woman," said Cassie, feeling her heart swell with gratitude.

"I've learned so much from her over the years," Eamon said. "In some ways she has become a work mother to me. I ask her advice about all kinds of things. We're very lucky to have her on this trip. She hasn't accepted the invitation in a few years because she's been so busy promoting her cookbooks. I wouldn't be surprised if she got her own show."

A server appeared with a long, white plate, which he placed between them. "To start, we have an amuse-bouche—a Scottish salmon tart with goat cheese foam, a beet dumpling, and a savory cannoli of butternut squash topped with microgreens from our kitchen garden."

The three bites were topped with tiny flowers and microgreens. Cassie took a short video and snapped a few photos, making sure to get a macro shot of each, focusing on the tiny herbs, backlit in the glow of the evening light.

"These are almost too beautiful to eat," she said, continuing to photograph the small pastries.

"Bonsoir," said Marc, who seemed to appear out of nowhere. "Your first wine is a 1990 Perrier-Jouët Belle Epoque champagne." He poured the wine from a green bottle adorned with white and green art nouveau flowers.

"Oh, hello again," said Cassie, happy to see him.

"She hasn't tried anything yet. She's too busy photographing it," teased Eamon. Marc smiled before turning away to serve another table.

Cassie's eyes darted up with panic. "I need images for my notes," she said, feeling the need to defend herself.

"You're one of *those*, huh?" said Eamon, looking down at the menu.

Cassie felt her cheeks flush with embarrassment.

"I'm kiddiiing," he said after too many seconds of silence.

"I'm starting to believe that you take pleasure in messing with people," Cassie said playfully.

"There is some truth to that," he said, smiling. "I like making people sweat."

Cassie felt her skin tingle, and she wondered what else he could have meant.

She took a bite of the salmon tart, which melted in her mouth, sweet and salty. The beet dumpling was beautiful: magenta puree encapsulated by a thin, silky skin that had been pinched together tenderly. Finally, she turned to the cannoli, an inexplicably thin pastry crust piped full of a yellow puree. It crunched under her fork, the butternut squash and fresh thyme spilling out onto the plate.

"Thank you for inviting me to the tasting earlier," Cassie said once she had finished scribbling notes into her notebook. "That was really kind of you."

"I'm glad you came. These trips can get kind of lonely if you stick to yourself the whole time."

"I was surprised they assigned us in pairs."

"It's a new thing," he said. "Not everyone is cut out to be on the road all year eating alone. Viand is trying to build a system where the team can review restaurants and have a life."

"How's that working out for you?" Cassie probed.

"Good, I guess. I'm a social person. I like to be around people. I had a hard time eating alone every night for months on end. I mean, it's okay at first, but then it's just a work trip and there is no one there to share it with. Meals are when we *connect* with people, you know?"

"Breaking bread," said Cassie.

"Exactly. Breaking bread. We do it with people. Besides, anyone who visits a restaurant based on our recommendation is going to be dining with other people, so in my mind, it's a critical part of the experience. How does a restaurant treat a woman versus a man? Do they pull out the chair for everyone, or just the women? How can I judge that if I'm dining alone?"

"That's a completely valid point. Gender bias is latent in all industries," said Cassie, remembering how much she struggled as a female lawyer in a male-dominated industry.

"It's especially bad in these high-end kitchens," Eamon admitted.

"I'm not surprised," she said. "I imagine how stressful it must be to work in a place like this. The work is so incredibly detail oriented, and there isn't much room for error." Her mind drifted to James and how he used to cook. It was so fluid. He had the ability to adjust recipes with an extra squeeze of lemon or more butter, and she understood now that it was because he had a great palate.

"Wild mussels with cauliflower foam, caviar, and uni," said their waiter, as two additional servers placed the next dish in front of them.

Cassie snapped a few photos, making sure to capture the elegant bowl that held everything in place. Satisfied, she picked up her fork and took a bite. When the first taste hit her tongue, she felt her entire body soften, as though she were surrendering to it.

"Oh my god," she exclaimed, eyes wide and excited. "This is insanely delicious. Each of these flavors is so pure—there is nothing superfluous," she said confidently.

"I couldn't have said it better myself," said Eamon.

The next course was a plate of red prawns served with fennel and tiny potatoes the size of marbles that were sweet and creamy, along with haddock velouté, prepared tableside.

"Can I ask you a personal question?" asked Cassie.

"Shoot."

"How did you get into wine? It seems very specific."

"It is. My family owns a vineyard in Sonoma, so I've been raised in the industry. I was very lucky. Wine has always been around—I was fortunate to have parents who knew a lot about it. So I guess I learned through osmosis, from them as well as from so many of their friends."

"You grew up in a winery? That must have been amazing," Cassie gushed, imagining what it would be like to grow up in a vineyard.

"There are parts of it that are great, but there are other parts that are incredibly difficult. Let's be clear, it's agriculture. There's much that is captivating about wine, but the truth is that it can wear on people."

"What do you mean?"

"Working with family can be hard. It's easy for everyone to have unrealistic expectations," he said, fidgeting with the silverware on the table, adding under his breath, "Especially my father."

"Sounds like something bad happened," said Cassie, realizing she had struck a nerve.

"Yeah, it did. It's part of the reason why I started writing. I felt like there was no opportunity for growth there. I still don't know how he expected me to learn the ins and outs of the business without teaching me. I kept asking for his mentorship, and for whatever reason, it just felt like he kept me at arm's length. I was willing to learn, but I think at the end of the day I realized that he isn't capable of being a good teacher. It's complicated."

"That's hard, but maybe he tried in his own way?"

"Maybe. Anyway—I've moved on. Viand has been great for me. It's an incredible vehicle to travel the world, stay in nice hotels, eat incredible food, some not-so-great food, but yeah, I like to go where the wind takes me."

It was a feeling Cassie could relate to, but she wanted to know more.

"Are you close with your father?"

"Incredibly. We are very similar people and we are very good friends, which is what makes the whole situation even more difficult. Let's talk about something else."

"Okay. What does it take to be a sommelier?" Cassie asked, changing the subject.

"A great memory—for geography, flavors, and minute details. I started out by working at wineries during my summers, and eventually started studying wine. I got lucky and was able to land nice jobs here and there—French Laundry, Auro, to name a few. I'm still working toward my Court of Master Sommeliers certification."

Their server appeared at the table next to them and waited for a break in their conversation. "Your next dish is sea bass with white asparagus, fresh peas, and mousseron mushrooms."

Cassie snapped into action but tried to be quick and not hold up the meal.

"Do you take a picture of every course?" asked Eamon, half joking.

Cassie took a deep breath and decided not to let it bother her. "I think we've already established that I'm a serial food photographer. What do you do to remember everything from a meal that you need to review?"

"I refuse to divulge my secrets," he said, grinning. His eyes sparkled in the now dark, candlelit room, and Cassie felt goose bumps rise on her arms and her heart skip a beat. "You sure ask a lot of questions," he added.

"I'm just curious. Everyone is so different, and there is more than one way to get the job done." She took a bite of the white fish, letting it melt on her tongue, buttery and creamy.

Eamon smiled at her and took a sip of wine but refused to answer the question.

"Enough about work," Eamon said finally. "Tell me more about you. What do you like to do for fun?"

"Fun?" Cassie laughed. It was such a foreign concept to her. Typically, she was always working, and when she wasn't, she was thinking about work. "I don't know. I like to run, I've been enjoying getting back into photography, and I guess you could say I read a lot." Eamon didn't need to know that she was typically reading legal citation guides or codes and statutes, not novels or restaurant reviews.

"I'm surprised I haven't run into you at any events in New York," he said.

"I guess you could say that I like being nondescript."

"That's clear. You're proving to be a hard nut to crack."

"What do you mean by that?" Cassie asked.

"You're difficult to figure out. I'm usually good at getting people to tell me their whole life story before the amuse-bouche."

"Sorry to be a disappointment."

"You're anything but," he said, and let the comment hang in the air for a few moments. "Okay, serious question. What vegetable are you?"

Cassie laughed, caught entirely off guard by the ridiculous question.

"Excuse me, what?"

"You heard me," he said, grinning. "Not your favorite vegetable, but rather what are you, and why."

"This is so ridiculous," she said, laughing. "I can't believe this is the conversation we're having in *this* restaurant." She looked up at the ceiling, begging for an out, but when she looked back at Eamon, he continued to stare at her with a smirk on his face. "Okay, fine. Let's see. I'm not quite sure. Maybe cauliflower?"

"Interesting. Seemingly innocuous but versatile enough to become anything: pizza dough, rice, soup, stews, pickles, whatever you want. A chameleon."

"Yep," she confirmed, unsure if she was currently cauliflower, or if that is what she wanted to become. "How about you?"

"I'm a potato," he said, his face curling into a giant smile, his answer scripted and well rehearsed. "Also a humble vegetable, but always the best part of the meal."

"Is it?" Cassie questioned, involuntarily scrunching up her nose in response.

"Obviously!" he added, excitedly talking faster and louder than before. "It's the side dish that pulls everything together. Thousand-layer potatoes fried in duck fat? Phenomenal. Potato chips and caviar? Perfection. Thrice-fried fries with curry mayo? Life-changing. Poutine with cheese curds and gravy? Delectable. Mashed potatoes at Thanksgiving? Irrefutably the best part of the meal. This is a hill I will die on."

"You're too good-looking to be a potato," Cassie said, the words slipping out before her brain could stop her.

"So maybe a purple potato?" he joked, grinning again. "Okay, next question. Why did you want to become a food critic?"

The question hit like a blow to the stomach and left her even more speechless than the vegetable question. Why *did* she want to be a food critic? Her mind raced around, but she didn't have a good answer. The past few days had felt like an out-of-body experience, and she still felt grossly unqualified for the job. After all, she was a lawyer with no restaurant experience. Hell, she wasn't even any good at cooking.

After a moment, she finally answered. "I want to bring experiences to life for people who either cannot have them or want to have them. It's that simple. I want to inspire people to get out and live: enjoy the food that is on their plate, take a moment to feel the sunshine on their skin, and to remember that there is more to life than simply existing. And maybe each review is a reminder to myself to do the same."

The servers came by with their next dish: a filet of duck stuffed with foie gras, served with sous vide beets and a small salad of pickled grape vine sprouts, accompanied by a Vosne-Romanée

Burgundy. It was almost as though Cassie could taste the presence of the earth itself, the connection between the wine, the vines, and the grain grown to feed the animals. She cleaned the plate, leaving nothing behind.

"This dish has such a strong connection to the place. I love the inclusion of the vine itself in this dish," said Cassie.

Eamon raised an eyebrow.

"What do *you* love about being a critic?" she asked.

"It's less about being a critic, and more about loving the culinary arts. Food is the fastest way to understand a culture, its traditions, heritage, and history. I also love that it's this living artifact and it's always changing—some dishes transform every time they are prepared, and others over decades. Recipes get passed down from generation to generation, and they tell a story, but instead of words there are spices, herbs, and specific cuts of meat."

"Kind of like wine?" she asked.

"Yes, but food is more malleable. Wine is a time capsule—it literally bottles a moment in time and freezes it until the future. It's incredible that we can open old bottles and get a sense of what the earth tasted like fifty or a hundred years ago. It's such a trip."

"That's such a nice way to think of it," she said. "That's how I used to think about photography. Film photography, that is."

As though he'd read her mind, he said, "Same thing, I guess. You're just freezing light onto film, no? One moment, captured forever."

"Exactly. It's magic." For the first time all night, she was starting to feel a little tipsy. She looked at the row of nearly empty wineglasses and instinctively reached for her glass of water, drinking the entire thing in one go.

The next dish was a Chaource cheese foam and caramelized brioche, drizzled with hazelnut oil and a champagne reduction, followed by the restaurant's famous dessert, Lemon Waves, a thin ribbon of baked pastry topped with spheres of sorbet and slices of green apple so thin that they appeared luminescent. Served next to the main dessert was a tray of petit fours—one chocolate, one cherry, and one pistachio.

"And for your pairing, a glass of 1983 Arton Armagnac," said Marc as he poured golden liquid into small fluted glasses. "Enjoy."

She took a sip of Armagnac and savored the caramel, cherry, dark chocolate, and lavender flavors.

"How do they make this?" she asked.

"It's basically brandy, distilled wine, but made in a more rustic, artisanal way."

"How do they get it to taste like lavender?" she asked. "Is it some sort of infusion?"

"No, it's just a flavor compound that comes out of the process. Armagnac is cool because there are so many small growers who produce on their private farms, and the smaller the batch, the more unique flavors come out." Eamon held the glass up to the light, studying it before taking a sip of the dark brown liquid.

"What are you doing?"

"I love watching the Gibbs-Marangoni effect, which is a result of the surface tension caused by the evaporation of the alcohol. It is an indicator of the amount of sugar and alcohol. Nerdy explanations aside, I think it's mesmerizing."

Cassie had never really looked at how a liquid moved in a glass, but he was right, it was hypnotic. She took out her camera and tried to capture the phenomenon, rather unsuccessfully.

Eamon extended his hand across the table and asked, "Hey, can I see your camera?"

Cassie froze. It wasn't a very expensive camera, which made her self-conscious, knowing how gear-focused real photographers could get. "What for?" she asked.

"Come on, just let me see it."

"Ugh, fine, just don't judge me." Cassie passed her camera across the table.

"Why would I judge you?" Eamon asked, fiddling with the buttons.

"I don't know. Camera nerds get judgey."

"I'm not a camera nerd. Maybe a wine nerd, or a music nerd, but certainly not a camera nerd," he said, before lifting the camera up to his eye and snapping a few photos of Cassie.

"Hey!" Cassie raised her hands up to block the lens from seeing her face. "Who said you could do that?"

"Who said I couldn't?" Eamon flashed his megawatt smile at her before handing the camera back.

"This review is supposed to be *a-NON-y-mous*," she said with an air of authority, even though she had no idea what she was talking about.

Cassie stuffed the camera back into her bag, embarrassed, violated, and a little giddy at the same time. Why would he ever want to take a picture of her?

"I just want you to be able to remember tonight, you know, with more than pictures of your plate," he said, looking at her directly, his eyes shimmering in the candlelight.

"That's really nice of you, thank you," Cassie said, letting her guard come down a little bit.

"You know," he said, fingering the cut crystal snifter in front of him, "when I first met you, I thought you were going to be one of those women's magazine writers—the ones who don't eat anything, send dishes back to the kitchen, and complain the whole time. But I can tell that you are a true foodie at heart. You would be amazed how many people come on these trips and don't even enjoy it. It can be hard work eating large meals so frequently. But not for you. It's almost as though you're coming at it with a virgin palate. Each bite is an epiphany—a whole new world opening in your mind."

"Isn't that what these chefs want? I guess I'm just trying to be as open and receptive as possible so that the experience can take me wherever it needs to. And for the record, I agree with you. I think food is art, and it *should* evoke an emotional response, whether that's memory, nostalgia, or even a little fear of the unknown. They say that smell has the strongest tie to memory and can trigger one even decades later."

"I can tell you one thing. This will certainly be a meal that I remember for decades, and it wasn't just the food," said Eamon, smiling at her, his hazel eyes unwavering.

She leaned back in her chair, holding her glass of Armagnac, and paused to take in the scene around her. The sun had now set, and the room was dim, warmed by the glow of the chandeliers above. Cassie listened to the hum of the room; the clink of silverware and glasses, the chatter, and laughter—all sounds of life being *lived*.

"WOULD YOU LIKE to tour the kitchen?" asked Marc, once all their plates had been cleared.

"Yes, please," said Cassie, grabbing her phone and her camera.

Marc led them through the restaurant, through a set of double doors, and into the kitchen, which was jarringly bright compared to the soft glow of the restaurant. The kitchen was in peak service, and everyone was moving quickly. Orders were coming in, dishes were ready to serve, and Cassie clung to the walls trying not to get in the way. The kitchen felt like a completely foreign world compared to the dining room, where the servers moved at a controlled, confident pace. Here they moved quickly, matching the pace of the kitchen as the chefs executed each dish.

Even in the middle of service, the kitchen was clean and orderly, and the cooks were positioned at their designated stations. Framed on the walls were reviews, awards, and photographs of the chef with celebrities, presidents, and dignitaries from all over the world.

"Chef, this is Mademoiselle Cassie and Monsieur Eamon."

"Chef Moret," said Eamon, with a nod of his head.

"Hello," said Cassie, waving her hand awkwardly.

"How was your meal?" asked the chef, taking a moment away from the expo station.

"Wonderful," said Cassie. "I loved how each dish made a connection to the land, the seasons, and the region. Bravo."

"Yes, that is what we strive for," he said. "I'm so glad you enjoyed it."

FOLLOWING CHEF'S CUE, Marc led them out of the kitchen and through an unmarked door. A light turned on, illuminating a stone staircase that led to the basement.

Cassie could feel the temperature drop as they descended into the darkness deep beneath the kitchen. Once they reached the bottom of the staircase, Marc flipped on a switch, revealing an impressive wine cellar carved into the earth that smelled like damp clay. The room was shaped like a vertical trapezoid, with racks of bottles of wines on either side, naturally chilled by the surrounding cave.

"These used to be active champagne cellars," said Marc, "but today we use them for wine storage. In fact, they are part of an intricate underground network connecting neighboring Champagne houses for miles. In World War One, around twenty thousand people lived in these caves for years at a time to escape the bombing."

"That's incredible," Cassie said. "How many of the Champagne houses were used for support during the war?"

"Most of them. Pommery, just next door, was a school, and the caves under Veuve Clicquot and Ruinart were hospitals."

Carved into the chalk walls were markings, graffiti, of names, initials of young lovers encircled with hearts, drawings, and crosses that identified small altars. Cassie craned her neck to look up at the ceiling, inspecting the carvings as though they were ancient cave paintings. She took a step backward and accidentally bumped into Eamon.

"Excuse me," he said, with a sparkle in his eye that made Cassie feel like she had been struck by a bolt of lightning. He put his hand on her shoulder as a gesture of apology, but as they drifted apart again, his hand migrated to the small of her back and lingered there as though he didn't want to let go. His hand felt especially warm in contrast to the chill of the cellar, and she yearned for him to touch her again.

"Crayères means 'chalk pits,'" Marc continued, "and they are a type of cave typical here in the Champagne region. They were originally cut by the Romans, who dug something like three hundred quarries underground, some as deep as thirty-seven meters. Our restaurant is built on the history of this town, this community, and on the craft of Champagne. We do everything to capture this place in every dish. We hope you were able to get that from the meal."

They wandered around the space for a few more minutes. Eamon pulled bottles off the rack to examine their labels, and Cassie looked around, letting herself soak in the significance of the underground refuge.

"I should get you back upstairs," said Marc after a few more minutes, leading them back to the staircase.

"Incredible," Cassie whispered into the darkness.

28

Cassie woke up early the next day to finish her Viand review. She breezed through it and then focused on her post for social media. The posts were getting easier to write, and she wanted to keep her reels simple, but with a cinematic touch. She ordered a pot of coffee from room service and sat down at the small desk tucked into the corner of her room.

Building her reel in Instagram, she selected a set of clips that each highlighted something specific about the dinner: the bubbles in the glass of her champagne, the sunset, the dining room, a tray of appetizers, the sea bass, the desserts, and the flickering candelabra that sat on the sideboard next to their table. She then set it to classical music and added copy over the video: "Domaine Les Crayères in 15 seconds." She then set to work on the caption.

An Evening at Les Crayères, Reims

It's been 278 days since you left, but today I miss you even more. You would have loved everything about Domaine Les Crayères—the architecture, the cuisine, and most of all, the champagne. We would have had a glass before dinner, overlooking the manicured gardens, imagining what life could be like if we moved to France.

Chef Christophe Moret (@chefchristophemoret) takes us on an evocative journey through the region, including his favorite seasonal markets, neighborhood farms, multigenerational cheesemongers, and ultimately through the vineyards that grow the grapes used to make champagne. If cuisine is truly art, then the kitchen is his canvas, the ingredients his paint, and his story about the region of Champagne is told on the plate. The flavors take us to places of his memory, and some of the dishes into his family's kitchen, modernized but with the same heart. We are simply passengers, here to enjoy the story he chooses to tell.

We would finish the meal, sipping Armagnac and getting lost in each other's aromas, now mixed with the smell of the kitchen and the delicacies of Les Crayères.

Wish you were here.

#EatPostLike

Feeling accomplished after posting her own reviews, a thought crept into her mind; maybe she would post one more on @NewYorkSecretDiner. The restaurant was so incredible, it surely had to be included. She picked a few stills and tapped out the caption on her phone:

Les Crayères, Reims

France has many good restaurants, but few are as dedicated to Champagne as Le Parc at Les Crayères in Reims. The restaurant, built on top of a maze of Champagne caves, lives in an art nouveau château that has since been meticulously restored. Today, the restaurant is run by Chef Christophe Moret, who has transformed the restaurant from what could have been a dusty mausoleum into a vibrant showcase of the region. All the ingredients are sourced locally, exhibit supreme freshness and quality, and are prepared with an acute attention to detail to best present each ingredient with its most pure flavor, but also with a level of decadence inherent to the French sensibility.

The menu changes every night based on what is in season, with a small handful of dishes that are always in rotation. To my delight, Chef and his team incorporated unlikely ingredients from the surrounding community into each dish, including locally sourced meats and cheeses, garden-fresh produce, and even snippets of the vineyards that surround the estate.

Le Parc at Les Crayères may be one of the most romantic restaurants in the world, which is convenient considering it is also a hotel. Book strategically.

#NewYorkSecretDiner
#NewYorkSecretDinerOutofTown

Almost instantly, the post had over one thousand likes and fifty-seven comments, one of which was from David.

@DAVIDMAKESMONEY: Whoever is posting this, I will find you.

WITH ONLY A few hours until the train back to Paris, Cassie headed downstairs for breakfast. In the hotel's café, she saw Eamon already seated at a table near the glass wall, having a cup of coffee.

"Good morning. May I join you?" she asked.

"Of course," he said, clearing his laptop off the other end of the table, making room for her.

He signaled to the waiter with two raised fingers, and within moments there was a second pot of coffee on the table.

"Pourrions-nous, prendre un deuxième petit-déjeuner, s'il vous plaît?" he said to the waiter.

"I hope you're hungry," said Eamon. "Hotel breakfast is one of my guilty pleasures."

"How is breakfast a guilty pleasure?"

"I just love it. I love ordering too much. It's so decadent first thing in the morning."

Cassie's skin tingled with goose bumps, and she found herself fantasizing about what else he might have meant by something being "decadent first thing in the morning." The thought surprised her, and she shook her head as if to throw it from her mind.

The waiter brought over a large tray with a basket of fresh pastries that came with a plate of different jams and butters, a glass bowl of freshly cut fruit, a tasting of different juices, and a singular pale blue soft-boiled egg served in a white porcelain egg cup. The top of the egg had been scored and surgically removed, then topped with a generous mound of black caviar.

The waiter poured Cassie a glass of champagne from a bottle chilling in a nearby ice bucket, before returning to the kitchen.

"I'm sorry," she said while taking pictures of the scene.

"The camera eats first, right?" he said. "Take your time. I know I was giving you grief last night, but seriously, I'm used to it—all these trips are the same."

"I still find it a little embarrassing," she confessed.

"I would argue that there are more embarrassing jobs. This one, not so much."

She dipped the spoon into the egg, then spread the gooey egg and caviar onto a piece of toast. She popped the bite into her mouth and let her head fall to one side with pleasure. "Mmmm, delicious."

"Caviar, like truffles, always works best on simple dishes. It needs to be the hero."

She could see why Eamon liked breakfast so much—especially this breakfast. It was decadent, luxurious, and extravagant.

"I had a really nice time last night." He paused, and then said, "You know, I'm glad we met."

Cassie was speechless. "Oh, yeah, me too. It was really fun." She thought about their moment in the cellars, his hand holding the small of her back longer than it should have, making her feel fluttery inside, even now in the light of day.

"Your post was really beautiful," he said, before taking a bite of toast. "Very ethereal. You've got a nice style."

"Oh, you follow me?" she asked, now blushing. She looked down at her phone to check the stats on her posts and was surprised to see that her @EatPostLike reel was doing very well. She had gained a few thousand new followers, and it looked like her post was well on its way to going viral.

He laughed. "Didn't notice, huh?"

"Honestly, no? My account has been growing really quickly. It's been kind of hard to track."

"Yeah, with this many likes, you'll be an influencer in no time," he said with a smile and a wink.

"I don't know about that . . ." She cringed at the word *influencer*. It was a far cry from *counselor*. She had been so proud of her career for such a long time. She loved being a lawyer. She enjoyed preparing cases, finding the bits of information that would make an argument bulletproof, and, in truth, she even adored all the documentation the job demanded. But it was everything else that broke her heart— the incredibly long hours, the abusive culture in her firm, and always needing to play defense against her coworkers. She never felt like everyone was on the same team; it was almost like they were always in competition with each other—because they were. Nonetheless, Cassie was still struggling with the idea of leaving her identity as a lawyer behind completely—even temporarily.

Eamon poured himself another cup of coffee and dumped two packets of Splenda into the black liquid.

"Splenda? Aren't you supposed to be—"

He interrupted her. "Shhh, I know. It's humiliating that I put it in my coffee. It's a guilty pleasure. I've tried to switch to just black coffee or even regular sugar, but I just can't."

"It will be our little secret," she said.

"Thank you. I would be mortified if Rebecca or Kelly ever found out."

"Funny," she said, realizing that Splenda was a major taboo for food and wine people. "How have they not noticed already?"

"I'm very diligent. But you seem trustworthy."

"More than you know," she added truthfully.

"Hey, do you follow @NewYorkSecretDiner?" Eamon asked, after checking his phone.

Cassie froze. "Um, of course, doesn't *everyone*?" she blurted out, trying to seem natural. She had completely forgotten that she had posted to that account too.

"Apparently he was here last night. I just saw the review."

"No way," said Cassie, feeling her cheeks get hot and her hands suddenly clammy. She made a mental note to delay any New York Secret Diner posts by a few days next time.

"I wonder if I could figure out who he is—he must be staying in the hotel." He looked around at the other people in the restaurant, scanning for someone who looked like a secret restaurant critic. "Don't you know him," Eamon asked, "you know, from New York?" Her heart was racing at this point; she was desperate to deflect attention in any direction. Her mind started to spin; she had been too careless, and Eamon was surely going to find her out, and then he would never respect her again.

"No one does. He's an enigma," she said. "He's arguably the one restaurant critic who has perfected the anonymous review."

Cassie reached for a glass of champagne, taking a big swig. What if he figured out that she was posting as @NewYorkSecretDiner? She would surely be sent home immediately as a fraud, and she would never know if she could actually cut it as a critic.

"Isn't that the truth," he added, before looking down at his watch. "We need to leave in an hour," he said. "Are you packed?"

"Yes, although I could stay here for the whole trip."

"You and me both. But we have a flight to catch."

Copenhagen

29

The group landed in Copenhagen around 9:00 p.m., the sky exploding with orange and pink as the sun started its journey toward the horizon. They boarded the Sprinter van waiting for them at the airport and made their way into the city center, driving along the waterfront.

The van turned and started to cut into the city, which looked like it was straight out of a fairy tale; picturesque buildings lined waterways filled with sailboats, houseboats, and day-to-day motorboats used to get around the city. There was not much vehicular traffic, but the bike lanes were packed with people on stylish cruisers.

Kelly stood up in the front of the van. "Hi, everyone. Hope you all are having a great time."

The group applauded in response.

"Tomorrow is a research day. Use it wisely. Friday, we have a group reservation at Noma, which as you know, is currently ranked number one in the world. We will be leaving the hotel at five o'clock on the dot, and our reservation is at six. Noma is currently serving their Vegetable Season menu, and I've only heard good things. Due to the difficult nature of securing reservations, we had to book a group table. I realize many of you know people at Noma, so please try to be discreet about why we are visiting. It is important they do not realize that we are one of the review teams for Viand and that this is their final review in the judging process."

THEY PULLED UP in front of the Admiral Hotel, an old quayside maritime warehouse that overlooked the water. Upon first glance, the hotel was in a modest but robust building, once used for military purposes, but it had recently undergone extensive renovations to convert it into a chic hotel that attracted young business travelers. Once inside, Cassie's eyes drifted over the large, weathered timber beams and columns, and the contemporary Danish furniture adorned with soft hygge touches like sheepskin hides, candles, and antique art that filled the walls.

After checking into her room, Cassie wandered through the labyrinth of dimly lit hallways and down to the restaurant to get a bite to eat. She spotted Ben at the bar, already halfway through an order of steak frites. Cassie leaned up against the bar, suddenly feeling how tired she was from the day of travel, her feet starting to throb under her body weight.

"That looks delicious," Cassie said, feeling her stomach rumble.

"Want some?" Ben offered, generously pushing the plate toward her.

"No, I'll get my own. I'm starving," she said, looking around for a bartender or a waiter.

Ben swiveled his barstool around so he was facing her directly. "I couldn't ask you earlier, but how was Les Crayères?" he asked in a sweet but prying way. She didn't mind.

"Les Crayères was enthralling—there was so much thought and consideration that went into every part of the visit: the hotel, the grounds, breakfast, the cellars, and of course, dinner itself. I wish we could have stayed longer."

"Yeah, that's how it always is. You only get to stay one or two nights in the really nice hotels. Otherwise, they put us up in places like this." He used his fork to wave around the room, which was cave-like, with dim, moody lighting.

"I think it's kind of romantic," said Cassie, watching the low light of the candles flick over the weathered wood bar top. "It's no château, but it's still nice. Better than home."

"I think it's dark and depressing," he said with a frown, "but I shouldn't complain. I'm technically homeless. I gave up my apartment a few years ago, so now I just bounce from assignment to assignment, staying in Airbnbs whenever I need to fill the gaps."

"Wait, what? You don't have a home base?"

He laughed. "Not anymore. Why would I? I was only home a few days a month. Why pay rent. I call it 'freebasing.'"

"But don't you miss your own bed?"

"Not when I can't sleep in it—ever."

"What about your things? Your clothes, furniture, your *stuff*?"

"I have a storage unit. I moved out, put all my stuff in storage, and got on the plane. It's basically my walk-in closet, which, typically, I could never afford."

"So what do you do when the weather changes?"

"It's called minimalism, sweetie. But every few months I fly back and I swap out wardrobes, or I buy things on the road. We don't really need all that much."

"That's dedication," she said, still trying to get the bartender's attention. "I don't think I could be away from my apartment for that long."

"Yeah, it takes a certain type. It's not great for my dating life," he confessed.

"You're not dating anyone?"

"Not at the moment. It's too hard when I'm on the road. Just taking life as it comes, I guess. What about you?"

"My boyfriend died about nine months ago."

Ben dropped his fork onto his plate with a *clank*. "Oh my god, how tragic. I'm so sorry."

"He was in a car accident. He died instantly."

"How tragic."

"He was my best friend. I miss him terribly every day. But I know he's always with me. I've felt his presence a few times on this trip, which has felt very special."

"Why don't you take a seat?" Ben asked, now looking at her in a pitying way. It was one of the worst parts about losing a partner—how desperate everyone was to make her feel better.

"Really, I'm fine. Thank you. I'm going to send my order up to my room. I want to be ready for tomorrow."

"Okay, I'll be here if you change your mind."

"Thanks, Ben, I really appreciate it."

THERE WAS A knock on her door, and the waiter brought in a tray of food and a bottle of Chablis. She thought it might have been excessive to order the entire bottle, but quite frankly, she didn't care. There was work to do, and she needed something to help her settle in.

He left the food on the desk, and Cassie lifted the stainless-steel cloche to take a few fries off the plate. She would tackle the steak part of her meal later. She opened the bottle of wine and poured herself an embarrassingly generous glass before sticking the bottle back into the ice bucket that came with it.

She didn't know where to begin, so she pulled out her phone to text Ruby.

CASSIE: What do you know about Noma?

RUBY: Not a lot. That it is nearly impossible to get a reservation. It's the #1 restaurant in the world, and they use some crazy ingredients.

CASSIE: Everyone is really excited.

RUBY: Loved your last review, by the way. I'm living vicariously through your posts.

CASSIE: As you should. Please know that I wish you were here.

RUBY: Am I the one you're writing these posts to? 😂

CASSIE: I think you know the answer to that question.

RUBY: You're no fun. How's it going otherwise?

CASSIE: Good, I feel like I'm starting to find a groove.

RUBY: Do you need any help?

> **CASSIE:** Maybe with research? I have no idea what to expect from Noma, and it's arguably the most important review thus far.

> **RUBY:** When are you going?

> **CASSIE:** The day after tomorrow . . .

> **RUBY:** You got it. I'll circle back.

Cassie spread out all her reading materials across the bed: local magazines swiped from the hotel lobby, her computer, and the small stack of journals she had stashed in her bag. She started with the journals—James must have an entry for Noma. Once she located the Denmark section in one of the books, she found Copenhagen, and then notes on the restaurant.

Tucked into the back of the book, she found a stack of newspaper and magazine clippings on the restaurant—a few from its opening, some from the fermentation lab, new book releases, and spotlights on the chef himself. It was not lost on her that James had a habit of collecting physical clippings in such a digital era, a memory that instantly brought her back to Sunday mornings in James's sun-drenched living room when they would sit on the sofa with a pot of coffee and the Sunday *New York Times*, listening to Van Morrison's *Astral Weeks*. She could vividly remember the sound of the newspaper opening and closing, the aroma of coffee and toasted croissants, the waxy feel of the weekend magazine inserts, and the smell of the damp ink that left its trace on her fingertips.

James had scribbled notes in the margins and had highlighted the articles calling out particular dishes that featured everything from ants to jellyfish, techniques like fermentation and torching, and notes on how reservations would sell out almost instantly. James had even created a list of tricks on how to score a reservation—a clear indication that he was indeed trying to get one. And then Cassie saw a small note scribbled at the bottom of the page that felt like a dagger ripping into her heart:

Noma is arguably the most important restaurant in the world right now, led by a chef who has challenged society's assumptions about what we consider to be edible, but also about how we cook. Is the cuisine defined by the ingredients found in Copenhagen or by the creativity with which those ingredients are manipulated? Either way, Noma has found a way to capture the flavors of the region in a way that tells a story about where they are in the world and their perception of that place.

Time is a critical piece of the puzzle in this kitchen; some components take years to prepare. How much of this cuisine is dependent on freshness—or the opposite, its age?

A question weighs on me: Would Cassie appreciate it?

Did he intend to bring her to Noma? She felt her heart skip a beat, and then the familiar knotted feeling traveled up her throat until she couldn't bear the pain anymore. All her memories of him came flooding in at once, and she longed to see him again, to hear his voice, to feel his skin against hers. She felt frustrated that he was gone and that there were still so many unanswered questions. Perhaps they could have gone on the Viand review trip together, as a duo. It could have been so romantic.

Cassie felt her mind grow quiet. And in that moment, she realized the saddest thing of all. His death was the catalyst for her taking a sabbatical, mustering the courage to take a chance on a new life, a new career, and accepting the Viand invitation, even if it was meant for him. She wouldn't be here without him—or without his absence.

Then she felt the tears start to flow. She let herself cry, heavy and hard, exorcising the grief from her system—at least momentarily.

Once she was out of tears, she got up to wash her face and gather herself. She crawled back into the same spot on the bed. She looked down at the journal and realized she'd missed another note scribbled in James's handwriting.

France, Spain, Italy, Croatia, Austria, Germany, Denmark, Netherlands.

Had he been planning out a trip for them?

30

The next morning, Cassie rolled over and looked at the clock. It was later than she expected, and she got out of bed and took a shower before calling down to the front desk for a pot of coffee to be delivered to her room. Once she was able to settle in to her research again, she started scouring the internet for reviews from major publications, trying to absorb as much information about the chef and the many iterations of the restaurant, including pop-ups all over the world, as she could. She was getting more and more nervous reading about dishes like head of cod, served with wood ant pesto, others made with plankton, soups made with squirrel meat, and a reindeer "feast" that included reindeer heart tartare, sweetbreads, and tongue served yakitori style.

Cassie felt her stomach turn and she took a big swig of coffee. She felt intimidated by the descriptions of the dishes—was this a meal she could even enjoy?

Bzzzzzz.

RUBY: Okay, I think I've got some info for you.

CASSIE: I'm all ears.

RUBY: By no means is Noma traditional fare, but, in Anthony Bourdain's words, the chef "changed the whole world of gastronomy." They forage for ingredients (think wild herbs, seaweeds, mushrooms, etc.) and use fermentation in some way in almost every dish. They are also known for using unconventional ingredients like insects, traditionally discarded cuts of meats, and invasive shellfish. They "push the boundaries of what is considered edible and encourage diners to rethink their perceptions of food."

CASSIE: Can't wait. 😑

RUBY: I know it sounds intimidating, but it's seriously one of the most influential restaurants of the twenty-first century, you should consider yourself lucky to be going there.

CASSIE: I know. I think I'm just in my own head on this one.

RUBY: Think of it as research. No matter what, it will be an incredible experience! Have you ever heard of the one-bite rule?

> **CASSIE:** No—this sounds like a trick moms play on toddlers.

> **RUBY:** 😂 It basically is. No matter what it is, just try a bite. If you don't like it after that, you don't need to eat any more, but you absolutely have to take that one bite.

It seemed like a fair price to pay for being invited on this incredible gastronomical adventure.

> **CASSIE:** Okay, deal. At least this menu is designed around vegetables, not whale meat.

> **RUBY:** You've got this! Send updates! 😳

The next night, the group arrived at the restaurant, which was situated on a thin strip of land with water on either side. Cassie followed as they walked down a long, linear boardwalk flanked by tall summer grasses and wildflowers. On their right they passed by three glass greenhouses, and then finally arrived at the main entrance, a wooden façade in the iconic shape of a house, with a single unmarked wooden door. A host opened the door and welcomed the group into a dark, wooden room that felt secluded but welcoming, through a glass atrium that filled the space with daylight, past a farmers' market–like display of fresh produce, past the open kitchen that buzzed with chefs and servers, and into the dining room. The room resembled an old farmhouse, with simple wood trusses made from solid timber and, above, a simple slatted roof with a skylight running down the middle. Reclaimed beams were arranged as vertical pillars and stacked upon one another to create a large service station that ran down the center of the room, a hub of activity for the servers and runners. Wide oak floor planks ran the length of the dining room, then turned onto the surface of the walls, making the space feel warm and cozy. On two of the walls, large windows opened to the west, looking over a field of wildflowers, the bay, and the city beyond. It was a picturesque spot that felt like they were in the middle of the countryside, not in a large metropolis.

She loved how the space felt like a village: a collection of buildings that each had their own purpose and function in the operations of the restaurant. She snapped pictures of everything she could, from the simple displays of garlic hanging on the walls to the enormous team of chefs busily working away in the open kitchen. The restaurant had been carefully considered, both from the vantage point of a guest, but also for the functionality of a chef and his world-class team. She took it as foreshadowing for the rest of the evening: if they had thought this much about the design of the restaurant, the food was sure to be sensational.

THE GROUP TOOK their seats at the table, adorned with ceramic chargers, linen cloth napkins, and crystal wineglasses that were impossibly thin. Cassie chose a prime seat in the corner of the restaurant; on one side, there was a large window overlooking the water, and on the other a clear view of the kitchen in the next room. She was seated in between Rebecca and Ben and was excited to hear their thoughts throughout the meal. Eamon and Kelly were across the round table, busily inspecting the place settings.

"Welcome to Noma," said their waitress. "I'm Pia, and I'll be your server tonight. Who will be having the wine pairing?"

Everyone except Rebecca raised their hands. "I'll have the juice pairing," she said confidently.

"One juice and four wine pairings. I'll be right back." Within a flash, Pia was gone.

"I hope you like weird wines," said Eamon, looking right at Cassie, although presumably addressing the whole table.

"Is that a challenge?" she asked, not even knowing what challenge she might have been expecting.

The sommelier arrived at the table and served the first wine, Les Varrons, an organic Chardonnay from Jura, France, by Domaine Labet. It was bright and acidic, with salt and a distinctive funkiness. Cassie raised her eyebrows at Eamon as she took a second sip of the wine. He smiled at her, as though he knew the range of delights they were in for. For a moment, Cassie started to worry—her mind flashed to reindeer tongue, her stomach starting to twist into a knot. She looked over at Ben, who was filming on his phone, excited and giddy for the meal.

"Have you been here before?" she asked under her breath.

"No, but I've been trying to get in for years."

"Do you know what we're in for?"

"Vegetables?" He shrugged. "Are you nervous or something?"

"I might have read too much . . ."

"Ha! I've done that before. Now I let myself go into restaurants blind, let the experience wash over me," he said, gesturing to the ceiling. "Try to not think about it," he whispered. "This is one of the best restaurants in the world. Everything is going to be mind-blowingly delicious. At the very least, it will be cerebrally interesting."

"As long as we're not eating brains," whispered Cassie, careful not to let anyone else hear.

Ben was not as coy—he let out a comical snort, choking on his wine.

THE FIRST DISH was presented to the group, carried by a small fleet of waiters and chefs who placed each dish on the table at the same time: fresh herbs in a terracotta pot. Cassie glanced around the table, frantically looking to see if anyone knew what to do. Eamon picked off a leaf and ate it. Rebecca spent a full minute smelling the herbs, rubbing the leaves between her hands and then cupping her hands over her mouth, inhaling deeply. Ben focused on video, taking cinematographic shots of the potted plant, presumably for TikTok. Cassie focused on taking photos of the dish, every few frames looking up to see if anyone had figured out what to do with the damn thing. And then, while shooting macro photographs, she saw the end of a clear glass straw poking through the herbs.

"Oh! There's a straw!" she exclaimed excitedly, pushing her face toward the straw and straight into the bush of blooming oregano, inhaling its fresh aroma as she sucked up a creamy warm liquid. It was a soup, but it took her a few minutes to figure out exactly what kind of soup—it was sweet and buttery and soft. And then she placed it.

"Potato!" she cried, her eyes darting across the table to Eamon.

Eamon's eyes sparkled in return, and he submerged his face into the tiny herb garden. "Point proven, once again," he added, after coming up for air.

She tried to sip it slowly, savoring the sweet flavor and velvety texture, but it was too delicious. And then she slurped

loudly, desperate for the last few drops of soup. She was mortified and put the pot down awkwardly. Moments later, she heard
a similar gurgle coming from everyone else at the table. It was
ridiculous—and she couldn't help but laugh quietly to herself,
which was met with a smile from Eamon across the table, straw
still pursed between his lips.

"That was fun," said Rebecca, now glowing with delight. "I
love a surprise."

"I'm sure we will be in for more twists and turns during this
meal," said Ben.

The sommelier poured the second bottle of wine, a 2019
Trauben, Liebe und Zeit Weiss No. 10, a fifty-fifty Chardonnay and
Pinot Blanc blend from Franz Strohmeier in Austria. The liquid
in Cassie's glass was cloudy, which was off-putting at first glance.
Eamon was clearly excited, and he vigorously swirled the glass on
the table, aerating the wine, before holding the glass in front of
the light to examine its color, finally bringing the glass up to his
nose. He cupped the glass near his face and took a deep breath, inhaling the aroma. He smiled quickly to himself, and then brought
the glass to his lips. He took a sip and passed the wine around his
mouth from cheek to cheek, softly gurgled it, and then swallowed.
"Exquisite," he whispered, before downing half the glass.

Then the next dish: a small tart of glazed nasturtium flowers
alongside a sea buckthorn and black currant fruit leather arranged in the shape of a butterfly adorned with tiny purple flowers and herbs. One by one, the diners picked up their butterfly
by the stalk of fresh lavender that held it together and slipped it
into their mouths.

Cassie felt her anxiety start to melt away, maybe because of
the wine, but also because, mercifully, there wasn't a last-minute

menu change and she was spared eating a fermented fish head, or something equally terrifying.

She watched Eamon from across the table, observing how comfortable he appeared. It was as though he didn't even realize how intoxicating he was, and from her seat, she had enough distance to not be sucked into his gaze or his magnetic, charismatic allure. She had seen him do this same thing with waiters and waitresses, baristas, hotel concierges. It was just how he navigated the world—with a powerful charm that opened doors, solidified relationships, and created opportunities. It was a gift, Cassie told herself, and nothing more than that. It wasn't personal. It certainly wasn't her. For Eamon, it was business.

The next dish was a thick stalk of white asparagus sprinkled with saffron salt, served with candied pinecones seasoned with seaweed and a whole elderflower blossom, meant to be eaten in one bite. A seaweed tart followed, made with sugar kelp, herb paste, and topped with a tangle of vibrant green seaweed. It was salty, almost briny, and reminded her of walking down the beach in Maine, where her family used to summer when she was a child.

"Wow, I feel like I was just transported to the beach," she said, holding her hand in front of her mouth, still savoring the flavors.

"Isn't food *magical*?" said Rebecca, waving her hand in the air. "Each plate of food is telling a story, leading us down a path to explore something new—an uncharted world that we discover through our palates. I don't know about all of you, but I think it's pure alchemy."

"Meanwhile, creating new connections and new memories," added Ben, pressing his finger to his temple as he looked around the room.

"What are you doing?" asked Cassie.

"Hitting Record in my brain. I want to keep this memory forever."

"Isn't that what your social feed is for?" joked Cassie.

"Ha!" Ben bellowed. "Yes, of course. But it would be nice to keep memories like this up here too." He tapped his forehead again. "Besides, it's nice to have a few memories that are just for me, and not my followers."

"I hear that," said Cassie.

"I don't understand you kids," said Rebecca. "You put so much effort into social media, and you're missing out on so much of *life*! Go read a book in a park, wander around an art museum, fall in love with a stranger at the bar over too many martinis. *Live!*"

"Sometimes I wish that social media didn't dominate my life so much," Ben confessed. "I feel like I spend too much time on it and I probably care too much about what my followers think."

"So put the damn thing down," said Rebecca, in a motherly tone.

"It's not that simple, Rebecca," said Ben, starting to get defensive. "These apps open doors—this is part of my job now. Social media is how I've built a name for myself, it's how I find stories, it's how I connect with people. It's become an essential tool for my career."

"It didn't used to be like that. It used to be all about *who* you knew and who *they* knew. That's how you would find a good story."

"Isn't that another way of saying *gossip*?" Cassie teased.

"Yes, honey, it was gossiping, and it worked. But you had to find the pulse—what restaurants were up-and-coming, and which chefs were becoming the next hot thing. Today, publications review too many restaurants that are already buzzy or in the conversation somehow, and then the reviews are 'you've heard about this place, now let us tell you more about it,' which isn't terribly interesting. Readers want to be surprised, and more than that, they want to know that the writer has done the work to take them on an extraordinary journey."

"Our generation puts in the work too. We just use our fingers to do the walking," said Ben with a laugh. He took a swig of wine. "The biggest difference is that most critics now have a persona to maintain. It's a personal brand, baby!"

James had straddled the two worlds: going incognito like a traditional critic while maintaining an incredibly large digital footprint with hundreds of thousands of followers. It was a remarkable feat, and once again, she felt a sense of awe and appreciation for him and the world he had built for himself. She wondered if she would ever be able to pull something like that off, to gain that level of fame on her own terms. She was used to being successful—in law school and in her career—but this still felt like uncharted waters. She let her mind slip for a second, fantasizing about where else she might be able to go. Australia? South America? A culinary tour across Asia? The thought made her stomach twist with excitement.

The next dish was a black sphere charred beyond recognition that had to be cut open with a steak knife, revealing a glassy, caramelized onion cooked with elderflower. Then a cucumber dolma, a tightly wrapped cylinder of cucumber that had been dehydrated and then rehydrated and stuffed with beechnut cream, garnished with flowering herbs. Next, a quail egg, topped with a dried plum and rose hip "chorizo" that was spicy, salty, and had the same umami qualities of a meat-based sausage. This dish made Cassie sit back in her chair, chewing longer than she should have, savoring every moment of its presence in her mouth.

"How do they do that?" asked Cassie blankly.

"What?" asked Ben.

"Make fruit taste like meat."

"Fermentation. The fermentation lab is where so much of the innovation happens at Noma," said Pia, interjecting.

"Of course," said Cassie, remembering the articles she'd read about the innovative lab.

"How are you enjoying the meal?" asked Pia.

"It's incredible," said Cassie, knowing that was a vague answer. "Horizon expanding."

"You should come back for our game menu next season," she said, while opening the next bottle of wine.

"Surely," Cassie lied, "if I can get a reservation." She would not be coming back for game season.

"There are always tricks to the system," said Pia, now filling new wineglasses with a 2017 Frank Cornelissen Munjebel Bianco from Etna, Italy.

Across the table, Eamon and Kelly were engrossed in conversation, talking about Big Sur and the hot springs at the Esalen Institute, swapping stories of midnight soaks and naked hippies. Cassie felt a twinge of jealousy, wishing that she felt free enough to go skinny-dipping at midnight with a bunch of strangers, something she knew she would never be able to do, because she was too shy, too inhibited.

The next dish arrived, a small bowl of morels cooked in brown butter served with maitake mushroom broth, complex and unctuous. The morels were harvested the year before, pickled and preserved, and served with a hand-carved appetizer fork. The concentration of flavor brought images of the woods to her mind, from the mossy forest floor to the tree canopy high above. This dish was followed by marigold flowers fried in an incredibly light tempura and then salted, served with an egg yolk dipping sauce. Then walnut "tofu," surrounded by grilled rose petals, topped with a sunflower seed mole, herbs, and tiny flowers, and a caramelized milk tart stuffed with cheese and thinly sliced black truffles, the flavor nutty and savory.

"That's better than sex," Cassie overheard Eamon say from across the table, eyes closed and head back in rapture.

Kelly giggled, shushing him.

Cassie felt like she was spinning, and it wasn't the wine. She was overwhelmed. She knew nothing about food like this: the techniques, the ingredients, the science, or the process. She felt herself starting to spin out, so she took a deep breath and found calm by looking at the water.

Did it matter, she asked herself. Most of the diners here wouldn't understand all the techniques either. Wasn't part of the allure of fine dining the immersive nature of a restaurant? It surely wasn't about the necessity of eating. Dining, specifically this kind of dining, was art. It was about the technique, ingredients and concepts coming together in such a way that it revealed the true beauty in the craft and, ultimately, created a sense of emotion and wonder.

She let herself float for a moment, taking in the room, looking at the other diners, who were clearly in awe of the meal, fully captivated by the creativity, discipline, and technique it required. Cassie looked out over the water, at the city beyond lit up in a golden hue, and over to the kitchen, where the chefs were hard at work. One of them, a handsome chef with salt-and-pepper hair, blue eyes, and arms adorned with tattoos, looked up at her. They locked eyes for just a moment, and then he smiled before looking back down at his work. Even though he was practically in another room, she felt electricity surge through her body. She turned to her notebook, trying to make herself look busy, hoping that no one at the table—especially Eamon—had noticed.

Then they were served a small beeswax cup filled with flowers and crunchy bee pollen, followed by a presentation of a large shawarma, or at least what looked like a shawarma, adorned with roasted onions and rosemary, cut tableside. Pia explained that it was not made from lamb or chicken, as is traditional, but instead from celery root and truffles, before it was cooked on a spit for hours. One of the chefs used a large knife to slice off thin pieces of the "meat," plating it with greens, roasted apple, and red currants, before smothering the plate in a brown "jus." Cassie cut off a small bite and was surprised by how much it tasted like meat. It was earthy, salty, sweet, rich, and incredibly delicious.

"Well, this is way better than the shawarma cart in my neighborhood," said Rebecca, practically licking her plate.

"No kidding," agreed Ben, soaking up the jus with a fat slice of sourdough bread.

Mercifully, there was a pause in the service, giving the group a few moments to digest. Cassie found herself looking over at the chef in the kitchen numerous times, greedily craving that electricity in his light blue eyes. Occasionally, their gazes would meet, causing Cassie to blush once again.

Ben leaned over to her and whispered, "That hot chef keeps looking over at you."

Cassie felt her cheeks flush red, embarrassed that Ben had also noticed. "No, he's not," she managed to choke out.

"Um, yes, he is, and he's rather steamy." Ben fanned himself with his notebook. "He's surely not trying to catch my eye. Trust me, I've tried."

"You're imagining things," she said, staring into the florals on the table, trying to play coy. She waited for the table to completely dissolve into conversation before she stole another glance at the hot chef, whose blue eyes glanced up to meet hers, followed by another quick smile and a bite of his bottom lip, showing his pearly white teeth. He too was being reticent, busily working and shouting "yes, chef" in unison with the rest of the kitchen.

The first round of dessert was a glass-like tortellini filled with rose hip fudge, flower petals, and wood sorrel. The inside was sweet, jammy, and tasted of cooked plum. And then the final dish: a small potted purple oxalis plant surrounded by fresh herbs, which gave Cassie a feeling of déjà vu.

"And we've come full circle," said Kelly, picking up the hand-forged garden trowel that came with the plate. She cut the dish in half, revealing a layered cake of rose-scented ice cream in a chocolate pot topped with edible chocolate dirt.

"How was everything?" asked Pia, as an army of servers cleared the final set of plates.

"Extraordinary. So creative," said Ben, clearly impressed.

"We are thrilled to hear it. Tonight, things are a bit different. Today is the summer solstice, and we are closing early for our team celebration. We hope you will stay and join us."

"We would love to," said Kelly, surprised by the invitation.

Once Pia left the table, Kelly leaned in. "This is their annual solstice staff party—it's a true honor to be invited. If the rumors are correct, we're in for a fun night," she said, giddy with excitement.

31

The group moved into the lounge, where Eamon ordered a magnum of biodynamic wine. The sun started to set, lighting up the sky in a beautiful range of pink, orange, and purple hues. Cassie watched as the kitchen gathered for their final meeting, going through the evening's service, and the chefs started cleaning their stations. Patrons slowly started to leave, audibly praising the restaurant as they teetered down the boardwalk and back to the street.

As soon as the last table had left, the music grew louder, and the lights were turned down. Within a few moments, a table had been set up outside and was covered in large tubs filled with wine and beer and a spread of snacks and small bites for the staff. Cassie was too full to try anything but was impressed by their staff meal: platters of boiled seafood were put out with dishes of melted butter, loaves of rye bread, and a colorful spread of pickled fish and vegetables.

A small band set up in front of the restaurant, letting their music spill out over the water and into the city beyond. It was an idyllic summer evening, the sky glowing cobalt blue, and the air warm and comforting on the skin.

Once it was clear that the staff was outside and no longer working, the group got up and started to mingle, introducing themselves to the chefs and praising their work. Cassie mean-dered around the party feeling out of place, trying to keep herself busy by snapping photos of the building, the gardens, and the party. As she was photographing the city skyline, she felt some-one standing next to her. It was the handsome chef from the kitchen, who was even more attractive up close, his eyes a pale blue that appeared white-hot compared to his salt-and-pepper hair. His arms were covered in tattoos of vegetables, knives, and butchery diagrams.

"Hej," he said, smiling at her. "How was your meal?"

"Incredible," she said. "Thank you for everything. It was truly memorable."

"I'm glad you enjoyed it. I'm Nils."

He put out his hand, and she slipped hers into his palm, feel-ing the size and roughness of his skin—war wounds from the kitchen: callouses, cuts, and scarred-over burns. She looked up into his eyes and felt her skin tingle involuntarily.

"I—I'm Cassie." She felt herself trip over her words.

"Where are you from, Cassie?" he asked, his blue eyes unwav-ering.

"New York."

"I've always wanted to go to New York. You must tell me every-thing about it."

"I don't know, there's not much to say. It's busy, everyone is busy. It's not as beautiful as it is here."

"Naw, but it's *New York*, it's the best city in the world."

"Yeah, sure. It's nice. There's lots to do, I guess. How about you?"

"I grew up in Rørvig, which is a little more than an hour away. It's a sweet little harbor town where people like to vacation."

"What is it best known for?" she asked.

"Cheesecake and beaches," he said, adding, "There are some good restaurants there too."

"Did you like growing up there?"

"As much as anyone does when they are growing up. I wanted to be in the city, so I was anxious to leave." He took a sip from his bottle of beer and bit his lower lip to catch a lingering drop. "Do you want something to drink?"

"Um, sure," she said, and they started to make their way toward the bar. He poured her a glass of wine, pink and cloudy, its smell sour and sweet.

"Where do you live in New York?" he asked.

"Manhattan." She didn't want to talk about New York, or her life there, or James, so she changed the subject. "What's it like working here? Do you love it?"

"Yes, this group, they've become like family to me. We *are* family. It's exciting to be here, working so hard. It takes dedication, but it's worth it." His hands were now waving around, animated with excitement. "Chef is so inspiring; I believe he is a true genius. I'm learning so much from him and the entire team. It's the kind of experience that can define a career forever. But enough about that. Do you want me to show you around?"

"That would be incredible," she said, excited to see behind the scenes.

They walked down the cobblestone "street" that connected the different buildings of the compound, from the old warehouse to the glass houses. He opened the door to one of the greenhouses, which was overflowing with fresh herbs and microgreens planted in boxes flanking the walkway and in planters hanging above their heads. The aroma was overwhelming, fresh and verdant. Nils reached up and pinched a few leaves off a plant, popping one in his mouth before handing her one.

She brought the leaf to her nose, smelling its sweet and powerful aroma. "It smells just like the first dish—was this used in our meal?" Cassie asked.

"Yes, the herb pot? That's such a great dish. We try to use as much from the property as we can. Our team harvests right before service so that everything is as fresh as possible."

In the greenhouse, Cassie noticed clusters of herbs and plants, some she recognized but many she didn't. It felt like a botanical garden; there were rare specimens from all over the world growing here, carefully tended to by skilled botanists.

"Come with me, I want to show you something," he said, leading her out of the greenhouse and into the long white building where the offices were located.

He led her into a small white-tiled room, filled with racks of labeled jars covered with kitchen towels and big stainless steel prep tables. She noticed an intimidating selection of scientific-looking equipment along one wall, which made the room look more like a medical lab than a kitchen.

"Welcome to the fermentation lab. This is where most of the behind-the-scenes work happens. This is where we create our housemade miso pastes and garums, our kombuchas for the juice pairings, and the pickled elements of the dishes."

She looked around and smiled, not sure how to react.

"Yeah, I guess it looks like nothing without anyone in here. Everyone is outside, enjoying the party. But this is—how do you say?—*where the magic happens*."

She laughed. "Welcome to *Cribs*, the Noma edition."

He didn't get the joke.

"Go on," she said, kicking herself.

"I don't get it. My English isn't that great. That's just what Chef says." He was embarrassed too.

"No, your English is really good! Go on, I shouldn't have said anything."

Nils opened the door to a small walk-in on the far wall of the lab. To Cassie's surprise, it was not cold inside; instead it was hot like a sauna, the air thick and funky. He pulled out clear sous vide bags filled with pickling plums, pickled cabbage, coriander, and a jar of tiny black pickled morel mushrooms she recognized from the meal.

"There's some sort of pickled element in every dish," Nils said.

"How much experimentation goes into the fermentation part of the restaurant?"

"So much. There's a whole team dedicated to it. A team of chefs who are constantly testing different ingredients, methods of preservation, and the duration of time. Time is perhaps the most critical ingredient. Oh, you must taste this," he said, reaching for a small plastic container and a spoon. He dipped the spoon into a brown paste and handed it to Cassie.

"What is this?" she asked nervously.

"Fermented grasshopper. Don't be nervous. You already ate it."

"I did?"

"You did." He was smiling now, taking pleasure in her feeling uncomfortable.

"I thought this was a plant-forward menu?"

"Plant-forward does not mean vegan," he corrected.

Cassie cautiously brought the spoon to her lips, taking a small bite of the paste. It didn't taste like insect; instead it tasted almost like a nut butter, with a distinctive pickle-y sour note.

"It's quite delicious," she said, pleasantly surprised.

"I know. It's remarkable—before modern civilization, people would harvest in the late summer and the fall and preserve everything from meat to fish to fruit to vegetables so that it would last through the winter. It's actually unnatural to have fresh ingredients throughout a whole calendar year. You've heard of pickling, no? Well, pickling is a form of fermentation, which humans have used as a preservation technique for millennia— they did it to keep food from spoiling, to make bread, alcohol, yogurt, cheese, and sauces like soy sauce. And there are some incredible health benefits to fermented foods that are alive with bacteria. I think you call it 'probiotics'?" He started pulling more jars off the shelves, looking at the labels and checking the dates before he continued talking. "Try this. It's a cherry that has been pickling for two years," he said, pulling a pink, wrinkly cherry, stem still attached, out of a jar. "We serve this with five-year-old roses." It tasted wild and complex, latent with flavors that were hard to explain. "One of my favorites are lacto-fermented gooseberries." He fumbled around some more, opening small glass bottles and smelling them, before placing them under Cassie's nose, the aromas ranging from bright and acidic to bold and savory.

"Chef built this lab so that we can experiment for experiment's sake. Only a fraction of the ingredients in this lab make it onto the plate. What's cool is that we can create completely new ingredients that then sit on the shelf of the kitchen. Things like aged apple vinegar, mushroom garum, wild rose vinegar, or corn yuzu hot sauce, to name a few."

"How do you use them?" Cassie asked.

"We've found that these fermented elements are quite

powerful—they act as flavor bridges that connect disparate ingredients and complete a dish."

"How much experimentation does it take?"

"Sometimes it can take a while, and by that I mean years, for us to figure out how to best deploy these flavors, but when new dishes come together, the flavors are wildly surprising and exciting."

"Thank you for sharing this with me," Cassie said, her mind blown.

CASSIE FOLLOWED NILS out of the greenhouse and into a seating area where picnic tables had been set up. There was a greenhouse on either side, and the sitting area was framed with tall berry bushes. From where they sat, Cassie could see the rest of the party beyond, where people started to dance on a makeshift dance floor with festoons of lights overhead. Nils leaned down and picked a handful of bright orange and pink berries that looked like raspberries, but jucier.

"What are those?" Cassie asked.

"Cloudberries," said Nils. "Do you not have these in America?"

Nils was standing very close to her, and she felt her voice drop a few decibels to almost a whisper. "Um, I don't think so."

Suddenly, she noticed that the temperature had dropped a few degrees, and she wished for the sweater that she'd left with her bag in the other room. She was starting to feel the compounding effect of all the wine, her head feeling soft, the usual anxieties that ran through her mind now quiet.

He held one in front of her mouth, gently letting the skin of the fruit touch her lips. Cassie looked up, locking her eyes with his, letting her mouth open just enough for the berry. He gently pushed the berry into her mouth and used the side of his thumb to slowly caress her lip. Cassie felt her body rush with goose bumps, and without breaking eye contact, she pressed her tongue to the roof of her mouth, popping the fruit open, and releasing the sweet juice. "Thank you," she whispered. His face was inches away from hers, and the air was thick with tension.

He didn't say anything. Instead he ran his thumb along her lip a second time before pushing his hand under her ear and into the nook at the back of her neck, gently tracing her hairline with his fingers and bringing her face to his. His lips were soft and pillowy, and Cassie felt herself let go, the stress falling away from her body. She let the weight of her head fall into his hand. Slowly, she opened her mouth, feeling the wetness of his tongue against hers. He still tasted like cloudberries, with a slight bitterness of hops.

Nils pulled his head back and looked at her, almost as if he was studying her face. He used his finger to move a strand of hair and tuck it behind her ear.

"You're very beautiful."

Cassie felt her face flush again. She had never been good at receiving compliments, and she didn't want to say anything to ruin the moment. So she raised herself up on her toes, met his mouth with hers, and returned the compliment with another kiss.

32

The next morning, Cassie went down to the hotel lobby for breakfast, hiding behind her black cat-eye sunglasses. She had a pounding headache and was so hungry she felt weak. She saw Ben and Eamon at a four-top on the outside patio and headed in their direction.

"Can I join you?" she asked.

"Good morning, sunshine," said Ben with a twinkle in his eye. "You had quite the night, huh?"

"Um, what are you talking about?" she asked, not wanting to bring it up.

"You and that hot chef," said Ben.

She felt her face get hot. She thought they had been alone.

"Latte, please." She ordered before the waiter could even say hello. "And a Bloody Mary." A cocktail felt like the only logical way to get through breakfast.

"Make it three," said Ben, with a wink.

Eamon hadn't said anything to her; in fact, he was facing the other way, looking out over the water.

"So, who was the hottie?" asked Ben. He was unrelenting.

"He is a chef at the restaurant. He was very nice. He gave me a tour."

"A *priii-vvaaaa-te* tour," added Ben.

"So mature, Ben," Cassie muttered, sneaking a glance at Eamon from behind her glasses. "Yes, he was nice, I had a nice time. God, does anyone have any Advil?"

"Here you go," said Ben, handing her a small white tube filled with pills.

"Occupational hazard," she said, trying to excuse having too many drinks.

"So, tell me everything. Did you go home with him?" Ben asked, shocking Cassie with his brazenness.

Suddenly, Eamon pushed his chair back and stood up, leaving the table.

"What's with him?" asked Ben as he took a sip of his Bloody Mary.

"Maybe he's jealous," said Cassie.

"Oh, wait, what?"

"Yeah, I've started getting some vibes from him, but who knows."

"What kind of vibes?" Ben was now leaning into the table, clearly living for the drama.

"You know, *vibes*. Seemed like he was just paying a little bit more attention than normal. He invited me to a champagne tasting before dinner the other night, and then we had a long, decadent breakfast at the hotel. I'm probably reading into it, but it felt really nice and relaxed."

"He's usually very professional, and he usually sticks to himself during downtime. You must have impressed him in some way."

"Probably by taking photos of every dish," she joked, rolling her eyes.

"Yeah, he's old-school."

"Wine guy," Cassie concluded. "Nonetheless, I'm fairly confident he's going to be a jerk to me for the rest of the trip." She wondered if he was actually taking an interest in her, but she pushed the thought out of her mind, sure that he was the kind of guy to keep his personal and professional lives separate.

"Who cares? Tell me what happened last night!"

"Not much, honestly. We kissed, we walked around, we danced, he put me in a taxi, and I went home."

"I'm not sure if I believe you," said Ben, laughing.

"I'm not ready for much more than that. I don't know, his English wasn't great, and I felt like the chemistry was a little . . . *off*. I don't know how else to describe it. I mean, he is a beautiful man, but there just wasn't a ton of spark, you know? Besides, I weirdly still feel like I'm in a relationship. Like James is just on a long work trip. I don't know how else to explain it."

Ben frowned and took a minute to stir his drink.

"I'll never be able to really understand. I've never lost someone who was that close to me. But I think you need to live your life. You deserve to have a little fun and a little romance too."

Cassie perked up a little and gave Ben a sly little smile. "He was really hot," said Cassie, before picking up the menu and fanning herself with it. "Like *really* hot."

Ben raised his glass toward her. "To the hot chef."

"To the hot chef," said Cassie, and they clinked glasses.

"So are you going to see him again?" Ben asked. He was relentless.

"I don't know. Do we even have time?"

"I think you should see him again—you know, see if that spark ignites."

Cassie wasn't convinced. "Maybe." She looked down into her lap.

"You got his number, right?"

"I gave him mine."

"What is this, the 1950s? Cassie, you need to go get what you want!"

"I don't even know what I want," she blurted out suddenly, surprising herself with her honesty.

CASSIE SPENT THE rest of her day writing her reviews and editing her photos and videos from Noma. Slow pans of the field of wildflowers and wild grasses, cut to the entry sequence, then a shot of the kitchen, the dining room, and then detailed videos of each dish, accented with macro stills that captured every dish from the tiny flower petals to the microgreens carefully placed on each plate. Even through the small screen, Cassie felt excited by her representation of the meal.

She took a break to go through the Viand review, adding her notes and personal comments about the experience. She was feeling more and more confident, both with her reviews and her opinions about flavor. She was starting to understand what tasted good to her and what flavor combinations worked particularly well for her palate. More than anything, she was becoming more comfortable with succumbing to the dining experience, letting the experience take her to a new place, mentally and physically.

She flashed back to James—and how he used to poke fun at her when she was feeling uncomfortable. "When you're nervous, you go into control," he would say, as though to remind Cassie of her fatal flaw. It infuriated her, but he always managed to do something to defuse the confrontation—he would trail a string of kisses up her arm and onto her neck, or a glass of her favorite wine would appear. He had that magic touch.

Noma, Copenhagen

I know you have always dreamed of visiting Noma for the cuisine, the ingredients, and the hospitality, and there is nothing I would have wanted more than for you to be here with me. The restaurant is known for its whimsical and genre-bending dishes, which are even more wonderful in person than in the glossy magazines that you spent so many years studying. To be a guest at Noma is to have a front-row seat at the main stage of their kitchen—and what a treat it is to be part of the show.

We tasted the Vegetable menu, an exploration through the garden with awe-inspiring presentations of ingredients we so often take for granted. Take, for example, the potato, usually served baked, fried, boiled, steamed. Here they return the potato to its humble beginning, the ground, but in the world of Noma, it arrives in the form of potato soup served in a terracotta pot, topped with a garden of herbs. While potatoes are often a favorite staple of a meal, it was refreshing to be surprised by this dish. It was a hint of what else was to come.

Other dishes are crafted from ingredients that are transformed through experimental cooking techniques; onions that are cooked until they resembled lumps of charcoal, with sweet, almost gooey centers, fermented ants that taste of pickled ginger and lemongrass, or plums, dried and fermented until they could be easily confused with cured meat. Noma is constantly expanding our perceptions of the definition of cooking, what we consider to be edible, and what it means to be delighted by a meal.

While each dish is interesting and exquisite, the hospitality is what really steals the show. The team, which comes from all over the world, is a well-oiled machine. Each individual player works in sync with the rest of the team; they greet guests in unison, which is overwhelmingly heartfelt, and then each one peels off to do their individual jobs—as a chef in the kitchen, a runner, a hostess operating flight control over the restaurant, or a server. The flow between the players was fluid and dynamic, and the synergy created an electric current that carried through the entire evening. And no detail goes unnoticed. From the extraordinary wine pairings to the genre-pushing desserts (mold pancakes, for example), each element of this meal at Noma was carefully considered and executed with the highest level of precision. It is clear that this team has worked very hard to deliver a performance of this caliber, and do they deliver.

Noma has changed me, just as you have.

Wish you were here.

#EatPostLike

Cassie hit Share and watched the upload progress bar tick across her screen. She scrolled mindlessly for a few minutes, liking occasional posts from some of her favorite accounts. And then a text message popped up.

> **NILS:** Hej, beautiful. It was so nice to meet you last night. I hope you're having a wonderful day.

Cassie smiled into the bright blue light of her phone.

> **CASSIE:** Hi, thank you for the tour. I had a really nice time.

> **NILS:** I would love to see you again 😊

> **CASSIE:** I'm sorry. I have to work tonight. 🥺

It wasn't a lie. She had one last meal to review in Copenhagen. It was an early dinner, and she could probably meet up after, but just the thought of staying up late felt exhausting—especially with the remnants of a hangover still in her system.

NILS: What about later?

She didn't answer. He was very forward, and it made her uncomfortable—but in a way that she kind of enjoyed. She threw herself onto the bed and let her mind wander to Nils for a few moments. His soft, full lips, his intense gaze, and the colorful tattoos that traveled up his forearms, disappearing under the folded sleeves of his white T-shirt. She could faintly remember the smell of him—like smoke and sweat—or was that just the smell of the kitchen?

It had been so long since she had been touched, and she was still pulsating from the way he kissed her. How his finger gently traced her forearms and how he looked at her with so much intensity.

33

She had an hour before dinner and decided to walk to the restaurant. She needed some air, and she thought the walk might help clear her mind. She sent Rebecca a text that she would meet her there.

Cassie walked south and then northwest, making her way to Gothersgade, a boulevard that cut through the city, past the King's Garden, the teal spires of the Rosenborg Castle, and the Copenhagen Botanical Gardens. The gardens were green and lush, and she felt a pang of longing at seeing groups of people scattered on picnic blankets across the grass.

She turned south again and walked through Copenhagen's trendy Meatpacking District, arriving at the restaurant right as they were opening for the evening. It was housed in a blue and white industrial building with "Kød og Flæskehal" in large metal letters over the awning. Inside, the décor was equally utilitarian: white subway tile, sheet metal bar tops, exposed HVAC ducts, and reclaimed wood that was chipped and weathered.

"Welcome to Kødbyens Fiskebar," said the hostess. "Do you have a reservation?"

"Yes, and there is one more joining me," said Cassie, looking down at her watch. Rebecca wouldn't be there for another thirty minutes. "I'm early. Can I just get a drink at the bar?"

"Of course," said the hostess, directing her to the large island bar in the middle of the restaurant.

Cassie ordered a glass of sparkling wine and enjoyed the first sip—chilled, fruity, and effervescent. She pulled out her phone to check her messages. Nils hadn't texted again, but now with half a glass of wine in her system, she had the courage to message him back.

> **CASSIE:** 8:30?

> **NILS:** Fantastic. Meet me in front of the Tivoli Gardens.

Cassie toggled over to Instagram and saw a message from David on @EatPostLike. She hadn't noticed that he started following her.

@DAVIDMAKESMONEY
What an incredible trip. I know James always wanted to go to Noma. How was it?

Cassie wasn't sure how to respond. She figured he was still grieving, and once again, he was looking to her for comfort.

@EATPOSTLIKE
It was amazing. How are you?

@DAVIDMAKESMONEY
Were you just in France too? I thought you were the girl who worked all the time.

> **@EATPOSTLIKE**
> I took some time off. You know, it's been a hard year.

Cassie was a little annoyed that he was being so nosy. Why did it matter to him?

> **@DAVIDMAKESMONEY**
> I didn't realize you were so into food.

> **@EATPOSTLIKE**
> What's not to like?

> **@DAVIDMAKESMONEY**
> When do you come home?

> **@EATPOSTLIKE**
> I'm not sure yet.

There was a part of her that didn't want to come home at all. New York just reminded her of James and her job, and it all filled her with such sadness. She liked the idea of just staying on the road, living out of a suitcase, and seeing the world.

> **@DAVIDMAKESMONEY**
> We should get together soon.

> **@EATPOSTLIKE**
> That would be nice.

She was lying. She didn't want to see David again, maybe ever. She wasn't sure that she wanted to see any of James's friends again. She wanted a clean slate, a new beginning, for her career and her social life.

@DAVIDMAKESMONEY
I can come meet you.

David was like that. He liked to flaunt his money in ways that were insulting to other people. Worse than that, he had the emotional intelligence of a newt, and he was notoriously terrible at reading the room. He dated aspiring models whom he met on Tinder and spent an ungodly amount of money on them, taking them out to fancy dinners, reporting back to James that his dates never ate any of the food—a detail that bothered James so much. "Why doesn't he ever date someone interesting?" he would lament. "It would be so fun to double date." Cassie would roll her eyes; she didn't like David all that much, and she liked his girlfriends even less.

Just then, Rebecca walked into the restaurant and spotted Cassie at the bar. Cassie was relieved to have an excuse to end the conversation with David.

@EATPOSTLIKE
I have to go, talk soon.

"Five on the dot. Living up to your advice, I see. Do you want a drink?" asked Cassie, handing her the cocktail menu.

"Sure," Rebecca said, perusing the cocktail menu before addressing the bartender. "I'll have a gin martini, three olives," she said confidently, turning back to Cassie. "I'm incredibly excited to eat here. The menu is entirely seafood—some of the freshest in the world—which is the only way one should eat in the summertime. Especially oysters. But truth be told, I'll eat oysters any time of the year."

"What do you love so much about oysters?" Cassie asked.

"What's not to love?" Rebecca asked, her hands now clasped in front of her chest as she looked up toward the ceiling. "They are the most delightful treasures—briny and salty and sweet. Haven't you read *Consider the Oyster*? It's mandatory reading in my opinion."

Cassie tapped *Consider the Oyster* into her phone and lined up a digital version to read later. "Are you working on a new seafood book?"

"Technically, no," Rebecca said, before taking a sip of her martini, "but I'm always doing research for recipes. I'm hoping to be inspired tonight."

"Ladies, are you ready to be seated?" asked the hostess.

"We are," said Cassie.

"Follow me."

ONCE SEATED, THEY looked over the menu. Each dish was listed as just a few ingredients, but she knew that fish was always best when prepared minimally.

"Hm," Rebecca said. "Seems like we're going to need to order à la carte here. What's looking good to you?"

"I'm curious about the scallops, the razor clams, mussels—"

"Oooh," Rebecca interrupted, "what about the fjord shrimp, asparagus, hake, and the Norwegian crab?"

"Sounds great—get everything," Cassie joked.

"Are you okay to split the dishes?" Rebecca asked. "My body cannot handle this much food anymore."

"Of course," she said, taking note on how to order when there wasn't a tasting menu.

A waiter stopped by the table who looked like he was descended directly from Vikings: a tall blond wearing thick-rimmed glasses, with a beard so long that it rested on his impressively muscular chest. Rebecca ordered for the both of them, peppering through the list of items quickly as the waiter scrambled to write everything down.

"You can always tell a New Yorker by how they order food," Cassie said.

"Isn't that the truth? Even a short time in New York can engrain an ordering style. I refuse to make people wait for me—or my indecision."

"Same," Cassie added, taking comfort in how New Yorkers just understood each other.

The waiter came back with a bottle of Danish white wine that he poured into two delicate wineglasses, followed by a platter of Marennes oysters that came with an herbal vinegar sauce and fresh lemon, served on frozen beach stones.

Rebecca swooned over the oysters, drenching them in lemon juice before picking one up and slurping it into her mouth. She chased it with a bite of potato bread slathered in sea lettuce butter and another squeeze of fresh lemon.

"So, what was your impression of last night?" she asked Rebecca.

"In a word, magnificent," Rebecca said. "I think it could possibly be the restaurant of our time. They are doing so many innovative things there: new techniques, new flavor combinations, new ways of presentation. It's pure art. They are the avant-garde."

"Did you see the fermentation lab?" asked Cassie. "It was . . . impressive."

"We did. It must be such an *education* to work there. I would give anything to stage at Noma—but my intern days are *loooooong* behind me."

"What do you mean?"

"So many of these high-end restaurants are built on a culture of free labor. Chefs from all over the world travel to work at starred restaurants for free, under the guise of education. It's been criticized as exploitation, especially considering how much they are charging the diners."

"Sounds a little bit like law," Cassie said, raising an eyebrow.

"Were you . . . a lawyer?"

"I am. I was. I don't know what I am anymore."

"That's relatable. Most people don't pursue food criticism as a career—we all start out doing something else."

"What did you do before?"

"I wanted to be a novelist, but I fell in love with cooking. Worked my way through the newspapers, the magazines, and then finally to my own books."

"I know them. We used to cook from them all time."

"Used to? Sent them to the curb already?"

"No, that's not what I meant. My life is kind of . . . upended right now."

"I get it," said Rebecca. "Things go bad at home, so you take off for a life on the road, jumping from trip invitation to trip invitation. It's fairly common. Then people get addicted to the lifestyle, and they never leave."

Next, the waiter brought over a large bowl of Limfjord blue mussels cooked in cider, fresh herbs, and double cream that filled the table with a sweet, maritime aroma. For a second, Cassie's heart panged—remembering the nights she would go out with James and how they would eat mussels at their local in New York. Fortunately, the preparation was different enough that she was able to refocus her mind.

"So, what got upended, exactly?" Rebecca asked after scooping a plump mussel into her mouth.

"James, my boyfriend, died in a car accident nine months ago." Cassie was relieved that she felt comfortable enough to share this secret with her new comrades, this little clique she trusted, even after a little more than a week together.

Rebecca gasped loudly, which echoed through the restaurant. "Oh, how *tragic*," she said, reaching her hands across the table. "I'm so dreadfully sorry. There's nothing worse than losing a lover."

"He was more than my lover," Cassie said. "I wanted to marry him. We were good together. He was an accountant, he had a stable job, and he gave me the space I needed, the space my career needed. I used to be completely and utterly dedicated to my job."

"Doesn't sound like you had much room in your life for a man." Rebecca frowned.

"There's some truth to that. But James was so patient with me. And God, I pushed him away, I held him at arm's length. I feel so *guilty* about it now." Cassie felt her throat start to pinch, forcing the tears to well up in her eyes.

With impeccable timing, the waiter arrived at their table. Cassie dabbed her eyes with her napkin, desperately trying to hide the fact that she had been crying.

"Here you have the fjord shrimp with a ramson emulsion, and

Norwegian crab served with sea lettuce, nasturtium, sour cream, and house-made potato chips."

"Thank you," said Rebecca to the waiter, in a tone that suggested he should get lost.

"I was horrible to him," Cassie confessed, "and all he wanted was to be with me. I'm still not even sure why. But he wanted to travel, get married, and probably have kids."

"You couldn't have been that horrible to him. Sounds like he was a stable guy who loved you dearly. He was there for you."

"He was, and it annoyed me. It's awful. I'm a terrible person."

"No, you're not," said Rebecca in a soft, hushed voice. "It sounds like you needed something else from the relationship. Something he wasn't giving you."

"I think what I needed was *adventure*. I needed excitement and *passion*, but I made it very clear that my career came first, before him, before our relationship. So he hid a lot from me. I don't know, maybe he didn't want to make me jealous because I could never get away from my desk."

"So now you're burdened with guilt, because you can't go back and fix it?"

"Yes. And I've realized just how wonderful he really was. It's killing me to think about what we *could* have been, had I only known the truth. Since he died, I've learned about the other sides of his personality he didn't want to show me, maybe because he didn't want to get hurt either. He built this incredible business without telling me, and he was really, really good at what he did."

"Does that make you envious?"

"Without a doubt. I'm used to being very good at things—

school, studying, law, working hard—but my success has always come at a cost."

"I completely understand that feeling. It's difficult to be a strong, independent woman. Men have different expectations when it comes to relationships."

"I can only imagine what it was like in your generation," said Cassie, looking at Rebecca, who was radiant with beauty, her silvery hair backlit by the window, and her red lipstick still perfectly applied, somehow.

"Well, sweetie, that's why I never *really* settled down. I loved my work, and quite frankly it made the men in my life mad. So . . ." Rebecca trailed off and took a sip of wine. It clearly wasn't weighing on her. "Look, don't get me wrong, it would have been splendid if one of my marriages had worked out, but they didn't, and it seemed like every time something ended, another incredible man showed up in my life."

"Are you seeing anyone now?" Cassie asked.

"No, but who knows who I might meet tomorrow."

The next few dishes were beautifully presented, like precious little jewels. Razor clams topped with olive oil and chives, circular cuts of raw brill served with charred pearl onions and pink pickled onions, and Danish white asparagus alongside bright, orange roe and edible flowers.

"This is delicious, but not terribly filling," Rebecca said after the last course.

Cassie nodded in agreement, wishing for another plate of everything.

"So, you seemed close with one of the chefs from Noma last night," Rebecca said, with a knowing smile.

"Gah!" Cassie threw her head back in frustration, humiliated. "Does everyone know?"

"I can see a tryst brewing when I see it. Don't be embarrassed— you should take a lover, especially after what you've been through."

Take a lover. The phrase rumbled around in Cassie's head. It seemed incredibly old-world, but also liberating, like something Ruby would do. Why couldn't she do the same?

"I have to confess something," Cassie said quietly.

Rebecca raised an eyebrow and leaned one ear closer to Cassie.

"I have plans to meet Nils after dinner."

"Good girl," Rebecca said, beaming with pride. "I have no doubt that whatever is in store for you will be *titillating*."

CASSIE AND REBECCA left the restaurant around eight o'clock, and it was still light out. The streets were filled with people sitting at cafés, riding their bikes, and gathering in parks. The Danes were relishing the extended hours of sunshine.

Cassie hugged Rebecca goodbye and started to make her way toward the gardens. She had heard of Tivoli but didn't know what to expect. She started feeling nervous about seeing Nils again and picked up her pace. She didn't want to be late.

34

It was 8:20 when Cassie arrived at the gardens, and the plaza in front of the main gate was swarming with people. She found a bench across from the park's entrance and took her phone out of her purse so she would be sure to hear it ring. As she waited, she people watched, finding herself jealous of these incredibly happy, beautiful people. They seemed so radiant and full of life. Maybe it was the infinitely long summer days, or maybe it was the Danish way, but something about this place was making her envious for something different in her life.

AROUND 8:45, CASSIE was growing impatient. There was still no sign of Nils, and no message on her phone.

> **CASSIE:** Hi—are we still meeting?

She tapped the message into her phone, nervous that she was in the wrong place, or had mixed up the time.

A few minutes passed. Nothing.

Then her phone buzzed.

> **NILS:** I'm so sorry, I got stuck in the kitchen. I thought I was going to be

able to get off early, but there's a big group here tonight. I'm not going to be able to make it. I'm so sorry.

Her heart sank with disappointment.

CASSIE: I understand.

She put her phone back in her purse. This felt weirdly like payback for all the times she bailed on plans with James because of the office. She deserved to be stood up.

She sat for a moment, quiet and still, watching the people flow in and out of the park, through the plaza, and on their way to their happy lives. She was jealous that they had someplace to be, friends and families to rush off to meet. Instead, here she was, alone, halfway around the world, with nowhere to go and no one to be with. Once again, she felt untethered, spinning.

Cassie felt her throat tighten, the piercing pain that comes before the tears. Rejecting them, she chose to stand up and walk toward the entrance of the park. She was in Copenhagen, damn it, and she wasn't about to go back to the hotel to sit in her room alone. She wanted to see this Tivoli—with or without a date.

CASSIE PURCHASED HER ticket and entered the park, instantly feeling transported away from the bustling metropolis of Copenhagen and into an enchanting world of gardens, follies, and whimsical rides shaped like vintage cars, space rockets, and flying dragons.

She walked over to the manmade lake, filled with miniature boats floating calmly across the surface of the water. Behind the lake was a roller coaster that resembled the sinuous shape of a dragon, rising above the trees and looping through the air. Every few minutes, a train of people would scream in chorus as they zipped and flipped along the undulating track. Next to the roller coaster was a red-and-green four-story Chinese pergola, framed by a broad old weeping willow.

She watched the kids running around, parents trailing closely behind, teenage lovers walking hand in hand, and tourists snapping photos of the different attractions.

Cassie walked around the lake, past the hanging gardens, the orangery, through the bamboo gardens, looping back until she came upon a white Middle Eastern castle-like building with a large water feature in the front. It was reminiscent of the Taj Mahal, but smaller and adorned with thousands of tiny glowing lights, now visible as the day faded into evening. She walked down the path of the building, curious to see what was inside, passing through an open-air café.

"Cassie?"

It was Eamon. Shit. He was sitting at one of the tables, laptop out, writing.

"Hi. What are you doing here? Aren't you supposed to be on assignment?" said Cassie.

"I'm wrapping up now. Aren't *you* supposed be on assignment?" Eamon seemed equally surprised to see her in the park.

"I was. I was supposed to meet someone here."

"Oh, your new friend?" he asked with a biting tone in his voice.

"Well, I was stood up." She looked down at the floor, kicking a pebble out of the way. "So, what are you doing here?"

"My assignment was the restaurant inside the hotel. Who

would have ever thought that there were *two* starred restaurants in Tivoli Gardens?"

"Seriously?"

"Seriously. And more than forty food and drink establishments. This place is a city unto itself."

Eamon closed his computer, placed it in his bag, and stood up. "Walk with me. Please?" he said, his voice soft and disarming.

Cassie nodded, and the two made their way down the gravel path into the heart of the park.

"So. What happened earlier. I'm sorry. I got emotional."

"I was wondering about that. It's not like you to just up and leave."

"I didn't like seeing you with that guy. I don't know why—I know it's not my place—but you know, chefs are a different breed. They are different from us."

"What does that mean?"

"They can be a bit rough, let's say. I don't know how else to put it."

"Okay, well, Nils was a complete gentleman. Besides, why do you even care? We don't even know each other."

Eamon was quiet for a moment. "Well, what if I want to get to know you?"

After a few moments, she finally responded. "What do you want to know?"

He leaned in, as if to whisper a secret in her ear, and breathed, "Everything."

"That's not terribly specific," she joked, feeling her prickly defensive nature start to soften. "Besides, I'm not that interesting." She flushed.

"But you are," he said, in a way that made her skin tingle with delight.

The sky was fading into a deep cobalt blue, and the lights of each ride were competing with the next, reminding Cassie of old neon bar signs.

"What do you love the most about writing?" she asked.

"Probably the exposure. I've had the privilege to travel all over the world with one purpose: to eat and drink amazing things."

"I'm sure you've been to some amazing places."

"I have. The wine business has some truly incredible events, which are usually hosted at starred restaurants. I guess you could say that I've been at the right place at the right time."

"Sounds like it."

"How did you get started?" he asked, his arm grazing hers, making her feel fluttery on the inside. *Did he do that on purpose?*

"Oh, I just fell into it," Cassie quipped; it had become an easy way to explain her situation. After all, it was the most honest thing she could say.

"We all did, I guess," Eamon confessed. "I don't know anyone who went to school to become a restaurant critic. It's something people discover later in life. Even for those who love cooking."

"So, what do you love about restaurants?" Cassie asked.

"I love the idea that you're entering someone's world, and that it's an experience that can be completely transformative. One person, or a team of people, has deliberately created a place where their food, their ideas, and their vision come alive, and we get to be guests in that world for a few delicious hours. It never ceases to amaze me how immersive restaurants can be. It's almost like going to the theater, but we get to be part of the show."

"It's as though we become actors on their stage," added Cassie.

"Exactly, you get it."

AFTER AN HOUR, Cassie started to recognize the glowing light displays and realized that they were walking in circles around the park. Their conversation flowed freely, and they walked slowly, bumping into each other every few steps. She wondered if she was just being clumsy or if it was subconsciously intentional. Surely, he must have noticed by now.

They stopped in front of a tall ride called the Star Flyer. "Come on," he said, grabbing her hand and pulling her toward the entrance.

"Eamon, I have my bag with me. Aren't there lockers or something?"

Without giving her a moment to think twice, Eamon stashed their bags in the bushes, making sure no one was looking.

"This seems like an honest town. Besides, it's just a few minutes."

Cassie groaned but obliged, following him onto the ride.

"Just know, my camera is in there, and if it gets stolen, you're dead."

"It won't," he said, his face beaming with an arrogant smile. "Besides, my laptop is in there too. We'd both be fucked."

The ride operator led them to two swing seats and buckled them in. Cassie nervously fidgeted with the chains, and then they slowly rose into the air, above the park. She swung her feet, suddenly aware of how far off the ground they were and how high they were about to go. The higher the ride went, the more she could see of the city, the lights of the park spinning below her. It seemed like the whole place was shimmering, the city duplicating itself along the surface of the water, twinkling in the reflection. The ride climbed to the top of the tower, spinning rapidly, causing the swings to tilt dramatically, pushing the riders even farther out over the boundaries of the park. Eamon reached over and grabbed her hand. She looked up at him, surprised. He locked eyes with her and smiled, his chiseled face catching the glow of the ride's changing neon lights.

As THE RIDE came back down, their hands remained intertwined until they came to a stop. Reluctantly, she let go and stood up, walking unsteadily toward the exit, as adrenaline surged through her body.

"See? Still here," he said, pulling her bag from its hiding spot.

"Thank God. Are you hungry? I'm weirdly hungry."

"Didn't you just eat?" Eamon asked.

"The seafood didn't stick with me too long. Don't get me wrong, it was incredible, but we split everything so we could have a taste, and what we had wasn't terribly filling."

"Well, good thing there are *forty* restaurants here."

"Okay," Cassie prodded, "since you're the Tivoli expert, where should we go?"

"Well, what do you want?"

"Nothing fussy. It's been a lot of . . ."

"Fussy food?" Eamon interjected.

"Yeah, I don't want to complain, but it's been a lot."

"Oh, I get it," he said. "Some trips all I want is an enormous salad, and some all I want is a juicy cheeseburger."

"How about the Food Hall?" said Cassie, pointing across the park. "I bet they have a burger there."

"Excellent choice."

They cut through the crowds of families and tourists to a modern pavilion made of large, undulating glass panels and gilded flutes. Once inside, the space turned into a maze that navigated around individual boxlike bars surrounded by stools and, above, illuminated signage. In between each food stall were tables and chairs and potted trees that made the room feel like they were outside, dining al fresco. There was an array of culinary choices, from traditional Danish smørrebørd to pizza, sushi, French bistro, Mexican street food, North African, Indian, and of course, an American-style grill.

"Why do we need to travel anywhere else?" she joked. "It seems all the major food styles are already here."

He laughed. "What are you hungry for?"

"I kind of want to try as many things as possible. Is that crazy?"

"Not at all. Where should we start?"

"When in Denmark," she said, pointing toward the smørrebørd sign.

They walked over to the food stall and took a few moments to familiarize themselves with the menu.

"I haven't had any traditional Danish food on this trip yet, and I know exactly what we should order," said Eamon, his neck straining toward the menu.

"Go for it," said Cassie. "Just make sure you order some wine."

Cassie moved away from the bar and grabbed a table. She watched Eamon at the counter as he ran his hands through his wavy hair and pointed crudely at the menu. She liked his look, rough but curated. He looked like he could thrive both on a vineyard and in a major city, wonderfully mercurial.

"No wine, just beer," he said, dropping two brown bottles onto the tabletop. "Chin-chin," he said, raising up the bottle for a cheers.

"So, what did you order?" she asked.

"We've got fried cod cakes, salmon salad with trout roe, Swedish shrimp, and liver pâté, because I can never say no to pâté. And a big fat cheeseburger."

"Yes!" Cassie cried. "I'm so excited. I can't wait for that cheeseburger," she joked.

"You might have to fight me for it."

"Bring it on," she said, feeling her stomach rumble. "So, tell me, what do you love about this life? You're on the road all the time—it must be difficult to be so nomadic."

"To be honest, you get used to it. And then you start needing it. Even a few weeks at home starts to feel like too much." Eamon picked up her hand and traced his fingers along hers, making her entire body tingle. "But that said, there's nothing I love more than being at home at the winery. You should come see it sometime."

"I would love to," she said, wondering if the invitation would ever come to fruition. "It sounds wonderful."

A runner appeared in front of them and presented a wooden board covered with Scandinavian toasts. He described each one quickly, having clearly done it numerous times before. Cassie looked over the spread, piled high with mounds of bright, glistening pearls of caviar, lingonberries, fresh microgreens, and prawns, freshly boiled with their heads still intact, served on pieces of dark rye bread.

"I never would have thought that Danish food would be so amazing," Cassie confessed.

"You're not the only one. It's not the first place people think of when it comes to cuisine, but it's become a leader in the last decade. I feel as though the Danish are doing something very cool; they are building on a heritage of fresh ingredients and a farm-to-table culture while making it more modern."

"Exactly. Fermentation is an old-world technique, and it is being used in such an innovative way here." Cassie recalled the previous night in the lab. "At least from what we tasted at Noma, and it's clear that their influence is spreading all over this city."

"It's so true."

Cassie cut off a piece of the salmon salad toast, making sure to capture a generous heap of greens, capers, and bright orange roe. "This looks amazing," she said before bringing the bite to her mouth. She felt the small beads of roe popping, releasing their bright, briny liquid, which perfectly cut the mayonnaise-rich smoked salmon salad. She felt herself slow down, chewing the bite methodically. When she could chew no more, she swallowed and sat back in her chair, taking a moment.

"That good, huh?"

"Yeah."

Then the burger arrived. It was impressively large, almost like a caricature of an American burger, served on a wood cutting board, with the handle of a steak knife sticking out of the top.

"Finally!" Cassie rejoiced, pulling the board closer. "I probably should have had this for breakfast."

"Hangover was that bad, huh?"

"Killer."

Cassie pulled the knife out of the burger and cut it in half, revealing oozing cheddar cheese, sautéed onions, and the pink, still bloody meat in the middle.

"Mmmm, medium rare, just the way I like it."

"There's no other way," said Eamon, watching as she inspected the sandwich. "Only psychopaths eat their burgers well done."

"And steaks," she added.

"Lunatics," he confirmed, nodding.

She picked up half of the cheeseburger and brought it to her mouth, gently squeezing it in a feeble effort to keep the ingredients from sliding, sending the juices from the meat running down her forearms. She was so hungry that she didn't care; she committed to the burger, taking an impressively massive bite. She closed her eyes, letting the flavors of cooked onions, pickles, cheddar cheese, and grass-fed beef swirl around her mouth. She chewed until it seemed impossible to chew anymore, swallowed, and opened her eyes. A smile curled across her face. "Damn, I needed that."

"This might sound creepy, but I love watching you eat."

"Yeah, that is a little creepy," she responded, before smiling at him and taking a swig of beer, feeling light and almost effervescent from the attention.

"You could be a mukbang star," he teased.

Cassie paused, beer halfway to the table. "What is mukbang?"

"It's when people eat on camera." Eamon took another bite of food. "It's oddly satisfying."

"Sounds like a fetish."

"I wouldn't *necessarily* call it a fetish. More like market research. I think it's important to understand all the food subcultures on the internet, no matter how weird they might seem. But that's not the point. I love to watch how much enjoyment you get out of what you're eating. It's as though you've never tasted anything so delicious before." His attention was fully on her now, his piercing hazel eyes holding her gaze.

"Maybe I haven't," she teased, her cheeks full of burger. Which was the complete and utter truth—she had never been to restaurants of this caliber before, and she had never been able to let herself truly enjoy food. Now it was primal—an understanding of food as a necessity, as a symbiotic relationship with the earth, and as a source of pleasure.

"I don't believe you."

"I spent a good part of my life eating mediocre, overpriced midtown salads."

"Ooooh, yeah. Those are sad."

"Very sad. This burger, on the other hand, is giving me life. You might not get the other half if you wait any longer." She wasn't kidding.

"You can have it; it will give me more time to watch you."

Cassie gave him an exaggerated eye roll as she picked up the second half of the sandwich. She took a bite and moaned audibly, throwing her head back erotically.

"How was that?" she asked after she finished chewing.

"Academy Award winning," he said, grinning. "Were you in *When Harry Met Sally*?"

Cassie laughed. "I completely forgot about that movie."

"Well, your reenactment was spot-on. You know, you're pretty funny."

Cassie choked. "No one has ever, ever, ever called me funny. Uptight. Certainly. Myopic. Without a doubt. But funny? No. Way."

"I think you're funny."

"You're trying to flatter me." Cassie wanted to change the subject. "And you should stop. How's the pâté? Everything you dreamed of?"

"It's not as good as in France, but that's to be expected."

He paused and fidgeted with his beer bottle. "So, I take it you're not seeing anyone at home?" he asked brazenly.

Startled, Cassie said, "Why do you say that?"

"Well, after last night. You know—that guy at Noma."

"Well, it seems that was a one-off." She felt her cheeks go hot with embarrassment.

Eamon looked smug, if only for a second. He turned and looked across the restaurant.

"If you really want to know, I *was* seeing someone. I was in a long-term relationship, but"—she paused, taking a deep breath—"he died last September."

"I'm sorry to hear that. What happened?"

"Car accident."

"I'm so sorry," he said, his eyes now soft and empathetic. "How long were you together?"

"Long enough to not be able to consider any other future for myself."

"How so?"

"We had been together so long that in some ways I felt like I was already married to him. I was fiercely loyal, even though I realized after he died that he had been lying to me for a long time."

"Lying to you about what?"

"Everything. His entire existence. It's been a mental burden, that's for sure."

"Go on," he said, taking a sip of beer.

"He had another identity. It wasn't like he had another family and kids in another state, but yeah, he was living a double life."

"My friends accuse me of that. Some of them know that I

review for Viand, but not many of them. We're supposed to be stealth and operate in the shadows." He lifted his hands in front of his face and wiggled his fingers, pantomiming an imaginary veil.

"I'm still trying to get the hang of the role of an elusive restaurant critic. Seems like I have something to learn from him—and you, apparently."

"That's the attitude. I'm not the best at it, to be honest," he confessed. "I don't even use aliases to create reservations. I guess you could say that it matters less to me than it probably should."

Cassie suddenly felt his leg subtly pressing up against hers under the table, and she was too scared to move, fearful that she would break the electric current running between them. She wondered what it would feel like to run her fingers through his hair, tracing the dark blond waves until the point where they met his scalp.

"So, what about you?" Cassie asked, trying to be nonchalant. "Are you seeing anyone?"

"I've been in and out of some things, but nothing has stuck."

"Why not?"

"The truth is, I don't like that many people."

"That is a complete lie. You could become best friends with a brick wall." Cassie laughed. "You're hands down the most charismatic person I've ever met."

Eamon looked up at the ceiling, questioning her statement. "Eh, I guess you're right," he said. "After all, I'm a potato." He flashed a Cheshire cat smile that made her insides turn to pudding.

THE TWO BOUNCED from vendor to vendor, trying spicy and sweet pork buns wrapped in pillowy rice cakes, bites of sustainable sushi made from crab harvested from just outside Copenhagen, and Asian fusion lobster rolls, something Cassie never would have thought existed. Eventually, Cassie was so full she couldn't take another bite.

"I'm tapping out," she said, putting her hands over her stomach. "I don't think I've ever eaten this much in my whole life."

"We conquered this food hall. What's your rating?"

"A beautiful representation of all culinary continents, five stars."

Eamon laughed, and said, "Come on, let's get you home."

They stood up, bellies full, and made their way out the door and back into the park. The rides had all shut for the night and were not moving, but their lights were still on, filling the dark sky with halos of color from pink to yellow to blue. The park was relatively empty, with a few other stragglers walking under the moonlight. They walked in silence for a few moments, gently bumping into each other every few steps.

"I'm really glad you're on this trip," he said, before adding, "The usual cast of characters is infinitely better than being alone, but it can be difficult to make long-lasting friendships. I'm sure you will be surprised to hear that critics can be terribly acerbic, and sometimes these connections can be . . . superficial." He paused. "And transactional. But you're different. I don't really know how to describe it, but you're so real. Plus, I appreciate that you bring new ideas and thoughts to the conversation—it's really refreshing. You're open-minded and hungry, and I'm not just talking about the food."

Cassie looked up at him. "What do you mean?" He was more handsome than ever, backlit by the colorful blinking lights of the rides.

"You're so eager to learn about us—this world—me." He paused again and looked down at his feet, shifting his weight nervously. "You're different. I don't know how else to put it." And with that, Eamon suddenly wrapped his arm around Cassie's waist, the handle of his computer bag pressed into her lower back, and with the other hand, he pushed a strand of her hair behind her ear. He kissed her once, lightly, on the lips, as though he was trying to wake her from a deep slumber. He smiled, almost giddy with delight, and leaned in again, this time kissing her intensely, his tongue exploring hers, warm and soft, as his hand caressed her cheek and traced the lines of her neck.

He stepped back and slipped his hand into hers. "I'm sorry. I've wanted to do that for a long time. I couldn't wait any longer," he said, before pulling her in for another kiss. "I never knew I could be so turned on watching someone eat a burger."

Cassie laughed out loud. "Well, I guess there's a first time for everything."

She looked at him, her eyes darting from eye to eye and down to his lips, and he kissed her again, this time slowly and deliberately, savoring her as though she were a fine wine. Cassie felt herself completely liquify in his arms, and she let him drink her in.

They stayed there for a few minutes, under the blinking lights of the abandoned rides and the moonlight above, before the security guard came around for his final sweep of the evening and asked them to leave.

Rome

35

Roma," said Rebecca as she stepped out of the van. "I've missed you!" She took a deep breath of the hot summer air in a way that told of previous liaisons in the Eternal City.

The group tumbled out of the van, tired and hungry. They'd had an early morning flight from Copenhagen to Rome, and it seemed everyone was a little on edge. It was the second week of the trip, and the group was settling into a groove. They had their designated seats in the van and fell back into the usual conversations when they were in transit. What's the most decadent meal you've ever had? Best brand trip? Bucket list restaurant? The most surprising locale for cuisine? Cassie stayed quiet during these conversations, sometimes pretending to sleep, listening to the impressive stories that would make any frustrated nine-to-fiver explode with jealousy.

"Ladies and gentlemen," said Kelly, gathering the group in front of the hotel, "welcome to Rome. We are here for four nights, so make the most of it. There is so much to see, but remember that you have reviews to do. I hope you make the most of our stay at the Hotel de Russie. This is one of my most favorite hotels in the entire world."

Cassie had spent the entire flight working, desperately trying to complete her reviews from the day before, edit photos, and schedule her next posts in an Instagram planning app. She never would have imagined that social media would be so much work—and now she understood why people said that it was a full-time job. She was starting to develop a good rhythm; every few hours she would log in, reply to comments, check her DMs, leave comments on other people's posts, and check the metrics for old posts. She spent extra time studying the posts that had been successful and taking notes on similar posts that performed even better. She wondered how James managed it all without her ever knowing.

From outside of the van, Cassie looked up at the simple, white, rustic building and frowned. It didn't look like much on the outside, aside from the large, art deco–style glass awning. Upon closer inspection, she noticed that the staff were wearing tailored blue suits with black top hats and were standing in front of heavy brass doors. She handed her bags to a bellhop and followed the group inside to the barrel-arched lobby, filled with parlor palms and lush tropical plants. Flanking the arches were white marble busts on pedestals, staring blankly into space.

At the end of the hall, a large picture window framed the courtyard outside, peppered with orange canvas umbrellas, and at the far wall, stone steps ascended into a terraced garden that became less and less manicured as the edges blurred with the forest beyond. Trailing vines dotted with small, white flowers hung off balconies, filling the warm, summer air with the smell of jasmine.

She stood for a moment, weak in the knees, remembering all those hours she'd spent at the Strand drooling over the glossy travel guidebooks. New York felt like a different planet now, her existence there a lifetime ago. Here she was, standing in the courtyard of this incredible hotel, feeling like the star of her own movie.

One by one, each person checked in at the desk and eventually made their way to the end of the corridor, stopping next to Cassie in front of the picture window.

"Wow," said Ben, in a rare moment short of words.

Rebecca just sighed and kind of giggled to herself.

"Good memories?" Cassie asked.

"The best," said Rebecca, with a secretive smile. "But I don't kiss and tell." She fanned herself with an ornate mother of pearl folding fan.

"Of course you don't," said Cassie.

"It's so nice to be back in Rome. It's *such* a romantic city." Rebecca tapped Cassie on the shoulder with her fan, now folded tightly in her hand, before making her way to the elevator.

While Cassie was admiring the view, Kelly slipped in next to her. "Don't forget to check in," she said. "That is, if you ever want to leave the lobby."

"It's just so beautiful," said Cassie. "I've had so many 'pinch me' moments already, but this hotel is sending me to another level of awe. How did you even find this place?"

"I have my ways," said Kelly with a wink. "Isn't it wonderful? Picasso used to stay here. I just love hotels with history."

"I don't know if I've said it to you yet, but thank you. Thank you for inviting me on this trip. It's been everything I've needed."

"That's wonderful to hear. We've been loving your reviews, and it's been fun to see your new account blowing up. I think it's great you created an account that you're the face of. Not everything needs to be anonymous."

"Thank you. It's been really fun to express myself in a new way," she said honestly.

"Okay, I'm off. Enjoy Roma!"

AFTER CHECKING INTO her palatial room, Cassie headed to the courtyard for lunch, laptop in hand. She felt foolish for not already having a plan of all the places she wanted to see in Rome; if only she had bought one of her beloved guidebooks.

Cassie sat down at a table near the back of the courtyard, close to the stairs that rambled up to the rustic garden wall and into the park beyond. A few tables over was a two-top with two handsome middle-aged men immersed in conversation, smoking thin, white cigarettes. Looking at them, she felt an appreciation for how Italian men dressed—simple, in well-tailored linens and nice leather shoes. They seemed so at ease, and for the first time in a long time, she didn't feel a pang of envy. They were just two good-looking men, enjoying their lives, like she was enjoying hers. She credited it to the fact that, for the first time in months, she was more comfortable bearing the weight of her grief, and as a result, she felt lighter and more comfortable in her own skin.

The waiter came to the table, and she fumbled her way through the menu, attempting to order a salad, knowing full well that she would eat whatever arrived. She opened her laptop and started searching through Google Maps, dropping pins on the sights she wanted to see. The Colosseum, the Roman Forum, Campo de' Fiori, and gelato shops. Yes, she had to try as much gelato as time would allow.

"There you are," said Eamon, sitting down at her table. "Have you eaten?"

"I just ordered," she said. "How's your room?"

"It's okay," Eamon said flatly. "This hotel is a bit old, no?"

"You're a snob. The rooms are *gorgeous*!"

"I know," he said, smiling impishly. "I just wanted to get you going."

She clicked her tongue at him disapprovingly, before giving him a smile in return.

Eamon signaled to the waiter across the courtyard. "I believe it's spritz o'clock," he said. "Due spritz di Aperol, per favore."

"Oh, you speak Italian too?"

"All the wine languages," he said with a wink. "Where are you reviewing?"

"Hmm, let me see . . ." She pulled out the folder with her itinerary in it. "I don't have anything today, but tomorrow is Il Pagliaccio and the next day is La Pergola."

"Then we dine together at La Pergola."

Two large balloon glasses filled with a bubbly, bright orange concoction arrived at their table, along with a tiered silver tray of salty snacks: pretzels, potato chips, and peanuts.

"This is civilized," Cassie said, picking a pretzel out of the dish and putting it in her mouth.

"The Italians have mastered aperitivi culture. They truly have life figured out."

"Cheers," she said, raising her glass up before taking a sip. The taste was curious, bitter and sweet, with a slight flavor of orange and rhubarb. "Well, this is delicious," she said after a few large gulps.

"Oh, yeah, these are dangerously good. Hey, let me show you around Rome. I know the city pretty well, and it will be faster than fumbling around with Google Maps."

"How do you know all these cities so well?" she said, frustrated.

"That will be you soon enough. That's the thing about these trips—once you do a good job on one, the invites just keep coming."

"Noted," she said, taking another sip of her spritz.

AFTER LUNCH, CASSIE went up to her room to freshen up, taking a moment to enjoy the luxuries of the room: the Carrara marble bathroom, the beautifully scented soaps, and the excessively pillowy towels. She changed into a red A-line sundress and slipped on a pair of white sneakers. She completed her look with a swipe of red lipstick and a pair of white cat-eye sunglasses that felt especially summery.

Cassie stepped out onto the street and into a blast of intense heat that felt shocking after the cool, air-conditioned lobby. She looked around for Eamon and spotted him leaning up against a seafoam green vespa, sunglasses on, looking down at his phone. He was wearing a short-sleeve powder-blue denim button-down over a white T-shirt, the sleeves rolled up to show his muscular arms, his veins tracing his biceps. He looked so cool and relaxed and—dare she think it—sexy. She clicked a few photos of him before he looked up and saw her.

"Now, that's a dress," he said looking her up and down. "They are going to love you."

"What do you mean?"

"Oh, you'll see."

He handed her a white helmet before putting his on.

"Safety first," Cassie said.

"I knew you would want a helmet. I usually don't wear one."

Eamon straddled the bike and gestured for her to get on with a quick nod of his head. She paused. There was no graceful way to do this. She swung her leg up and over the back of the bike, organized her skirt, and tucked her feet onto the pegs.

"Andiamo," said Eamon, as he started the engine.

THEY DROVE DOWN Via di Ripetta, which looked like a significant thoroughfare on the map, but in reality was a small cobblestone street with narrow sidewalks on each side. They zipped past shops that seemed as though they had been there for centuries, family-run meat shops, wine stores, pharmacies, shoe stores, and the tabacchi shops that doubled as cafés.

They hadn't been riding for more than five or ten minutes when Eamon pulled the bike to a stop, got off, and started to make his way to a corner café.

"I need a coffee," he said, grabbing her hand and pulling her inside.

The café was small and modest, with only a few places to sit down—rickety two-tops pushed against the storefront. She was half expecting a large menu, like one you would see at a Starbucks, but instead there was a small chalkboard with a handful of items scribbled in chalk that she could barely make out.

Eamon looked at his watch. "One o'clock, too late for a cappuccino." He stood at the bar, in front of a middle-aged gentleman who was not terribly welcoming. "Due caffè, per favore."

"Un momento," the man responded, turning around to the espresso machine.

Cassie looked around. "Where do we sit?"

"We don't," said Eamon with a flash of a smile. He pulled out his phone and scrolled around on the map. "I'm still trying to get my bearings, but I think we're headed the right way."

Cassie could feel people—the men, specifically—looking at her. She could see their heads turning out of the corner of her eye.

Eamon leaned to whisper in her ear, briefly placing his hand on the small of her back, and in a low voice, rumbled, "I told you they would love you."

Cassie smiled, a little embarrassed, but now distracted by his seductive growl. The feeling of his breath on her neck made her entire body tingle, and she longed for him to lean into her again.

The barista placed two small saucers with small white demitasse espresso cups filled with dark, murky coffee in front of them. On the side of the saucer was a small cube of sugar and a tiny silver spoon. Cassie dropped the cube into the cup, stirring until the sugar started to break up and dissolve. Eamon pulled two battered Splenda packets out of his pocket and stirred them into his coffee.

"You carry your own Splenda stash?" she asked, teasing.

"It's Italy. I have to," he said with a shrug and a naughty smile, and downed his espresso in two quick gulps before going back to studying the map.

Cassie blew on the surface of the coffee, nervous to burn her tongue. She finally mustered the courage to take a sip, and it was just as strong and bitter as it smelled. She grimaced and brought the cup to her lips again, finally finding the sugar at the bottom in the last sip.

"That was unpleasant," she said, wiping her mouth and drinking the glass of water in front of her in one go.

He had been watching her intently, playing with his lips. "That's why I bring my own sweetener. Italian coffee can take some getting used to. Are you ready for your whirlwind tour of Roma?" Eamon gestured to the door.

"I was born ready."

THEY WHIZZED ALONG the labyrinthine streets that wound through the city, zipping down quaint cobblestone residential streets, past intricate Baroque façades, through palazzos filled with bistro tables next to babbling fountains, and past gated portals with glimpses of the elaborate gardens within. Every few blocks was another church, and almost as frequent, decorative fountains carved into the shapes of lions, dolphins, and mythical nymphs that bubbled with fresh drinking water delivered to the city via Roman aqueducts.

Cassie had her hands wrapped tightly around Eamon's solid, muscular waist, hanging on as he wove through the traffic of the city. Cassie held on, feeling Eamon's abs flex underneath her arms with every twitch of the bike.

"So, where did you learn how to drive?" she shouted nervously.

"When I was in college, I spent my summers in Europe," he said. "Why?"

"Um . . . nothing."

"What?" he shouted.

"Could you slow down?" she shouted back.

"Am I making you nervous?" he asked, that Cheshire cat grin peeling up at the corners of his mouth, as he started to weave the bike like they were going through a slalom course.

Cassie tucked her head down, pinched her eyes shut, and gripped even tighter to his trunk. "Please slow down!" she shouted back. She hated feeling out of control, on the back of this bike, her life in his hands. Her mind flashed to James, and all of the terrible scenarios she had crafted around the accident.

Just when it felt like the canyon of streets would never end, and Cassie's arms were tingly and numb, they turned into a colossal piazza that was the length of two and a half football fields and filled with people: tourists snapping photos, lunchgoers under broad, white canvas umbrellas, and groups of teenagers sitting on the base of the central obelisk, chatting and taking selfies.

Eamon stopped in the middle of the piazza and parked the bike. Cassie hopped off and stepped back from him, her heart pounding with fear. "What the fuck, Eamon? Why are you driving like such a maniac?" she shouted.

"Easy, easy," he said, trying to calm her down.

"Don't *easy* me. Are you trying to kill us?"

Eamon paused, realization dawning. "I'm sorry, I wasn't thinking. I didn't mean to scare you." He reached out to touch her shoulder, but she whipped away from him.

She felt the need to repeat herself, a tear now rolling down her cheek. "Why didn't you slow down when I asked?"

Eamon took her hand in his and kissed her palm tenderly. He looked her in the eye, with a pathetic, apologetic look on his face. "I'm sorry. Please believe me, I didn't mean to scare you." He kissed her hand again. "I just wanted you to hold on tighter to me." His solemn look now turned into a flirtatious grin.

"Ughhh," Cassie moaned, hitting him on the shoulder. Her anger had flushed away now that her feet were on solid ground. She tucked herself under his arm, taking comfort in the weight of his body on hers. "Come on, let's walk," she said, hoping to calm the adrenaline that was surging through her body.

Cassie stood in front of one of the fountains; rising high above was Neptune battling an octopus that was trying to pull him under the water, tentacles wrapped around his muscular legs, as the god was about to thrust a spear into the animal's head.

"They used to flood this piazza and hold mock naval battles here, can you believe that?"

"What? Seriously?" She looked around the gigantic square, trying to envision the lower levels of the buildings blocked off, and how much water it would require to fill the space. It was mind-boggling, but also an incredible visual. She wondered if it was true.

"Yeah, so, Piazza Navona sits on top of the Stadium of Domitian," Eamon read from his phone, "also known as Circus Agonalis. The stadium was used almost entirely for athletic contests."

"A proper tour guide would have this memorized," she jested, leaning into him with a pointed elbow.

"Well, you get what you pay for." He flashed her a big smile that made her heart melt. "Come on, it's time for our next stop."

They climbed back onto the vespa.

"Just no more crazy driving," she said sternly.

"Yes, boss," he said, before lurching back onto the streets of Rome.

36

E amon wound through the city, cutting through small neighborhood piazzas and across major thoroughfares, into the heart of Rome. He slowed down and parked the vespa, tucking it between two Smart cars. He was clearly looking for something, turning in circles and trying to see down the tight, narrow streets. Eamon stopped referencing the map on his phone and instead looked around, relying on memory.

"Do you know where we are?" she asked.

"I think so. The next stop on our tour is somewhere . . . right"—he kept walking, looking up and down the streets, trying to navigate—"around here."

"Are we lost?"

"No."

"Are you sure?"

"Yes."

"Do you want to look at the map?"

"No."

Even though they were clearly lost, Cassie weirdly felt at ease. Typically, she would start to panic in a situation like this and want to take control. Instead, she welcomed the unknown and feeling dependent on someone else.

She started to wander a little, looking in shop windows, at the fragments of centuries built, rebuilt, and repurposed in such a magnificent old city. She looked down a street and saw a familiar-looking edifice—the Pantheon.

"Is this what we're looking for?" she called out to Eamon, who had wandered off in the other direction.

He walked over to her and looked in the direction she was pointing. He stopped, looked at the iconic building, looked back at her, took her face into his hands, and kissed her squarely on the lips. "You're leading this tour from now on," he said, as he slipped his hand into hers and pulled her toward the Pantheon.

"Good thing I paid attention in art history," Cassie joked.

They wove through the crowds of people, between the towering columns, and queued in a single-file line so that they could enter the building. Once inside, the space expanded into a vast rotunda with square coffers lining the dome, terminating in a singular oculus that was open to the sky, which made it feel mystical and almost surreal.

Cassie moved to the center of the rotunda and stood directly under the oculus. She paused for a moment and looked up at the sky through the circular opening. The dome of the Pantheon seemed to darken and fall away, and the sky deepened in saturation—a blue, metaphysical dot that seemed both disconnected from reality and, at the same time, a focused snapshot of it. A bird flew over the oculus, and many people audibly gasped, followed by whispers of "Did you see it?"

Cassie refocused her gaze on the beam of light that pierced the opening and cut through the volume of the space, landing on Eamon, who was standing across the room, looking at his phone. He was perfectly illuminated in the beam of sunlight, the atmosphere around him hazy and ephemeral. Cassie took out her camera and snapped a photo of him glowing in that magical light.

BACK ON THE vespa, they cut across the city again and found themselves in the busiest intersection of Rome, whipping around the roundabouts along with the other cars and scooters. They made their way past the Monumento a Vittorio Emanuele II, to the Roman Forum, which was once the heart of the ancient city but was now occupied by tourists and feral cats.

They parked the vespa again and walked into the Forum, following one of the self-guided routes through the notable ruins. They roamed through the campus punctuated by the remaining columns that were once part of enormous marble temples, victory arches, basilicas, and fragments of buildings with mosaics and frescoes that illustrated daily life at that time.

Cassie imagined the Forum in Ancient Rome; the fragments of the city gave her just enough information to reconstruct it in her mind. The sky was starting to turn a golden and pink hue, bathing the white marble columns in orange light.

"Isn't it wild to think that this was a vibrant city *thousands* of years ago?" asked Cassie, camera out and snapping photos of the ruins. "And they were able to build all of this without modern technology?"

"I can't get over how many times this city has been built and rebuilt," Eamon said, looking off into the distance. "Rome is comprised of layers of city built upon previous cities."

Cassie snapped a quick photo of Eamon without his noticing.

"Just like people. We build ourselves as one thing, fall apart, and then create a new self, and build out that person on top of the old one. Burying our secrets one by one over time."

"Oh yeah, Miss Brooks, what kind of secrets do you have buried in there?" His arms were now wrapped around the small of her back, pulling her side to side in an awkward kind of dance.

"I'm actually a spy," she joked, smiling impishly before kissing him among the ruins and the cats.

He pulled back and looked at her. "I have a confession to make," he said, before looking at his feet awkwardly.

Her heart started to race, and her eyes zoomed across his face, looking for a clue. Did he hack into her phone? Could he know about @NewYorkSecretDiner? Had he known that she had been lying this whole time?

"I saw you," he said assertively.

"Saw me where?" Her mind shuffled through the options. What could he have seen her doing?

"The airport. You walked in on me in the shower, you sneaky devil, you."

Her body flushed with a wave of relief, and she threw her hand onto his chest, strong and solid. "Oh my god, are you trying to give me a heart attack?"

"Um, yes," he said. "That was not the response I was expecting. You were acting all coy in the airport, trying to make it seem like nothing had happened."

"I'm so sorry," she said, after letting out a cathartic laugh. "It's true, I was pretty horrified in the moment, but the truth of the matter is that the sight was very, very nice." She punctuated the comment by poking him in the sternum.

"Nice, huh?"

"One I'll never forget," she said, before crawling under his arms and sneaking another kiss.

"How's the tour been?" Eamon asked as they walked back to the vespa, hands intertwined.

"You have a future as a tour guide," she joked, "but you've left one critical thing off the itinerary."

"What's that?" he asked.

"Gelato. I still haven't had it, and we've been in Rome for more than twelve hours. It's practically a sin at this point."

"Well, then, we need to sort that out," he said, before mounting the scooter. "I have just the place in mind."

After a few minutes, Eamon cut northeast on Via Venti Settembre, and they entered a picturesque part of the city filled with embassies, bureaucratic buildings that occupied entire city blocks, and palaces that had been converted into art museums. He turned and drove down a side street, eventually parking in front of a modern shop with large windows and spiraling green topiaries flanking the doors.

He slipped off the vespa and offered Cassie his hand.

"Signorina, il tuo gelato," he said.

The shop was sleek and modern; the floors were white tile with smaller inset black tiles. Black chalkboard graphics gave recommendations, and the walls were lined with stainless steel drums and glass jars of milk. A large glass freezer case cut through the shop, and inside were numerous trays of colorful gelato that were organized into four categories: Fruit, Classics, Creamed, and Specialties.

"This place is completely natural. They don't use any additives or preservatives, and they make the gelato fresh every day depending on what is in season," Eamon said. "It's my favorite."

Cassie perused the offerings, her mouth watering with excitement. Lemon cream, raspberry ricotta and meringue, Parmesan, creamed corn, cassis, persimmon, summer fig, bergamot, tiramisu, creamed coffee, watermelon cream . . . the list went on and on.

"Oh my god, how do you even decide?" Her head was spinning.

"Well, I like to do a combination. One fruit, one nut, one cream—or chocolate, depending on my mood. So tonight I'm going to have wild strawberry, pistachio, and salted caramel. Pistachio is my constant. I always order it. It's my litmus test to judge the gelateria."

"Excellent strategy." She nodded and perused the case while Eamon ordered. She decided on Parmesan, fig, and blue honey with walnuts. "I'm going for the cheese plate combo," she joked. "After all, we skipped dinner."

"Ehh, sorry about that," said Eamon.

"Don't apologize. It's good to give my stomach a break after so many large, decadent meals. Have we even hit the halfway mark on the trip yet?"

"Almost. There's still a lot of meals left to go."

The man behind the counter handed them each a rather large tub filled with gelato and topped with a waffle disk that had been dipped in chocolate.

"I added the waffles—hope you like it," Eamon said, handing her the cup and a plastic spoon.

They sat down on one of the narrow benches outside the shop, their bodies pressing against each other.

"So, what's the verdict? How's the pistachio?" she asked.

"Nutty," he said. "One of the best pistachio gelatos I've ever had. The other one was in Venice—that one was *special*. How's the Parmesan? I was curious about that one."

"Here, try it," she said, pushing the cup in his direction.

He took a small scoop and licked the spoon so that Cassie could see the ice cream starting to melt on the surface of his tongue. She took a moment to study his face: his sharp, chiseled cheekbones, wild eyebrows, and his firm jawline that cut back to his neck. He looked up and locked eyes with her, and she lost herself in the hazel that faded from green to brown to amber—so colorful and intricate, they looked like small universes unto themselves.

"What?" he asked, looking at her suspiciously.

"Thank you for a wonderful day," she said, and kissed him, savoring the pistachio and salted caramel flavors that lingered on his lips.

37

Cassie was starting to settle into a nice rhythm on the trip. She had found a balance of being able to see each city in addition to thoroughly researching each restaurant, so she felt prepared going into each review. The next day was no different. She drew a bath, where she read reviews and past articles about Il Pagliaccio, followed by some time on her phone editing photos from the past few days, writing her captions, and building reels for Instagram. She posted a reel from the day before, this time keeping the caption short and sweet, but in the same format.

A day in Rome

We once considered visiting Rome, a trip I have always dreamed about. We talked about drinking affogattos at local cafés, wandering the halls of art museums, and packing a picnic lunch to eat in the shade of the Colosseum. That version of the story was never meant to be, and instead another story, my story, is being written.

I have fallen in love with Rome, jasmine scented, its streets paved with the histories and day-to-day dramas spanning thousands of years. The city is wild and sophisticated, rustic and romantic, simple and yet more complex than any of us will ever fully understand. There is healing to be had here under the Italian sun; it is a place of rebirth and rejuvenation, and I too have been reborn.

Wish you were here.

#EatPostLike

Cassie hit Share, and then toggled over to @NewYorkSecret-Diner to reply to a few DMs and check the comments on the account. She reposted some beautiful images of fine dining in New York, and then reshared her @EatPostLike post to stories, hoping to gain a few more new followers.

A few moments later, she saw a message from David to @New-YorkSecretDiner pop up, and her heart started racing.

@DAVIDMAKESMONEY
CONSIDER THIS YOUR LAST WARNING!

Cassie waited in the lobby for Ben, who was her dinner date for her review of Il Pagliaccio. Ben rounded the corner walking swiftly down the hall, wearing white trousers, a white button-down shirt, and a fitted blue blazer.

"Don't you look the part?" Cassie said, giving him air kisses on both cheeks.

"June in Rome—is there anything better?"

"Something's different about you," she said. "Oh, this is *your place*." She emphasized this with a tug at his lapel. "Your happy place."

"Italy, baby. I love it here. Come on, the car is waiting for us."

Ben calmly opened the car door for her and made his way around to the other side. As soon as the door shut, he turned to her and excitedly said, "Cassie, tell me *everything*."

"About what?" She was playing dumb.

"Oh, come on, it's *obvious* something is going on between you and Eamon. We've all noticed the flirtatious looks between you two, and conveniently, it seems you both are always missing at the same time. Something is brewing."

"Okay, fine. Yes, we've been . . . canoodling. But nothing's really happened."

"Canoodling," he said suspiciously. "I need details."

"I ran into him at Tivoli Gardens randomly. I went to meet— um—it doesn't matter. When I was there, I ran into Eamon as he was wrapping up his review, and we hung out in the gardens, talking. We shut down the park, us and the teenagers. You know, he's actually really funny and fun to be around."

"Oh, you *like* him," said Ben, raising his eyebrows for effect.

"Yeah, I think I do."

"Cuuuteee," he said. "So do you *like* him like him? Or is this just a trip fling?"

She hadn't really thought about it. "Wait, a trip fling is a thing?"

"Oh yeah, honey. They are the best. You're on a press trip together, and you're joined at the hip, you have these amazing shared experiences that you wouldn't have otherwise, you fuck each other's brains out for a week, and then you get on the plane and never see them again except occasionally on social media.

And then you just like their photos, send heart eyes to each other once in a while, and that's that."

"That's so not me," said Cassie, a little insulted. She hadn't thought about Eamon in that way, and it suddenly made her heart drop into her stomach.

"Oh, okay. I see it now—you're trying to land the man," he joked. "Trying to get a ring on that finger."

"No, that's not it. It's unfair to assume that all women are just out in the world trying to get married. We have other goals and aspirations too." She felt herself getting flustered—men always assumed one thing or the other.

"Yeah, yeah, yeah," he joked, waving her off. "Well, I can tell you that I'm usually up for a little *sumthin, sumthin,* if you know what I mean." His eyebrows were dancing again.

"Yeah, I know what you mean," she said, rolling her eyes.

"Okaaay, Miss Perfect. So you've kept it PG?" He seemed to be losing interest without the promise of salacious details.

"Unfortunately for you," she said in a sheepish tone.

"It's true." He laughed, rolling his head back. "I live for the gossip," he said, turning to look out the window.

At least he was honest.

During dinner, Cassie kept spinning around Ben's comments about Eamon. Was she just a trip fling to him? After years of being in a long-term relationship, she had forgotten about the self-doubt that dating inflicted. The roller coaster of emotions, riding from the highs of wonderfully exciting moments to the lows of worry and anxiety.

More than that, she wanted all the writers on the trip to take her seriously. She wasn't a journalist, or even a writer for that matter, but she wanted to try. She had this new opportunity to prove herself, to improve her writing and her reviews, and to see where this world could take her. Maybe it was just her type A personality kicking in, but she wanted to be a good critic, and she knew that it would require time, education, and patience.

38

Eamon and Cassie were strolling hand in hand through Campo de' Fiori, a market located in central Rome, looking over wood crates filled with fresh artichokes, whole chestnuts, tomatoes on the vine, and tiny wild strawberries no bigger than a penny. She rubbed her thumb along the inside of his hand, feeling like her whole world was protected there in his palm. They meandered through the market, in and out of the stalls, shaded from the intense sun by large canvas umbrellas. Eamon turned around, smiled, and then kissed her deeply, his mouth still tasting like sweet strawberries, before pulling her along to the next vendor. She floated alongside him, letting her eyes wander over the market goods and out into the piazza beyond.

Walking in front of her, his hand still holding hers, he looked back with that wide, bright smile, except his face was not his—instead it was James's. Shocked, Cassie stopped, relieved to see him once again.

"Where have you been?" she asked, curious.

"I've been here—the whole time. I never left you," James said, using his finger to gently push a loose strand of hair behind her ear, the sun now warm against her face. She closed her eyes and savored the warmth of the light, her heart feeling whole and healed. "I told you we would come to Rome," he said, leaning in to kiss her tenderly on the lips, and then again on the sensitive spot on her neck, just

above her collarbone, "I've always wanted to bring you here, and you deserve the best."

She looked up at him and studied the irises of his eyes—green, with a slight aquamarine tint, like a high alpine lake. He kissed her one more time, and she closed her eyes again, savoring his lips, just as she had remembered them.

Cassie sat up in bed, startled, her arms flailing as she searched for James, and found nothing but the hotel pillows beside her. Confused and disoriented, she got up for a glass of water, before curling back into bed to watch the sky turn from dark blue to pink, to orange, and eventually into day. Her mind flooded with the visceral details of him: the way that he smelled, the way the skin on his chest felt when she would tuck her head into the spot just below his shoulder, the way his eyes would shimmer when he was excited about something. Once her heart stopped racing, an overwhelming sense of calm came over her—she was sure that he was okay. That's what he was saying, right? That he was okay, and that he had brought her to Rome, in his own way. After reading his journals and going through so many of his posts, she realized that this trip had *always* been his dream, but was it hers?

A beam of morning light came in through the window, illuminating her room in a golden hue. She went over the dream again and again, recounting each word James had said to her, reveling in the feeling of his presence, even if it was only in her imagination. When he was alive, he was a grounding force for her, someone who made her feel so comfortable and secure, she never had to take risks on her own. She was happy with the status quo— law, routine—because he was so safe. Was she doing the same thing with Eamon? Was she starting to become too dependent on him? Or was this just a fling? Did the others think she was being unprofessional? Would anyone on the Viand board take her seriously if they found out? Did she even belong there? Could she have a future as a critic?

She laced up her running shoes and set out for a run. She was desperate to clear her head and find her center again.

She ran south on the Tiber, dodging vespas and older women out doing their shopping before the heat of the day set in. She crossed the river, circled the Castel Sant'Angelo, the iconic cylindrical castle, and then ran up the wide Via della Conciliazione toward the Vatican. She weaved through the curved colonnades that framed Saint Peter's Square, and bounded up the steps of St. Peter's Basilica just as the Vatican guards were opening the doors. There were a few people waiting to enter, and she filed in behind them, passing through the tremendous portico of the cathedral.

Cassie walked through the doors and into a dark, cold vestibule, then passed through the second set of doors and emerged into a colossal space with enormous gilded arches topped with intricately painted rotundas high above her head. She stopped and let her head fall back, her eyes feasting on the view. The church was awe-inspiring in scale, opulence, and detail. Beyond, glowing arches led into smaller rooms that surrounded the center altar, likely reserved for prestigious families and dignitaries. "Wow," she gasped, as she forced herself to keep walking so that she wasn't blocking the entry.

She crossed over to the side of the nave, steering clear of people there to pray. Two bright beams of light were cutting into the space from the ribbon of windows that sat underneath the cathedral's dome, drawing her into the center of the immense church. She walked slowly, her footsteps quiet and inaudible, tracking the perimeter of the building while she looked at the different altars, chapels, and statues of saints. The basilica made her feel tiny and insignificant. It was, without a doubt, the most opulent display of wealth and power that she had ever seen.

Just then a choir filed into the nave, preparing for rehearsal. Cassie sat down on one of the creaky pews and waited for them to settle in, letting her eyes wander. The choir started singing a slow harmony that filled the gigantic arches of the basilica, before one singular voice rose above the others, the sound simple and angelic, the notes lifting as if to heaven and beyond. Cassie felt her throat pinch, her eyes pool, and she let the tears fall as the music washed over her.

She thought about the last nine months, and the weight of it all—the responsibilities, the grief, the stress. She wanted to feel light again—carefree. She wanted to let go.

And just then, the voices of the choir intensified alongside the soloist, the music getting louder, the sound amplified by the architecture of the church. Her heart started to pound in her chest, and she let the music carry her to where she needed to go.

"Thank you, James," she whispered to the sky. "Thank you for bringing me here and for giving me this new life."

CASSIE CAME DOWN to the lobby at five o'clock on the dot, and Eamon was sitting waiting for her. He was dressed sharper than normal, wearing a linen suit that was tailored to his fit, muscular body. Cassie was dressed more conservatively, in a black business-chic dress, paired with her now signature bold red lip.

"You look nice," Eamon said, standing up to greet her.

"Thank you," she said. "Are you ready to go?"

"Ready as I'll ever be."

They loaded into the car and started to make their way to the restaurant, which was on the far edge of the city. Cassie was quiet, watching the city fly by, her mind still in St. Peter's with the heavenly choir.

They pulled up in front of the Rome Cavalieri hotel under a giant portico, the underside peppered with retro light bulbs reminiscent of a Las Vegas marquee. Eamon opened the car door for her, and she hopped out, leading the way into the lobby of the hotel, which was an eighties version of luxury, adorned with historical oil paintings, overstuffed furniture, gigantic crystal chandeliers, and an impressive circular staircase that wrapped around the lobby.

"I feel like I've stepped back in time," she said under her breath.

They took the elevator up to the restaurant. As Cassie stepped out, she was awestruck by the floor-to-ceiling windows that looked out over the ancient city. From the glassy perch, they could see the entirety of the city, from the Vatican to the surrounding suburbs to the mountains off in the distance.

The maître d' sat them at their table: a generous two-top on the terrace, oriented diagonally so that both seats were optimized for a view over the city, the dome of St. Peter's Basilica off in the distance.

The waiter brought two glasses of complimentary bubbly and handed a hefty menu to Eamon. "Ca' del Bosco Cuvée—enjoy," said the waiter, before slipping off into the kitchen.

Eamon opened the menu, and after a few moments looked at Cassie, leaned in, and said, "You're not going to believe this. This—is a water menu. An entire menu of *water*."

"Seriously?"

"Oh, you heard me right. An entire menu dedicated to water, organized geographically and by mineral content. There are fifty-five on this menu. I've counted."

It was ridiculous, but Cassie stared at her menu, expressionless.

"Have you made a selection?" asked the waiter.

"Is there a water pairing?" asked Eamon.

"Yes, we will send the chef's recommendation."

"Fantastic," said Eamon, clapping the menu shut and handing it over. Once the waiter was gone, Eamon confessed, "That would have sent me into decision fatigue."

Cassie couldn't help but laugh. It was preposterous to her.

"Finally, a smile," said Eamon. "What's going on? You're being awfully quiet."

Cassie looked down, fidgeting with her phone. "Am I?"

"You are," he said. "Is something wrong? You've barely said a word since we left the hotel." He wasn't going to let it go, apparently.

Cassie was silent, and instead of responding, she watched the bubbles climb up the sides of the glass. She wasn't used to such direct confrontation. Usually, when she would go silent, James never said anything; he let her run off to the gym or the office, patiently waiting for her to come back around.

"Hello?" Eamon asked, now looking at her directly. He was not giving up.

Cassie squirmed under the pressure. "I know, I'm sorry, I just . . . feel overwhelmed."

"Overwhelmed about what?" he asked.

"This," she said, gesturing between the two of them. "Us."

"Okay," he said slowly. "I thought we were having a good time here." He sat back, as though he was reconsidering everything that had happened over the last week.

Cassie said nothing, and they were quiet for a few moments, letting the sound of the restaurant fill the emptiness between them.

"I'm pretty sure we've been having a good time," he blurted out. "What changed? Did something happen? Did someone say something?"

And there it was—he hit it square on the nose. She turned her head and looked out at the dome in the distance, remembering the sound of the choir from earlier that day.

"Who was it? Ben? You were with him yesterday, right?"

"It's not about Ben," she said finally. "It's not about anyone specifically. Look, I want to be taken seriously on this trip. I don't want a trip fling to derail this opportunity. And as you know, when romance is involved, it's usually the woman who is discredited."

Eamon sat back in his chair and looked at her. "So you think this is a trip fling?" he asked, a tone of annoyance creeping into his voice.

"I don't think either of us knows yet," she said defensively.

"Look, Cassie. I know you've been through a lot, and I don't know what happened in your previous relationship, but I like you. I'm really attracted to you, and I want to get to know you better."

"I just don't know how much I have to give," she said, being completely honest. "I don't even know what I want. After James died, I found all this—stuff—paraphernalia. Turns out he was a restaurant critic, and he kept it completely hidden from me. He had lied to me for the whole time we were together, and although I've read some things that indicate that he wanted to tell me, he never did. I still feel very betrayed, and I don't know if that piece of me will ever feel whole again."

"Understandable," he said, looking down at the place setting in front of him, fidgeting with a salad fork. "Is that how you got on this trip?"

"No, I entered the competition myself." She lied before she could stop the words from coming out of her mouth. "But this trip was always a goal of his."

"And now you're here."

"I am, and I can't even tell you how far away from my previous life I feel. It's like I'm a whole new person."

"Seems to me like you're a natural. You have a very confident voice."

Cassie laughed. "Yeah, based on what you've seen on social media."

"Isn't that enough?"

"Is it?" She laughed again, nervously. "I'm sure it takes more to be a proven critic."

"Not these days. Besides, it sounds to me like you want to stay on the Viand team," he said, a mischievous smile inching across his face.

She cracked a smile. "Yes, yes, I think I do."

THE REMAINDER OF the evening was a decadent blur. First, a parfait of foie gras that was a plate of frozen foie gras with dehydrated berries that melted in the mouth, coating the tongue with creamy fat, cut by the acidity of the fruit. Then marinated mackerel on caponata, a modern presentation of eggplant, olives, and capers in which the ingredients were arranged in straight lines, so it looked like a painting.

"So, tell me," Eamon asked, "are your posts written to James?"

Cassie felt the blood drain from her face. "I know it's lame, but yes. I guess I feel like I owe it to him."

"Do you miss him?" he asked.

"Of course, but every day gets a little easier. I've gotten better at riding the waves, I guess. I once read that grief is love with nowhere to go, and somehow it helps. It made me realize that I needed to refocus all that energy—and I think posting on Instagram has become that channel. A place to put my love—for the world, for this food, and for myself."

"That's a healthy way to think about it," he said, "as long as it's making you happy."

"I can see how it looks like I'm living in the past and hanging on to something that isn't there anymore."

"Are you?" he asked gently.

"I don't think so. I know he's gone. And I'm strangely relieved that the person I was then is gone too."

The next dish arrived: seaweed, scampi, and squid, sautéed in garlic and butter, served with a simple broth, followed by a modest bowl of tortellini topped with minced herbs. Before taking a bite, Cassie photographed the plate and examined it closely.

"I've read about this dish," she said, suddenly remembering an entry in James's journal. "It's like Italian xiaolongbao. This is the chef's signature dish."

"Well, let's give it a go."

Cassie scooped up one of the glistening pieces of pasta in a gilded spoon, so that she could examine it at eye level. The pasta was so thin that it was almost sheer, barely containing the liquid inside. She put it into her mouth and pushed her tongue to the roof of her palate, releasing the warm and unctuous carbonara sauce in a quick explosion of cream and salty pork.

Eamon stopped after the first bite and dropped his silverware onto the plate. He closed his eyes and chewed, very slowly and tenderly. She watched him pass the bite around in his mouth, the muscles on the sides of his jaw flexing in a way that was undeniably sexy.

"I like watching you eat," she said, now relaxed and at ease.

"See what I mean?"

"I'm joking, obviously," she said, trying to make light of the truth.

"I don't think you are," he said with a wink.

"Eamon?"

He stopped chewing and looked at her. "Cassie?"

"Thank you for being so patient with me. It's been a hard year."

"I know it has, but you're here now. Let yourself enjoy it. Trust me, I've spent lots of time not enjoying myself on the road, because I was eating alone, or I've been paired up with some crusty old guard restaurant critic, or an influencer who is more interested in taking photos of themselves with the food than focusing on the experience or, heaven forbid, the skill required to make such a meal. But *you*—you are a breath of fresh air. You get it. You understand the craft, and how much hard work is required to make it in the culinary world."

"No, I don't," she protested. "I've never set foot in a commercial kitchen."

"Maybe. I'd argue you understand hard work. You know what it means to put your blinders on to get it done. I know because I see it in you. You know how to do your research, and I've watched you during our downtime—on the bus, in the airport. You're constantly googling and researching so you know what questions to ask."

Cassie felt her face go hot. She didn't realize that Eamon had been watching her so closely. "I don't know about that. I'm just doing what feels right. But I have to be honest, it's been great to work side by side with you, Ben, and Rebecca. She's been doing this for what, thirty or forty years?"

"She'll never tell. And somehow she never ages. She's a marvel," he said.

"Truly," Cassie agreed.

The team of servers brought their next dish. "John Dory fillets with squid and shrimp," the waiter whispered.

The dish was presented on a white ceramic steam infuser filled with hot rocks, lemon wedges, and fresh herbs. The waiter poured hot water over the stones and captured the steam under a glass cloche, further cooking the fish with the herbs and fresh citrus.

"So, what do you want to do after this?" she asked. "What's your five-year plan?"

Eamon laughed. "Five-year plan? I'm not sure I've gotten that far. Honestly, I'm enjoying going wherever life takes me. It's a big world out there, and there's so much to see—and eat."

"But you can't do that forever."

"Oh, Cassie," he said, and sighed. "You're such a pragmatist."

"Don't you want some stability?"

"Right now, no. I want to see what life has to offer. You could say that I'm tumbleweeding. So far, it's been working out in my favor. I would like some company on the way, however," he said, the corners of his mouth curling into a smile. "This would be so much more fun with a good partner in crime."

Cassie smiled, flattered.

"Why are you asking?" he asked.

"I guess I'm just trying to understand the road map here," she said. "Where do people take this as a career?"

"I've seen people take it in so many directions. Some become staff at major publications, some continue to freelance, some write books, others go home and become house cats."

"House cats?" she asked curiously.

"Writers and editors who stay in the office."

"Ah, I get it now."

"Some create their own magazines, and some settle down in exotic locales. Some simply travel whenever they can—once a month, once every three months, whatever they can do. Okay, your turn. What's your five-year plan?"

"I don't know. I'm still trying to figure out my one-month plan."

"Is there something tying you down?"

Of course, she still had a full-time job. After all, she was only on sabbatical, and she was supposed to return to her job in just over a month. Part of her knew that this trip was just a fleeting distraction and that at some point she would have to walk back into the office and be a lawyer again. Even though she hated her job, she knew she couldn't completely quit; she had spent three years in law school and months after that studying to pass the bar exam—she was committed.

"No," she said, unsure if she was lying or not.

DESSERT STARTED WITH a selection of cheeses that were served tableside from a wooden trolley. Cassie looked through the glass case like a kid in a candy store, lusting over the spread of cheeses, some soft and creamy, others hard and crystallized, and some with dark blue veins cutting through them. The waiter cut slices from his favorites for the table, including a Parmesan from his hometown, which he recommended that they cover with olive oil and a few drops of balsamic vinegar from Modena. The combination was beautiful—creamy, luxurious, and cut by the crisp acidic flavor of the vinegar.

Although Cassie was full, a tempting dessert arrived in front of her called the Sun, made from three different types of chocolate, passionfruit, and carrot. The small tart was presented on a backlit plate that glowed like the sun.

"And now, for our third dessert," said Eamon, winking at Cassie as he watched the waiters appear with yet another dish: a round red sphere of raspberry sorbet topped with white chocolate custard that melted the sorbet dramatically onto the plate. A final plate of macaroons and tarts completed the meal, along with a glass of Amaro Averna.

The sky had turned a beautiful cobalt blue, and the city was illuminated by glowing orange lights. They paid the bill and paused to enjoy the light summer breeze before heading back downstairs, where a black car was waiting for them.

Eamon picked up her hand and kissed the back of it. "I hope you're not tired," he said. "I want to show you something."

THEIR CAR PULLED up at a dark intersection, and Eamon opened her door and took her hand, leading them down a winding street toward the sound of running water. They turned the corner and saw the Trevi Fountain, its façade lit bright white and the pool a brilliant aquamarine. The sound of the water was deafening, echoing off the buildings surrounding the piazza, filling the area with a hushed sound that created a sense of intimacy. The fountain looked entirely different from what Cassie remembered in those small, glossy guidebooks that she once poured over in bookshops. In reality, the fountain was all-encompassing, and filled all her senses with awe and wonder.

"How did you know I've always wanted to come here?" she asked.

"I just did," he said with a smile, "but I thought you should see it at night."

"We should make a wish," said Cassie, feeling around the bottom of her bag for coins. She came up with two dirty pennies, gave one to Eamon, and held hers tightly between her thumb and her index finger.

"Wait—" he said. "You have to toss it a certain way. You have to throw it with your right hand, and over your left shoulder." Eamon demonstrated, turning his back to the rushing fountain.

Cassie also turned around, held up the coin, kissed it, and threw it into the vast pool, unable to hear it splash over the roar of the fountain.

"What did you wish for?" he asked, slipping his hand into hers.

"More pasta," she joked.

Eamon pushed a strand of hair away from her face, and said, "I think we can make that happen," before leaning in to kiss her.

THEY DECIDED TO walk back to the hotel, wandering through the dark city, the air hot and thick, filled with the smell of jasmine. As they walked, their hands were intertwined, Eamon holding tighter than necessary, like he never wanted to let her go. Every few blocks, he would spin in front of her just so he could get a good look at her face, before smiling and leaning in to kiss her, his eyes wild with excitement.

It took them a long time to make it back to the hotel, and when they got there it was dark and the front door was locked, the lobby empty. They whispered and giggled as they fumbled with their key cards to get into the front gate, rode up the elevator, and stumbled into the hallway outside of his room.

"I don't want this trip to end," Cassie confessed.

"Me either," Eamon said. "I feel like I'm in an alternate universe, and I just met the most amazing, perfect girl."

Cassie blushed. "I don't know about that . . ." she said.

Eamon leaned in to kiss her, soft and gentle. "Do you know how beautiful you are?" he asked, cupping her cheek in his hand. "You're courageous," he said, kissing the palm of her hand. "And intelligent." And now the inside of her arm. "Radiant." He worked his way up her arm, kissing every inch until he reached the small of her neck, making her insides feel hot and gooey.

"Is this a bad idea?" she asked, heart pounding. She didn't want to ruin the moment, but she knew she had to ask.

"How could it be?" he asked, now walking his fingers along her collarbone in an imaginary march.

"Aren't we supposed to be colleagues?"

"Not really—we're all independent contractors here. There's no HR department telling us what we can and cannot do."

She hesitated.

"Come inside," he pleaded, "just for one glass of bubbly." Both of them knew full well it would be more than one drink.

Venice

39

The group stepped out of the Venezia Santa Lucia station, descended a short flight of stairs, and was immediately greeted by the Grand Canal, the major aquatic thoroughfare that cut through the city of Venice. A water taxi was waiting for them, and they hesitantly handed their bags over to the attendants. Eamon boarded easily, like he had grown up on a boat, gracefully hopping from the dock onto the hull. Cassie, on the other hand, awkwardly managed to get herself on board with the help of both attendants, and then immediately slid into a seat, worried she might lose her balance, and her dignity.

Ben sat down next to her and instantly started filming. "Come on, Cass, let's selfie," he said, holding his camera out at arm's length. Cassie dug her sunglasses out of her bag and made her best kissy face for Ben's followers.

Once everyone was loaded, the taxi began its journey south, slowly making its way along the winding canal. Everyone in the group had their phones out and ready, snapping photos and taking videos of the stunning city, catching glimpses of the picturesque side streets, horn-shaped gondolas, and noble waterfront palazzos.

Cassie took a moment to look around at her fellow travelers. Rebecca sat near the front of the boat, with a chic scarf wrapped around her silvery hair and a pair of large Prada cat-eye sunglasses. She looked like the epitome of old Hollywood beauty, an actress who had stepped out from a frame of an old movie. Kelly was on the phone, flipping through her folders of itineraries and documents, making sure that reservations were in place and everything was in order. Ben continued to film, now pointing out monuments and tourist attractions to his followers. And on the far side of the boat was Eamon, looking as cool and handsome as ever, calmly taking in the views of the city as if he had seen it all before, likely because he had. He caught her looking at him, and he bit his lip flirtatiously, sending a jolt through Cassie's body. She aimed her camera lens at him and took a few photos. There was nothing she wanted more than to tuck into the nook under his arm, so that she could lose herself in his intoxicating cologne, but calmer heads prevailed, and she stayed on the other side of the boat, admiring his beauty from afar.

The color of the canal was a beautiful teal that was reminiscent of a tropical locale. The canal was framed on either side by Gothic buildings that were built right up to the edge of the water, with docks and recessed inlets for boats to land.

As they passed the Basilica di Santa Maria della Salute, an octagonal cathedral adorned with statues and architectural filigrees, the mouth of the canal opened into an enormous waterway filled with everything from large sailboats with tall wooden masts to small, Chris-Craft wooden speedboats that looked like they were straight out of an old James Bond movie. Off in the distance Cassie could see small islands that were populated with Venetian Gothic buildings, domed churches, and spires reaching up toward the sky.

Suddenly, they turned into a narrow canal, passed under a

small bridge, and pulled up to a crimson dock where hotel attendants helped the boat land, then ushered the group into a small,
dark reception area and into the lobby of the Hotel Danieli.

As Cassie stepped into the gorgeous, light-filled atrium, she
gasped, completely overwhelmed by the scene in front of her. It
was a collision of architectural styles: Gothic, Italian Renaissance
with Islamic influences, rich with the textures of Persian rugs,
gilded ceilings, and Murano glass chandeliers above. Her eye followed the crimson carpet up a staircase that wound around the
interior of the lobby, reaching toward the skylight, capped with a
detailed stained-glass ceiling.

"What do you think of the hotel?" said Kelly, practically sneaking up behind her.

"It's . . . exquisite. I didn't think anything could be better than
the hotel in Rome, and yet here we are." Cassie gestured at the
lobby.

"Hotel Danieli is a very special place. The original palace
is from the fourteenth century and was the Palazzo Dandolo,
home of a multigenerational family that served as the Doges of
Venice."

"How do you know about all these amazing hotels?" asked
Cassie, in awe.

"I wrote for travel magazines for years. It was so much fun."

"Why did you stop?"

"Oh, you know. Money. Family. Babies. I needed to stop traveling, and I needed a consistent paycheck."

"Adulting," Cassie said compassionately.

"Exactly," Kelly confirmed. "Rest up. You only have a few hours
before the party. We will meet in the lobby at six o'clock."

"And if I want to see the city?"

"Head right over to Piazza San Marco, pop into Basilica San Marco, and pick one museum, if you must, either the Palazzo Ducale or the Peggy Guggenheim, but honestly, I would just wander and get lost in the streets of Venice. It's an incredible city. Just don't be late!"

"So, basically, I should have been asking you for tips this whole time?"

"Probably," said Kelly, as she handed Cassie her hotel key, a skeleton key on a weighty burgundy silk tassel that was soft and heavy in her hand.

CASSIE FELT TIRED from the travel, and all she wanted was to go for a run. She knew she would feel better after a little exercise. As she unpacked, she kept having flashbacks to the night before when they were tangled in Eamon's bedsheets, feeling the extents of each other's skin. She put her arm up to her nose and could faintly smell Eamon, a trace of balsam fir and ginger. Her body continued to vibrate with the memory of his touch and how he looked into her eyes, as if taking her in for the first time. She could feel his fingers running through her hair, along the back of her head, and onto the soft spots of her neck. She longed to feel his lips on her collarbones again, drawing an invisible line along her shoulders, moving into the nook under her shoulder blades and then down her spine to the small of her back, tender and vulnerable.

She felt like time had slowed down for them, making the night extra-long so that she had more time to explore him, studying the area where his abs met the bottom of his sternum, the insides of his arms, and his back, broad and wide. They stayed up sharing secrets about their guilty pleasures, where they wanted to travel to the most, favorite movies, and first loves while playing snippets from their favorite, formative teenage albums—quietly, so no one else could hear.

There was comfort in the silence of the night and under the blanket of darkness. Cassie felt safe with their secret, and for a few spellbinding hours, they felt completely alone in the world. Nothing else mattered. But once the birds started chirping, she felt a sense of panic and returned to her room, leaving Eamon alone in their sweat-soaked bedsheets.

DRESSED IN HER running clothes, Cassie felt like a time traveler as she passed through the lobby of the fourteenth-century hotel, heading out onto the street, crowded with tourists. She followed the pedestrian-congested streets until she got to Piazza San Marco, which opened into an enormous football-field-size square filled with just as many pigeons as selfie-snapping tourists. She cut through the short end of the square and started to weave her way through the labyrinth of a city, preferring the small, winding side streets to the large thoroughfares.

She let the city guide her, taking bridges to shortcut across the canals and the quaint backstreets lined with dark green mold climbing over the centuries-old stone walls. Once she was able to get away from the touristy areas, she began to understand that Venice was like any city—there were corner stores, pharmacies, shops, and offices. But the streets were made of water, and instead of taxis, there were gondolas.

When Cassie got back to the hotel, she drew herself a bath in the giant marble bathtub in her suite. It was the night of the Vi- and gala, and she was nervous about her first formal event with the team.

Bzzzz.

RUBY: Hey girl hey. How are things on the great food tour?

CASSIE: Incredible.

She snapped a photo of her current view, her red toenails poking out of the tub, her dress hanging on the back of the bathroom door, where she had hung it to steam the wrinkles out.

RUBY: OoooOooOOooo! What's the event?

CASSIE: The Viand Nominee and Achievement Awards Gala. It's not quite the final awards ceremony— kind of a warm-up for the big event that happens in the fall.

RUBY: I love a fancy party.

CASSIE: I know you do.

RUBY: 😆

CASSIE: I have to tell you something . . .

RUBY: I'm listening.

Cassie sent Ruby a photo from the taxi ride of Eamon looking out over the grand canal.

RUBY: Who is that? Paul Newman's son?

CASSIE: I guess I can see it . . .

RUBY: What's the story there?

CASSIE: I'm not sure, but I can report back that whatever is happening sure is hot.

RUBY: 🔥 🚒 You're making me proud.

CASSIE: Hahahaha. We're having a nice time. I'm trying to be careful, though. The trip ends in less than two weeks, and I'm sure he already has the rest of the year booked out with trips . . . and I'll be back at my desk in New York. 😔

RUBY: Cassie. I give you permission to change the plan. Go with the flow.

CASSIE: ?

RUBY: Don't come home yet.

CASSIE: Oh. I never even thought of that.

RUBY: Of course you didn't.

CASSIE: I don't even know if he really likes me—what if it is just a fling?

RUBY: First of all, who cares. You deserve to have some fun. And second of all, I'm sure he does like you. You're amazing, you're beautiful, you're wonderful, you're a goddess!

CASSIE: hahahaha

RUBY: I'm your #1 fan!

CASSIE: I know you are. And in case I haven't said it to you—thank you.

RUBY: You have. But I know you well enough to know that you have a tendency to be very guarded. So just try to be open to him, to this trip, to LIFE. Let him love you, Cass. Let him love all of you.

CASSIE: 🫶

At six o'clock on the dot, Cassie rode the elevator down to the lobby, taking a moment to check her outfit and her makeup in the elevator's antique mirrors. She was wearing the red Givenchy dress she bought in Paris, the shape tracing over her waist and onto her hips, the neckline's cutouts showing just enough cleavage to be considered sexy but professional. Her hair was pulled into a soft bun, and she'd accessorized with the gold sculptural earrings, gold shoes, bright red lipstick, and a pair of oversize black sunglasses that she tucked into her crimson clutch.

The lobby of the hotel was cleared out for the party, and guests were starting to trickle in through the front doors and into the main hall of the hotel, the marble floor reflecting the evening sunlight across the room. In the corner, tucked into the Bar Dandolo, she saw Kelly, Rebecca, and Ben, who were sitting down in ornate armchairs enjoying a glass of champagne.

"Beautiful dress, darling," Ben said, standing up to twirl her around. "It fits you like a glove."

"Thank you for helping me find it, darling," she retorted, before giving him an air kiss on either cheek.

"Chin-chin," Kelly said, handing her a glass of wine. "I know I've said this a thousand times, but thank you so much for coming. You've been such a delightful add to the group."

"Thank *you*," Cassie gushed. "Thank you for having me. The whole trip has been more than I ever thought it could be. I'll never be able to adjust to normal life ever again."

"Yeah," said Kelly with a shrug. "That's a thing."

"So, who is coming to this party?" asked Cassie.

"Quite a few of the nominees will be here, as well as some of the people we are honoring with other awards, lifetime achievement awards, and donors to the Viand Awards. Some, not all, of the review teams are flying in too—the Asia team, the Australia team, and a few people from the South America team. Also, our CEO, COO, you know—the usual players."

"But keep your eyes peeled," added Ben. "There will be quite a few star chefs here tonight, and it's a great opportunity to ask questions for upcoming stories."

Her mind flashed back to the awards ceremony party she'd gone to with James in New York, glittering with the who's who of the culinary scene, at least in the United States.

"Is this more of the European representation?" she asked.

"Exactly. We know it can be hard for teams to travel, so we move the parties to different cities around the world. Plus, it's more fun that way," Kelly added.

Eamon stepped out of the elevator wearing a white dinner jacket with black trousers, a crisp black bowtie, and a small red rose on his left lapel. He walked over to the bar, greeting everyone with air kisses. "Sorry I'm a few minutes late, I got stuck on a call."

"Mmm-hmmm," Kelly said, handing him a glass of champagne. "You look thirsty."

"How did you know?" he asked, raising his glass to everyone in the group.

Wow, Eamon mouthed silently to Cassie, looking her up and down as though he was devouring her with his eyes. She could smell his cologne, cedar and lemon verbena, and she thought about peeling off his jacket and unbuttoning his shirt one button at a time.

Cassie looked around, appreciating the moment. Here she was at this beautiful party, surrounded by a group of talented writers whom she truly admired, feeling like she had finally cracked the code. Her new Instagram handle was doing well, her numbers were growing, and she felt like her content was getting better every day. Her writing was getting better, and she was more confident in what she had to say. She felt like a new woman, standing there in that Venetian hotel, and for the first time in months, she thought of James and didn't feel that familiar colossal wave of grief. Instead, it just felt like he was there with her, for a moment, telling her that he was okay, and she was going to be okay too.

And in that moment of calm, she knew she didn't want to go back to law. For the first time, Cassie felt clarity about what she wanted to do next, and what kind of path she needed to take so that she could build a new career. She didn't have a road map, and she certainly didn't have a plan, but she sensed the potential and it excited her. Like anything, she knew that it would take hard work and dedication, but she felt confident that she could turn this opportunity into something bigger for herself. For the first time in years, Cassie felt happy.

"Shall we start exploring?" Kelly asked. "There are activations in every room, and I want to be sure to see everything before the awards show at eight."

"Let's go," said Ben, camera ready.

THEY MADE THEIR way through the lobby, stopping to admire the ornate ice sculptures, decadent displays of caviar tins and fresh oysters, seasonal vegetables fried tempura style, and bites of fried spaghetti topped with Parmesan cream, presented on a stick like a lollipop.

"This is like a Best of Venice food tour," joked Ben, panning around the room with his camera. "I love it."

"Usually, these parties have a little bit more of an international feel, but since we're in Venice, we decided to highlight local chefs," said Kelly. "I think it's nice to have a specific focus."

When no one was looking, Eamon tucked behind Cassie and pressed his body against hers, whispering in her ear, "You look absolutely incredible, Cass. I can't keep my eyes off you."

Her chest filled with butterflies, and she felt excited and

empowered. "You don't look half bad yourself," she joked, turning around to meet his sparkling eyes.

"Thank you," he said, refusing to break eye contact with her. "I'm having a hard time putting this into words, but I can't get over you." He gave a small shake of his head. "That dress . . ."

"Ben deserves all the credit."

"I'm glad he's not wearing it," he joked, before leaning close and saying in a low growl, "I can't wait to take it off you."

Her skin shimmered with anticipation. She couldn't wait for the awards ceremony to start—and end. She thought about tracing her fingers along the Laguiole wine key tattoo inked into the inside of Eamon's biceps, onto his chest, and around the hook-shaped scar on his abdomen.

When everyone had tried all the dishes, they made their way upstairs and into the formal dining rooms of the hotel, which was lined with fourteenth-century portraits of popes and had glittering chandeliers. There were more tables with more culinary delights: bites of creamy burrata ravioli, hazelnut gelato, tiny fried crabs served with polenta, and cups of black squid-ink pasta topped with edible flowers. A band was set up in the corner of the grand room, playing to partygoers who sipped champagne and chatted with the chefs working the tables.

The next floor was the restaurant of the hotel, decorated with gold and navy damask wallpaper, red velvet chairs, gold-framed glass and mirror wall panels flanked by delicate red sconces, and a mirrored ceiling that reflected the scene of the canal deep into the restaurant. They passed through the dark dining room and onto the balcony, where they were greeted with a blast of evening sunlight that covered the party in a warm orange hue.

Waiters carried trays of Campari spritz cocktails that looked like glowing red orbs, served with slices of fresh orange, and guests nibbled on canapes as they visited the different tables covered in decadent displays: seafood towers filled with shrimp, snow crab, oysters, clams, and freshly boiled langoustine tails, six large copper pots filled with different kinds of risotto simmering at a low temperature, intricate, multicolored stained-glass raviolis stuffed with smoked salmon and cream cheese, and a bread display that looked like an abstract sculpture.

In between bites, the group shared the moments from their day in Venice.

"Oh my god, you guys, I had the most incredible gelato today," Ben said, showing the group the clip on his phone. "It was from this tiny gelateria, Bacaro del Gelato, and the stracciatella was to die for." The group of critics erupted into conversation, each sharing their opinions on who made the best gelato in Venice, and the conversation quickly spiraled into the best gelato in Italy, with people reminiscing about cones from Florence, Positano, and Cinque Terre.

"I'm more of a cicchetti woman myself," said Rebecca. "Handsome bachelors always love a good aperitivo." She raised her Campari spritz toward the center of the group.

Not far off in the distance, a massive Star Clipper with its sails raised came into view, inspiring oohs and ahhs from everyone on the terrace. The boat crossed through the lagoon, slowly weaving through the archipelago and past the dome-topped islands in the distance. Cassie posted a few photos of the view to her stories, along with a photo of the impressive seafood tower.

A waiter came by with prepared bites of Cappelli spaghetti cooked with butter and fresh lemon and topped with a spoon of

Italian caviar and parsley. Cassie felt the little hairs on her arms stand up with delight, and her whole body reveled in the flawless combination of flavors.

She looked over to Eamon, who was also clearly enjoying the dish. "Let the caviar be the hero," said Cassie, before flashing Eamon a big smile.

As the group chatted, Cassie let her eyes wander over the other guests: chic, wealthy couples, familiar-looking chefs she recognized from magazines and TV shows, PR people, and then—David? Across the terrace, she spotted a familiar face. David, James's old friend, was dressed in a tux and a pair of circular black sunglasses. Her heart started to race—it couldn't be him, could it?

Still watching, she took a step back and discreetly took cover behind Eamon's shoulder as he chatted with Ben about caviar pairings. Could it really be David? Surely, he was in New York, eating at an overpriced steakhouse, not here, in Venice, at the Viand gala. But then David saw her and started walking in her direction with urgency.

"Cassie, what a surprise," he said, leaning in to give her an air kiss on each cheek.

The mere idea of feigning happiness at seeing him made her sick to her stomach. He was the last person she wanted to see.

"Yeah, um, nice to see you, David."

"What are you doing here?" he asked pointedly.

"Um . . ." she stammered, trying to move out of earshot of the group, but David refused to budge. "I'm, um, here with the Viand Awards."

"Oh, really?" he asked, hostility creeping into his voice. "I had no idea that you were into food. Aren't you a lawyer?"

The group suddenly started to hush around them, and Cassie could tell that Ben, Kelly, Rebecca, and Eamon were now tuned in to her conversation with David.

"Uh, yeah. You knew that. Didn't you know that I write on the side?" she lied.

"I missed that detail," he deadpanned. "You know, it's funny, James never mentioned that you were a writer."

Cassie knew that she was cooked.

"Oh, he didn't?" She squirmed, wanting the conversation to be over so she could run back to her room and cry.

"No. I know James was @NewYorkSecretDiner," David said, his voice growing louder. "And I know that you have been posting on his account. I know about the award he won, and the invitation for *him* to review for *the Viand Awards*," he shouted. The party suddenly hushed, and everyone turned to see what was happening. "I know it was you. I know that you're impersonating him. Or should I put it this way—you stole his *fucking* identity."

David held his phone in front of her face. "You're the one posting on James's account. It's you. I know it's you."

Cassie's heart sank. There it was, the image of the clipper that was supposed to go on @EatPostLike but instead was posted on @NewYorkSecretDiner. Her stomach dropped, and her entire body was hit with a wave of nausea.

"Um, I'm not sure I know what you're talking about," said Cassie.

She nervously looked around her new group of friends, this wonderful group of people she had gained so much respect and love for over the trip. She didn't want to disappoint them.

"Did you seriously think I didn't know?" David asked, almost insulted. "He was my best friend. I knew everything about him.

Of course I knew that he was @NewYorkSecretDiner. Food was one of the things we had in common. When you were working weekends, who do you think he called to go out? Me. You never understood or appreciated his passion for food or the culinary world—and he knew it. Did you seriously think you could hide this from me?"

"Um . . . I can explain," Cassie said, her heart racing and her mind unable to form any sort of logical explanation.

"It's a very simple question, Cassie. Did you take over James's Instagram account?"

Cassie hated it when people used her name in an accusatory manner like that. It made her feel like a child.

David didn't wait for her to answer, instead continuing his barrage. "You were sloppy, Cassie. You used his account to promote yours, and you clearly didn't think anyone would notice. I did. You should have answered my messages, Cassie. You didn't, so I booked a flight, and here you are."

"Um . . . I—I . . ."

"How could you? This account was James's life's work, his passion project, and you're just going to *take* it from him after his death? You're disgusting," he said sharply. The last word hung in the air like a spoiled piece of fish, and was followed by gasps from the crowd.

Cassie took a moment to look around, a feeling of overwhelming heaviness coming over her. She had managed to ruin this beautiful party, filled with important chefs, restauranteurs, critics, and Eamon. Oh, Eamon—it seemed as if he liked her for who she really was, despite her lies and deceit.

"I'm . . . I'm sorry," Cassie sputtered as she ran for the door.

BACK IN HER room, Cassie frantically packed her bags while tears streamed down her face. She was mortified—embarrassed for being found out, for letting James's secret be revealed, for being so damn *sloppy*. She felt like a fraud, an interloper. She didn't belong here. *How could I be so stupid?* she thought, the negative talk in her mind blaring louder than ever.

Cassie did the only thing that made sense in that moment: she booked a flight home to New York.

New York

40

The next day, Cassie landed at JFK, and she walked off the plane feeling broken, her face swollen from crying. She had spent the duration of the flight staring off into space, unable to focus. She just gazed out the window, watching the clouds float by, feeling the tears fall down her cheeks.

She knew that this was the end, that there was no way anyone else would invite her on another trip after they knew that she had stolen her dead boyfriend's famous Instagram account and leveraged it for herself. What once seemed like an honorable thing to do—bring life back to James's passion project—now felt like a complete betrayal and an endless source of embarrassment.

Cassie tapped out an email to the HR department at her firm: *Good afternoon, my trip was suddenly cut short. I'm available to come back to work tomorrow.* With that email, more than any other, she felt like a complete failure. Just a few days ago, she had decided that she didn't want to return to law, hopeful that she had found a new path, but here she was groveling to get back into her personal hell. She wanted to disappear, but the thought of sitting at home and doing nothing felt worse.

On Monday morning, Cassie put on her best navy blue suit and snapped into her old routine. She made a green smoothie, drank it before leaving, and took her usual commute, stopping for a cup of coffee at the shop around the corner from her office. She hadn't come up with a story to explain *why* she was back early, but she knew it would come in time. Ran out of money? Missed the office? It didn't really matter; it was a lie. She just needed enough of an excuse to get people to stop asking.

When she got to the floor of her office, she rounded the cubicles and arrived at her desk—cleanish, but now covered in a veil of dust. Her ZZ plant in the corner was looking sad and thirsty. Ruby had not been watering it like she had promised. Cassie picked up the plant, walked it over to the office kitchen, and put it in the sink, dousing it with water.

Unsurprisingly, Ruby was standing in the doorframe, as if on cue.

"What the fuck are you doing here?" she asked, always to the point.

"It's a long story. I'm not ready to talk about it yet," said Cassie. "I thought you were going to water my plant?"

"I got busy. Why are you back? I thought it was going so well?" Ruby asked.

"I got made. Found out."

"By who?" asked Ruby.

"David."

"Who is David? Sorry, I'm catching up on a lot here."

"James's childhood friend. Apparently, he knew about @New YorkSecretDiner when James was alive, and he came to Venice to find me because I was avoiding him online. He is weirdly invested in it. He said that I disgraced James's work and reputation."

"What happened?"

"He caught on to me—he started following me on Instagram and he noticed that I was sharing my posts on @NewYorkSecret Diner to help grow my following. He confronted me at the party in Venice and completely humiliated me."

"Motherfucker."

"I know."

"So—just to be clear—you were pretending to be @NewYork SecretDiner?"

"Yes, Ruby! You know all of this. I accepted the invitation as @NewYorkSecretDiner—as James." Cassie felt her voice rising out of frustration. "That was how I was invited on the trip. But it was obvious that they were going to figure it out, so I stopped posting on James's account and I created my own. But now I'm sure that I will never be invited back on another trip, and none of these people will ever take me seriously again."

There was a pause. Ruby poured herself a cup of tea and added a generous dollop of oat milk, turning the liquid from black to brown.

"So, question. Did anyone from the trip confront you after this . . . altercation?"

"No, I just left. I completely panicked. I bought a plane ticket and left on the first flight out. I couldn't bear the shame."

"That sounds like you. But, again, just clarifying here: Did anyone at Viand tell you it was an issue that you accepted the invitation on James's behalf? You were still doing the work, weren't you? Experienced or not, you were doing good work, no?"

"Honestly, I don't even know. I just bolted. I was horrified. Maybe keeping it secret meant more to me than it did to anyone else. All I know is that it was important to James that the account be anonymous, so it was important to me. It certainly meant something to David. He was *pissed*." Cassie rolled her eyes dramatically, her frustration about the situation pouring out of her.

"Okay, okay, but who on the trip told you that this was an issue?"

"Stop lawyering me," snapped Cassie. "I was wrong. I was wrong for taking over James's account, and wrong for lying to everyone. I didn't deserve to be there in the first place." Cassie dropped her head, letting the tears fall.

Ruby sweetly put her arm around her and let the silence fill the break room. After a few moments, she said, "I know you're embarrassed, Cassie. You've been through so much this year. Give yourself a break. You don't have to be perfect, and you certainly don't always have to be right. I think at the end of the day you'll see that this was just a bump in the road."

"Maybe," said Cassie, sniffling. "I was just ready for something else. I got a taste of something new, and it was *exciting*. And, oh my god, Ruby, this world—I can't even describe how wonderful it was to be on this trip, surrounded by such intelligent people, staying in bucket list hotels, eating at restaurants that most people only dream about. I was ready for a big life change, and it felt like I had found it. But now I'm back here, back where I started." Cassie paused for a minute, before adding, "The thing I keep coming back to, over and over again, is the fact that James lied to me for so long. How was I supposed to know what was going on—or the nuances of the situation? How was I supposed to know who was in on James's secret? How could I have known that David knew all along that James was @New YorkSecretDiner?"

"You couldn't have known, Cass. And frankly, it was really

shitty that David didn't say something to you after James died. It was like he was holding that over you to prove that he was closer to James than you were. It's bizarre."

"You know, it was nice to be away and with a group of people who knew nothing about James. It was a fresh start, and it felt really good. They didn't look at me with pity, they didn't feel like they needed to walk on eggshells around me. For a few short weeks, I was free of this nightmare. Free of this fucking job, my fucking dead boyfriend, this fucking city." Cassie could feel the rage starting to bubble up—it all felt so unfair. "And then this guy—*this* guy—shows up and ruins it all. They will never take me seriously again, and why would they? I'm nothing but a fraud."

"Aw, Cass. You're good at everything you do," said Ruby, trying to reassure her.

"That's not true."

"It is. And I bet you were doing a great job at the reviews too." Ruby shrugged. "I'm just surprised you didn't tell anyone."

"Once a secret diner, always a secret diner," said Cassie.

"But why? Why does it matter?"

"Again, it just felt like it was important to James. He put so much effort into maintaining anonymity, it seemed like he would have wanted it to stay that way."

"But just so I understand, no one else on the trip had a secret alias?"

"Not that I know of. I don't know—maybe it is a crazy constraint I put on myself. Maybe it doesn't matter."

"Would it matter to his followers?"

"Absolutely. The mysterious identity is part of the fun."

"But you have your own account now—couldn't that just be your digital identity?"

"Absolutely."

"And you want to keep doing it?"

"I do. It's been so nice to get out of this office and do something that isn't doc review. It felt good to create something, instead of always trying to tear something apart."

"Can you go back?" asked Ruby.

"Could I, or should I?"

CASSIE'S PHONE RANG for the fifth time that day, and she quickly silenced it. It was Kelly—calling to scold her, Cassie was sure. It had been a few days since she left Venice, and she still hadn't spoken with anyone from the trip.

Where are you? the text message read.

Cassie ignored it. But just a few minutes later she received another text message.

> **KELLY:** I know you left Venice. Please call me. I just want to make sure you're okay.

Reluctantly, Cassie called her back, waiting a few seconds for the call to connect, followed by the signature ringtone of an international call.

"Cassie?" Kelly answered, clearly panicking.

"Hi, Kelly. Yes, it's me."

"Where are you?"

"I'm in New York."

There was a pause. "Okaaaaay." Kelly was clearly not happy.

"I'm sorry. I panicked. The only thing I could think of was to come home. I was freaking out."

"Look, Cassie, I get it. It was a stressful situation. I just wish you had talked to me before booking a ticket back to New York."

"I'm sorry for disappearing like that," said Cassie, realizing the implications of her actions for the first time.

"I've seen some shit on these trips, but I've never had anyone just *leave*. It doesn't make me look good, you know?"

Cassie felt guilty—she hadn't thought through how the situation would play out when she booked a one-way ticket back to New York. She didn't think about Kelly, Viand, or even the restauranteurs whose business depended on how many stars they would be awarded. "I'm sorry. How can I make this up to you?"

"Come back. We need you in Barcelona in five days. Do whatever it takes to get your head right, but please come back. The owner of Moments has asked for you, and you, specifically."

"Seriously?"

"Seriously," Kelly repeated. "No one would have guessed that you didn't have the credentials or experience. I think we all assumed that you were diligent about doing your research. Your reviews have been wonderful. You come at this from a different perspective—now I understand why—but with that comes a new way of looking at a restaurant. It's refreshing. Additionally, you've been a pleasure to travel with, you have gotten along well with everyone in the group, you ask the right questions, you're curious, and your photos are exquisite. You deserve to be here. But I'll be honest, you've put me in a tough situation. I vouched for you to be on this trip, and I can't find anyone else to fill your spot at this point. I'd really appreciate it if you came back and finished the trip. The hotels are already paid for, so please, just come back and finish."

"Let me think about it."

CASSIE FELT TERRIBLE. She had acted impetuously and hadn't thought through the consequences of her leaving—not necessarily for her, but for everyone else. After all, this was a job, and she was expected to deliver her work.

It was the middle of the afternoon, and Cassie took a moment to look out of the office window and watch an afternoon rainstorm blow into the city. It passed quickly, dropping a sudden barrage of rain onto the city streets, before rolling up the Hudson River.

She thought back on the trip, fully acknowledging what an amazing opportunity it was. Not many people got the chance to travel across Europe, spending time in some of the world's most iconic cities, eating at world-renowned restaurants. And of course, there was Eamon. She had so many apologies to make.

> **CASSIE:** Hi David, can we talk?

> **DAVID:** I said everything I needed to in Venice.

> **CASSIE:** I want to apologize. I was wrong. I know how much you loved James, and I'm sure it felt like just as much of a betrayal to you as it would have to him.

> **DAVID:** . . .

> **CASSIE:** I'm sorry.

> **DAVID:** Thank you, Cass. We both lost someone we loved. You

deserve to be happy, and if this
makes you happy then so be it.

CASSIE: It's not about that . . .

DAVID: But it is. And you've represented
him well. James would have been proud.

CASSIE: 🖤

"Cassie, welcome back. We have you on doc review," said
Bryce, the new middle manager on the team. "I need your notes
by morning."

"Um, thank you. I'm still getting my bearings, and there hasn't
been time to be properly briefed on the case," she stammered,
knowing that the ask was impossible after looking at the stack
of three file boxes now in her cubicle. "And given that I'm coming back after some extended time away, I don't think tomorrow
morning is a realistic timeframe for me to go through all of these
documents."

"I don't want excuses," he said. "I want it done by nine a.m."

"Bryce, this isn't reasonable. I'm happy to provide a timeline,
but tomorrow morning isn't feasible."

"I want it in the morning," he said sternly, before looking back
at his phone and walking away.

Cassie seethed. This guy—the new guy—was flexing to show
his power over her, and there was nothing less incentivizing
than middle management trying to establish power. She knew
this was going to be a problem, and if they weren't working well

together from the get-go, they would probably continue to butt heads throughout the duration of the case.

Cassie looked at the stack of file boxes and felt sick to her stomach. None of these inter-office altercations were new to her, but today, they filled her with rage.

CASSIE WALKED INTO Bryce's office, knocking on the door as she entered.

"Can we discuss this deadline?" she asked, trying to keep calm despite the ringing in her ears.

"Cassie, I'm not interested in hearing your excuses," he said. "This is clearly outlined in your job description. We need it tomorrow, so I recommend you get to work."

"Well, Bryce, I don't work that way anymore. This is an unrealistic timeframe, and I'm not going to agree to set myself up for failure." She paused, suddenly fearful to say what needed to be said, because she knew it was the only way forward. "I think. I think . . . it's time for me to go." She paused. "Yes," she confirmed, "it's time."

"You're quitting? Now?" he asked, flabbergasted.

"Yes. I quit. Right now!" She spun on her heel, suddenly desperate for fresh air. It was the only thing that could calm her now.

"Good luck, sweetheart. I'll make sure you don't get another job in law in this city."

"Maybe that's for the best," she said, before stopping by her cubicle to pick up her purse and blowing Ruby an air kiss across the pen. Without missing a beat, Ruby caught the kiss in midair and smooshed her closed fist against her chest.

Barcelona

41

The taxi pulled up in front of the hotel, the Mandarin Oriental, a large stone building with a tremendous three-door stone portico and uniformed bellmen standing outside. The hotel was converted from an old bank, the first story comprised of large, rustic blocks of stone, and then smoother stone as it rose up toward the sky, reminding Cassie of the art deco–style buildings in New York.

She passed through the entryway and followed the navy blue carpet adorned with flowers over a bridge that crossed through the atrium and into the main lobby of the hotel. She passed by ornate, lacey white screens on either side that helped her eyes adjust from the bright Spanish sun to the dark, intimate lobby with gilded mirrors overhead.

After checking in, she looked down into the atrium and saw Ben, Kelly, and Rebecca having breakfast. Her stomach twisted into a knot, and she felt a wave of anxiety roll over her. She doubted her decision to come back and questioned if she should have stayed in New York.

AFTER A SHOWER, Cassie took some time to rest in her hotel room. She stretched, meditated, and did everything she could to put herself in a better place mentally. She felt exposed and vulnerable. Was still in the process of mentally unpacking the fact that she had quit her job—officially. Just the thought of being *unemployed* filled her with panic, self-doubt, and fear.

Cassie looked at the clock: 1:17. She was late, and she didn't want to keep Kelly waiting.

KELLY WAS SEATED at a table in the garden terrace, vigorously tapping away at her phone. The table was neatly tucked into a dreamy verdant niche, with overgrown vines crawling around the banquette, climbing to cover the trellis above.

"I'm sorry I'm late," Cassie said, slipping into one of the high-backed wicker chairs across the table. She was nervous about getting too close to Kelly—she had no idea how this conversation was going to go.

"Hi there. I'm happy to see you," Kelly said, looking down at her watch. "I was starting to get nervous that you didn't get on the plane."

"I'm really sorry for making your job difficult," said Cassie, her voice soft and full of remorse.

Kelly paused. "I'm just thrilled you're here. Now that you are, can you tell me what happened? Exactly."

Cassie took a deep breath. She owed it to Kelly to tell her the truth, and now was the time.

"James, my boyfriend—he's gone," Cassie sputtered. "He's the one who won the culinary journalism award. He died in September, and I recently discovered his Instagram account when I was clearing out his apartment. I . . ." She paused and took a deep breath. "I started posting on his account, pretending to be him. I know, it's horrible, and hard to explain. I guess you could say I was jealous. I just wanted a taste of his life, the one he kept hidden from me. Anyway, I saw your invitation, and I was so desperate for something new, a fresh start, that I accepted. On his behalf," she added, unsure if it would make the story seem any less horrible.

"Okay," Kelly said, waiting for the rest.

"David is James's best friend. He has been messaging me for the past month or so, but I ignored him, which clearly upset him. So he came to find me."

"Wait—James never told *you* about @NewYorkSecretDiner?" Kelly asked.

"No, I found out after he died." Cassie's heart sank. Hearing it laid out so simply made her feel like a morally corrupt person— like a thief. "Look, I know it sounds terrible, and it is," Cassie finally choked out. "I shouldn't have done it, and I feel horrible about it in retrospect. It was devastating to learn that he had another identity and another life that he just kept hidden from me. I felt completely betrayed, left out, and angry—*on top* of my grief. I saw your message, and all I wanted to do was run away from my pathetic life, run away from the sadness, and have my own adventure."

"Well, I'm glad you came," said Kelly. "You've been doing a great job. Your reviews have been phenomenal. You get it."

"Well, that's a surprise, because I have felt like I've had to put in so much work just to understand the *basics* of the culinary world. I feel like a fish out of water."

"You can't tell from over here," Kelly said kindly. "The truth is that most of our readers experience a restaurant from an untrained perspective. They aren't looking for flaws in a sauce or a slight hiccup in service. They want to experience the magic that a restaurant can offer. They want to be wowed, so sometimes a critic who has the same vantage point can offer a fresh, honest review."

Cassie was relieved that Kelly had an open mind and was beginning to appear like she was not going to hold the incident in Venice against her.

"But I must be honest, this is a business and you're here to do a job. I just need your review, and I need it done well. I know you've been through a lot, and this is clearly triggering for you. Can you do it? Can you give me one last review?"

"Of course, Kelly. I'm just so grateful that you gave me this opportunity. I'll do anything to make it up to you. I'm sorry I just . . . left. I didn't know what to do."

"We don't need to talk about it anymore," said Kelly. "One question, though. What happens next for you?"

"I'm not sure, and for once, it's nice not to know."

THE NEXT MORNING, Cassie booked an afternoon session at the ancient baths in Barcelona. She needed to get out of the hotel and find a way to recenter her mind before her review that evening. It was almost as though she could feel a new wave of depression creeping in, this one so big and dark it was starting to scare her.

She took the long way, walking down the Passeig de Gràcia, one of the high-street shopping areas of Barcelona, an expansive, tree-lined boulevard lined with nineteenth-century architecture reminiscent of Paris. She cut through the Plaça de Catalunya, around the large fountains circled with flower beds, and continued south on La Rambla with its undulating street tiles that resembled little waves. The tall, mature trees provided shade for the street, which acted like an open-air mall. She wandered through the Mercat de la Boqueria, Barcelona's famed open-air market, through the maze of food stalls selling fresh fruits and vegetables, shimmering local fish on beds of ice, and wheels of cheese. Butchers sold everything from cuts of meat to cooked sausages to entire legs of ham, which hung from the signage. There were chocolatiers, tinned fish purveyors, flower shops, and of course restaurants selling local Catalonian delicacies.

After the market, she cut back northeast toward Ciutadella Park and turned on Passeig de Picasso before arriving at Aire de Barcelona, marked with a substantial wooden portal and a smaller man door cut into it, with a metal plaque on the side of the wall that read, "Time Does Not Exist."

She checked in and followed the hostess to the changing room, where she put on her red one-piece swimsuit and wrapped herself in a thick, white robe from the spa. She followed the signs to the pools, descending a flight of stairs into the main bath hall. She turned a corner, heading down a dark, barrel-vaulted hallway flanked on either side with tall metal lanterns, and a sliver of the pools came into view. She walked through the corridor, once part of the ancient Roman Forum in Barcelona, now restored to create a modern spa hidden well below the city. New slabs of white marble lined the pools, some long and thin, following the shape of the vaulted architecture, and some snaking in and out of the massive piers that held up the building above. The rooms were dark and lit with small, latticed votives, but the pools themselves glowed a brilliant aquamarine.

She dropped her robe on a lounge chair and lowered herself into the caldarium slowly, walking down the steps and into the glowing body of water. She took a deep breath, feeling the heat on her calves, on her thighs, and then on her chest as she sunk into the healing waters.

Cassie let her mind grow quiet for the first time in days, listening to the sound of the water and the echo of the room. She felt the mass of the building, the thickness of the walls, the earth surrounding the underground pools, and she took another deep breath, further slowing her heartbeat and calming herself. She closed her eyes and floated in the water, feeling the water dance across her skin, the sound of the room muted in her ears. She let herself lose track of time, let herself disappear into the secret oasis buried deep below the bustling streets of Barcelona. She wanted nothing more than to feel light and unburdened by the weight of everything that had happened over the past nine months—she wanted to be at peace.

Once the water started to feel overwhelmingly hot, she got out of the caldarium and into the cold plunge, inching her way into the frigid water before submerging herself completely, the water so cold her lungs clenched in her chest. She stayed underwater for as long as she could, then rushed to the surface, gasping for air. And in that moment, she felt the heaviness of her grief begin to lift. She closed her eyes and let go.

She let go of the stress, the anxiety, and the mental weight she had been carrying about James's death and the lies that she uncovered. She released the imagined life that she had created in her mind, scenes that played constantly through her head: the dinner dates, trips, parties, neighborhood walks, and other defining moments that would never be.

But she knew that she had been mourning more than just James; she was also grieving a substantial part of herself—the woman who was entirely dedicated to becoming a lawyer, the woman who had sacrificed her own happiness and the happiness of her loved ones for her career ambitions, the woman who was willing to put it all on the line for success. She had enormous guilt about wasting all that time and money on her education for a singular career—guilt that had been eating her up inside. Sitting there in the ancient aquamarine pool, she could see a new vision for herself for the first time: one where she could find happiness and create her own destiny.

It was time to move forward.

42

Cassie was relieved to realize that the restaurant she was to review that night was in the hotel. Moments was an acclaimed restaurant that was run by a mother and son team from Catalonia, and had been awarded quite a few Viand stars over recent years.

As she waited to be seated, she admired the room, which could only be defined as "modern opulence." It was filled with white linen–covered tables and white upholstered chairs that seemed to float above a champagne-colored rug. Above, curved ceiling panels were covered in clouds of gold leaf, illuminating the room with a warm, amber hue. On the far side of the room, floor-to-ceiling glass panels framed a dense, junglelike wall of tropical plants, giving the room another layer of luxury.

"Hello, beautiful," said Eamon from behind, surprising her.

"Eamon! I—I wasn't expecting you," she stammered. "I thought Rebecca was assigned with me tonight."

"Surprise," he said, flashing her a smile. "I traded with Rebecca, and as you know, she's a romantic at heart."

Cassie's face ran hot.

"We will seat you now," said the hostess, leading them to a table in the middle of the dining room.

Cassie was mortified. Her palms started to sweat, and her heart started to race. She wasn't ready for this conversation.

They sat for a moment in awkward silence, until their waiter came by to offer water and wine. They both gladly accepted the sparkling cava, Cassie taking a large gulp to calm her nerves.

"Tonight's meal is inspired by Salvador Dalí and his tome, *Les dîners de Gala*. We have reimagined dishes once served by the legendary surrealist artist, and the recipes that inspired the creation of this restaurant. We hope you enjoy."

Cassie awkwardly looked around, nervously scanning the tables for any familiar faces. She did not want to have another uncomfortable encounter in public.

"So," said Eamon, "what the fuck?"

"I know, I'm sure you have a lot of questions."

"I do."

"Where do you want me to start?"

"The beginning."

"Well," she said, pausing to take a drink of water. "First of all, let me say that I'm sorry I lied to you. I'm sorry I lied to everyone. This whole situation has been a little"—Cassie paused—"difficult to navigate, and clearly, I did not do it well."

"Thank you, but can we back up? Can you start at the beginning?"

"Sure," said Cassie, taking a deep breath. "Remember when I told you about James, my boyfriend, who was living a secret life? Well, he was @NewYorkSecretDiner, and he never told me. He lied to me for *years*, and although I had some indications that he wanted to tell me, he never did. So, when I discovered this decadent, delicious life he was living without me, I wanted to taste it for myself. I wanted a bite of the forbidden fruit. And kind of by accident—but maybe it wasn't an accident—I just started . . . posting. And taking myself to nice meals and accepting invitations—like this one."

"So, you've been posting as @NewYorkSecretDiner?"

"I was. But I realized that it would be too hard to keep it anonymous with all of us on the same trip. So I started my own account."

"@EatPostLike," said Eamon. "It's a beautiful account. You've done a nice job with it."

"Thank you," said Cassie, shaking off his comment. "Anyway, I got caught. Turns out, a few people knew about @NewYorkSecret Diner, David being one of them. He got suspicious that I was posting and flew to Italy to prove it."

"Moneybags," said Eamon, and followed with a swig of sparkling wine.

"He's in banking. Now that I think of it, it's totally like him to jump on a plane to try to prove a point. Probably in business class, no less."

"Is there any other way to travel?" said Eamon.

"You've been on too many press trips," said Cassie jokingly.

"Guilty as charged. I like luxury."

"And decadent breakfasts, apparently."

Eamon smiled and took a sip of his wine. "You know me well," he concluded.

Cassie circled back; she wanted to wrap up the conversation. "Look, it was important to James that the account be secret. I was trying to honor that. No one else knew, other than my best friend at home. I guess what I've learned this week is that the people who loved James and knew about the account didn't want it to live on without him—which I think is crazy, because it was anonymous. Nonetheless, he didn't specify his digital legacy in his will, so we will never know exactly what James would have wanted. To me, it didn't make sense to let the project die with him—I wanted it to live on. It was a piece of him that I could keep alive, to keep him with me in my own way. Maybe that was not the right decision. Anyway, the long and short of it is that I'm sorry for lying to you."

Eamon was quiet for a moment and fidgeted with his fork, spinning it slowly. "I appreciate you being so honest with me," he said, "but I still have questions. You're a lawyer? Is that right?"

Cassie gave an awkward nod.

"What made you want to take over his account in the first place? It seems like a very un-lawyer-y thing to do."

"I was just so tired and incredibly burned out. I was exhausted from constantly fighting for respect at my job, sick of the grueling hours, and dissatisfied that I never got any shine. I never got credit for my work, never got to experience any perks, even though you know the top brass was out wining and dining the clients every night, with their huge T&E budgets. I got tired of feeling so *invisible*—feeling like I was wasting away in the office. I couldn't do it anymore."

The first dishes arrived on small plates of different shapes. One was carved out of horn, in the shape of a teardrop, with brioches stuffed with pickled mussels. Prawns in broth and eels coated in beer batter, topped with a green dollop of pureed herbs, arrived in a glass bowl.

Cassie didn't touch her plates but kept talking, while Eamon listened, chewing.

"So . . ." She paused. "I just quit my job—officially. I was on sabbatical before, but I quit, officially. I have no idea what I'm going to do next."

"That sounds scary," he said, with a bite tucked into one cheek.

"It is, but I'll have to figure it out. I can't go back. I'm just— *done*. I'm done with the bullshit, I'm done with the late hours and feeling like my work isn't appreciated. I'm fucking *done*. I have more to offer the world, and right now, this feels good. It feels right, you know?"

"And it tastes delicious," said Eamon. "You should really try the prawns."

Cassie tasted each element with small bites, and then popped the shrimp into her mouth, which exploded with flavor.

"Wow," she said, still chewing.

"Right?" said Eamon. "Delicious."

She continued, "You know, everything was so *vanilla*. Even before James died. I was just going through the motions. Work, gym, home, work more. There was no *passion*, no spark. This trip has really opened my eyes to what life can be like—what it's like to be constantly surprised, delighted, and, of course, well-fed. I feel like my whole body is surging with creativity. I just want to learn more, see more, *eat* more. I've really loved meeting all of you, and meeting the chefs, and seeing how much passion and imagination they put into their craft—something so ephemeral as a plate of food. It's truly inspiring."

The next dish was a plate of three gently cooked quail eggs served in a buttery crust filled with an equally buttery leek cream, and topped with a generous spoonful of jet-black caviar. Cassie broke open the runny yolk of an egg with the tip of her fork, videoing as it oozed into the caviar and covered the tart.

"Now that's what I call food porn," she said, before taking a bite.

"So, I take it you're staying in the influencer game?" Eamon asked.

"Why do you say that?"

"You're still taking pictures of your food."

"The algorithm must be fed," she said with a shrug. "Just please know I'm sorry, Eamon. I am sure you hate me now, but I hope one day you will forgive me."

"I like it when you grovel," he said with a naughty smile. "You know, it's funny. You were so angry about being lied to, and then you went and did exactly the same thing."

"Yeah, I've been beating myself up about that pretty badly," she confessed. "I can honestly say that I had no idea that I would care for all of you so much, or that we would all bond as a group on this trip."

"Some trips are special," he added.

"I also hope that you know that I haven't felt this comfortable around someone in a long time," Cassie said quietly. "I finally feel . . . *alive.*"

"Cheers to that," said Eamon, raising his glass. "To life being lived."

LEAVING THE RESTAURANT, Cassie and Eamon slowly walked toward the elevator, bumping into each other every few steps. It was the last dinner of the trip, and she didn't want the night to end.

They stepped into the elevator, and Eamon pressed the button for his floor.

"Can I join you?" Cassie asked before slipping her hand into his and looking up into his dark hazel eyes, the rings of green especially prominent.

"I would love that," he said, leaning in to kiss her as the elevator rose up to his floor.

They barely made it to the door of his hotel room, stopping every few feet to kiss, veiled by the darkness of the hotel hallway that was only illuminated by stark spotlights in front of each door.

Once inside, Eamon opened the mini fridge and pulled out a mini bottle of champagne.

"That's going to be a very expensive split," said Cassie, remembering the colloquial term for the bottle size from their visit at Les Crayères.

"Look at you, using wino language," he said, before running his fingers through his wavy hair. "Don't worry, it will be worth it." He popped open the bottle and poured two glasses, handing one to Cassie. It felt cold and refreshing in her hand, and even better as the first sip slid down her throat.

"So, what happens after all of this?" asked Cassie, suddenly feeling self-conscious again.

"Well, I'm headed to Southern France to cover their summer rosé festivals. Do you have another trip lined up?"

"No," she said. She hadn't even thought about what she was going to do next. "No plans."

"Why don't you come with me? There will be sunshine, seafood towers, and rivers of rosé. I could use the company, and you would be a perfect partner in crime." He reached out for her hand, bringing her wrist to his mouth, kissing it tenderly, slowly making his way up to her elbow.

"Hmmm, sounds nice," she said.

"There are lots of starred restaurants in Southern France that you could review. You are starting to develop a unique voice; you should really build on it. The last thing you should do right now is go back to New York." His lips had made their way to the back of her neck, and instinctually, she dropped her head to one side, further exposing her skin to him.

Cassie knew he was right. Maybe it would be nice to go. Sit on the beach, decompress, learn more about wine production and the food of the region. Besides, who didn't love a seafood tower?

His hands wandered over her body, tracing the lines of her rib cage, moving along her waist to her hip bones and up her abdomen. He kissed the back of her neck where it met her shoulder, and she reached back to his head, running her fingers through his soft hair, exposing her body to the sky as his hands traveled up to her breasts.

He took off his shirt, his skin bathed in moonlight, his body muscular and statuesque. She leaned in to kiss his chest, following the lines of his collarbone to where it met his shoulder, tasting the faint saltiness of the sweat on his skin.

"You're absolutely delicious," he said between kisses.

"Yeah, but you're a potato. You're always the best part of the meal," she said, and she meant it.

THE NEXT MORNING, Cassie woke up in his bed to the sound of birds chirping. The sun was just starting to come up, slowly turning the sky from purple to blue.

Instinctually, Cassie looked at her phone, one eye pinched shut for a few minutes while she let them adjust to the morning light. She scrolled through Instagram for a few minutes, looking at photos of model-esque influencers posing on beaches, a feeble attempt at aspirational content. Did they really think those posts would inspire her to book a ticket to some random island? She toggled over to Gmail and deleted the string of spammy emails from online shops and publications, saving the ones that seemed mildly important to read later when she was more awake. She read the headlines on the news, and then went back to Instagram, now more mentally prepared to go through the comments on her latest post from the day before. She had shared the incredible junglelike bar of the hotel, with rattan shading devices that made it feel like an exotic locale. After replying to a few of the comments, she scanned her DMs, going through them one by one and carefully answering questions and making recommendations—lighthearted responses peppered with emojis.

One DM caught her eye.

Hello, I'm the editor of Global Traveler magazine, and we are looking for a new restaurant correspondent, effective immediately. Kelly from the Viand Awards recommended that we reach out to you. Do you have time for a call in the next few days to discuss the position? We would need you to be in Portugal next week. Please send a few times that would work for a call.

Sincerely,
Margaret, Global Traveler

Cassie reread the note a few times, her hands trembling with excitement. Maybe she could make this work!

She leaned over to Eamon, who was still sleeping, and kissed him on the lips, waking him up.

"I have to go. Thank you for a wonderful night."

Eamon propped himself up on one side, his hand tucked under his head. He was shirtless with the sheets wrapped around his waist. His skin was glowing in the light of the early dawn, and she watched his abs move with every breath. She traced her finger down the center of his body, feeling his sternum between his pecs and the soft tender part where his abs met. He wrapped his arms around her naked waist and pulled her closer. "Do you really have to go?"

"I think I should. We have to leave for the airport in a few hours."

He kissed her again, pulling his body against hers. "I'm going to need about thirty more minutes of your time," he said, flipping her over onto her back, pinning her hands down on the mattress, and kissing her again, morning breath and all.

ON THE VAN ride to the airport, Cassie and Ben were sitting in the last row, chatting quietly. It felt like the last few moments they would have alone, and Cassie wanted to be sure to give him a download of everything that had happened.

"I'm going to miss you, Ben. I can't even imagine this trip without you," she confessed.

"I'm so glad you were here, too. Hopefully we'll be able to do another trip together—that is, if the powers that be want it to happen. Ooh, maybe next time we can do the Asia circuit for Viand or something—wouldn't that be amazing?"

"That would be incredible. I can't even imagine."

"Singapore is beyond special; you would absolutely love it.

There's such incredible food on all levels, from the street food to fine dining. And Seoul! They are living in the future over there."

"I would love that, but I doubt I'll get invited on that trip," she said, full of uncertainty again.

"You never know," Ben said with a smile, bumping his shoulder into hers affectionately.

"Thank you for being such a wonderful friend," Cassie said. "I was worried you would never want to talk to me again."

"You know I live for the drama! Besides, who cares? I hope someone takes over my account when I'm gone."

"I don't think anyone could fill your shoes," Cassie said. "They are too fabulous."

Ben laughed, loud as always. "You're absolutely right."

INSIDE THE TERMINAL, the group said goodbye to Ben before he ran off to catch a flight to Melbourne, waving back to the group as he walked away.

"It's always a delight to travel with Ben," said Rebecca, watching him pass through security. "It's like he's here for one minute, and then before you know it, he's off to another lust-worthy destination. It's another reality being a full-time travel writer."

"The dream," Cassie said under her breath.

"You too can have the dream, sweetie," said Rebecca with a wink. "I should go, but I want to say one thing to you. I know you got upset when that man approached you in Venice . . ."

"About that, I'm so sorr—"

Rebecca raised her hand and put it over Cassie's mouth. "Stop. Stop apologizing—to us, to yourself, to anyone! This is your life, and you get to live it however you want. And you know what? Life is messy, we make mistakes, we walk down the wrong road, but it's the *mistakes* that make for great stories. So let them happen—stop trying to plan and control everything. Just let go and live your life for *you*, unapologetically."

Cassie opened her arms and gave Rebecca a hug. "Thank you. I'll do my best."

"I must go, sweetie. Do keep in touch," said Rebecca, giving Cassie an air kiss on the cheek before rolling her suitcase through the terminal and disappearing into the crowd.

Cassie wiped a single tear from her eye and excused herself to go to the ladies' room. She left Eamon and Kelly sitting at the airport café, drinking terrible cappuccinos and eating stale croissants. But instead of going to the bathroom, she cut across the terminal and went to the airline desk.

CASSIE CAME BACK to the café invigorated, smiling and giddy.

"What's the smile for?" asked Kelly. "Are you excited to head home?"

"Yes, I think so," she lied.

"Well, make sure you reach out when you get back. Let's go for a bite," said Kelly, packing up her belongings. "It's time for me to go. Thank you both for coming on this trip—it was truly memorable. Maybe too memorable," Kelly joked, giving Cassie a hug. "You like to keep people on their toes, don't you?"

Kelly turned to give Eamon a hug, then left for security, leaving Cassie and Eamon sitting in the overly lit café. Eamon leaned in. "I saw you at the airline desk. Does this mean you're coming to France?"

Cassie put her hand on top of his. She took a moment to feel the warmth of his skin, taking him in. He was such a beautiful man, any girl would be lucky to have him, and a part of her wished that she could go with him.

"Not today, but maybe I'll meet you there," she said with a coy smile. "I have things I need to do first. Save me a glass of rosé."

She reached across the table and put her hand on the side of his face, soft and freshly shaven. She ran her fingers through his beautiful hair, anchoring her fingers in the nook where his head met his spine, and pulled his face toward her. She kissed him, sweetly and tenderly, before pulling back to look at him once more.

"Thank you," she said. "Thank you from the bottom of my heart. Thank you for seeing all of me."

He sat back and bit his lip. "You're a surprising one, Cass." He looked down at his cappuccino and then back at her again. "I guess we should get going, then. I hope I'll see you around."

She kissed him maybe for the last time, savoring the softness of his lips and the taste of his mouth, before standing up and grabbing her bags. "You will," she said with a knowing smile. "I'll see you on the internet."

Acknowledgments

First, I want to thank Steven Salpeter, who brought this opportunity to me and believed that I was the best writer for the job. Thank you for rooting for me, and for sharing your knowledge and wisdom throughout this process. This project certainly wouldn't have happened (and probably wouldn't have been finished) without you. Thank you, thank you, thank you.

I have so much gratitude for the Assemble team for giving me the agency to turn this into the story that it has become. Much of this book was inspired by my own life, and I am appreciative to have had the opportunity to make it as authentic as possible. I'm grateful to Jack Heller for having the vision, and to Caitlin de Lisser-Ellen, Madison Wolk, and Jiayun Yang for all the help throughout the process.

To the team at Avon—thank you for your patience. Ariana Sinclair, thank you for your thoughtful notes that have made this book stronger. Additional thanks to Kathleen Cook and Shelby Peak for your behind-the-scenes work to get this book ready to go to print.

Thank you to Ben Setiawan, Natalie Compton, David Graver, Georgette Moger-Petraske, Prairie Rose, and *all* of my fellow travelers—there are literally too many to name. A special shout-out to those who helped me while I was working on this book: Ali Rosen, Emily Saladino, Joey Skladany—thank you for sharing your experiences and for brainstorming with me. I still believe that some of the best conversations happen in the back of a van while traveling to an unknown destination.

Additionally, I want to thank the PR teams that invited me on trips that inspired many of these scenes: Bernadette Knight, Drew Warren, Lauren Nodzak, Annie Taplin, Sarah Bessette, Alyssa Faden, Ana Calle, and so many more. Your trips defined an enormous chapter of my life, and I'm eternally grateful. Thank you for trusting me with your stories.

Thank you to Ted Buenz, who shared tales of handmade food critic identification posters found in New York City restaurants—it was a vision that stuck with me and inspired this book. And to the critics themselves: Ruth Reichl, Pete Wells, and so many more. Thank you for being my muses. I hope to share a negroni with you one day.

Big thanks to the food bloggers whose diligent documentation brought so many of these meals to life for me. I couldn't have written this book without the countless blog posts, Instagram posts, photos, and detailed reviews of meals that I was unable to have in person. Additional thanks to the chefs, restauranteurs, and creatives who express themselves so beautifully through food and drink.

Jennifer Pelka, your influence is all over these pages. Thank you for teaching me about food; how to taste, where to eat, and how to write about it. I'm ever grateful to you for starting Gastronomista with me so many moons ago, it has been a vehicle that has taken me all over the world and continues to open doors. It all started with you.

To the fierce, incredible women in my life who inspired Ruby in one way or another: Rammy Park, Jennifer Pelka, Miriam

Peterson, Jamie Berg, Felicia Martin, Louise Levi, Liz McDonald, Meredith Kole, Amanda de Beaufort, Amanda Linhart, Sarah Parrish, Colby Ricci—stay wild. I love you all.

Les Baker V.—you're a wonderful comrade and travel partner. Thank you for being the best, always.

Big thank you to Kenna Wells for recommending wines for some of the meals in these pages. I'm counting down the days until we can share a glass together again.

I also want to thank Jessie Hernreich for reading early drafts of this book when I was too shy to share it with anyone else. To Holly Rasmussen, thank you for helping me cross the finish line, despite the worst possible timing. At least there was champagne.

Pedro, thank you for always believing in me and trusting me. Your travels inspired me to find my own way to see the world—and my vehicle has been food and drink. Thank you for supporting me, despite this not being part of the plan.

To my mother, Bonnie, thank you for always being my greatest cheerleader. While Cassie is a bit of me, she is also inspired by you. Now, please stop working and go travel—you've earned it.

To Joy Johnson, thank you for exposing me to fine dining, and for helping me fall in love with it. You have inspired me so much, and I treasure the memories of meals we shared in Paris, New York, and beyond.

To my husband, Zac Stevens: Thank you for your patience, endless support, and most importantly, for letting me be me. You have always given me the space to explore, learn, and create on my own terms. It is the best gift you have ever given me. I love you.

Finally, to Odin, my sweet boy. I can't wait to show you the world.

About the Author

EMILY ARDEN WELLS is a partner with the Colorado-based architecture firm Move Matter / Architects and owns a digital media agency called Five O'Clock Creative, where she has won awards for her photography and food styling. She cofounded the award-winning cocktail and spirits website Gastronomista.com and is considered to be one of the first cocktail influencers, having inspired generations of content creators. Her writing has been published in *Elle*, *Glamour*, *Saveur*, CNN, and O, *The Oprah Magazine*, among others. She lives in Colorado with her husband and son. *Eat Post Like* is her first novel.

www.emilyardenwells.com
IG: @gastronomista_